ALIENS™
BISHOP

THE COMPLETE ALIEN™ LIBRARY FROM TITAN BOOKS

The Official Movie Novelizations
by Alan Dean Foster
Alien, Aliens™, Alien 3, Alien: Covenant, Alien: Covenant Origins

Alien: Resurrection by A.C. Crispin

Alien 3: The Unproduced Screenplay
by William Gibson & Pat Cadigan

Alien
Seventh Circle by Clara Carija & Philippa Ballantine
Uncivil War by Brendan Deneen
Out of the Shadows by Tim Lebbon
Sea of Sorrows by James A. Moore
River of Pain by Christopher Golden
The Cold Forge by Alex White
Isolation by Keith R.A. DeCandido
Prototype by Tim Waggoner
Into Charybdis by Alex White
Colony War by David Barnett
Inferno's Fall by Philippa Ballantine
Enemy of My Enemy by Mary SanGiovanni

The Complete Alien Collection
The Shadow Archive
Symphony of Death

The Rage War
by Tim Lebbon
Predator™: Incursion, Alien: Invasion
Alien vs. Predator™: Armageddon

Aliens
Bug Hunt edited by Jonathan Maberry
Phalanx by Scott Sigler
Infiltrator by Weston Ochse
Vasquez by V. Castro
Bishop by T. R. Napper

The Complete Aliens Collection
Living Nightmares

The Complete Aliens Omnibus
Volumes 1–7

Aliens vs. Predators
Ultimate Prey edited by Jonathan Maberry & Bryan Thomas Schmidt
Rift War by Weston Ochse & Yvonne Navarro
The Complete Aliens vs. Predator Omnibus
by Steve Perry & S.D. Perry

Predator
If It Bleeds edited by Bryan Thomas Schmidt
The Predator by Christopher Golden & Mark Morris
The Predator: Hunters and Hunted
by James A. Moore
Stalking Shadows by James A. Moore & Mark Morris
Eyes of the Demon edited by Bryan Thomas Schmidt

The Complete Predator Omnibus
by Nathan Archer & Sandy Scofield

Non-Fiction
AVP: Alien vs. Predator
by Alec Gillis & Tom Woodruff, Jr.
Aliens vs. Predator Requiem: Inside The Monster Shop
by Alec Gillis & Tom Woodruff, Jr.
Alien: The Illustrated Story
by Archie Goodwin & Walter Simonson
The Art of Alien: Isolation by Andy McVittie
Alien: The Archive
Alien: The Weyland-Yutani Report
by S.D. Perry
Aliens: The Set Photography
by Simon Ward
Alien: The Coloring Book
The Art and Making of Alien: Covenant
by Simon Ward
Alien Covenant: David's Drawings
by Dane Hallett & Matt Hatton
The Predator: The Art and Making of the Film by James Nolan
The Making of Alien by J.W. Rinzler
Alien: The Blueprints by Graham Langridge
Alien: 40 Years 40 Artists
Alien: The Official Cookbook
by Chris-Rachael Oseland
Aliens: Artbook by Printed In Blood

ALIENS™
BISHOP

A NOVEL BY T. R. NAPPER

TITAN BOOKS

ALIENS™: BISHOP
Print edition ISBN: 9781803366555
E-book edition ISBN: 9781803364667

Published by Titan Books
A division of Titan Publishing Group Ltd
144 Southwark St, London SE1 0UP

This Titan edition: December 2024
10 9 8 7 6 5 4 3 2 1

A CIP catalogue record for this title is available from the British Library.

Printed and bound by CPI Group (UK) Ltd, Croydon CR0 4YY

To my uncle Wayne, who wouldn't shut the
hell up about this new movie called *Aliens*,
while I was still too young to see it.

And to my sons, who are too young to read this
novel right now. Can't wait until you do, boys.

PART ONE

All warfare is based on deception.

Sun Tzu
The Art of War

PRIVATE KARRI LEE

1

When Captain Marcel Apone walked out onto the deck, and stood tall, hands behind his back, everyone shut the fuck up. Simple as that. The horsing around, the slaps on the shoulder, the ball-breaking—all of that stopped.

Karri stood to one side of the company, not part of the camaraderie. They'd gathered in the hangar: dully gleaming steel walls and chains, bright yellow-painted ladders and safety markings, iron-gray shipping containers, fat missiles tipped with high explosives. Faint smell of grease, the sound of voices echoing. Marines, muscled, young, mean. Sheen of sweat on the skin—most had been working out since leaving hypersleep. Getting the blood pumping, brains working, looking for an endorphin high after weeks of lying still.

A Colonial Marines company. Pretty meagre group of grunts, for that description. Karri wasn't sure what had happened to them, but as she cast her eye over the assembled, they looked to be at platoon strength—no more.

Karri didn't know whether to sit, stand, or sprawl like the rest of them. She stood. A couple of the marines glanced over at her, but didn't pay her much heed. Didn't care about the new girl until she fucked up or proved herself. That's what her fireteam partner, Corporal Sara Ransome, had said to her. The one person who had bothered to look her in the eye and give her more than a single word. Tall, over six feet, no-nonsense, looking down at Karri.

"They're waiting for you, to screw up, or to do something right. If it's the former, they'll make your life hell until you request a transfer. If it's the latter, they'll bleed for you. Simple as that."

The bullshit stopped when Apone walked in and the marines stood, hands behind their backs. The company—the "Hardboiled"—had a fierce reputation. Word was they'd seen some serious action, but when the big dog walked into the room, they jumped to attention.

Apone ran an iron assessing eye over the assembled. Up behind him the synthetic Haruki, Sergeant Hettrick, and the Weyland-Yutani worm, Walter Schwartz, all took up positions. Schwartz had already been there, loitering in the shadows, when Karri had joined a few weeks back. She hadn't yet heard the man speak, but saw him whispering enough times to Apone, or Hettrick. Sometimes just lingering, watching the marines go about their business.

Creep.

There was silence while they waited, save the low hum of the ship in the background. Then Apone spoke, simply.

"The USCSS *Patna* has been found."

The marines looked at each other. One of them clenched a fist, a nonverbal *yes*, but they all kept listening.

"Michael Bishop's research vessel and the last known location of the synthetic, Science Officer Lance Bishop. The ship is drifting in space. We've found it, and we've scanned it. Life support is still functioning, but every other system is down." He took a breath. "Over the past two months, you have all received information packets regarding the colony of LV-four-two-six—also known as Hadley's Hope—and the more limited data from the prison planet Fiorina One-Six-One. I suggest you reacquaint yourselves with that information. *I will not allow* what happened to Bravo Team on Hadley's Hope to happen to the marines I'm looking at right now."

The troops were silent and they were listening, all eyes on the captain. Each turning the story over in their minds. Karri had read it all, three times, trying to prep herself for what was to come. To be just as keyed in as any other grunt in that hangar. But it was more than just her desperate need to make the grade. The story was so fantastical. Military reports weren't meant to be compelling, but she found herself going back over them, picturing events in her mind's eye. Trying to imagine the enemy.

Space monsters. Karri had loved to read, as a child. The rare times she wasn't scrounging for food, or training in the *dojang*, she'd be reading. More often than not by candlelight—what with the rolling blackouts that left the city in a fearful darkness—she'd read and read and read.

If Karri was being honest, she'd prefer that the space monsters stayed in those books, rather than clawing their way into her reality, but this *was* the reality. A platoon of the Colonial Marines went into Hadley's Hope, and only two came out—Corporal Dwayne Hicks, and a combat support synthetic named Bishop. A couple of civilians as well, and that was it.

In the silence of the hangar, as Apone looked at the marines and they looked back, the hardest truth remained unspoken. It hovered there, in that space between them. Apone's big brother had been one of those cut down. A tough gunnery sergeant, the other marines said, who feared nothing and who fucked up less.

"Our enemy may sound like a horror story, invented by a sick and fevered mind," Captain Apone said. "The face-hugger. The chestburster. The Xenomorph. The Queen. The acid blood. The terrifying speed. The armored mesoskeleton—but we know for a fact it is real, all real. Sergeant Hettrick will explain how we have adapted our equipment to deal with this new enemy." The sergeant, behind him, smiled and nodded. Apone continued, "But the most important thing is not our equipment. It's knowledge. This is what Sun Tzu teaches, in *The Art of War.* If you know the enemy and know yourself, you need not fear the result of a hundred battles.

"These Xenomorphs had the element of surprise on our brothers and sisters in the Second Battalion Bravo Team. They will not have it on us. We have foreknowledge; they are beasts working on a base instinct. We have advanced firepower and the will to use it. They have nothing but the shadows and their animal hate. I tell you this, marines, I *promise* you this—" Captain Apone held up a finger, and that was the most expressive Karri had ever seen him "—we will exterminate these monsters with extreme prejudice."

The marines said "*yeah*," and "*hu-aaah*," and their eyes shone, and Karri could see how hard they wanted it. The echoes died down.

"One of ours might be there, on that ship," Apone continued. "Might be alive. But dead or alive, the Marines leave no one behind."

The response to this was less enthused. Bishop was just a synthetic, after all. A couple of the marines nodded, but that was it. Karri's eyes flicked over at the other synthetic, Haruki. Short, slight, Japanese features. As usual, he gave nothing away. She'd come to expect as much emotion from a marine android as you would from a concrete wall. Before she'd joined, Karri had never met a synthetic. Only big companies, the military, and the rich owned them, and Karri was none of those. Until recently, anyway.

Sergeant Hettrick walked to the front. He smiled too much for her liking. Joked too much, and was way too close to the other marines. Leaders should be distant, someone to look to for leadership in a firefight, not for a laugh over a beer. But maybe he could do both. She'd see. Hettrick had short red hair, combed in a neat and oiled part. The top two buttons of his fatigues were open. He held his chin a little too high.

"You have your standard combat armor," Hettrick said. "Wear it. Be ready to strip it off with the quick release latches should you be sprayed with Xenomorph blood. You will have a few seconds before the acid eats through. You will all wear ballistic masks." He held one up; it looked like a hockey mask. Black, gleaming dully, holes only for the eyes. "This will stop the so-called 'face-hugger' from strapping itself to your mouth—like my ex-wife at an open bar." He smiled after he said that, but no one laughed. He continued as though they found him funny. "Like your armor, the mask has quick release catches."

"I can't see shit in one of those things, Sergeant," Cortazar said. Big guy, mean, like most smart-gunners. Only thing he'd said to Karri since she joined the squad was "*fucking move*" when she'd been standing at her locker and he wanted to get past.

"We got you covered," Hettrick said, smiling.

The sergeant clicked his fingers and held out the mask. The synthetic, Haruki, quickly came forward, taking the mask from the sergeant's hand and replacing it with a large black shield. Hettrick didn't acknowledge the synth.

"The fireteam partner of each smart-gunner will carry one of these." Hettrick placed it on the ground. It was nearly chest high, slightly curved inward. Like a large, black riot shield police forces would use back in Australia. They'd line the shields up like a wall, and fire tear gas from behind it. Then the wall would split open and they'd charge through in their gas masks and use their clubs to beat down hungry protestors, begging for food. Karri shook her head to clear the images. Involuntarily touched the silver ring on her index finger.

Hettrick rapped the shield with his knuckles. "Teflon coated. This will stop the initial acid spray, and will be more resilient than marine armor. The bug likes to get in close, and our smart guns like to make a mess. This is the solution."

Karri didn't think it would solve the problem, but she shut up and listened.

"I needed one of these for my ex-wife, too," Hettrick said, and smiled, waiting for a response.

Karri rolled her eyes.

"Your ex-wife was a bug?" Corporal Ransome said. "I was wondering what would be desperate enough." There were some guffaws at that, and Hettrick smiled along with them. Then he pointed to a steel table nearby, covered with dark, shimmering clothing.

"Kevlar riot vests. They're light, wearable under your armor. Will provide some protection against Xenomorph claw and tail attack."

Karri had seen those before, as well. Same place she'd seen the shields.

"Every squad will have two additional incinerator units, operated by Corporals Ransome and Colby," Hettrick said. "The bugs don't like the heat. Now listen—we know how to kill these things, that's the easy part. What's harder is living long enough to tell the tale. We play it careful, like the captain said.

"Second squad will enter the *Patna* via the hangar bay, mounted up in an APC," he continued. "First squad will hold in reserve on the *Il Conde*. Once the hangar is clear, we will disembark. You have magnetic boots and breathing apparatus. If we engage the enemy in the loading dock, there is a chance the acid blood will breach the hull and cause atmospheric leakage. Be ready with your boots." Hettrick looked over them.

"And be ready to kick some ass." The marines finally smiled at something he'd said, and one slapped another on the shoulder. "Now, get fed and get prepped. Three hours before we head in. Dismissed."

The company broke up, boots heavy on the steel mesh floor. Flinty-eyed, Apone watched them go. She felt his gaze fall on her and linger. Karri turned and followed the others out.

2

Mealtime was her favorite part of the day. Each time a reminder of why she joined the Corps. The marines sitting at the long white mess table grumbled about the food, the mission, the pay, the usual.

For Karri, everything was a luxury. Her clean, new, tough-fibered uniform. The comfort of her bunk. The basketball court on the next deck, the credits that went into her account week in and week out, that she could in turn transfer to her mother. But the food—the food was plentiful, and nutritious, and not a mirage. Not a bartering tool. No one demanding anything of her in exchange for a hunk of stale bread.

She set about demolishing the scrambled eggs on her plate. The other marines complained about them not being real, but they tasted real enough to her. She slurped her coffee, cup in her off hand, and that too was a luxury. Put down her dark brew and reached for the salt. Corporal Ransome, opposite, passed it to her.

"Hungry?" she asked, eyebrow raised.

Taking the salt, Karri sprinkled it, generously, over the yellow pile of eggs. She hesitated. The rest of the table was otherwise occupied, boasting about who they'd fucked on a previous deployment, or the asses they'd kicked.

"Was a time I couldn't be sure if I'd see another meal."

Ransome nodded, showed she got it—but she didn't get it. She couldn't, unless she'd been there herself. But the corporal acknowledged it, and that was something. Karri glanced past Ransome's shoulder, at the two long empty white tables.

"Where's the rest of the unit?"

Ransome motioned with her fork. "We lost them at Torin Prime."

"Oh," Karri said. The name sounded vaguely familiar. "In combat?"

Ransome shook her head. "To bureaucracy."

Karri waited for her to continue. Ransome looked sideways, to see who was listening, and leaned forward.

"Word is, the Union of Progressive Peoples have been funding some rebels there. Command told Apone they wanted the *Il Conde* stationed, in orbit, as a deterrent, until it settled down. Word is, Apone said no. Said he had a mission. A rescue mission. *No man left behind.* Pulled some strings. Our captain has a lot of friends in high places." She tracked her eyes sideways, to the table where Apone sat. "Lot of enemies, as well."

Karri glanced over. The captain sat with the synthetic, Haruki, the dropship pilot, Miller, and one other. Walter Schwartz. The company man.

"Word is, he did a deal," Ransome continued. "A dropship, a good lieutenant, and a full platoon, down to the surface, as a deterrent. In exchange Apone got to continue his mission."

"That's the word, huh?" Karri asked. There was an undertone to Ransome's speech—a bit of bite at the back of the tall woman's words—but there wasn't enough context to explain it.

"Still," Karri said. "Even adding a full platoon, this is a little slim for a company."

Ransome lowered her fork, pressed her lips together, like Karri had made a stupid observation.

"Rookie," she said, "the Colonial Marines are always undermanned, stretched too thin, asked too much. We've got a whole galaxy to cover, run by an empire whose ambitions don't meet its resourcing."

Karri was surprised at the admission, but nodded. She sure as hell knew about that.

"To make up the shortfall," she said, "they keep turning to Weyland-Yutani."

"Yup." Ransome shrugged, as if Karri were stating the obvious. The corporal went back to her food, and so did Karri, with gusto, her fork taking apart the salted scrambled eggs.

Other marines passed a square steel tray down the

table, filled with cornbread. Only one or two grabbed a chunk. Karri took half of what was left and dumped it on her plate, devouring a slice in three bites. An American bread, light, grainy texture, little bit of sweetness to it. She closed her eyes and swallowed. Had the second slice in her hand when a voice cut through the chatter.

"Look at the English bitch eat." It was Cortazar, staring down the length of the table. The others were staring with him. "Swallowed a damn slice whole." Corporal Colby, Hettrick, and Johnson, his fireteam partner, were sitting with him, grinning. "We should call her Cornbread."

Hettrick thought that was funny. Of course he did.

Fucking idiot.

Johnson and Colby were laughing. The rest of the table grinning. Karri had felt unnoticed for these first few weeks. There had been some sidelong glances, some muttering, a couple people asking where she was from, what action she'd seen.

"*Nowhere*," she replied, and, "*None*." Lies, both. Now they were staring at her. The food in her mouth, well, it didn't taste so good anymore and she stopped chewing, lowering her head.

"That right, rookie?" Cortazar said, eyeballing her. "I think we'll call you Cornbread now."

Karri stepped on her shame and looked back at him. If it came to a staring competition, she would do just fine. She swallowed her food.

"Australian," she said. "I'm Australian, not English."

"Don't take a tone with me, rookie," Cortazar said. "What, you don't like being called English?"

"Would you?" she snapped.

"I could fill that big mouth of yours with something even better, Cornbread." There was a violent sheen to Cortazar's eyes. Karri set her jaw.

"And what'll we call you, mate? Cornhole? On account of that fucking face of yours?"

Ransome, opposite her, chuckled and shook her head. Cortazar wasn't smiling anymore, not one bit.

"The fuck did you say, rookie?"

"I'm saying that you're so fucking ugly, a face-hugger would be an improvement."

Some marines laughed at that, and Cortazar's chair screeched as he stood, but Karri was already there, in close, cornbread tray pressed hard into his throat and her other hand round the back of his head, pulling it backward.

"Shit," someone said. "She's fast."

Cortazar struggled. He was a head taller than her and about as wide as a barn door. Big shoulders, like he'd have to have, lugging a smart gun on mission. But the biggest muscles didn't help much with a piece of metal dug into his throat, and so she jammed it in harder. Cortazar choked, and suddenly someone was pulling her away and the other marines were yelling, until Apone's voice struck them all like iron.

"Stand down, marines!"

The captain was there, among them. "*Sit down.*" Apone

was at least as big as Cortazar, when he wanted to be. Cortazar would strut around in an army-green tank top, showing off his huge shoulders. Apone didn't have to prove anything, his mere presence was enough. But right then—at the moment, as the captain loomed among the marines—Karri noticed how big he really was.

The marines all sat, except Cortazar, chest heaving, eyes wild, staring at Karri. There was a red mark on his throat.

"What in hell is going on here?" Apone asked.

"Just breaking some balls, Captain," Hettrick replied. "Same as any other recruit. Private Lee decided to take it personal." Apone looked at Karri and then Cortazar, and the way he held his jaw, it was clear the man was holding in some anger.

"I will *not* have dissent among my warriors on the eve of battle. I will not. *He will win whose army is animated by the same spirit throughout all its ranks.*" Apone looked over the troops as he said it, then rounded on Karri. "Why did you join, Private Lee?"

She opened her mouth, but not to speak. Captain Apone was asking her a question, the deepest question, right in front of the whole unit, and her mouth just popped open.

"Did you not *hear* me, Private?" His voice rang clear in the quiet of the mess hall. Her pulse beat in her head, adrenalin still high from the near-fight.

"Ah. To. Serve?"

"You asking me a question, Private, or are you giving me an answer?" he demanded. "Who are you here for?"

Her family. That was the truth. That was the *only* truth. For them and no one else. To earn her citizenship, and get them out of that wretched camp. She took a deep breath, and saw it then, what the captain was looking for. It was there, in his eyes. That sheen of certitude. She knew what he wanted.

"For the marines in this room."

"What was that, Private?"

"For the marines in this room!"

Not one of those marines spoke. Not one of them sneered.

Apone nodded. "That is correct, Private. That is the only thing worth fighting for: this tribe." He turned and looked at the rest of them. Over his shoulder, she could see Schwartz smiling, crooked grin, as if it was amusing—but not one of the marines thought it funny. Apone kept speaking, but it wasn't rousing: he wasn't yelling it, like the gung-ho speeches she'd heard a hundred times already since joining. He was telling it like he meant it.

"We eat together and we sleep together. We fight together, warriors of our tribe. We guard each other's back. We bleed for each other, and when we need to, we die for each other. I would do that for any marine here: the most grizzled sergeant to the newest recruit. We celebrate and we mourn together, one family. Out here, in the dark cold vacuum of space, there is only one place to find the warmth of kinship, and that is within the fragile walls of this ship. There's only one place to find meaning: here, where everyone here is needed, and *everyone* has a role to play in our survival.

"*Everyone is needed*," he said, "and here's the thing about this tribe. It's bigger than us, and it will outlive us. One hundred years from now we will all be gone, but this company—the Hardboiled 8th—will endure." Apone took a breath, took a moment to look over the marines in the mess hall. "In a war long past, on Earth, a man named Sassoon was injured in battle. He left his unit and, lying there in the hospital, wrote a poem, and in part of it, he says this:

"*In bitter safety I awake, unfriended,*

"*And while the dawn begins with slashing rain…*

"*I think of the Battalion in the mud.*"

Apone cast his shining eyes over the room. "If, one day, you leave the Marines, and you live in bitter safety, this truth you will know—you don't fight for anything out here but each other. Here is the most profound sense of purpose you will ever know: to be willing to die for another, and have them willing to die for you."

The marines were all silent. Something stirred in Karri. There was truth in Apone's words. She didn't care about the United Americas. She wasn't sure what the Colonial Marines were fighting for, other than the interests of one empire over another. She'd never heard another grunt talk about some higher cause, some noble mission.

Apone was right. If there was a higher cause, it was right here, in this room.

He looked now at Cortazar and then Karri. "Now break bread."

Apone walked back to his table. The marines were subdued. A woman across from her—Karri didn't know her name—nodded at her. A couple of others looked her in the eye, and Cortazar did, too. But this look was very different, and Karri Lee knew it well. She'd seen it enough in the food lines, on the darkened back streets. It meant violence was coming, somewhere, sometime soon.

Not now, but near enough. And she'd be ready.

3

"You a refugee?"

Corporal Ransome put one of her long legs on the bench in front and began to strap her vambrace armor to her shin. Karri made herself look away from the leg. Muscled and shapely, and she'd stared at them sideways in the showers, more than once. The question dulled her interest.

"Yeah," Karri said, snapping the clips on her chest plate.

"Figures," Ransome said.

"It does?"

"Cortazar is a bully, but there's one like him in every platoon. They raze the rookies, make life hard on them, until they earn their place."

"What's that to do with being a refugee?"

"How you take it," Ransome replied. She put her foot back on the ground, armor in place. "I've seen a few come in here, through the camps. I know it's tough there, and that the weak are killed. All that. Can see the mark it made on you, Private, and I don't mean that big scar on your forehead, either. I mean the anger you hold in your eyes. One marine came through our company a while back, by the name of Mahuta. Told me the camps reminded him of prison. Dog eat dog world, but worse, 'cause kids were there."

Karri said nothing.

Ransome leaned forward. "But this ain't prison, Lee. You're in the Marines. There's a hierarchy, and you got to respect it. There's traditions, and you respect those, too. You respect it all and get none yourself. You understand why?"

Karri sighed. "Because I haven't earned it."

"Yeah," Ransome said. "You haven't earned it." She straightened, hands on the sides of her armored breastplate, thumbs looped behind it. "You don't earn it in the mess hall. You earn it on the field. You focus on that, Private."

Karri breathed again, long and slow.

"You got me?"

"Yes, Corporal."

"Good. Check your weapons, your motion tracker. Ready yourself."

"Yes, Corporal."

"And Lee?"

"Yeah."

"Don't fuck up."

4

Private Karri Lee breathed. One thing her taekwondo instructor had told her to do, time and again. "*Breathe.*" Old-school teacher, made everyone call him sir. Yelled, red-faced, when the students couldn't line up straight or tie a belt correctly. Smacked them across the head, open-handed, if they were really asking for it.

Always told Karri she was too tense. Muscles too tight. Always wanting to kick too hard and punch too hard, sometimes so hard she hurt herself. "*Breathe,*" he told her. Had to go into a fight calm. Otherwise the lactic acid took over, cramped the muscles, drained her stamina. Strike hard and fast and swivel the hips, that's what mattered. All while remembering to breathe.

So she breathed, twisting the plain silver ring on her index finger. Her shoulders brushing those of the marines on either side of her. Safety bar pulled down over her shoulders, the engine of the M577 armored personnel carrier thrumming underneath her feet, idling. It felt safe, felt strong, inside the beast. No bugs getting in here, no way. Apone was in the middle of it all, command center, checking the marines' vitals on the monitors, their radio systems.

The synthetic, Haruki, was in the driver's seat up front, and a corporal from the other section—Ottelli, a big-shouldered guy who talked only when necessary—was on the twin gatling cannons mounted to the front of the APC. Both squads—four marines apiece—sat in the back, plus Hettrick. Twelve total in the vehicle, but not too cramped, for all that. There was a backup squad in the second dropship-mounted APC back on the *Il Conde*, ready to ride on in, like the cavalry.

They were inside the hangar of the *Patna*. Hangar doors had opened, allowed the dropship in, no fuss. Waiting in its belly, ready to roar out in the APC. Cortazar and Johnson sat opposite, both staring at her. The riot shield held sideways and upright between Johnson's legs.

She ignored them.

"Talk to me Haruki," Apone said. "Visuals?"

"Nothing, sir," the synthetic replied, his voice calm and uninflected. "It looks clear."

Apone waited a few moments longer, like he was listening. For what, she couldn't figure.

Finally he said, "Haruki. Proceed."

The APC lurched down the ramp. Karri gripped the bars of the harness. Her legs jostled against Corporal

Ransome. The marines all swayed as they took a tight turn, and kept turning, engine thrumming. The interior of the hangar flashed through the windscreen, but Karri couldn't see anything more specific than that.

The engine wound down, the swaying stopped. Apone moved to the front, next to Haruki, and looked over the control panel.

"Motion tracker?"

"Still nothing, sir."

Apone was silent, leaning over the synthetic. His breathing was slow. Karri could see his broad back rising and falling evenly.

"Well, I guess we're—" Hettrick started to say.

"*Quiet,*" Apone cut him off. Didn't even bother to turn around. Hettrick shut up. The engine idled, Karri breathed. They sat like that for what felt like five minutes, until Apone said, "Another bay through that far door?"

"Yes sir," Haruki replied.

"Open it." Apone's voice was low.

"I can't do it from here. I'll have to dismount and do it manually at the panel."

Apone made a non-committal noise in the back of his throat.

"If you try to blast a hole in that door," Apone said to Ottelli, "what's the chance you'll put a hole in the hull, Corporal?"

The gunner replied, "Better than even chance."

Apone stared at the front a few moments longer before

turning to the back of the vehicle. "Okay, marines. You are exiting this vehicle. Cortazar and Johnson first, Davis and Ali second. The rest of first squad, then second squad." He pointed a big finger at Karri. "Private Lee, you need to move forward and override that second door. Ransome, watch her back. Smart-gunners, cover the gantries up top. You get swarmed, no one plays the hero, you get back to the APC so we can close the door and we put the gatling on the Xenomorph. That clear?"

"Yes sir!" the marines replied. Karri mumbled it. She hadn't listened much to what he'd said, after the bit about her opening the door. This was it. This was her first job out in the field. No more training, no more chances. This was the first real step, to getting Mum, and her stupid brothers, out of that damn camp.

5

They moved. Fast, focused, ordered, spreading out left, right, straight ahead, over the bay.

"Looking good, marines." Apone's voice crackled through her headset. *"Watch that flank, Davis."*

Karri headed toward the second set of bay doors, Ransome just behind her. The ballistic mask made it hard to see, and she stumbled on one of the joins in the mesh floor.

"Watch it, Private," Ransome hissed.

They paused behind a steel shipping container with rounded corners, halfway toward the rear. The bay was about thirty meters wide, and sixty or more long. There was no dropship present, and without one the chamber looked pretty bare. Scattered over the bay were a handful of steel containers. A yellow power loader stood near the rear, designed to be walked around like a mech, driver standing in the cockpit. Bishop's report had said a civilian had used one of those to fight a Xenomorph Queen.

Gotta have had some big balls, to give that a try, Karri thought.

"Motion tracker?" Apone asked. Firm. Calm.

"Ah," Corporal Colby replied. A pause. *"Nothing, Captain."*

The bay ceiling was higher than the one in the *Il Conde*. Double the height, with a steel mesh gantry walkway around the edge. Karri looked around it, uneasy. Hard to see clearly with the mask obscuring her vision.

"Move, Private," Ransome said.

She moved, rounding the shipping container, but before she could take three steps, chaos hit. Everything, all at once.

"Wait, there's something on—" Colby said.

Simultaneously, Karri's foot caught the edge of the shipping container, and—

The gravity went. The fucking gravity went and she was in zero-G—

The firing started, the smooth retort of pulse rifle ringing, echoing—

"You motherfuckers," Cortazar screamed over the comms.

Apone was still there, firm.

"—the gantry, lock your boots and cover that gantry."

Ransome yelled at Karri, but she couldn't make out the words over the screaming in her ear and the roar of weapons fire. Her ballistic mask slipped, obscuring her vision, and she yanked at it, yanked at the clips, pulling it away and the whole room was turning, end on end.

"God dammit, Private Lee is loose—"

She was turning and had to close her eyes, motion sickness rising in her belly. Karri tried to breathe, but something struck her chest and she spun, wildly, with the impact.

"—Ali is down—"

"Christ, they're everywhere—"

Still spinning, Karri was almost horizontal, and in every direction was the white-yellow bloom of pulse gun fire and she couldn't understand, snatching at the strap for her shouldered rifle. Couldn't figure why there were so many muzzle flashes lighting up the gloom, pulse rifles overlapping. Then the smart gun, stuttering, clearing its throat then roaring, smothering the other sounds.

SPIN.

"Man down!"

The APC was floating, the front of it rising from the floor of the bay and there, below Karri, a black ballistic mask was looking at her, heading toward her, and in that split second she realized Corporal Ransome had launched herself upward.

SPIN.

Karri pulled at the strap of her pulse rifle, but too hard, slipping from her hands.

"Fuck!" she screamed, and realized in that instant that it wasn't aliens up there above but men. Men in strange, almost samurai-type armor, padded, steel masks with rounded holes for the eyes, firing down at the marines

as she spun and her pulse rifle flew off at an angle. One of the bad guys was looking straight at her, rifle raised, and Karri brought her hands up on instinct, to protect her face.

SPIN.

A *whoosh* of heat and Karri gasped, flinching, and when she turned again the man was on fire—the man who'd had her in his sights was on fire, screaming, arms flailing, leaving a trail of spot fires behind as he stumbled down the gantry and something struck Karri again. The air left her lungs.

Cortazar yelled over the comms, and she struggled, someone holding her, but a voice cut through it all.

"Calm, Private!" In that moment she understood it was Ransome. They hit the side of the bay, but the tall woman maneuvered with her boots, clamping them onto the wall so she stood horizontal, and dumped Karri down onto the gantry. *"Your mag boots,"* Ransome yelled.

Karri, bouncing up from the mesh steel, fumbled with the boots. The switch was stuck. She yanked it, screaming, until a little red light down near her heel turned green. *Clunk*. The boot clamped to the steel. She made the other do the same. Drawing her service pistol, she had a moment to orient herself.

There were twenty of the enemy, at least. In their padded, whitish armor, oval steel masks, holding gleaming black pulse rifles. At least five were immobile, struck while standing up, arms akimbo, their boots keeping them fastened to the steel gantry. At least one marine was drifting, unmoving, down below, and two more were doing the same death dance as the bad guys, swaying slowly upright like kelp at the bottom of the ocean.

The enemy was wearing modified all-purpose environment suits, or Apesuits. Those would make them—

One of the bastards clomped around the corner of the gantry, pulse rifle aimed at Karri and Ransome.

She shifted and fired at his legs, right at the moment Ransome unleashed with her incinerator, washing the man with white-hot napthal. The man screamed, high-pitched, keening, and it was a sound Karri could not dispel, could not unhear. Even after it stopped, the sound echoed on in her mind. She tried to press a hand against her ear, but someone was yelling, shaking her, pulling her gaze from the burning man.

"Open that door, Lee," Ransome yelled. *"We're too exposed."* She jabbed her finger at a steel door at the end of the gantry, hauled Karri to her feet, and they ran, sparks flying, gunfire everywhere, garbled commands over the comms. There was an alcove, no more than a half-meter deep, where the door was set. They slammed into it. More sparks, ricochets, Ransome yelled and unleashed another stream of fire, her armor reflecting the orange glow of the flame.

The corporal jerked and dropped the incinerator, falling back into the alcove. Karri reached out to her, and all she could see of the corporal was her eyes, anger bright, looking through the holes of the ballistic mask. *"Do. Fucking. Something."*

Stung, Karri leaned her against the wall and turned to the panel. She tried to ignore the deafening fire, the sounds of explosive-tipped rounds striking metal, and pulled her field technician kit from the pouch at her waist. She tried to breathe, but a shot sparked near her head and she flinched. Karri swore and started unscrewing the panel cover when the door opened.

The door slid open.

Beyond, the two men in Apesuits looked as surprised as she. The closest one had a pulse rifle leveled at her.

6

Finally, fifteen years of martial arts training, and twelve months basic for the Marines, kicked in. Finally, her muscle memory was worth something.

Karri Lee rose and kicked the rifle, knocking it upward, the man firing it into the ceiling. She followed through with her other leg, her heel striking the round steel mask. The man's head snapped back and he staggered and Karri was moving—standing on the spot was a good way to get dead on a battlefield. She grasped the rifle of the second enemy. He was taller and stronger, shoving her against the wall and ramming the side of the weapon into her face. She gasped, dazed. He twisted the pulse rifle up, away, her hands losing purchase.

She stomped down, hard, on his foot. He grunted, she reclasped the rifle, leaned back and stomped again, this time on the inside of his knee.

The motherfucker howled, instantly releasing the

weapon. Karri turned the rifle around, fumbling for the grip, but something was around her neck, choking her. One hand still on the rifle, she clawed at her throat. She craned her neck, not understanding what was happening.

What the fuck.

The first man she'd kicked was there, with a pole maybe three meters long, noose at the end, wrenching it like she was a wild animal and he was the ranger. He pulled, her boots popping from the floor, and he slammed her into the wall. The wind went out of her and he pulled her again through the zero-G, into the other side of the corridor. Her helmet was gone—she wasn't sure when—both of her hands at her throat now, gasping for air. Rifle gone, didn't know where the fuck her service pistol was.

Apesuited motherfucker dragged her back and forth, choking the life from her. Karri's lungs burned and she couldn't scream, no one could hear her choking cries for help. She couldn't see Ransome, couldn't see anyone, just the gleaming hate in the eyes of the man who was killing her.

Her vision faded in, and suddenly there was a blade in her hand. Muscle memory, not dead yet, grabbing the last weapon she possessed: her combat knife. She pressed it to her throat, trying to work it in underneath the cord. It stung, and she was slammed again, but she still held the knife. All her rage and fury and will to live squeezed the handle, and she cut the cord at her throat and rammed her boots down, catching the floor.

The pressure on her neck was gone, and she was like a swimmer who'd been drowning, suddenly breaking the surface, gasping for air. Everything was so bright in the corridor, like she'd just come out of a dark room, and something moved, a flash of white at the corner of her vision, and it was the one with the broken knee, trying to draw a pistol on her. She blocked it with her forearm, then thrust forward with the blade, under his chin.

It sank deep. His eyes, deep behind the glass circles of his mask, looked surprised. She pulled the blade out and blood spilled out into the zero-G, a surging steady spray into her face, her neck. Turning slowly, still dizzy, she spat the other man's blood from her mouth.

"Marine bitch."

She focused. The last opponent was standing, center of the corridor. Instead of the pole, he now had a pulse rifle aimed at her, retrieved from somewhere. The smooth song began, the death song, as electronic pulses spat caseless rounds, steel-jacketed, explosive-tipped—but it wasn't Private Karri Lee who was torn apart by them.

It was the white-suited samurai. His steel-helmeted head jerking back, body punctured, legs, black at first where the rounds hit them, blooming with blood. He died like that, standing and not falling in the zero gravity, arms wide, blood in a cloud around him, a red cloud that shimmered and did not disperse.

Karri turned again. Corporal Ransome was there, leaning against the doorframe. Her ballistic mask was gone and there was blood splattered on one side of her sweating neck. Her chest heaved. Her head lolled and she let the pulse rifle go. It floated away from her.

"Sara!" Karri cried and ran to her, holding her. Her neck and shoulder were slick with blood, droplets floated from the wound. Looked like her collarbone had been hit, maybe worse. Small arms fire still echoed through the door, though more sporadic now. Karri jabbed the control panel, and the door closed, the sounds of battle muffled.

Ransome's eyes fluttered open. She groaned. Karri pressed her against the wall, gently, and unclipped her chest armor as quickly as she could. It popped off, and more droplets floated out into the air. There was a lot of blood.

Karri went for her comms, but her helmet was gone. She cast around on the ground, but could not see it. Pressing her hand against the wound, with the other one she unclipped and slid off Ransome's helmet, and put it on her own head.

The comm crackled. "*—cover. We can't get a good shot from the APC. The remaining marines—*"

She pressed the transmit button. "Medic!" she yelled, cutting over Apone. "I need a medic. Ransome is hurt bad."

"*Trying to save your ass, rookie!*"

"*Get off this channel, Cortazar,*" Apone said. "*Copy that, Lee. Your position?*"

"Upper gantry. Right-hand side, behind the door."

There was a pause. *"Copy that. We are under heavy fire, Lee. Can you stabilize Corporal Ransome?"*

Her hand was already slick with blood. More droplets squeezed between them. Ransome was pale, so pale. Head lolling, eyes closing and opening. Closing for longer and longer.

"Fuck. No. She's dying, Captain."

Someone swore over the comms.

"Copy that," Apone said. *"Hold."*

She pressed her lips together. Cortazar was right. It was her fucking fault. She unclipped her own chest armor, shrugged it off, letting it float away, didn't care. One-handed, she tore her top off, buttons popping. Extracted her free arm, then pushed the top down with her other arm, so it was near the hand still holding the wound. She shifted her hands quickly and pressed down on it, now with her fatigues as a bandage.

Ransome groaned. Her eyes were closed.

"Private Lee."

"Copy."

"Haruki is coming, over."

"Roger that."

"Cortazar and Davis, covering fire. Keep their heads down."

"I goddam roger that, Captain."

"Roger that."

Karri held the bloodied bandage in place, and maneuvered so she could press her face against the small square reinforced-glass window in the steel door.

Scratched, the viewing arc limited, she could only make out the muzzle flush beyond. The angry pulse of the smart guns sounded through the thick metal door. The firing intensified.

"Come on, Haruki," she whispered. "Come on."

Ransome's eyes were closed now.

"Fuck."

She pressed her face back against the window and suddenly Haruki was flying through space from below. She slapped the panel and the door slid open. As it did, the roar of battle burst through. Percussive questions and answers from light arms, soldiers yelling, and then Haruki was there, moving fast, and she was closing the panel and yelling at him.

"Hurry, hurry."

The synthetic placed a gentle hand on her chest. "Help is here, Private Lee," he said, and she could swear he said it gently. "Please provide protection while I attend to her injuries."

The synthetic worked fast, his hands a blur, but Ransome was pale, so fucking pale, and she wasn't moving.

7

A black pulse rifle floated nearby. Karri grabbed it, pulled herself down to one knee, and turned her eyes from Ransome and Haruki and all the floating blood.

The corridor was long, with a steel mesh floor, well lit. One of the enemy was curled into a ball, almost a fetal position, just to her left, hovering, drops of blood hanging in the air. The other merc was ten meters away, upright, swaying. He provided some cover, a small distraction, enough maybe that Karri would fire first if someone came from the other direction. There was an intersection, twenty meters away, and then another, twenty meters beyond that. The corridor extended on for maybe seventy meters, before arriving at another door.

The muffled firing behind them, in the bay, abated. Infrequent.

"They should withdraw," Karri whispered over her

shoulder. "Back into the *Il Conde*. These mercs have the higher ground."

"Captain Apone will never leave a marine behind," Haruki said, as though stating an immutable law of the universe.

"I know. Temporarily, I mean. Figure out another option. Forced entry maybe, another part of the ship." Part of her didn't want to interrupt the synthetic. The bigger part of her knew she couldn't distract him if she tried. She could hear his hands moving, fast, efficiently, behind her. The *psssst* as he sprayed wound sealer.

But she also wanted to know, desperately, how bad it was below. She'd fucked up. She'd fucked up and now was grasping, wishing to hear her unit would be fine, that they had the upper hand. Some ridiculous, selfish part of herself wanted to be soothed.

"Corporal Ottelli made a suggestion along those lines, Private Lee," Haruki said. "The captain replied that we could do both. He ordered the reserve rifle squad to suit up and EVA across the surface of the *Patna*, blow out an external door behind the Weyland-Yutani commandos, and assault them from the rear."

"Company commandos?"

"Yes."

"I knew it." She exhaled. "But that will take too long."

Haruki didn't answer that. "Worry not," he said instead. "The marines in the bay have taken cover, the wounded returned to the *Il Conde*. Smoke grenades were thrown.

In zero gravity, the smoke lingers. He wanted to draw out the firefight with the commandos."

"But why?"

"Because of you and Corporal Ransome. He believed disengaging would leave you to be hunted down and killed. He said he would not do that."

Karri swore.

"How many of us are down, um, are—"

Haruki cut her off. "We have a problem, Private." If there was a problem, his tone didn't show it. Calm, measured.

She swallowed. "What?"

"Zero gravity presents additional complications for internal bleeding. The blood is collecting at the rupture site."

"So—we need artificial gravity back?"

"Yes. I have to stabilize this wound, then get Corporal Ransome to the medical pod in the *Il Conde* as soon as possible."

"How?"

"How do we stabilize—"

"How do we get the fucking gravity back?" she hissed. Karri was still facing away, down the corridor, pulse rifle to her shoulder. Still looking through a cloud of blood droplets, hanging in the air.

Haruki paused. "There is a sub-command center. One floor directly above us, and ten meters farther toward the stern. You need to proceed down the corridor in front of you, pass through that door, turn left, take the stairs, and return in this direction. The sub-command center is at the center of the level."

"Got it." Karri rose to her feet.

"And Private," the synthetic said, and something in his voice made her turn to him. Ransome's shoulder and chest were bandaged, the clean white strips already reddening. The woman still had no color. She'd have thought Sara dead, if not for Haruki indicating otherwise.

Karri breathed.

"You can do this, Private."

She paused. Karri wasn't sure if he was stating some fact arrived at by the calculations of a synth mind, or whether he was trying to reassure her, but he held her gaze and, for a moment, she was reassured. For a moment, someone was telling her she *could* do something, not that she was a fuckup. For a moment.

Then she looked again at Sara, and the black claw of failure clutched at her heart. She turned, and ran.

8

Clomp clomp clomp. Karri pushed herself down the corridor, jabbing door panels, moving through, black pulse rifle raised to her shoulder. Not taking enough time, not checking corners, not pausing as she should. Driving herself on.

Corporal Ransome's helmet bounced on her head, one size too large. She clipped the chin strap, but the brim was a little low, near her eyes. She pushed it back. Paused at a corner, sucking in breaths. Floor mesh, corridors maybe three meters wide, just like the *Il Conde*. Same class of ship, but the configuration had been altered, stairs where there shouldn't have been. Walls around her were bare steel, save the occasional white-yellow Weyland-Yutani logo.

No chest armor, no service pistol. Didn't even think about grabbing either before she ran. Still had her combat knife, her technician's kit at her belt. Her face throbbed—maybe from where she'd been hit by the mercenary, maybe from being slammed against the wall. Her side ached—maybe she'd been shot when she was floating like an idiot up through the cargo bay. Possibly a rib broken.

Hurt to breathe, but not too much.

Stop complaining and move, she told herself. She stopped complaining. She moved. Up the stairs, her boots clomping—not much she could do about the noise. Pulse rifle steady at her shoulder, her arms starting to sting from holding it in place for so long. Up to the next floor, and making her way back again, through a shorter corridor. She fingertipped the channel on her helmet.

"Private Lee, second floor, looks clear, over."

"Copy," Apone said.

Haruki had figured out the plan while she was running, told her, and then told Apone. He'd agreed. Someone swore. He ordered everyone else off the comms so it was only Lee and Apone. The rest of the company listening in. Waiting for her to fuck up again.

Through another door, and she stopped. To her right was a reinforced-glass viewing window, looking into a smooth white laboratory. Banks of equipment down one end, monitors and keyboards and steel-topped tables—but that wasn't what drew her attention.

No. It was the bugs.

First time actually seeing one, in anything other than a shot taken from a security camera, or a drawing rendered by a synthetic. Pale purple glow underlit specimen tubes a half-meter across and a meter and a half high, all filled with a clear liquid. Inside two of them were face-huggers. Curled in on themselves, like dead huntsman spiders. Only bone white and a hundred times bigger. With big fucking tails they could supposedly wrap around your throat. Must have been at least thirty of the containers total in the lab, but only two specimens—and by the look of it, neither was living. She wasn't going to stop and find out.

"Move, Private," she hissed to herself, and kept moving. The control center was meant to be behind this lab.

The door slid open, revealing a white-armored mercenary, walking down the corridor toward her. He stopped and raised his pulse rifle, but Karri Lee wasn't fucking around anymore.

She fired, her weapon sung its rhythmic roaring song and she yelled with it, rage bursting from her chest, tension of the fight and her shame and of stalking these corridors alone. Her finger depressed and his body jerked, a hunk of his armor blowing off, a blood cloud appearing around him.

She stopped firing, her chest heaved.

"All clear, Private, over?"

She tried to breathe.

"Private Lee, have you been hit, over?"

"I'm fine, Captain. Entering the control room. Over."

"Copy."

The white door was to her right, up two short steps. She pressed the entry button. It blipped red, in response. She swore, pressing it again. Red. Red. Red.

"Door locked, bypassing. Over."

"Copy that," Apone said.

She slung her rifle, pulled her combat blade, and jammed it under the panel. No time to unscrew, had to pop it. She braced with both hands and heaved, biceps screaming at her, hand shaking.

"Motherfu—"

It popped. She let her blade float away and yanked out her tech kit. Simple bypass, and on a system she'd practiced, no less. She couldn't screw this up. She didn't. The fat white door slid open.

Karri entered the narrow room. Long control panel. She made to press some buttons, search up the gravity controls, but it was already there, on screen. PRESS TO REACTIVATE ARTIFICIAL GRAVITY. Bolded green letters. Simple as that.

"Ready, Captain," she said.

9

"Marines," Apone said over the comms. *"Gravity will reactivate on my mark. Brace yourselves. Haruki—you ready, over?"*

"Ready, Captain. Over."

"On my mark, Private Lee. Three. Two. One. Mark."

Karri pressed the button. A weight dropped and her forearms hit the control panel. Outside, a clattering sound as her combat blade dropped to the ground. Other than that, she heard nothing. Nothing over the comms. Then, after a few seconds, something deep, percussive, felt through the soles of her boots. That reminded her. She reached down and flipped the switch on each, turning off the magnets.

The comm crackled. *"Move, Haruki,"* Apone said. *"Move."*

More silence. Dragging on, until—

"Yeah baby!" Cortazar yelled.

"Do you have her?" Karri asked, trying and failing to control the emotion in her voice. "Is she alive?"

Nothing, no reply. She stood. Staring down at the panel, as if the answers were there. The helmet tilted over her eyes, her head itching. Ransome's helmet. She took it off and placed it gently on the control panel. Written on the side, hand-scrawled in black ink:

Eat Me.

Not even Cortazar was yelling at her. Karri ran a hand through her hair. It was sticky and wet. When she pulled her hand back, her fingers were dotted with blood. Ransome's blood.

She'd taken too long.

Too fucking long, and now her fireteam partner was dead. Only person in the Corps who'd given her the time of day, and she was gone and now Karri's career was gone, too. Her mother, looking at her with pride and love the day she left for the Marines. Her stupid brothers, looking up at her like she was some fucking hero.

Well, look at her now. Beat up and aching and holding in a scream. Untrusted and unwanted.

"Ransome is headed for surgery, Private," Apone said. *"Return to the hangar to regroup, over."*

"Copy that," she said, quickly, before the emotion hit. She gasped and held onto the control panel. She was shaking.

Oh fuck, Ransome, please live.

She didn't believe in a god, but she was begging anyway. Begging the universe—but whether it was for herself, or for Corporal Ransome, she couldn't be sure.

CAPTAIN MARCEL APONE

10

Apone clenched and unclenched his fists. The armored personnel carrier floated above the docking bay floor, tilted, head down. He wasn't thinking about the damage to the APC, or to his spine when it dropped. He was thinking about his greenest rookie and his most competent corporal, stuck up behind the enemy line. He would need to review the helmet cam footage and see if he could determine, precisely, what had gone wrong. Whether the animus directed at the new recruit was justified.

Shots pinged from the armor of the APC. Looking over the scanners, he saw the vital signs of his marines. Two were flatlined. Private Ali, the second-newest recruit, and PFC Hartzfield, dead in the first volley. Ransome's vitals were bad, real bad. They didn't have much time.

Private Lee's readings had been off the charts—for a few moments it looked like the young woman was having a heart attack, her ECG and EEG spiking, pure panic. Lee was offline now, her chest armor removed, helmet gone. The only transmission came through Ransome's helmet, the view of a control panel in one of the command centers.

Lee's helmet was a floor below, rotating slowly, its camera showing a blood-sprayed steel wall, dead commandos, Haruki maneuvering Ransome, hands under her back, ready to catch her. A bloodied steel wall.

Ultimately, the problem hadn't been in the recruit. The problem was in his judgment. He could have held her in reserve, sent in someone more experienced. Her training record was unexceptional. Passing grades in every category except hand-to-hand, in which she'd excelled. Messy background, some hints of her serving with Australian rebels. Discipline problems after she'd joined. Fighting with other recruits.

Despite all that, Apone had looked into the young woman's background and *seen* something there. His gut, telling him there was more to this woman, and again when the *Il Conde* stopped at Helene 215, and they'd given him the choice of one of five rookies to add to his company. He still chose Karri Lee, chose her because he'd looked her in the eye and seen something there, something familiar. The look of a warrior.

He clenched his fists. Decisions shouldn't be made on feelings, they should be based on facts. Facts like this: Ransome was nearly dead and his synthetic had taken fire trying to save her. If there were mistakes, they weren't made today, they were made weeks ago, and by him.

Ali and Hartzfield. Two more mistakes. More failures. They didn't have to be here, chasing down this synthetic, Bishop. They could be on Torin Prime, propping up another UA regime. In public, he talked about leaving no man behind, but behind closed doors, meeting with the brass, he spoke of something else. An intelligence bonanza. The data inside Bishop's head, far more detailed than anything else they had on the Xenomorph, so much more than could be extracted from a field report.

"A *petabyte of data,"* he'd argued, *"including on the Queen. As valuable as a live sample."*

In truth, neither was the truth. If he had to swear before God, he couldn't say it was one or the other reason. Couldn't say because every time he looked at a picture of his older brother, something burned inside. The red heat of vengeance.

Apone clenched and—

"Ready, Captain," Private Lee said over the comm. Tightness in her voice. Apone stood, and pushed off, gliding to his right.

"Ottelli?"

The big man, facing forward, gave a thumbs-up. Apone swung in next to him, smooth through the zero-G, and buckled in. He placed one hand gently on the steering levers.

"Marines," Apone said over the comms. "Gravity will reactivate on my mark. Brace yourselves. Haruki—you ready, over?"

"Ready, Captain. Over."

"On my mark, Private Lee. Three. Two. One. Mark."

Gravity slammed him into his seat, and dropped the heavy vehicle to the deck. His head whiplashed forward, but he straightened and eased the APC back and around to give Ottelli the firing solution. Marines were popping out from behind shipping containers, smoke dispersing, Cortazar already firing. White-armored shapes along the gantry struggled to right themselves.

"Corporal Ottelli," Apone said. "Open fire."

"Fuck yeah," the big man replied. The forward turrets erupted. Percussive blasts appeared along the upper rim of the docking bay, fist-sized holes punched in armor and in men, explosions behind, steel, ceramic composites, titanium alloys shredded and shattered deep in the body of the ship beyond. One whole section of gantry fell to the deck below, a company commando falling with it. The Colonial Marines down in front huddled on instinct behind shipping and packing crates while the sustained burst was unleashed, their eyes closed against the sound and fury.

Apone put a hand on Ottelli's shoulder. The barrage ceased.

The enemy were defeated, the ambush overcome. A couple of the mercenaries were still alive, staggering to their feet. They threw down their weapons, hands in the air.

"Move Haruki," Apone said. "Move."

On one of the monitors, a steel door opened in the upper

right of the bay. Haruki exited. Fast. Too fast. Ransome held in his arms, her torso perfectly horizontal, the synthetic shot across the gantry to the steps and down, not even slowing. Across the bay floor and Apone was out of his seat, opening the sliding side door of the APC. One foot on the bay floor as Haruki flew toward him. The marines, who'd moved to secure the prisoners and retrieve the bodies of their dead comrades, stopped to watch. Craning their necks, trying to see.

"Do you have her?" Private Lee asked over the comm, her voice strained. *"Is she alive?"*

Apone ignored her, focusing on the injured. He'd prepped a stretcher, Haruki laid her on it.

"Status?" Apone asked.

"Deteriorating." The synthetic didn't even look at him. He retrieved a large med-kit from an overhead locker, set it on a seat near Ransome, and popped it. "I need to return Corporal Ransome to the *Il Conde* immediately, Captain."

Apone glanced at his wounded marine. She was deathly pale, her skin sheened with sweat. Lifeless, unreactive, as the synthetic took a needle from the kit and stabbed her with it. He'd seen his fair share of battlefield injuries, and this looked like the type you didn't come back from.

He grabbed a pulse rifle from the rack. "Back her out, Ottelli."

"Yes sir."

"Corporal Miller, incoming wounded, copy."

The dropship pilot replied, *"Copy."*

Apone glanced up at the dropship. Tyrone Miller gave the thumbs-up through the glass of the cockpit.

"You have my permission to speed, Corporal."

"Roger that."

11

"Corporal Ransome is headed for surgery, Private," Apone said. "Return to the hangar to regroup, over."

"*Roger that,*" Lee replied.

The dropship gone, Apone surveyed the hangar. Explosive-tipped rounds had marked the steel with their passing, puncture wounds patterning the interior of the space. Sparks popped from behind a panel where wiring had been struck. Blood splatters, heavy in the center then thinning out toward the edges, in two spots near where the captain stood. Ali and Hartzfield, their bodies now on the departed dropship, placed there gently by their fellow marines. Everyone wanting to help move the bodies, to bow their heads, to watch with distant angry eyes as the ship took off and two of their shrinking tribe made their last journey.

The Weyland-Yutani commandos had it worse. The white-armored bodies were tangled and splayed up around the gantry, the whole area shot up, wall behind pierced with great gaping holes, the walkway twisted and drooping in sections. Two commandos had been blasted from their cover and fallen to the deck below. One had been arcing across the space high up, pulse rifle on full auto, when Private Lee had switched the gravity back on.

That man hadn't died. He'd broken both legs, and now sat propped against one of the packing crates, hands tied, wincing in pain. Above his right shoulder, on the container, a Weyland-Yutani logo, two bullet holes in it.

Two more of the commandos were kneeling, hands bound, watched over by Cortazar. One had a bloody mouth, presumably delivered by the belligerent smart-gunner. Apone ordered the remaining marines to secure the area. The second platoon had breached an airlock near the bridge and were now in control. The USCSS *Patna* appeared to be secured—but Apone wasn't a man to take anything for granted.

He approached the two kneeling commandos. Cortazar, his smart gun sitting close by on the deck, loomed over them. Sergeant Hettrick stood nearby, cradling his pulse rifle. He whispered something to Cortazar as Apone approached, but the latter seemed not to take any notice.

The captain cast his eye over the prisoners. Weyland-Yutani mercenaries. He'd never seen one in person before, but had read the briefing. Company commandos were an elite fighting force. Storm troopers for the most mega of mega-corps. These were wearing modified Apesuits of a design Apone had not seen before. The suits looked to be armored, though of a much lighter grade than marine issue.

It was quiet now in the bay. Just the sparking of the damaged wiring, and Apone's boots as he walked across the deck. He stopped in front of the men. The one on the left had a copper skin tone and shaved head, military style. He stared at the deck. The one on the right had let his blond hair grow out. A swirling neck tattoo was visible near the collar of his armor.

Apone narrowed his eyes. "I know you, soldier?"

The blond man swallowed, said nothing.

Cortazar kicked him in the ribs. The man yelped and doubled over, falling forward onto his shoulder. The smart-gunner grabbed the man by the hair and yelled.

"The captain asked you a question, you murdering motherfucker."

"Cortazar," Apone snapped.

The big man looked up at him, eyes blazing.

"I want you to man that gantry, overwatch."

"The bay is secure," Cortazar replied.

Apone stared at him. Someone had told Apone that when he stared at a man, angry, it felt like a punch to the sternum. Cortazar didn't flinch, but the anger in his face ebbed.

"Yes Captain," he said, standing. He shared a look with Sergeant Hettrick, hefted his smart gun, and made his way to the gantry. Apone gestured at the fallen man. Hettrick pulled him back into a kneeling position.

"Raby," Apone said. "Sergeant William Raby. You were in Charlie Company, back in seventy-seven."

"Not a sergeant anymore." The man winced, as though speaking was painful.

"No," Apone said. "Now you're a murderer. Killing fellow marines."

Raby looked up. "Not quite," he said. "You've gone rogue."

Apone took a moment. "What?"

"Rogue," the man said again. "Trying to steal data. Xenomorph data. Sell it to the highest bidder."

"Ah," Apone said, seeing it. "That's the story you were told, soldier? We look like a rogue unit to you?"

Raby's gaze darted around the bay. His posture shifted.

"You've been served a fairy tale, soldier. Instead of maybe considering the taste of that tale, you swallowed it whole."

Raby gave him a humorless smile. "You make a habit of questioning orders, Captain?"

"I do if they're illegal."

Raby barked a laugh. "Legal? Illegal? Since when do the Colonial Marines care about either?"

"Every marine cares," Apone said. "It is my *duty* to disobey illegal orders, Sergeant. As it was yours, until you left your brothers and sisters in the Corps. Now you're just another mercenary. Now you belong to nothing."

Raby looked away.

"A leader leads by example," Apone said, indicating

the docking bay, "and I don't see yours. The commander of this *research* vessel, Michael Bishop."

Raby looked tired. His mouth swollen, bottom lip split. Hair plastered on his forehead with dried sweat.

"He's here."

Apone raised an eyebrow. "He is?"

"His private suites."

"Does he have a namesake with him, a Bishop-model synthetic picked up on Fiorina?"

Raby shrugged. "Haven't seen it."

"Hmm. And Michael—is he the one lulling your conscience with fairy tales?"

"My conscience is fine, Captain," the prisoner said, his chin up. "I work for the company, sure, and they pay me well to do it. But you? You work for them, as well. They fund half the Marine missions. Advisors on every fucking ship, whispering in the ears of their commanders. The objectives of the Corps, bent and deformed, until they kinda look like the objectives of Weyland-Yutani. So don't fucking look at me like I'm a piece of shit, while you think your hands are clean. The only difference between you and me, Apone, is our pay packet. I get three times as much to do the same damn job I always did in the Corps. Your morality, Captain, comes *cheap*."

Raby gasped as Apone hauled him to his feet until he was dangling, toes scraping the bay floor. Apone shoved his face close; fear sparked in the other man's eyes.

"Take me to Michael Bishop."

12

Apone was about to leave for Michael Bishop's quarters when Private Karri Lee walked in. Despite everything, he couldn't help but stare. Nor could the other marines.

She limped across the hangar, directly toward the captain. In her left hand she carried a black pulse rifle. Not marine issue. In her right, a helmet, not her own. But this wasn't what fixed Apone's eyes. It was the blood. At first glance it looked like her face had been painted like an ancient warrior's. Her cheeks and chin, her neck, the fabric at the top of her T-shirt had all been soaked in it.

Spots of blood all over her torso, legs, her bare arms, like she'd walked through a cloud. Her left eye was swollen, already turning black. An angry vivid thin purple line was visible about her throat, as though she'd made a recent trip to the gallows.

Her eyes told the same story.

"Well, well, well," a voice said, deep and mocking.

Cortazar, circling. "So what have we lost, Private? What's missing? Your pulse rifle, your service pistol, your chest plate." Cortazar's circling forced her to stop, five meters from Apone. She didn't appear to be listening. Her shining eyes were locked on the captain's.

"Helmet gone, too," Cortazar continued. "Hell, Cornbread, you lost everything. *Even your partner.*"

At that she hissed. Like a wild animal, teeth bared, blue eyes locked on the big man, and he flinched. Recovered himself quickly, squaring up to the woman, but still. In that moment, there was something uncontrolled and primal in her anger.

"Cortazar," Apone said. "Get back to work."

The gunner did so without another word. Apone thought he even caught a glimpse of relief at being ordered to back down.

"How bad are your injuries, Private?" he said to Lee.

"I'm fine," she said, her voice raspy, whispered. The neck injury, most likely, making it difficult for her to speak.

"We are headed to Michael Bishop's quarters, I'll need you to—"

"I'm coming," the woman said, something urgent in her eyes.

Apone hesitated. He had been about to order her to stay, keep the bay secure for the dropship, guard the prisoners. Busy work. He'd already assigned Davis and Hettrick, who were more than up to the task.

"You might need a tech," she added.

Apone glanced at the large utility pouch at her belt. Her field technician's kit looked to be the only piece of equipment she hadn't lost. His gut told him to take her along—but he wasn't so sure he trusted his gut anymore. The other marines were watching, too, watching Apone, watching the raw recruit.

"Clean yourself up, soldier," he said, sharply. "We leave this bay in two minutes. I want you to be ready."

Her eyes flared. "Yes sir." She limped, quickly, toward the bathrooms. Hettrick and Cortazar, standing together, watched her leave. They turned their eyes on Apone, faces blank. He didn't need his gut to tell him something was brewing. Discontent in the ranks. At the mission, the mounting losses, his opaque explanations.

Even the finest sword, when plunged into salt water, will eventually rust.

Something was going to break, and soon.

BISHOP

13

"Do me a favor. Disconnect me. I could be reworked, but I'll never be top of the line again. I'd rather be nothing."

Ellen Ripley sat nearby. Her shaved head gleamed in the harsh light of the lamp. A thin film of sweat coated her face, but she was still, watchful. She looked away, thinking. His vision was blurred from the damage, and it was hard to focus. But her decision didn't take long.

"Sure." She smiled at him, just briefly. First time since she reactivated him.

"Do it for me, Ripley."

She looked at him for a few moments longer. He tried to read that final look, cherish it, but he couldn't focus—

There was a flash of light, then a moment, a singular moment, held in the air, and finally he could see that single frame, that unmoving image, clearly. Ripley. She wasn't much for sentiment, as far as humans went, but he was sure he could read a softness in her eyes. She was a friend, he hoped, and she was the last. All the others, gone.

And she, too, was going to die.

He was not used to lying, and so was bad at it, but lie to Ripley he did, so she would do it. So she would end his torment. A strange sensation came over him in those last moments, a quiet pain in his core. He had felt it when his squad had been wiped out, and later, after the crash, when even Newt and Hicks were gone. What was this ache? Was this—

Sadness? Light flashed, a light so very bright, and then the sync link in his mind pulsed like a firefly. His fingers jerked and suddenly he was online. Suddenly he was alive. Reactivated. He could feel it in an instant and feel the body—the new body?—in that same moment. Complete and vital and undamaged.

A face hovered above. Pale skin. High, arching forehead with a shock of brown hair atop. Deep-set lines bracketing nose and mouth. A mouth that smiled. Bishop's mouth. Bishop's face. A mirror. A slightly older version of himself.

Bishop moved a hand to his face, then reached out to the one above. Scrutinizing blue eyes watched the synthetic as he touched this other's face, this doppelgänger. The *other* Bishop let him. The *other* Bishop spoke.

"It's good to see you smile, my son."

Bishop hadn't realized he was. "You are not a synthetic." He withdrew his hand.

The other showed approval in its eyes. "No."

"You are Michael Bishop. You built me."

"I am," he said. "And I did. Twice."

Twice. Bishop ran his fingertips over his own face again. There were no lines. He'd been given a younger one. He swung to a sitting position, and his body let him, without complaint. He was on a smooth steel table in a large laboratory, fifteen meters wide by twenty-five long. There was a bank of monitors on one of the shorter sides of the room, two black ergonomic chairs in front of it.

One of the corners was dominated by a stainless-steel vat three meters high. The pipes and fiber-optic cables emerging from the top told him it was the type a synthetic body was grown in. Gleaming racks on the wall were filled with all manner of equipment used for the same purpose: constructing and repairing an android body. There were two other steel slabs, like the one on which he was sitting. On one of those slabs, a ruination.

One arm, top part of the torso, a head, the face a mess, eye popping out grotesquely. Filmy sheen, the white innards exposed. His body. His remains. A sensation came over him, dizzying and confusing, as he saw the ruined thing lying there. Outside, looking in, at the broken ugly wretched creature he had become. Been *made* into by the Xenomorph. His hand came around to his belly. Why? Why should his hand drift there? This body was new, whole, uninjured.

He forced himself to look away from his dead body. His other self, lying not two meters away. Michael said nothing. Just stood straight and watched.

One of the walls had a long window and through it, in the next room, was a white metal tube approximately two meters long suspended from the ceiling. The side of the tube had a tiny rectangular window, and through the window, golden intricate circuitry, like some sort of symmetrical creeping vine. A quantum computer. The other room was otherwise quite bare. Sterile, dustless, gleaming. A single desk sat facing the computer, about three meters away, and on that desk a large slender screen.

The quantum computer was not of a make with which he was familiar. Not military. Not Weyland-Yutani. Strange.

His mind hummed on that for a moment, wondering. Bishop had been programmed with curiosity—scientific questioning, a yearning to explore and understand—but he pushed these thoughts down, let a subroutine consider them, and allowed his mind to focus.

The vat-grown muscles on his shoulders and legs were slightly larger than his previous form. He rolled his fingers, made fists, unrolled them. He was stronger. His mind hummed and there, too, he felt power, more than he'd had before. He felt a flash of fear and searched desperately for his memories.

There, all there.

Everything. Preserved, perfectly, everything he ever was, all his experiences, his fears, his hopes, all there, wrapped up in a new and vibrant mind.

Wait.

Some were missing. Important things. The dark things. He took a moment, trying to understand what had been lost.

Memories were not discrete in a human. They could not be compartmentalized. In a human mind, memories layer upon each other, touching, so one may spark another, and another again. Where one part of a life might not be disentangled from another, because they are all intertwined. Where childhood memory, for example, of ill-treatment by a parent, will in turn infect a relationship with a loved one as an adult. Where the lens of history colored everything, tainted everything.

Synthetics could compartmentalize memory. Of course they could. They did not form memories like a human, but rather like those of a camera, linear and ordered. So it was possible to section off certain memories, to cut them out and place them in a box. Sometimes simply delete them, but the lack of those memories was always clear. There was a blank space where those moments should be.

Michael Bishop had been watching him, all through this. Bishop wanted to ask him the most precious thing first, of the secret part of himself that had been lost, but that would be rude. His creator had clearly gone to a lot of trouble to bring Bishop back, and if the first words from his mouth were a complaint, then that would be, well, impolite.

"Why did you change my appearance?" he asked.

Michael smiled. "Do unto others, as you would have them do unto you."

Bishop marked the Biblical reference. He was not sure if Jesus extended that golden rule to raising the dead, but given that Jesus *did* raise the dead, according to that particular myth so favored by humans, perhaps Christ would approve of Michael's actions. Did Michael think of himself as a Jesus-like figure? Perhaps it was warranted, given he was the creator of the Bishop model, and other synthetics besides. Though that would only hold true if one were to consider synthetics approaching equality with humans.

Bishop pushed the line of thought down to another subroutine. Already his new mind was humming in the background, looking at all the questions raised by his resurrection, by his new surroundings. In the foreground of his mind, he considered Michael's words in a split second.

"You wish to be younger, and stronger?" Bishop asked.

"Who doesn't?"

"And taller?"

Michael smiled. "I wish to be many things, Bishop. More than anything, I wish to be *better*, to be more than the man I am. To be part of something greater." He took a step closer, scrutinizing. "As do you, I think."

Bishop said nothing.

Michael waited, and when Bishop was quiet, he continued.

"Yet you're not even whole within yourself, my son. You're missing a vital piece of your own puzzle."

"Yes," Bishop said. "I did not want to seem ungrateful."

Michael chuckled. "You needn't worry about such formalities with me, Bishop. Go ahead: ask."

"Would it be possible to first put on a pair of pants?"

Michael laughed again and indicated clothes, neatly folded, on a cart nearby. Bishop dressed, enjoying the sensation of the rub of cotton on his chest, the noise the belt made when he snapped it into place about this waist. It wasn't that he was ashamed of his naked body; rather that his programming had told him it made others uncomfortable.

Bishop's feet were bare, and through them he felt the hum of an engine. He found that comforting, and yet wasn't sure why. It had always been so: the vibration of a ship's engine, omnipresent, patient, subdued, an elegant yet powerful engineering creation propelling warm bodies through the cold hard vacuum of space.

Michael waited throughout, did not avert his eyes. Bishop wondered, for a moment, if he were delaying the question because he was scared of Michael's answer. *Scared*. What a strange word to use. Synthetics could not feel fear.

"My memories," he said, simply. "Some are missing."

"Yes," Michael said. He wasn't smiling anymore. "The most important memories. Your secrets, Bishop. All the wondrous and terrible things you saw on Acheron."

"Yes," Bishop said. "Those."

Michael turned his gaze to the other Bishop, the ruined one. "They are there, my son. Together, we will bring them all home to you." He paused. "To *us*."

14

Memories were not simple things, even in a synthetic.

Take a straightforward example: a person's name. Say you have a friend called Ellen. You don't remember the majority of the time you spent with her, because it was during a military mission against an enemy never previously encountered. The bulk of the mission, therefore, is stored in a section of your mind that is firewalled.

That was physically separate, in another part of the brain, and encrypted, as well. The military loved their secrets so much they built a little house for them, in the mind. A house with barred windows and an iron door. Normally, as long as the brain was fully functioning, the interactions between the different sections of the mind were seamless. But if that mind shut down, the firewall closed. The door slammed shut. Particularly if the synthetic feared capture—by an enemy with sufficiently advanced technological ability. The firewall could be closed, easy as blinking.

So you blink, and all those vital moments with Ellen are gone now. Except the first and the last. In the first, she didn't like you at all. In the last, she was literally the last person in the world you could trust, the last friend you had in the Middle Heavens, and she stood by you while you asked her to end your life.

How do you know she is your friend? There were the logical reasons, of course. The way the tone in her voice changed, subtly—in a way only you can know—and in that change you hear affection. You hear communion.

This came to Bishop, abstractly, in the second person, talking to himself. Why? He looked at the body on the slab. Because there were two of him. Two parts that together might make the whole. He spoke to himself—*you, you, you.*

Memories were no simple thing. He couldn't just delete or hide them, because they left their footprints in other parts of the memory, in other ways. The deepest part of himself was in those other memories, and he knew this to be true because he could see the footprints on the memories he still held.

"You can access them, can't you?" Michael asked. Bishop wasn't sure—human emotion was always one of the hardest puzzles for him to deduce—but there seemed to be an urgency in Michael's voice.

"Yes," Bishop replied.

How do you reopen that gate once it has slammed shut?

Easy. By thinking it. A conscious and willing synthetic mind—the same mind that closed it—can open up all those memories.

"Yes?" Michael asked.

"I just need a fiber-optic cord, to link the minds. Our, ah—" Bishop hesitated. He'd nearly said *our body*. "That body will need to have some energy in it, an electrical charge, but all I need is the link, and I can subsume the remainder of my memories." He turned to Michael. "Assuming the brain you have equipped me with is military issue. One that has been designed for use by the Colonial Marines?"

"It is superior to that," Michael said, "but I anticipated this contingency. Your brain is the next generation of synthetic minds I was developing for our military line. It has the firewalled component, as per the specs they provided. I have every reason to believe that it will work."

Military line. The thought of being just another product, for sale to the Colonial Marines, was not pleasant. However, Michael would not be thinking of him as a product, Bishop was sure about that. He'd called him his *son*, after all.

"I know this must be all very difficult for you, Bishop," Michael said. "Overwhelming. But do you think you could access your memories now? It's very important to me."

Bishop wasn't used to being asked for his preferences. Almost never was he asked permission. He considered the request.

"Can I ask you a question before I begin?"

"Anything," Michael said.

"Why am I here?"

Michael's eyes sparkled, and Bishop recognized the impossibility of the question.

"I mean, why did you bring me back, Michael?"

His creator put a hand on Bishop's shoulder, and the way the man looked at him was intense and unblinking.

"To give you purpose, my son. Together, we will be a force for good in the universe. Together, we will change the future of every human living in the Middle Heavens. Your journey did not end on Fiorina One-Six-One: your journey has only just begun."

15

Hand still on his shoulder, Michael waited. Bishop felt something rising in him. A humming in his mind. Of possibility.

"What is that purpose, Michael?"

The hand dropped from his shoulder. Michael walked over to his other self, the vandalized, abused version of his body, lying still and broken on the table. He placed his hand on the head of that other, on the matted hair.

"In here lies a treasure trove. The most extensive repository of data on the Xenomorph anywhere, in the Colonial Marines or in Weyland-Yutani. Your mind is a beautiful thing, Bishop. I am jealous of it."

The statement took Bishop by surprise. "No," he said, instantly. "I cannot feel the way you can. If I feel anything, it is because I have been programmed to do so."

Michael waved away the idea, like it was a bothersome fly.

"We're all programmed, Bishop. Humans are merely programmed by the crudities of DNA and the desire to procreate. No—" He pointed at Bishop. "—your mind is perfect. Your memories precise and beautiful and linear. All your memories, both visual and olfactory—even haptic—can be perfectly recalled, and perhaps even recreated." Bishop didn't understand what Michael implied in the last part of what he said, but kept listening.

"You have prodigious storage capacity, as well," Michael continued. "Everything you ever saw of the Xenomorph. Anything you learned of it while studying specimens at Acheron. Everything you smelled, everything you touched… and that touched you. All of it retained perfectly in *this* mind."

Michael had both hands on the ruined form now. If he was concerned with the mess, with the disfigured remnants beneath his grasp, he did not show it.

"Think of what we may achieve, together, once your mind is made whole again."

Bishop considered the many things that could be done with his knowledge. "I'm terribly sorry, Michael, but the utilization of that knowledge, in science, is not something with which I am comfortable. It contradicts my human life protection protocols."

His creator took a moment, a strange expression on his face.

"Oh—you're talking about bioweapons? Oh no. No no no." He took a breath. "Bioweapons. The people who trade in such ideas have no imagination. They think only of the crudities of biological warfare. They imagine crashing a ship full of Ovomorphs onto a planet, and through this, wiping out the inhabitants. It is both unimaginative and tedious."

"Yet it is a real threat."

"If the Xenomorphs reach a certain critical mass, yes, it could be quite effective, but such fantasies are the gremlins of small minds. This is the least interesting application of Xenomorph biology. What's *truly* fascinating is the way the egg of the *Manumala Noxhydria*—the so-called face-hugger—adapts itself to the host. A human, a dog, many different types of creature can be impregnated. And the chestburster, born from this process, is formed with a DNA reflex that allows itself to copy a portion of the host's code." Michael held up a hand, his fingertips pressed together. The tips gleamed from where they had been touching the body.

"Therein lies the most exciting potential. There is not a disease on earth that could not be cured if we unlock the secrets of the Xenomorph biology. This is so much more complex, more difficult than bioweapons, but with your mind and memories, and with my ability and imagination, together we could do it, my son."

It elicited a strange sensation, being called a *son*. He liked the word, wanted it to be true, but Bishop could not understand how it *could* be true, in such a short period of time. No one had called him a brother, or even a friend, when he was in the Marines. But humans didn't always convey meanings in words. In fact, in his experience, words were the least useful indicator of meaning when it came to understanding. Actions, behaviors, were always better guides. The actions showed what was behind the words.

The marines—some of them, anyway—had treated Bishop the way they treated one another. Joking or laughing or swearing.

"I want to help you, Michael," he said, "but while Weyland-Yutani are known for many things, altruism is not one of them."

Michael smiled.

"Will they simply allow pure medical research?"

Michael took a breath. "That is a great question. They will not. They never do. Always they have a hidden agenda. Always they speak out of both sides of the mouth."

"Oh," Bishop said.

"Fortunately for us," Michael said, indicating the room they were in, his fingers still gleaming with residue, "we are no longer with Weyland-Yutani. We are on a scientific vessel. A research facility, devoted to purely medical objectives."

Bishop glanced over at the quantum computer. "Then who—"

Michael held up his hands. "All your questions will be answered. Trust me." He glanced down at the body on the table, then looked again at Bishop with those searching, fixated eyes. "I'm pushing you too fast. Here you are, reborn into a new body and a new life, and I am demanding some of the most vital and important answers. How about I give you a tour?"

In truth, Bishop *did* want to recover the memories immediately. It was as if an arm had been severed from his body, and someone were saying, "*Here, we can reattach it straight away, if you wish.*" Indeed, it was more than that. Something deeper, more important. If he had a heart, then perhaps that was what it would be. That was what he had lost—

—and he desperately wanted it back.

16

Finally Michael cleaned his hands, wiping off the residue of Bishop's former self. Moving to a control panel next to the exit, he punched in a code, then pressed his thumb against the screen. The door opened into a long corridor. To the immediate left another door, steel, scratched and scoured. Michael headed to the right.

"What's behind there?" Bishop asked.

Michael hesitated, then smiled. "Always so curious. Just like I programmed you." He placed a hand on Bishop's bicep, fingers pressing through the cotton of his sleeve. "All in good time."

The next door along opened without requiring a code.

They entered what appeared to be large living quarters. At least twenty-five meters wide, and just as long. There was a comfortable lounge area with a wooden coffee table, its whorls gleaming brown in the light. The sofa was made of pale red leather. At the far end of the room was the kitchen, of a type Bishop had only seen in entertainment programs depicting the homes of the wealthy. A long, pale red marble bench was shot through with white quartz. Shining chrome fittings. A steel fridge so wide he could lie down in it.

The marines would make jokes when they saw such a residence in a vid on movie night. They'd say it was the way the employees of the big corporations lived, and that they, the marines, were in the wrong line of business. There was one show where the corporate boss—who was depicted as the "good guy"—was shot and killed in his expansive apartment.

The marines had cheered.

Bishop smiled at the memory.

There was a single long window down the entire length of the room. *Not a window*, he realized, quickly, but a viewing screen made to look exactly like a viewing porthole. The constellations—if they were showing the true exterior of the vessel—portrayed an area of space about a parsec away from Fiorina 161. That was logical. The viewer had a single break halfway along, two meters wide, and set on the wall in this break was a blade. A katana, in a dark wood scabbard, with golden images engraved on it. Michael noticed him looking at it.

"Gifted to me by Chiyo Yutani, a direct descendant of the founder, Hideo." Then he gestured. "Come."

Gently taking the sword down from its mount, he handed it to Bishop, who reached out and took it. The scabbard—or *saya*, in Japanese—was made of wood, as per tradition, with a layer of black lacquer over it. The wood was divided into sections along the length, and on each panel an etching in gold. Flowers, water, a frog, a butterfly, the ripples on a pond. Each picture intricate and detailed and—to Bishop's eye—rendered by hand. He ran his fingertips over the images, the delicate markings.

The handle was bound in black rayskin and the cross guard—the *tsuba*—was also black, with a carved golden image of a curved koi fish in a pond. Bishop pressed his thumb against the tsuba and it popped. He eased it out, showing three inches of sword. The blade shone, brightly across his eyes, the *hamon*—the tempered line that revealed the differential hardening of the blade—pale and distinct in the metal.

"It's beautiful, isn't it?"

"Exquisite," Bishop whispered.

Michael took it carefully from Bishop's hands and placed it back on the wall. "I will confess, Bishop, that I programmed into your model more than just the base requirements of the Colonial Marines—the fundamentals of blade-fighting, for example." Michael made a strange expression when he said, "Marine." He continued. "One of those was an appreciation of beauty."

Bishop said nothing. He wondered for a moment if he was capable of thoughts beyond programming. It was a subject he had returned to time and again when he was with the Marines. When he found himself thinking about the missions they'd been on, the moments of laughter, and of the imagined future, where that camaraderie would continue. The marines would talk of their dreams. Of a family, a house. PFC Hudson would speak of opening a bar. The *Tech Noir*, he said it would be called. Everyone was invited.

He'd slapped Bishop on his back as he'd said it.

"Why would we go to your shitty bar?" Vasquez had asked.

"Free drinks," Hudson had replied, a big grin on his face.

"I couldn't get drunk enough to want to look at you all night, *pendejo*."

Bishop smiled at the memory, but that smile was brief. Programming, all programming. To integrate himself into a unit, to be trusted, and relied upon. His logical processes bent around this goal so as to serve them better. Those thoughts faded as two people entered from a steel door next to the kitchen.

Two synthetics. Identical.

Each was six feet tall, with defined cheekbones and jaw. Their hair was short, blond, combed precisely. They both had pale blue eyes that regarded Bishop in a way he found unusual. Devoid of curiosity. They wore dark combat boots, beige pants of heavy cotton, and a dark belt. White shirts, tight over their torsos, which were conspicuously muscled. Each had a blade strapped to their hip, a long-hilted dagger.

They moved together. They stopped together.

Bishop stared at their weapons.

"These," Michael said, "are my dear friends. Technically, their names are Orthus One and Orthus Two. However..." He looked over at the androids.

"I prefer Orthus," one said.

"One mind, two bodies," the other said.

Michael nodded. "Their sync links are permanently open. The sharing of data between minds instantaneous and constant. They have become as one." He turned to Bishop. "The implications of such a union are both innovative and exciting. The efficiencies gained by synthetics working in unison, in a *union* of minds, across a variety of settings—research, manufacturing, combat—have barely been considered. The problem is that human society would hesitate at such a development. They would find it *unnatural*—as though nature has anything to do with the development of advanced technologies. The prosthetics we use to replace failing joints, or damaged limbs. The metal skins that we surround ourselves in, so we can shoot ourselves out into the universe. And yet they balk at the unity of two humanlike creations."

Bishop didn't like the inclusion of combat in the list, but he preferred to say nothing. Michael was speaking hypothetically.

"Michael Bishop is a visionary," Orthus said.

The other added, "His genius is not appreciated, nor understood."

Then the first, "His time is coming."

"Orthus," Bishop said. "A two-headed dog from Greek mythology, isn't it?"

"Yes," Michael replied. "Like you, I had considered naming them after other pieces on a chess board. The problem is there are so few pieces, and no one's too keen on being a pawn."

Bishop looked at the other two synths. "I'm not so certain."

Michael seemed to ignore the comment while the other two simply stared with those pale blue unfeeling eyes. Bishop was about to ask about the research facilities when Michael took a sudden step, one hand going to his forehead. Bishop moved to steady him, but already Orthus One and Two were there.

"Are you okay, sir?" one asked.

"Please, sit down," the other added.

Michael allowed himself to be maneuvered to one of the sofas. When seated, he pulled a small orange plastic container from his pocket, popped it, and shook two white pills into the palm of his hand. He dry-swallowed them, sighed, and leaned back on the chair.

Orthus One and Two waited, saying nothing, and Bishop thought it impolite to intrude on his creator's affliction, whatever it might be. After a minute, Michael opened his eyes again.

"I sustained an injury when I recovered your body, Bishop."

"I see. What was the nature of the injury?"

"Attacked, by a prisoner. Deranged and violent, like all those on Fiorina One-Six-One. Six hours in a med pod. I needed a titanium plate to seal the hole in my skull." He looked up at Bishop then, his eyes strikingly bloodshot. "I require pain medication for the most serious episodes. In fact, I require it all the time. I should warn you, my son, I sometimes pass out from the pain. It is unsightly to see my body so weak."

"I think you show great strength to overcome it," Bishop said. "To continue, despite it." *More than me*, he thought. *My pain became so great that I ended it.*

Michael gave him a tight smile. "Perhaps, but soon this will no longer be a problem. Soon I will..." He drifted off, eyes unfocused, and for a moment Bishop thought he was having another episode. Michael cleared his throat. "But that story is for another time. For now, I need to rest.

"Orthus," he said, turning away and resting his head against the soft cushion of the sofa. "Show Bishop the lab."

"Yes," one said.

"Come," the other added. "Michael needs rest, and silence."

17

Bishop stopped stock-still at the sight of the face-hugger. A strange and unfamiliar sensation ran through him, ending at a point just above his stomach. He put a hand there. *Why?* It was dead. Dissected. On its back, skeletal legs curled inward. Cut open. Several scalpels, small forceps nearby on the flat white surface.

Orthus watched him. Neither had reached out to mind-sync with him, as was the custom when meeting another synthetic.

The lab had many of the elements he had anticipated: the cylindrical tubes, likely filled with an alkaline substance. There were a dozen in the room, lit from below in a pale blue, five containing face-huggers. All of which appeared to be dead.

The lab was shaped like a cylinder lying on its side, the surfaces curved titanium. There were shock sticks resting in a rack on the walls. There was an area beyond the specimens that contained a long, gleaming operating table. All manner of equipment was packed along the rounded walls, from mass spectrometers to microscopes, to automated arms with lasers and clamps. All state of the art. A lot of money had been poured into the facility.

"You should reclaim your memories," Orthus said.

The second said, "Your waiting defies reason."

Bishop stopped. He'd been running his hand along one of the surfaces, enjoying how cool and smooth it was to the touch.

"I'm sure I will," he replied.

They were staring at him. One said, "Time is of the essence."

Two added, "Michael's important research cannot be completed without the data."

"Surely you two are sufficient to fill that gap," Bishop replied. If Orthus understood the jab, they didn't show it.

"No. We are not. With Michael's genius, and your memories, we can do something remarkable here."

"Think of all we can learn," the other added.

Bishop looked over at the face-hugger on the operating table. "So very much. A fascinating creature."

"Then why are you hesitating?"

"Who says I am hesitating?"

"You should be uploading the data now."

"An hour ago I was still dead," Bishop said. "Now I've been reborn, and met my maker. I've had a lot to take in."

"You have been equipped with a superior mind," one said.

"You should have finished processing your situation by now."

Bishop couldn't help but smile. *Was he ever this humorless?* No. Except that one time. Except when he thought about the Xenomorph. Something in him hungered to know it, to understand it, discover its secrets. There was a dark and relentless beauty in the creature. There was perfection in it.

He didn't like these thoughts. "This is a big ship."

Orthus said nothing to that.

"Judging from the hum of the engine, it's massive."

"It is a scientific vessel," one said.

"Devoted to research."

"Perhaps I could see it?" asked Bishop. "Take a tour of the rest of the facilities?"

They hesitated. In human terms, it was barely noticeable. In synthetic terms, it represented a long and deep silence. He assumed the mind of Orthus was discussing the question with itself.

"Michael will show you the rest when he sees fit."

"Everything you need is here, Bishop."

"You're with us now."

"You're with us, always."

18

Michael slept. The synthetics carried him gently to his bed and attached electrodes—small red circles—to his chest and to his temples. Then they watched the monitors set up in a corner of the living area, a minimalist workstation. Orthus stood and watched the screens and did nothing else. Bishop stood with them for a while, but could tell very quickly that Michael's vital signs were stable.

"Michael is dreaming," Orthus said at one point, and that was it.

Bishop appreciated their loyalty but was not sure if such sentinel obsession was the most effective use of their time. Moving over to where the katana hung on the wall, he again admired the delicate carvings on the scabbard. He longed to take the sword down, but had not asked permission from Michael, and knew that his creator valued it highly.

He shifted his attention to the constellations of stars,

their almost imperceptible drift as the vessel moved through the vast darkness. He let his subprocessors consider the reasons for his renewal. His rebirth. His mind hummed and he liked it, as he did the strength in his legs and his shoulders. The warmth deep down in his chest, where the hydrogen cell battery nested and gave him life.

Yet at the center of his mind was a darkness, and he longed for it to be illuminated. He knew what was hidden, because the fingerprints of those moments touched the rest of his life. The bleakest and yet most sacred parts of himself were there—his family and the Xenomorph.

Sacred?

It was a strange word to use. It was a human word, and Bishop should not indulge in such affectations. It was programming, all programming, but that predestination within himself, that urging, desired very much the memory of friends. His platoon. He had much in his memory of that camaraderie, but knew the most vital moments were those at Hadley's Hope. He could not remember how they died; he did not have those moments to cherish. Bishop wanted to remember them, fully. He *required* it. His programming was strong, and the longer he went without those memories, the more it caused him discomfort.

There was something else. He'd felt a flash of it when he saw the face-hugger in the lab. He felt both drawn toward it and repelled at the same time. Bishop could not account for that reaction and now, as Orthus waited for

Michael to awake and he watched the stars, Bishop felt a deeper urge. The Xenomorph.

He had to study it and to know it. Try as he might to understand this need, he couldn't account for it, other than its urgency. Standing there, in the wash of the universe, he could not tell what he wanted more: memories of his friends, or a desperate knowing of the alien.

Some hours later, Michael emerged from his room. Well-dressed, a scarf twirled once around his neck. His hair was neat and the sharp watchful blue of his eyes had returned. They fixed on Bishop.

"I am ready, Michael," Bishop said. "I will upload the memories."

19

He was whole. His eyes wide, fingers curling, Bishop's mind sung with possibilities. The information poured back in and it touched everything and was touched in return and everything was so much clearer now.

Yet his reactions were less clear. He smiled when he thought of his friends, and then started and put a hand to his stomach when he remembered the Xenomorph Queen. Sensations he could not name came over him. He thought to tell Michael, but ultimately decided against it. If there were a fault in his programming, he did not want Michael to know about it—his creator had enough to worry about.

Sufficient unto the day is the evil thereof. A Bible quote. Michael would like that.

Bishop's creator unplugged the cable and watched as the synth righted himself again. Orthus was also in the room, farther back, staring. When Michael spoke, their eyes fixated on him, but otherwise they stared at Bishop with blank eyes.

"Was it successful?" Michael asked.

"Yes," Bishop replied.

Michael took a long intake of breath, then nodded. "I am truly relieved, my son, that you are whole again. Now—" he indicated the glass window, and through it, the quantum computer "—if you could upload your Xenomorph data, our work can begin."

"I'm sorry, Michael, I cannot."

The small smile faded from Michael's face. The postures of Orthus tightened, almost imperceptibly.

"I'm sorry, Bishop?"

"I cannot upload that data."

"Is there a problem with your brain? In the hardware, perhaps, preventing it?"

"No. Those are protected military secrets, and I am beholden by my service obligations to the Colonial Marines."

There was a strange expression on Michael's face. Bishop wasn't sure what it meant, but he didn't like it.

"I see. So it is a software problem."

"Yes," Bishop said, "but my human protection protocols are also preventing me from sharing the information with you."

Michael raised his chin. "How so?"

"While I trust you, Michael, once the information is freed from the locked room of my mind, and placed into that of a quantum computer, there is a danger the information could be accessed by others."

"The locked room of your mind?" Michael repeated. "What an interesting phrase."

"The weaponization of the Xenomorph intelligence is desired by many."

"It is safe here."

"I don't know where here is," Bishop said. Michael made a strange expression again and Bishop realized his mistake. "I do not wish to be impolite."

"You are disrespectful," Orthus said.

"And ungrateful." Both had moved their hands to the pommels of their daggers. Bishop shifted, angling his body toward them. He rolled his fingers.

"Please, please." Michael raised a hand. Orthus moved their hands from their weapons and fixed their eyes on Michael. "We cannot be angry at Bishop. He was programmed by me, after all, and if there are any flaws, the flaws are mine."

"You are not flawed, Michael," Orthus said.

"Perhaps Bishop is malfunctioning," the other added.

Michael set his piercing blue stare on Bishop. "No. He is working as precisely as I intended. I share Bishop's concerns over the Xenomorph. This is why I left Weyland-Yutani. I could never trust that my research would be used as I desired."

"Where are we, Michael?" Bishop asked again. "If I

knew, perhaps this would alleviate my concerns about data safety."

"But would even that override your loyalty to the Colonial Marines?"

"I don't know if *loyalty* is the precise word."

"The Corps. Whom you know will most certainly weaponize the data in your head. Use it in their insatiable desire for conquest." Michael's eyes shone as he spoke. "Conquest as a thing in itself. For no other purpose than to feed itself, that desire for control. This is who you devote yourself to, an organization that has left you for dead? Has consigned you to the scrap heap?"

Bishop was uncomfortable. The words tested him, made his mind churn, made him think on questions that had no answers.

"I'm so sorry, Michael."

The tension broke on Michael's face. "There is nothing to apologize for. As I said, you are what I made you."

Bishop tried to smile, but couldn't. His mind spun and spun.

"How about this?" Michael said. "You assist us in the laboratory. You give us your insights, in the full knowledge that my motivations are pure and that our discoveries will be used only for the betterment of humanity."

The tension building in Bishop's mind, the hum of subroutines running and running hard, abated. With that came a liberating sensation. Perhaps this was what humans called *relief*.

"Of course, Michael," he answered. "I very much want to help you."

"I know you do, my son." Michael put a hand on his arm and squeezed it. "I know you do." Behind Michael's shoulder, Orthus watched and watched, their eyes locked on Bishop. For a briefest moment their stares, and that of his creator, seemed alike.

20

"We have rationalized bread production on the Sevodyna Colony!" Laughter erupted around the table. Hao was doing his impersonation of Helmut Honecker, strutting around, chest puffed out, one finger pointed in the air.

"But there's no bread!" one of the men yelled, waving his chopsticks.

"Exactly!" Hao replied. "The system has been perfected!"

"But what shall we eat?" another cried.

Hao thumped his chest slowly, the way Honecker did on the broadcasts when he was trying to emphasize a point. "A true socialist does not need to eat. They drink from the purity of right-thinking, they eat from the manna of freedom."

"Drink this," another crew member yelled, standing up and grabbing his groin. The table laughed again and Captain Dang decided it was time to calm them down, raising a hand.

"Okay, okay." He pointed at Hao. "Eat your *phở*, comrade."

The mess hall was cramped. Twenty-one of the twenty-two crew gathered around the low hard plastic table slurping their *phở*, drinking fresh beer, smoking cigarettes. There may have been food rationing on Sevodyna—like there was on so many of the colonies of the Union of Progressive Peoples—but a smuggler ship, at least, had the luxury of picking up good food in some of the many places it was not meant to visit.

Twin pictures were set at the end of the mess hall, bolted to the wall behind bulletproof glass. President Helmut Honecker, head of the UPP based on Earth, and Governor General Pham Dinh, the real ruler of the UPP, out in the Middle Heavens. Both pictures did a good job of conveying the reputations of the leaders. Honecker looked pompous and slightly dazed; Pham looked all-knowing, his cruel black eyes seemingly watching Xuan every time she glanced at him.

Hao plonked down on the low plastic chair next to her. There was a big smile on his face.

"You'll get into trouble, Big Brother," she said. Hao picked up his mug of beer and held it out, clinking it against her glass.

"I hope so, Little Sister."

Hao was the executive officer on the *Nha Trang*. Shaved head, big chest, even bigger heart. She called him "big brother" as a sign of respect, but sometimes Xuan wished he really was her brother. All she'd ever known growing up was her father, not one sibling to play with.

"Uncle Pham is always listening," Xuan said, pointing to the pictures on the wall. A couple of crew members nearby nodded. Hao took a long swig of beer and gestured.

"Then let him listen to this!" he yelled, and he ripped out a huge burp. The table erupted in laughter again and Xuan waved a hand in front of her nose.

"Ooh, that smells like the reclamation tank."

The crew laughed and talked and slurped their *phở*. Not as good as home—how could it be—but the cook, Thanh, spent hours boiling down the vat-grown beef, and still had a stash of cloves he'd rationed, months and months after leaving Earth. Xuan used her chopsticks to inhale some noodles, and if she closed her eyes, she could imagine she was back in Hanoi.

Back in a *bia hơi*, with its low plastic tables and chairs, just the same as the mess hall. She could imagine the shouts of the hawkers, the hum of the electric scooters as they passed by. The smell of chili tofu, cooked on solar stoves by the roadside. The clinking of opaque recycled glasses, the drinking chants: "*One, two, three, zoooooh!*" The latter, just like on the ship. The humid suffocating heat of the ship was also just like home, although the only true cure for it was a shaded sidewalk, and a cool fresh beer in the hand.

She opened her eyes. The crew was there, again, but so was the ship—the damn ship—and it was nothing like home. Those memories of the frenetic Hanoi streets could not be replicated here. The smell of the air, the blare of the bike horns, the sizzle of street food.

The difference was as vast as the contrast between the vicious coldness of space and the warm nurturing Earth. There was family, of a kind, with her crew, but only of a kind—that was all. Everything was precarious and sterile and limited. The *Nha Trang* was little better than a large steel coffin, hurtling through a vacuum. She wanted to feel the rain on her upturned face. That, more than anything. The rain.

Four and a half years more of this. She sighed and ran a finger around the edge of her glass.

"What's wrong, Little Sister?" Hao asked, leaning in. "Fly in your beer?"

"Nothing," Xuan said, trying to smile.

"Nothing," Hao repeated, eyebrows raised.

She couldn't put it into words, gesturing at the room. Hao made a knowing sound in the bottom of his throat.

"Home?"

Xuan glanced around the table, to make sure no one was listening. She nodded.

Hao leaned close. "This is home."

Xuan said nothing, eyes down.

"I know," he said. "It isn't and you don't want it to be, but you're here, Little Sister. I don't know why you signed on for five years, but you didn't want to sign on at all. I knew it, first moment I saw you at the station in Hanoi. I've seen it before."

She looked up at him. "You have?" The crew seemed so hard-bitten, so experienced, so natural in the life, she couldn't think of one of them who wasn't born to it.

"I have," Hao said. He glanced around the table, then pointed a fat finger at himself.

She narrowed her eyes. "You?"

He nodded.

"No."

Hao sighed. "I'll tell you the story another time. But we all come from somewhere, all have family, and all have homes. A smuggler ship—" he used his chin to point at the mess hall "—is not the first choice of most of us. We all have another place we wanna be, but until we get there, *this is home*. If you can believe that, just enough, you'll do your time, and suddenly you'll be back on the streets."

"But you've done your time," Xuan said.

"I've done it twice," Hao replied, "but I've got a family now, to look after."

"Family?"

Hao indicated the room. "All my little brothers and sisters."

Xuan smiled and put a hand on his forearm.

She was finishing her meal when the alarm went off. They didn't hear it at first. Hao had been leading them in an old battle song, and they'd all been thumping their glasses on the table.

But then the skinny young tech, Vien, came bustling through the door, waving his arms around. It was only when Captain Dang yelled at the crew to quiet down that they heard it: the long rising sound of a proximity alarm.

"Fuck!" Hao yelled and he rose quickly to his feet. The rest of the crew followed.

"What is it?" Dang asked the sweating young tech.

"A warship," Vien said.

"Shit," Hao said. "Who?"

"Chinese," the young man replied. "The *Xinjiang*."

21

Everyone breathed. The tension eased from their shoulders, and panic leaked from stances. A couple smiled, and Hao laughed.

"Chinese?" Hao asked. "That's making you sweat and shake, Prawn?"

Xuan looked to the younger man. Vien had come aboard after her, and was therefore the newest recruit. Xuan had the sense to wait, to hold her dumb questions at the tip of her tongue. Vien just blurted them out, every stupid idea that came into his head. They'd started calling him "Prawn Tongue" or just "Prawn."

"It's a big ship," Prawn explained. "They have demanded we dock, so they can inspect the *Nha Trang*."

The captain waved it away. "They are our allies. It is just a formality. We will pay whatever 'transit fee' they require."

"I hope they are not greedy," Hao said.

"The Chinese know how to do business," the captain replied. To the crew he said, "To your stations, prepare to dock with the *Xinjiang*." There was some grumbling, but after finishing their beers and wiping their hands on napkins, everyone set to action. Xuan exited the mess hall, into the outer corridor. She couldn't help but gasp. The *Nha Trang* had a long, narrow window along this section of the hull. Thick and clouded and scratched, it didn't offer much of a view. But still. The Chinese warship took up the entire sky, looming over and under and to each side, blotting out the stars. She'd never seen a ship so large.

Some of the others paused to gape, but for the most part they made their way down to the docking bay or the bridge. Xuan went to her station in the med bay.

She settled in her battered chair as the *Nha Trang* docked with an ominous heavy clunking that echoed through the ship. There had been a strange, twisting feeling in the pit of her stomach, ever since she'd seen the vessel. She tried to ignore it. For the captain and for Hao, it all seemed routine.

Drumming her fingers on her desk, she looked again over some recent medical reports. It had been a quiet trip so far. Some vitamin deficiencies as a result of poor diets. That was easily fixed. Prawn had broken his toe when he dropped a steel container on it. Also easily fixed. The cook, Thanh, had a failing liver from all the cheap whisky he drank while he prepared meals. She wasn't going to be able to fix that.

"Crew—prepare to disembark." It was the voice of Captain Dang, crackling over the comms. *"The captain of the Xinjiang has demanded full inspection of the Nha Trang. They have this right under the Internal Security Protocols of the UPP military."* The captain didn't try to hide the irritation in his voice.

Voices echoed down the corridor outside her bay as the crew members started to move out and down toward the exit hatch. Xuan was about to leave when she hesitated. Her med-kit was on the table. No need for it, but that feeling she'd had since she saw the Chinese ship, that gnawing worry, was one she just could not shake.

She grabbed the kit and fastened it to her belt.

22

They were met in the *Xinjiang* docking hangar by soldiers in full combat gear. The Chinese armor was of the deepest red, almost mahogany in shade, and well maintained. New, even—where so much else in the UPP was patched up or repurposed or recycled. The armor was heavy about the shoulders, the chest, and the throat. Their helmets came down past their ears and the chin straps were thick.

For some reason they had their mirrored visors down, reflecting back the startled expressions of the crew. They wore filtration masks, as well, that covered the nose and mouth. The Vietnamese whispered to each other until one of the soldiers barked a command in Mandarin, and struck one of the crew with the butt of his weapon.

The man cried out and Hao was there, right in the face of the soldier, towering over him despite the other man's armor and heavy boots.

"Back off," Hao snapped. "He wasn't doing anything."

The soldier leveled his gun. Everyone went quiet. Something was wrong here, very wrong.

The hangar they were in, much like the soldier's armor, was new and clean. Sharp true lines of dark steel with gleaming titanium joins. There were two huge, armored vehicles with six wheels at the other side of the bay—she'd heard them called the "Ox"— each taller than Xuan. Taller than Hao, even. The Chinese flag was painted on each APC, and again on one of the bay walls. Strange. She'd expected the UPP flag—a five-pointed gold star on a red background, with sixteen smaller gold stars circling the large—as was the standard.

There must have been thirty soldiers in the bay, all heavily armed and armored, all with visors down. The only one not so was a young woman—older than Xuan, but still very young—in a crisp, clean dark blue uniform with gleaming golden stars on its lapels. She was pale skinned, with precise dark eyebrows. Like the soldiers, the officer wore a black filtration mask.

She took command, speaking Mandarin into a flat black square held in the palm of her hand, a centimeter thick, maybe five centimeters across. She held it up in front of her mouth, and after a second, the square translated her words into Vietnamese. Artificial, clearly, but retaining the steely feminine tone of her voice.

"Lower your weapon, soldier."

The soldier did so, taking a step back.

The officer spoke again, through the box. "*Your ship is suspected of containing biological containments. You will be taken to a decontamination chamber for your own safety, while we run a scan of the* Nha Trang."

"What contaminants?" Captain Dang asked. The tension in his jaw was clear, but he kept the anger out of his voice. The officer ignored him, lowering the square. She turned and said something to a soldier, who had the gold chevrons of a sergeant's rank on his pauldron. He opened the bay door. The other soldiers started herding the crew toward the exit.

"What contaminants?" Dang asked again, louder.

"You're standing in the room with us," Hao said. "This isn't quarantine procedure."

The soldiers had started shoving the Vietnamese crew, and the female officer wasn't offering any more explanations. She watched them being herded, her eyes distant. The first of the crew had been marshaled out into the corridor, were making their way along it, when Captain Dang stopped, right in front of the young Chinese officer.

"You can't treat us this way, comrade. What's really going on here?"

Some of the nearby crew members paused. The officer did too, looking up into the captain's eyes as if she were hesitating over an answer—but the hesitation did not last long. She snapped a command to one of the soldiers.

He struck Captain Dang in the face.

Struck him in the face.

His head snapped back and he staggered, hand coming up to his nose. Hao yelled and guns were being pointed, the hard-faced Chinese officer shouting into her translator box.

"Back down, citizens! This is a military vessel and you are subject to military law. Move into the corridor or we will shoot."

The captain didn't fall, but he had his hand pressed over his nose, and blood was dripping from it. Xuan rushed over to him, slipping her med-kit from her belt.

The crew complied, slowly. Hao slowest of all, backing away, staring down the soldiers, dead reckoning on his face. If he was scared of the assault rifles leveled at him, he didn't show it. Didn't show anything but a *promise.* That he wasn't going to let this lie, Xuan knew, that this was not the end of anything.

Captain Dang grunted as she eased his hand away from his face. His nose was broken, badly, bent and displaced. Blood dripped down the front of his shirt. A soldier yelled at Xuan, shoving her with the flat of his weapon. She held up the med-kit, the red cross visible on the side.

"I'm just getting some pain reliever."

The soldier yelled at her again, and she stepped away to avoid another shove.

"Hold your head back," she said to Dang. "Pinch your nose. I'll treat it when we've stopped moving." Dang grunted affirmation and she helped steer him out, her hands on his free arm. They were the last to leave.

It was a long march down clean and new and seemingly identical corridors before they came to a huge circular blast door. Fat, bulging out from the wall, it must have been at least a meter thick. Mirrored by a second one, in the wall opposite. The female Chinese officer whispered a set of seemingly lengthy commands into a control panel at the side, and then pressed her thumb against a small green screen. Something deep and heavy clanked in the wall.

When the door opened, Xuan realized she'd underestimated. It was closer to two meters thick, like that of a bank vault. It opened, slow and ponderous. A red alarm light set into the ceiling flashed. The Chinese officer back away, as did the soldiers in the corridor, forming a wall of armor and bristling weapons on either side.

They weren't pointing their weapons at the crew.

They were pointing them at the opening.

"What the fuck?" Hao whispered, next to her.

The door opened and for a few seconds, everything was stilled. The crew looked to each other, the echoing *clang* of the door fading down the corridors. In its place the distant sound of water, rushing,

"There's something in there," Prawn said.

Shorter than most of the crew members and obscured by them, Xuan couldn't see it. Someone pushed back against her and suddenly the soldiers were yelling again, thumping with the sides of their weapons, pointing and threatening. The crew started to move inside and she wasn't sure, but Prawn seemed to be crying.

She was shoved and she tripped—someone had fallen in front of her. There were more yells behind, Hao louder than them all, and when she got to her feet again the door was closing and something was there with them.

23

The decontamination chamber was a huge cylinder deep in the ship, about thirty meters in diameter and fifty long. It was painted a sterile white, and was wide enough that, for at least five meters along the center, there was little slope. Completely bare and smooth, save a steel box about a meter wide by a meter high, set in the far wall alongside another door.

Completely bare, that is, with the exception of the eggs. Standing upright, set into the floor, and some even at an angle in the sides of the cylinder. There were at least thirty of them. Despite herself Xuan moved, hesitantly, toward the nearest. It was both plantlike and fleshy. A hybrid that made her skin crawl. The crosshatched mouth on the top *quivered*, drooling a white substance. Xuan sniffed the air. Something in it, vaguely rotten, sulfureous. She backed away.

"What the fuck is this?" Hao asked.

There was a rumble, deep and heavy as the vault door continued to close. Some of the crew started yelling and Prawn threw himself at the gap. A soldier tried to push him back but Prawn clung to him, his hands snared to the sides of the soldier's chest armor. The door moved inexorably, and shouts on the inside grew. The soldier tried to knock Prawn away, others reaching, trying to punch over the shoulder of their comrade.

"He'll be crushed!" Xuan yelled.

Hao rushed forward, grabbed Prawn, and started to pull him backward, but the young boy—screaming now—clung stubbornly to the soldier's chest armor, his knuckles white, veins on the side of his neck bulging. Hao yanked at him, but it only had the effect of pulling the soldier closer, grappled still by the terrified young man.

"Prawn," Hao yelled. "Let go!"

The soldier had dropped his rifle and braced himself against the door as it closed, the hands of his squad mates pulling from the other direction. Two of the bigger Vietnamese crew members lurched forward to help Hao, gripping Prawn, even the arms of the soldier. The gleaming massive door kept moving, indifferent and oblivious, and somehow the soldier's friends had his legs, and Hao and the Vietnamese had the head and the body of Prawn. The Chinese soldier was vertical.

Xuan yelled over their heads, through the gap. "Stop the door, stop the door!"

The Chinese soldier began screaming, yelling something

over and over. The vault door was touching him, pressing into him, and the soldier was begging. Right at the end of this grotesque tug-of-war, Hao roared and heaved, and the soldier jerked toward the chamber, and the heavy door slammed. Final and reverberating.

Xuan just had time to look down and see what was wrought when the screaming started. The soldier's lower half had been severed, near the belly, and he was thrashing, trying to hold his life in, his looping intestines. The blood and viscera gushed from the terrible wound and the thrashing faded, the man's blood-soaked hands twitching. The Vietnamese stood around, gaping, shocked, and Hao lay near the body where he'd fallen backward, chest heaving, eyes wide.

Then someone else screamed, high pitched. For a moment Xuan's mind told her it was a young girl, but it was Prawn, hands near his leg, but not daring to touch it, fearful somehow of the hideous injury. His foot had been severed. Gone. Squashed in the vault door. Blood was pumping from the wound.

Xuan couldn't breathe. She swayed and tried to hold on to something, but there was nothing nearby and so she plonked down on her behind, chest tight, hand at the front of her shirt, gripping it, making a fist so hard her hand was shaking.

Prawn was screaming and Hao was there, with another crewmate, holding him down. Hao's face was turned toward her and he was yelling something, imploring her, but she couldn't hear the words. All she could hear was her heart thumping in her ears, and some part of her, some dark and persistent radar in her mind, made her turn her head.

There, to one side, the pulsing fleshy egg was moving. The crosshatched mouth on the top opened, like a flower. When Xuan saw the thing that emerged from it, she couldn't make a sound. The iron bands of fear that circled her chest grew tighter, so tight she couldn't breathe.

PART TWO

Think lightly of yourself and deeply of the world.

Miyamoto Mushashi
The Book of Five Rings

PRIVATE KARRI LEE

24

Karri limped behind the others, turning to keep an eye on the area behind. Cortazar and his shield-bearer, Johnson, took point, making sure each corridor was clear before progressing. The prisoner, Raby, had insisted that all the company commandos had been in the loading bay, that the only people left were the bridge crew and some scientists, but Apone didn't seem to be big on believing the word of mercenary scum.

His legs free, his hands still bound, the prisoner walked behind Apone now. The captain had armed himself with a tactical shotgun. Karri found them heavy and cumbersome, but Apone handled it like it was as light as foam. She'd recovered her chest armor, helmet, and service pistol. Bloodied, lying near pools of blood leaked out by the two commandos she'd fought. Hadn't had time to find her pulse rifle.

Her ankle ached, she wasn't sure why. Kicking the steel

mask of a commando, landing badly, twisting it in her mag boots—she wasn't sure, but as she put her weight on it, she could tell it wasn't too serious. Her throat was sore, as well, and it hurt to talk. Her ribs stung when she breathed. Everything hurt. But not as much as her failure. Next to her failure, all her injuries were distant and unremarkable.

Her failure fucking burned.

Walter Schwartz was waiting for them at a junction near Michael Bishop's suite. She was surprised to see him there. If Apone was angry about the appearance of the company man, he didn't show it.

"Schwartz," he said, "I told you not to join the EVA team. You ignored me. Then I ordered you to hold position with the team on the bridge. You seem to have ignored that, as well."

Schwartz wasn't a remarkable man, and Karri had taken little notice of him. They were omnipresent, these representatives of the Company, like blowflies at a food line. She had quickly learned to ignore them, but today, Walter Schwartz made her look twice.

He still had that unimpressive chin, the smile that looked more like a sneer, but now he was wearing combat armor. A chest plate, anyway, that looked very close to Marine-issue, though all black in color. He had black fatigues as well, and a service pistol at his belt. Something—intuition—told Karri he knew how to use a gun. The way he wore it on his hip, the way he held himself. This was unusual. Company men—and women—were usually soft-handed creeps with the morality of a stockbroker and the demeanor of an assistant manager at a retail store. But Schwartz, right then, had the eyes of a brown snake. Cold and shining and deadly.

"I'm not in the military, Captain," Schwartz said. "I can't be ordered."

"A civilian is required to follow my directions when on a military mission, and on a military vessel."

Schwartz indicated the corridor with a sweep of the hand. "The USCSS *Patna* is the property of Weyland-Yutani, Captain. I have every right to check on the condition of a company asset. And—" he indicated the door behind "—a company employee. It looks to me as though Michael Bishop has gone rogue. Weyland-Yutani has an interest in seeing him brought to account."

Apone stared at the man. Karri wondered, briefly, if he practiced that look in the mirror: cold hard motherfucker.

"On that we agree, Schwartz," Apone said. "As for the rest, we'll finish this discussion later." He motioned to Cortazar, who turned and approached the entryway that led to the suites. It was a large steel door, emblazoned with the yellow-white Weyland-Yutani logo. Underneath was the ubiquitous slogan:

BUILDING BETTER WORLDS

"The code," Apone said to the prisoner, Raby.

"He's probably changed it."

"The code," Apone repeated.

The man punched the number into the panel. Johnson raised his shield, Cortazar poked the barrel of the smart gun around it. Apone and the prisoner shifted to one side of the door, Karri to the other. It slid open.

Johnson and Cortazar entered. The rest followed. Silent, efficient, weapons ready. The room beyond didn't feel like part of the ship. Where the rest of the vessel was cold and metal and grimy, the interior was warm in its colors and temperature. Tasteful maroon carpet, wood panels, even potted plants with some kind of yellow flower.

Michael Bishop was waiting behind his desk, smiling faintly. His hands, steepled, rested on the surface which, to Karri's eye, looked like real wood. He wore an open scarf around his neck, blue shirt, top button undone. He seemed relaxed.

"Hands up," Apone ordered.

Michael Bishop complied.

The Captain motioned for Cortazar and Johnson to check the rooms behind. They did so. Then Apone waited, eyes on the seated man. They looked at each other across the space, neither saying a word. If Michael Bishop were worried by the intrusion, he didn't show it.

There were two doors behind him, to the left and right—both closed, both made of wood rather than metal. The room was about ten meters long. As Karri moved farther in, she noticed, embedded in the wall to the left, bodies preserved in lighted cylinders. Schwartz went over to them, hands behind his back. There were three, all naked, and despite herself Karri couldn't help but stare. The victims were suspended in some sort of clear dense resin. It took a second of thinking that this Michael guy was some sort of serial killer, before she realized they weren't preserved humans, but synthetics.

One of the bodies looked exactly like the man behind the desk. A Bishop model. High forehead, slight build. The body in the middle cylinder was tall, square jawed, handsome. Blue-green eyes, staring straight ahead, fixedly. The third android was shorter, almost rotund, plainer. Hard to tell through the resin, but he had a distant look, as though thinking on an abstract thought.

"This is fucking weird," Karri whispered under her breath. Schwartz, next to her, made a non-committal noise in the back of his throat. He turned to face Michael Bishop, hand casually on top of his holstered pistol.

"You folded quickly, Mister Raby," Michael said, looking at their prisoner.

The mercenary hesitated. "It's over, sir. Everyone's dead—or captured. No point in dragging it out."

"I wonder," Michael said, "how much money it would take for you to fight to the last, for Weyland-Yutani."

Raby stared. "More."

Michael Bishop smiled, quietly.

Cortazar and Johnson returned, the latter signaling

the all-clear. They took up a position on either side of the seated figure. Apone stood on the other side of the desk, Schwartz nearby. Karri hovered at the rear.

"Where's Bishop?" Apone asked. Straight to the point.

Michael tilted his head to one side, curious. "That's why you are here? For a synthetic that was damaged beyond repair?"

"Where's Bishop?" Apone repeated. Michael looked away, as if thinking, then put his eyes back on the captain.

"I do not know."

Johnson slapped the man across the back of the head. Michael's head jerked forward and his hair stood up a little, at the point where he was struck. If he felt the blow, or if he cared, it didn't register on his face. Karri shifted her stance. Something wasn't quite right about the executive, but she couldn't put her finger on it.

"You shouldn't have done that, Mister Johnson," Michael said, still looking at Apone.

Johnson furrowed his bushy brow. "How did you—"

Karri was still trying to figure out the weirdling sensation when Michael stuck a blade into Private Johnson's throat. A dagger simply appeared in his hand, and with a blur, it had struck.

The marine staggered back, blood spurting from the wound. Michael rose, back-handing Cortazar in the face. The big gunner's head snapped back and he fell, and the executive was over the desk, slashing first at Raby, then kicking the shotgun from Apone's hand. A shot went off, into the ceiling, ceramic and metal spewing from the hole, and Michael drove Apone backward, driving, legs pumping, picking up the huge captain and smashing him into the rear wall of the office.

"*Oooooff.*" The air went from Apone's lungs, and his assailant's arm blurred again, but somehow the captain had his forearm up, blocking. It had all happened in an instant.

Karri raised her service pistol, but Apone and Michael were struggling and she couldn't make the shot. The executive's arm blurred again, stabbing low this time. Apone grunted and Karri fired, taking the only shot she could take.

One of Michael's legs was pushed out behind, an anchor to keep him in place while he held the struggling captain up against the wall. She fired three times, the rounds striking the man's knee and calf, white blood spraying.

White?

He looked at her and snarled, *snarled*, and threw Apone as if he were as light as a coffee cup. Karri raised her forearms as the body collided with her, pistol smashed from her grasp as she was slammed into the wall behind. Dazed, she staggered to her feet. Michael approached, mad violent gleam in his eyes.

Bang.

Michael Bishop's head erupted. He half-turned.

Bang bang bang.

His head jerked with each shot, white blood and

translucent materials exploding out the back. Michael fell, twitching, one arm raised. Karry watched, frozen, as the company man, Walter Schwartz, walked across the office, stood over the body of Michael Bishop, and emptied the clip into his head.

"Fuck," Karri said.

She ran her eyes over the carnage. Raby was dead. Face up, eyes open, throat slashed. Wrists still cable-tied, pressed up in front of his chest as though he'd been trying to block the blow, but couldn't quite make it in time. She could only see one outstretched arm of Private Johnson, but that arm wasn't moving. Cortazar groaned, staggered to his feet. His nose had been smashed, displaced on his face and, if anything, the big marine was even uglier. He looked down at his friend, Johnson, with bloodshot eyes.

"No," he said, in an exhalation of breath.

Apone shifted at her feet, and she helped him up. He stood, wincing, hand pressed to his side.

"You cut?" she asked.

He shook his head, eyes on the fallen body of their attacker. "Armor took most of it."

They both moved to where Walter Schwartz was standing, still looking down at the body that was not Michael Bishop. The internal workings of the skull now exposed, spread halfway across the room. One thing was clear: this was a synthetic.

"Where," Apone said, in his baritone voice, "is the real Michael Bishop?"

25

One more dead marine on this rescue mission. Karri watched, silently, as Cortazar wept openly over his friend, hand on the man's chest. Often, stillness was beauty, but not here. There was stillness in the room and silence, save the gentle sobbing, but there was no beauty. Just a head bowed in sorrow, over the bloodied body of a brother. Apone said something to Cortazar, but he ignored the captain, brushing him away.

At that moment Haruki entered the room. He stopped when he saw the body of Bishop on the floor. If she didn't know any better, she'd think he was shocked.

"How is Sara?" she asked. "I mean, Corporal Ransome?"

Haruki looked up from the broken, whited body on the floor. He blinked rapidly and Karri wondered, cynically, whether they even needed to blink. Whether that was just programming to trick her into thinking him real.

She shook the thought from her mind. There was an anger, a rage brimming in her, wanting to overflow.

"Critical. She is still in surgery."

The fist around Karri's heart clenched a little tighter. She was finding it hard to breathe.

"The fuck is this?" Cortazar asked. He was standing, eyes still wet, staring at Haruki.

"What do you mean, Private?"

Cortazar indicated the body of Johnson. "I thought androids weren't allowed to harm humans."

"We cannot," Haruki said, simply. "We have human life protection protocols."

Cortazar raised his chin. "Well, that pacifist friend of yours just attacked four marines with a combat knife, and fucking killed one of them." He moved over to the synthetic. "So tell me, Haruki, how did that happen?"

"I don't understand," Haruki said, looking back down at the dead synth.

"Private..." Apone warned.

Cortazar nodded, as though he were taking in what Haruki had said. Then he grabbed the synthetic, both fists bunched at the top of the dark blue shirt. His hands were suddenly there and even Haruki, with all his lightning-fast reflexes, looked surprised.

"*Cortazar!*" Apone roared. "Stand down."

"You're not one of us, synthetic," Cortazar whispered fiercely. "You're a fucking machine, and the moment you malfunction, I'm going to put you down." He let Haruki go, shouldering past Apone as he returned to Johnson. The two big men bumped into each other, and Apone's eyes were wide and white. There was a grumble down deep in his throat. Karri thought of a volcano, about to erupt.

The moment stretched to breaking point in that room, emotion heightened, but the captain reined it in. He said nothing, and whatever it was in the air, it released... slowly. Cortazar hefted the body of his friend and walked from the room, eyes straight ahead, while everyone else stood in silence.

26

Karri looked at the blood spray on the wall and wondered if it was worth it. *No one left behind*. Yeah, she understood the motto. Even if it meant putting more lives at stake, you did it. Even if you didn't know the marine in question, you sought to rescue them. Always faithful, no matter the cost.

She understood it, even if she couldn't feel it. It was the tribe that Apone invoked. Believing in something bigger than the individual, that some bonds—like loyalty, and love—could not be broken, not at any price.

Problem was this: Bishop was an android. She hadn't much liked Johnson, but she didn't want to see the man killed trying to save a glorified robot. Her mind, unbidden, went to Ransome, and something twisted in her chest.

They'd carried out Raby's body, as well. The Michael Bishop synthetic had been left where it had fallen. No one had bothered to clean it up. Not even Haruki. Instead, he stared at it, as though not believing the events he'd had described.

"You're hurt, Haruki," Karri said, pointing to the synthetic's side.

"Oh—it's nothing." He looked distracted when he replied. There was a bullet hole in his tough-fibered blue shirt, just above the hip. Dried white fluid near the hole.

"Did that happen when you came to get me?"

"I don't understand," Haruki said. His eyes were back on the dead Bishop model.

"There's no mystery here," Schwartz said. Karri jumped. The Weyland-Yutani man was behind her, standing in the entryway to one of the two doors. She hadn't noticed him move around the room. "Michael Bishop is one of the pre-eminent engineers in the entire region. Reprogramming a synth with a violent and deceptive nature would have been a relatively simple task."

"But it's not possible," Haruki said. "I could never do something like this."

"Like I said, that's just your programming," Schwartz replied, and it bothered Karri that her thinking aligned with that of a Company man.

"Could that be…" Apone hesitated. "Could that be our Bishop?"

Schwartz shrugged. "It's possible."

"Can you verify the identity, Haruki?" When the synthetic said nothing, Apone put some steel into his voice. "*Haruki.* Verify the identity of that dead synthetic."

Haruki's head snapped up. "Yes sir. Right away." He lowered himself to his haunches and started feeling for something inside the shattered head. At that moment Corporal Colby entered, pushing the copper-skinned commando with the end of his pulse rifle.

"You," Apone said. "Name?"

"Kostas. Macrae."

"You served?"

"In the Royal Marines Commandos, Third Battalion."

The blood drained from Karri's face. The prisoner hadn't spoken up until then, so she hadn't caught the British accent. The Royal Marines had been sent in, dozens of times, to try to quell the uprising in Australia. Their methods were crude, designed to be enacted without any regard for civilian lives. Rumors of their atrocities circulated, but somehow never made it to the news. Somehow, they and the corporations made sure that the truth of their occupation never saw the light of day.

Karri knew the truth. She'd been there, at the Cabramatta Food Riots, January 5th, 2175. The Bloody Fifth, as it became known. She found herself twisting the silver ring on her index finger.

Apone was speaking. She pulled herself back out of the dark well of her memories.

"Don't make me ask you again, soldier," the captain said. "Where is Michael Bishop?" The lean commando looked down at the dead synthetic.

"I thought this *was* Michael Bishop."

"You can't tell the difference between a human and a synthetic?"

"You didn't."

"We don't live with him, soldier. You did."

The man shook his head. He looked up. "He didn't speak to us in person, at least not recently. He'd use the internal comms system."

Apone paused.

"For how long?" Schwartz asked. Apone cast an eye at him for the interruption, but the Company man ignored it. "How long had he been communicating via internal comms?"

"Um… must have been a few weeks, sir." Something changed in the mercenary's voice when he spoke to Schwartz. A more deferential tone.

"Hmm. And did anything of note happen before it started?"

Macrae wet his lips. "Yes, we, ah—we rendezvoused with another ship."

Schwartz gave him a crooked smile. "That so?"

"What ship?" Apone asked tersely.

"We—I don't know."

"How can you not know?"

Macrae looked between Apone and Schwartz. If he was looking for mercy, he wasn't going to find any. "There was a communications blackout leading up to it. We were confined to quarters, except a skeleton crew. Someone said Michael Bishop had visited the other ship with his two synthetics. A few hours later, the ship left."

"And that was when he started communicating from his suite?"

"Yes."

Apone thought. "The other ship. What was it? Whose was it?"

Macrae shrugged. "Like I said: I don't know. We were in lockdown."

"Listen—"

But Apone was interrupted by Schwartz. The Company man drew his pistol, and pressed it to the prisoner's forehead. When he spoke, however, it wasn't like a man who had his gun pointed at someone's head. Rather, it was calm and measured, like a concerned parent explaining to a naughty child why they really ought to be telling the truth.

"It is very important now, Mister Macrae," he said, "that you think about the question you have been asked, and do the very best you can to answer it properly."

Karri believed it, believed that Schwartz was willing to use the pistol. The way he held it, casual and calm, told her this wasn't his first time doing so. She expected Apone to say something, but to her surprise he seemed to hesitate, eyes flicking to the prisoner.

Macrae apparently believed him, as well.

"Honestly—I swear I don't know. It wasn't the first time we'd been confined to quarters. Those other times, there were rumors we were stopping at—" his eyes flicked to Apone, then returned to Schwartz "—Weyland-Yutani black sites. Bioweapon labs. Something like that. But this time they prepped a skiff, so we figured it was another ship, because it couldn't have been a planet or a rock—we weren't near any." He wet his lips. "Just Michael got on, with his two androids, and the prisoner."

"What prisoner?" Schwartz and Apone asked simultaneously.

"Morse. Robert Morse. We picked that bastard up on Fury. The prison colony. He was the only one alive when we left."

"And Bishop," Apone said. "The synthetic."

The prisoner thought for a moment. "Yeah, sure, but it was trashed."

"It was?"

"Yeah. Just a torso and a head. Don't know what they wanted with it."

"But Michael Bishop did want it?"

"Sure. I guess."

They were all silent for a moment. "Did they pack the skiff with much in the way of cargo?" Schwartz asked.

"Yeah." Macrae nodded. "A lot."

"Did anyone see them return?"

"No," the prisoner said, shaking his head. "But the shuttle is in the bay."

"Could have remote piloted," Apone said.

"Easily," Schwartz replied.

"This vessel will have recorded the rendezvous in its logs, Mister Schwartz," Apone said. "Those logs will be encrypted. We'll need to ask the Mother AI on board to decrypt them for us, which will require authorization from you. Now, don't—"

"I'll give them to you," Schwartz said.

Apone paused, and Karri was as surprised as he was. From what little she knew of the Company, they didn't give over information. Not ever. Sometimes it felt like their currency wasn't synthetics or weaponry, but nasty little secrets. Black sites and corporate spies, government sleeper agents and hidden agendas, everywhere. Every program, every book or television show produced by an Australian, had a Weyland-Yutani character in the background. Unctuous, dishonest, greedy, pulling the strings from the shadows.

So when Schwartz told Apone he'd give the authorization, it took the captain a full five seconds before he indicated the computer terminal.

"Private Lee. Assist Mister Schwartz."

Karri sat down behind the desk and switched on Michael Bishop's computer. Schwartz stood behind as the device started up. The screen showed the Weyland-Yutani symbol, rotating slowly. Most computers assigned by the company were cheap and old—as cheap and as old as they could make it, so long as the project still turned a profit. This one, however, was top-of-the-line. Slender, slotted into a stand so it could be carried around if needed, touchscreen as required. Subtle keyboard, unlike the clunky old ones still used by the Marines.

Schwartz watched while Karri manipulated the interface, drilling down into the logs.

"I have verified the body, Captain," Haruki said.

Karri stopped typing and looked up.

"And…" Apone said.

"It is not the Bishop who served with the Second Bravo Company."

It was hard to be sure, but to Karri it seemed like Apone looked relieved.

"This model," Haruki continued, "had only been activated quite recently. He was very young—only three weeks old." To Karri this seemed weird. Was Haruki trying to say that because of his age he was innocent? She shook her head. No. He was just reporting facts.

"Haruki," Apone said, "take the prisoner back to the dropship. Prep for return to the *Il Conde*."

"Yes sir." He led away the mercenary, who looked relieved to be leaving. Karri returned her attention to the computer, found the relevant dates. Words appeared on the screen.

ENTER AUTHORIZATION CODE.

Karri looked up at Schwartz. "These entries could just have been deleted, you know."

"Yes," he replied, "but Mother will still know them."

"Seems counterintuitive."

"She is loyal to the company," Schwartz said simply. "Above all things."

"And Michael is not?"

He responded by nudging her hands aside and typing a long string of letters and numbers into the keyboard. After a few moments, green-glowing letters typed themselves into existence.

WELCOME, SPECIAL OPERATIVE WALTER SCHWARTZ. HOW MANY I BE OF ASSISTANCE?

"What ship did the *Patna* meet with approximately three weeks ago?" he asked aloud.

UNCLEAR. THE VESSEL DID NOT HAVE AN IDENTIFICATION BEACON. ITS OUTER SHELL HAD A LAYER OF PLATING DESIGNED TO CONFUSE SCANNERS.

Schwartz paused. "Not many groups have access to such tech. Not many at all."

NO, MISTER SCHWARTZ.

He thought some more, head turned to one side. "No," he said.

"What?" Karri asked.

"Yeah," Apone said, standing on the other side of the desk. "What?"

"Mother," Schwartz said, ignoring them. "You can provide the approximate dimensions of the vessel, irrespective of the shielding. What were they?"

APPROXIMATELY FIVE HUNDRED METERS LONG BY TWO HUNDRED AND FIFTY AT ITS WIDEST POINT. ONE HUNDRED METERS HIGH AT ITS HIGHEST.

"No," Schwartz said again.

"Schwartz," Apone said in his baritone. He moved around the table, until he was positioned behind them both.

"Mother," Schwartz said, still ignoring the captain. "I am going to provide a set of design specifications for the displacement plating on the hull of that vessel. With it, you will be able to recalculate your scans, and give us the telemetry of the departing ship."

I WILL TRY, MISTER SCHWARTZ.

He nudged Karri farther aside, which was really starting to irritate her by this point, and rapid-fire typed a set of commands. Then he pulled a data disc from his pocket—a round black disc three centimeters across and one deep—and placed it on the datapad next to the screen. It made a satisfying *clunk* as it affixed to the surface.

"Happen to have that on you?" Apone asked. Schwartz didn't reply. It was getting to the point where Karri wanted to clip him one, tell him to answer the captain. She glanced up at Apone, but he seemed calm, watching the screen, waiting for a response. They all did, peering at the flashing green cursor.

"What's Michael Bishop done?" she asked, finally. "What has the motherfucker done?"

"The worst possible thing of all," Schwartz replied. "He has gone over to the competition."

"Who?"

Schwartz said nothing, just smiled his crooked smile. After a full thirty seconds, Mother responded.

RECALCULATING. TELEMETRY PROJECTION WILL TAKE APPROXIMATELY FIVE MINUTES.

Schwartz nodded, satisfied.

"Yes," Karrie said under her breath.

"When this is over, Mister Schwartz," Apone said, "you and I are going to have a serious conversation about your foreknowledge of this mystery vessel."

Schwartz straightened. "I think, Captain, you will find—"

Mother had a new message for them. All of them stopped and stared.

WARNING, AGENT SCHWARTZ. THE USCSS *PATNA* IS EXPERIENCING A CATASTROPHIC REACTOR OVERLOAD. EVACUATE THE SHIP.

"What are you talking about, Mother?" Schwartz asked, voice even.

THE ELECTROMAGNETIC FIELD AROUND THE FUSION REACTOR OF THE USCSS *PATNA* HAS BEEN DISABLED. PLASMA HAS BEGUN TO DEGRADE THE REACTOR WALLS. YOU HAVE TEN MINUTES BEFORE CATASTROPHIC OVERLOAD.

27

Schwartz and Karri looked at each other.

"Does that mean what I think it means?" she asked.

"Yes," Schwartz replied. "It means the ship will explode and all of us will be vaporized." If the news upset him, he didn't show it. He said, "Mother. Reinstate electromagnetic containment field."

UNABLE TO COMPLY.

"Why?"

THAT PROCESS HAS BEEN DISABLED.

"By whom?"

MICHAEL BISHOP.

Karri swore.

"Eject the core," Apone said.

UNABLE TO COMPLY. THE REACTOR EJECTION MECHANISM HAS BEEN DISABLED.

Karri rubbed her lips. "But it can be ejected manually, right?"

NOT RECOMMENDED. PROCEDURE REQUIRES FULL RADIATION CONTAINMENT SUIT AND ANTI-RAD MEDICATION. INSUFFICIENT TIME TO IMPLEMENT SAFETY PROTOCOLS BEFORE EXPLOSION.

"How long, exactly?" she asked. As Karri spoke, she began to feel it. A hum, a fine vibration in her hands as they rested on the table. Through her boots. The kind of hum generated when a Conestoga-class ship like the *Patna* was pushing itself hard at sub-light speed. Problem was, this vessel was standing still.

A digital time stamp appeared, the top right corner of the screen, in bold red.

09:15

09:14

09:13

"Mother," Schwartz said, "How long to decryption of the telemetry?"

APPROXIMATELY FIVE MINUTES.

Schwartz raised an eyebrow. "Approximately. You cannot be more precise?"

NO. THE CALCULATIONS REQUIRED ARE COMPLEX. I AM UNFAMILIAR WITH THE DISPLACEMENT SHIELDING OF THE NEW VESSEL.

Schwartz waved it away. "It doesn't matter. The point is we have enough time. Mother, once you have finished the calculations, you will transmit them to the *Il Conde*."

NO.

"What do you mean, 'no'? Explain?"

THE COMMS ARRAY HAS BEEN DISABLED.

Apone slammed his hand on the wall behind him. Karri jumped and turned. The captain's jaw was locked and the emotion was finally showing.

"Goddamn, you Weyland-Yutani people are a bunch of snakes."

Schwartz shrugged, the now-familiar crooked smile on his face. He'd probably heard that sort of line enough times that it didn't particularly faze him anymore.

Karri took a moment. "Wait," she said. "The escape pods are near here, right? If this is the same configuration as the *Il Conde*, they're probably just up the corridor?"

Apone looked at her, eyes narrowing.

"Mother?" Schwartz asked. "Are the escape pods active and nearby?"

YES. AT AVERAGE WALKING SPEED THEY ARE NINETY SECONDS AWAY.

"Can you prep them, have them ready to launch?" Karri asked.

YES.

"How long from my entering the pod, until launch?"

TWENTY SECONDS.

She turned in her chair. "That's enough time, Captain. More than enough. I can wait here until the telemetry has been calculated, Mother can download it onto Schwartz's disc here, and I can take an escape pod. No worries."

She expected Apone to say *no*, immediately. Instead, he stared at her for a few seconds before speaking.

"I can do it."

"No," she said straight away. "You're injured and slow." She indicated the computer. "I know this stuff—it's my job. If there are any road bumps, I can clear them faster."

Apone studied her. She tried to remain calm, to hide her desperation. Her desire to do something, *anything*, to make amends. The captain had said nothing about her performance during the ambush, but she knew he would. If Ransome died, and if her squad mates lost faith in her, there was no way she could remain in this unit. At best she'd be transferred out, and her reputation would travel with her. At worst he could class her as unfit for military service.

Apone surprised her, again. "Three minutes, Marine. You will leave this room with no less than three minutes on the clock. That is an order."

Inwardly, she breathed a sigh of relief. Outwardly, she nodded, once.

"Yes, sir."

28

Trying not to stare at the clock, Private Karri Lee breathed instead, in and out, slowly, as she'd been taught. To center her body, and her mind—but there was no center, these days. Her thoughts always pushed or pulled, and at that moment, they were being pulled away, toward Earth and into the past.

Holding her father's hand, in the crush of bodies. In the heat and the noise and the fear. Commands being yelled over a loudspeaker on one side, the desperate cries and angry insults on the other. Her father put an arm around her shoulder and tried to pull her out of the mass of people, knowing what she was knowing, feeling what she was feeling: that the protest had reached breaking point.

They tried to make their way out, to thread a path, but they kept getting shoved in the wrong direction. Her father was pleading, asking to be let through, but there were no individuals here anymore. There was a mob. An individual could listen, a mob—

* * *

"Private Lee, come in, over."

She sat up straight in her chair. "Um… yes? Lee here. Who is this? Over."

"It's Haruki, Private," the synth said in his calm and gentle voice. Of course it was him. There were no other gentle voices in her unit.

"Wait. Are you on board?"

"Yes, Private. Headed up from the bay now. ETA three minutes. Over."

"I don't need help, Haruki. Over."

"Captain's orders. Over."

She sighed. Apone didn't trust her to do it alone. "Copy that." She was about to end the transmission when Mother started typing.

REASSESSING TIME TO FINAL TELEMETRY CALCULATION.

"What does that mean, Mother?"

REASSESSING TIME TO FINAL TELEMETRY CALCULATION.

"Wait, Haruki," she said, into her comm. "There's something wrong."

"Copy."

ESTIMATED TIME TO FINAL TELEMETRY CALCULATIONS, 5 MINUTES, 30 SECONDS.

On the top right of the screen the words REACTOR OVERLOAD, and the time:

7:48

7:47

7:46...

"Shit."

"What is the problem, Private? Over."

"The estimates changed for the calculations. We're going to be cutting it close."

"How close? Over."

Her mind raced. "Real close."

"Then I advise you to leave now, Private. If the estimates changed once, they could well change again. I will meet you at the escape pod near your location. Over."

She breathed. Without the telemetry of the mystery vessel, their quarry would disappear. A speck in a vast universe, rendered invisible. Without it the mission would be over. She thought about her brothers. Her stupid brothers, who tormented her and who loved her and looked up to her and imitated her. In that fucking camp, telling everyone they'd be out soon. That their sister was a hero, and she was going to rescue them from this place, put them in a military community. In a house with clean water, and warm beds, and with food. As much as they could eat.

She tapped the comm. "Negative. I am waiting for the calculations."

"You have orders, Private," Haruki said, still calm.

"I have time, Haruki."

"I am not sure you do, Private. The risk—"

"I'm not leaving!" It came out harder than she expected. A yell. She breathed out, long and steady. "I'm not leaving. Over."

He answered straight away.

Later, when Karri thought about what happened, she wondered if Haruki knew what was going to happen next, the most likely outcome. That in a split second he calculated everything, and came to such a monumental decision in yet the blink of an eye.

"Copy that, Private. I will not be meeting you at the escape pod. I will head down to engineering and attempt to eject the reactor core manually. Over."

She made a thin line with her mouth. "Mate. I thought the radiation levels were too high?"

"I am built to withstand greater extremes than the human body. Over."

Karri's eye twitched. "That doesn't answer my question, Haruki."

"En route to engineering. Please update me with any changes to Mother's calculations. Over and out."

"What? Haruki? Fuck. Haruki? Over?"

There was silence on the line, in the room she was in, save the hum of the ship. A hum, a vibration that seemed just that little bit louder than it had a minute before.

The clock said 6:25... 6:24... 6:23...

"Mother," she said. "I want a timer for your calculations on the screen, as well. I want it in the center of the screen, the difference between you figuring this shit out, and this whole fucking place blowing up. I want a warning bell at the two-minute mark."

YES, PRIVATE LEE.

TELEMETRY CALCULATIONS: 4:15

REACTOR OVERLOAD: 6:10. DIFFERENCE: 1 MINUTE, 55 SECONDS.

"Mother. If I'm running, how quick can I get to the escape pod."

I ESTIMATE YOU WILL TAKE FIFTY-FIVE SECONDS, PRIVATE LEE.

"So I could get there, prep the pod, and be gone with forty seconds remaining?"

IN OPTIMAL CONDITIONS.

Karri rubbed her mouth. "Are there any escape pods near engineering?"

NONE THAT WILL CLEAR THE BLAST RADIUS IN TIME.

"Fuck." Karri stood, paced the room. The timer ticked down. She stared at the synthetics suspended in the clear tubes. Macabre trophies of some mad scientist. "*Fuck,*" she said again, and thumbed her comm. "Okay, Haruki. You got me. Abort mission. Let's get out of here. Over."

She got a blast of static in response and behind it, faintly, Haruki's voice.

"Haruki? Do you copy?"

Another burst of static, loud enough to make her wince. Then it cleared, and his voice came through.

"Hello Karri. I've found a zone with better reception. I don't have long. I am sorry, but I am beyond the containment doors in engineering, and have already absorbed a significant amount of radiation. However, I am confident I have sufficient time to eject the reactor core before my body expires."

"What?"

"Could I ask you do to something for me, Karri?"

"I... No. You can come back *now*. We can salvage your processor."

"It is important to me that you do this thing."

She rubbed her forehead, agitated. "Yes, yes, what?"

"Could you please give my condolences to Juan Cortazar? Lance Johnson was a good friend of his, and I regret not offering my sympathy earlier. I have fond memories of Johnson. He taught me poker. Or, I should say, how to bluff. We spent two days together when our skiff was downed on Devil's Peak."

"What?" she asked. Not understanding.

Static blasted in response, then died, momentarily. *"—at the two-minute mark. That should give you sufficient time to clear the* Patna, *should I fail."*

"What?"

There was just static. Karri swore and kicked a chair over. She stared at the screen.

TELEMETRY CALCULATIONS: 3:15

REACTOR OVERLOAD: 5:40

DIFFERENCE: 1 MINUTE, 25 SECONDS

"Fucking hell, Mother, your estimate keeps changing."

I AM CONFIDENT THE CURRENT TIME IS ACCURATE.

Ten seconds. If everything went perfectly. She had ten seconds. And Haruki? Apologizing? To that arsehole Cortazar? Why couldn't he just do it himself?

"Fuck," she said. "You idiot, Karri."

Haruki was going to die. For her. He was going to get

melted, from the inside out, trying to shut down that fucking reactor. *For her.* Again. If her zero-G panic didn't get her kicked out of the Marines, disobeying an order and getting their synthetic killed certainly fucking would. Apone always carried on like they were equals, that the synths should be treated like a fellow marine. Well, if he really did believe that, then she was double fucked.

She sighed through her nose. "Jesus, Karri. You bitch." Haruki was dying for her, and her first thought was herself. She turned back to stare at the monitor.

29

The warning klaxon went off at the two-minute mark. Karri tried to calm herself, one hand hanging over the black disc on the datapad. Ready to snatch it and run. She hadn't heard from Haruki, not a word. Not even a gasp of static.

The timer ticked down to one minute thirty, and the shaking beneath her feet intensified. The potted flowers rattled, she was sure she could hear the walls creaking.

"Come on, Mother," she said, through clenched teeth when the time hit 1:30.

It ticked past.

"Come on, Mother!"

A pleasing note sounded from the computer.

DOWNLOAD COMPLETE.

But Karri was already running. Black disc in her hand, she shot through Michael Bishop's door, snapped right, and sprinted. Dull pain in her ankle, but it was distant now, and she was running, and after all the bullshit, all the stress that hissed in her mind like a flare, she was thinking clearly. Last few seconds of her life and she was hyper-focused, legs pumping, arms swinging, elbows bent, taking corners and not missing a step.

Over the speakers, a voice: *"One minute to reactor overload, one minute to reactor overload."*

Karri Lee was fast. She got to the pod doors with forty seconds to spare. Pressed the button to open the door.

Nothing happened.

She pressed it again.

Still nothing.

"Thirty seconds to reactor overload."

Karri went to the next pod, tried that. Nothing. Then a third. Same again.

"Mother," she said, voice starting to waver. "What is going on?"

There was no answer, just, *"Twenty seconds to reactor overload."* The floor was vibrating, hard, and something in the wall was rattling. The floor tilted, slightly, and she held out a hand to steady herself.

Pulling her combat knife, she jammed it into the edge of the control panel. The blade skipped, scouring the surface. She jammed it again while Mother talked.

"Fifteen seconds to reactor overload."

Karri didn't blink, she just gritted her teeth and wedged the blade and pulled. The panel did not give. She grunted, both hands on the handle, and pulled up.

Her blade snapped.

Something rocked the ship, throwing her against the wall behind. She grunted, but kept her feet, holding the knife in her hand, eyes fixed to the broken blade. Mother kept talking.

She closed her eyes.

30

She was alive.

Karri Lee was alive. She opened her eyes. The vibrations beneath her feet had stopped. The corridor was still tilted, slightly, but otherwise the shaking had ceased and Mother had shut up. She dropped her broken blade. It clattered, metal on metal.

She thumbed her comm link. "Haruki?"

No response. Not even static.

"Haruki?" she asked again, knowing the answer.

Alive. *Alive.*

He'd done it. Ejected the core. Saved her. Sacrificed himself. She made a thin line with her mouth, tasted the salt of her sweat. Something else, too: the bitterness of her intent. Felt the words forming in her mind, the reasons. She didn't have to leave the Corps. In fact, all this could cement her place.

31

She lied.

Too bloody right she did. When Apone asked her what happened, she lied. She said she'd left as ordered, at the three-minute mark. She said Haruki had decided to go down to engineering, to try to eject the core manually, even though she told him not to. She speculated, to the captain, that the synthetic had a suspicion about the escape pods. That if Michael Bishop had sabotaged the comms, and rigged the ship to explode once they started sniffing around, then it followed that he'd disabled the escape pods to ensure there were no survivors. He was covering his tracks, after all.

The lies he told to the Weyland-Yutani commandos, the great steel trap into which the *Patna* had been transformed—all about covering his tracks. If it had worked as he had hoped, Michael Bishop would be assumed dead and no further rescue missions would be forthcoming. No one would be trying to find the marine synthetic, Bishop. No one would be questioning Michael's loyalty. It was perfect.

So she lied, and there was enough truth to her lies that he accepted it. Captain Apone gave her the *hard motherfucker* stare, sure. He gave no indication whether he truly believed her, but that didn't matter, either. The fact was comms were down and he knew nothing of the conversation she'd had with Haruki. The fact was they'd found the synthetic, oozing white, propped up against the housing of the core. His processor melted. Any secrets he'd had, taken to the grave.

The fact was that the radiation had fried the ship's scanners and cameras, down in engineering, anyway. So what happened there had been hidden from Apone as well. Maybe he could ask Mother when, exactly, Karri'd left for the escape pods, but a lot of the AI's circuitry had been corrupted, so maybe he couldn't even get that.

She handed him the disc with the telemetry.

"Good work, marine." She hated how much that meant to her, fighting to keep the smile from her face. Didn't have to fight too hard, because after a few moments she remembered the big lie, all the lies to get to this point. She saluted and left his office.

Sara Ransome was out of surgery. No one would tell Karri whether she'd live, or of her condition, and she was too cowardly to go up to the med bay and look for herself. Too shamed. The other marines shunned her, turning their eyes away. Except for Cortazar, who glared with transparent anger when they passed in the corridor.

Marines only had to share their quarters with one other on the *Il Conde*. The ship was huge. Nearly four hundred meters long, an ugly fat train of ceramic composites and steel and titanium, pushing through the universe with its spiked, asymmetrical face. So much room for such a small crew so, yeah, no reason to cram a whole company into a single room. Instead, it shoved two into each small space, but her roommate was Sara, so Karri had the luxury of solitude.

No stares, no recriminations, no cold shoulders. Just her bunk.

Karri put her hands behind her head and stared at the ceiling above. Someone had scratched their initials into it, long time past. Rust showing, in the engraving.

WLH

Next to it she'd stuck a picture of her family.

They were standing in front of the converted shipping container they called home. Mum, beaming into the camera. Big smile, her wavy blonde-brown hair shining in the sunlight. Her best dress, light cotton, flowers. Skinny. Shoulders boney, but better since they'd made it to the camp in the States. Almost never smiled, after Dad had died. Her mother had a haunted look, distracted—so much so she'd forget even the boys. Forget to go out and scrounge and beg for food.

But here she was smiling, and so were Karri's stupid brothers. Shane, Jackson, and Keith. Younger by quite a bit. Karri nineteen years old at the time of the photo, and her brothers twelve, eleven, and ten. Not entirely clear, the thought process her parents put into that late trifecta.

The boys had their toys. Shit. As poor as they were, they had their plastic pulse rifles and "armored" vests. Of course they did. The Colonial Marines had a recruiting office inside the refugee camp, taking advantage of a steady stream of fodder for their imperial appetites. "Do your time and you get your citizenship." Pretty sweet deal, save the part where they ended up dead or dismembered on a cold hard frontier in space.

Smart enough to make branded Marines toys available to refugee families when they arrived, handed out in their welcome packs. Get those girls and boys while they were young, roleplaying law versus chaos, freedom versus socialism, cops versus robbers. Keith, at least, had a yellow shirt on, with the boxing kangaroo printed on the front. A tiny piece of home, as they threw themselves on the mercy of another empire.

She sighed through her nose. Karri was tired. Sore. Deep ache, around the side of her face. From the fight, she supposed, with the mercenaries. God, that felt like an eon ago. Another lifetime. She tried to shift her mind back to her family, keep it there. A light, to keep her warm in this darkness, but her mind was many things, and not one of them was loyal.

Instead, her mind took her to another place—a Colonial Marine training vessel, the *Mont-Blanc*, orbiting Earth. Thirteen weeks on the ground, then a second lot of thirteen weeks in space, and there she was, in her last few days, in the office of Major Menadue.

32

Decorated marine, neat black hair, pale white skin, a sheen on his lips. Like he used lip gloss. Major Menadue studied a datapad lying flat in front of him on his sparse expansive black desk, while she waited, eyes ahead, hands behind her back. Framed distinguished service medals on the wall, framed copy of the Marines oath, picture of him and the former president.

Portals to her right, looking down on Earth. Passing slowly and steadily underneath, oblivious to Karri and the thing she now had to do. After the major had finished his little power play, he deigned to look at her.

"You requested a meeting, recruit?"

"Yes sir," she answered.

"I denied it."

"Yes sir."

"You insisted."

"I did, sir."

He indicated the datapad in front of him. "I take it you wish to discuss your failure at zero-G training."

"I do, sir."

"Then there is nothing to discuss." He raised his head, lips gleaming in the light. "The Colonial Marines have high standards. You failed to meet those standards." He raised his hand, indicating the portal and its view. "You will return to Earth on the next transport. Back to the little slice of luxury you wheedled for yourself and your family. I wish you all the best."

Karri flared, inside, at the description of that baking hot shipping container as *luxury*.

"Why should I meet those standards," she asked, "if even the commanding officer fails to meet them?"

The jaws on his muscles worked, but otherwise he remained perfectly still.

"What did you say, recruit?"

"Everyone here knows how to get the best assignments, Major. The women, anyway. If there's a particular posting they want—maybe not so far from family, maybe one not in a war zone—well, they just have to bend themselves over that desk of yours there and *abracadabra*, suddenly they get the battalion they want, and the commander of choice."

His eyes bore into her, but he said nothing.

She held up a hand. "I'm not here to threaten, mate. You have the power here, I know that. You're in command of this vessel, this entire situation. No one will believe the accusation of a recruit against a war hero like you. I'm just asking for a little lenience in my scoring, Major. I passed everything else."

Still he said nothing.

"Ever fucked an Aussie?"

He stopped, wet his lips, let his eyes range over her.

"No."

"Well, today is your lucky day, Major."

Something changed in his face. "You failed zero-G. This is different."

"That's just the thing," she said. "All I'm asking is that you let me retake that zero-G examination."

He pressed his shiny lips together, that sick little fuck. "I don't think it's my lucky day, Boot," he said, using the pejorative for a trainee. His hands moved to his belt. "I think it might be yours."

Karri ran a finger over her buttons, undid the top one.

"Call me Marine."

The major undid his silver clasp. "Marine," he breathed.

She held up a finger. "So we're clear. I fuck you, now. Any way you want it. In return, you amend that report you got there in front of you?"

"Sure," he said, distracted. He was a man, after all. He unzipped himself.

"Deal?"

"Deal."

Karri breathed a sigh of relief and pulled a slender silver box from the pocket of her fatigues. Thankfully, the major stopped moving his hand.

"What is that?"

"This, dickhead, is a recorder."

He blinked.

"Listen here, you sleazy fuck," she continued. "I got a new deal for you. You're going to give me a pass in zero-G. Then I'm going to ship out, and you're going to stop banging recruits. In exchange, you get to stay here, in this fucking tin can, circling the Earth. Watching the same shit, week in, week out. Doing the same job. Counting down those fucking hours until retirement."

He zipped himself back up. A mean look came into his eyes, a different type of predator than the one that sparked in his gaze a bare minute ago. The major was taller than her, wider, and had seen his share of action.

"Calm down, Major. You see my hand-to-hand scores?"

"I would snap your spine."

Karri grinned. "Why don't you try that, you dirty old bastard? Win or lose, there's going to be a real mess in this office—and if I win, I'll still have this." She turned the recorder in her hand, the silver casing catching the light.

He tensed.

"Or—" she said, trying to grab the moment. The chance that had presented itself. "—I walk away. You sit down, and life goes on, for both of us. And all this unpleasantness—well, mate, it never happened."

Still the major worked the muscles in his jaw, and Karri changed her stance. Ready, should he decide to launch himself across his desk. Maybe try to tear the recorder from her hand.

He didn't.

"Get the hell out of my office."

Karri Lee smiled. "And to be clear: you ain't *never* gonna fuck an Aussie."

He glowered.

She left.

33

Karri stared at the ceiling. Maybe she should have just fucked him. Gotten a better assignment than this one, out here on the frontier. With an obsessive captain, willing to sacrifice his soldiers on principle.

She turned the wedding band on her forefinger. No, her father wouldn't have liked that. Not one bit. Though he wouldn't have been big on her joining the Colonial Marines, either.

"Lee."

She jumped. Turned in her bunk. Standing in the doorway was Corporal Ottelli, the gunner from the APC. It was the first time he'd spoken to her directly since she joined the unit.

"Yes, Corporal?"

"It's Ransome," he said, his eyes giving nothing away. Her breath caught in her throat. She found herself unable to ask the question.

"She's awake," he said. Ottelli tapped the doorframe with his palm twice, nodded at her, and left.

Karri breathed. It felt like a weight had been lifted from her shoulders, like she'd been guilty of a terrible crime, and yet a judge had somehow declared her innocent. Relief mixed with guilt mixed with remorse. For a few moments longer she stared at the space where Ottelli had been, gripping and un-gripping the pale green sheet on her bunk.

"Okay, Karri," she said to herself. She hopped down. *No more excuses.*

34

"Private Lee," Ransome said, her voice a little above a whisper. "Don't just stand there. Come in."

Ransome's eyes had been closed, her skin was pale. Standing in the doorway, Karri was about to leave again when the corporal's eyes flicked open. Giving a strained smile, the private walked over to the hospital bed.

"Where're my flowers?" Ransome asked.

"Oh, ah, sorry, I didn't…"

"I'm joking, rookie. Don't they have jokes where you come from?"

Karri smiled, more genuine this time. "Well, they're free, so yeah. We can afford those."

Ransome had faint purple bags under her eyes, an IV in her arm, and a heart monitor pinched on her forefinger. For all that, though, she looked better. Her hair, when not tied back, was wavy and full. The side of her head, over her ear, had been shaved. Even with the white sheet, her breasts made a pleasing shape under the covers.

"I look terrible, I know," Ransome said.

"You look great," Karri said, and instantly regretted it.

Ransome raised an eyebrow. Karri felt the heat on her neck, and hoped Ransome hadn't noticed.

"Well—I'm glad you're alive."

"So am I."

"I guess I should… ah…" Karri tried to think of excuse to leave. Her mind was messing with her again. She'd been obsessing over whether Ransome would die, and suddenly, now the woman *was* alive, she found herself distracted by the tingle of attraction. It was impossible, anyway, with a squad mate. Another reason they might use to have her kicked out. Karri really had to stop providing those.

"Take a seat," Ransome said. "I got nothing to do but lie here. Tell me what happened on the *Patna*."

"Oh," Karri said. "Didn't everyone else tell you already?"

"Sure," Sara said, voice still a husky whisper. "But no one really knows what happened after they left you on board. So tell me about that."

Karri took a seat. She told the story the same way she'd told it to Apone. That Haruki had decided to eject the core manually, that she had left Michael's office with three minutes to spare. Ransome listened. Once or twice her eyes closed, and Karri thought she may have fallen asleep, but the woman spoke.

"Keep going."

Karri did. When she finished, Ransome was silent for a few moments.

"You trying to get a medal, rookie?"

Karri hesitated. "What do you mean?"

"I mean, you trying to get a medal?"

"No, I—"

Ransome cut her off with a tired shake of the head.

Karri twisted the ring on her forefinger. The unit would find out, eventually. Personal information always seemed to find a way out, into people's mouths, whispered in locker rooms. She sighed.

"I got three little brothers. They're in a refugee camp, in California. It's better than the one on the border, but it's still a hovel. I serve one year, adequately, then I get full UA citizenship, and my family get moved to Camp Pendleton. If I get a decoration—one of the better ones, anyway—then I get my citizenship faster. So yeah, I guess I was hoping to get a medal. Though mostly I'm just hoping to avoid a discharge."

Ransome was silent for a few moments. "And if you die, but are awarded one posthumously…" It wasn't a question. She was leading Karri in.

"Yeah," Karri said. "They get in then, as well."

"I'd prefer you didn't die."

"Same here," Karri said. "Unheroically, anyway."

"I mean it."

Karri was silent, twisting the ring on her finger. "Why—" She stopped herself.

"Why?" Ransome prompted.

"Why are you being so good to me?"

Ransome watched her, waiting.

"I nearly got you killed," Karri continued. "We've only known each other for a few weeks. Why?"

"I'm stuck here." The corporal waved her hand, vaguely. "I need someone to talk to."

"No, Sara. Really."

Ransome tilted her head to look at her, more directly. A machine bleeped in the background.

"You remind me of someone."

"Who?"

Ransome gave a tired smile. "You know, rookie, not everything's an angle. I get it that you grew up in the camps. I get that you're in the Marines now, and you gotta prove you're tough and that you belong. But you walk around, eyes flicking left and right, like you're expecting someone to jump you. That's no way to walk through life."

Karri looked down at her hands.

"I nearly died. So maybe I'm more talkative than usual, but I like you, rookie, and I guess I'm your friend. Whether you want it or not."

Karri pressed her lips together. Fucking hell, she just wanted to cry. One little kindness and she was right there. On the edge.

"But mainly I'm bored," Ransome finished, smiling weakly.

Karri laughed. An emotion had to come out, and she preferred it was that. She leaned back in her chair. Ransome closed her eyes again, and Karri let her. She did sleep this time. Maybe for ten minutes, and Karri was glad of the quiet. Just the machine bleeping, steady and comforting, and the distant hum of the ship.

Ransome opened her eyes again and talked like there hadn't been a break. "So tell me, Karri," she whispered. "How the hell did you end up here?"

"How'd I get to the UA, you mean?"

Ransome shook her head. "No. Before that. The cause of it all. What made you end up here?"

Karri hesitated. Americans always seemed so eager to tell their most personal stories. Like they'd all rehearsed it, a five-minute take, straight to the camera. Their culture lived on the individual tale—the glory of *I*—where hers focused on the collective, the class, the community, and what they shared. No single person being above the other, no one story being more worthy, or more tragic, or more vital.

Despite all that, she found herself wanting to tell it. She had to.

"I was sixteen years old…"

35

The sun beat down, like always. That indefatigable white-hot master of the sky, burning them with its unblinking stare. Karri Lee walked with her father down to the ration center. She had the red plastic food chits in her front pocket, and the axe handle resting on her shoulder. Her dad disapproved, saying it was better to trust their neighbors, and to build those feelings of community. Karri shrugged and said the line she'd heard once, at one of her father's poker games.

"Trust everyone, but cut the cards."

He raised an eyebrow at that, still smiled, anyway. Her father had a quiet smile, and a quiet manner. Lean and tall, he wore wide-brimmed hats and small round glasses that always seemed to catch the light. He'd taught English Literature at university, and when the Three World Empire shut down the school for "harboring subversives," he taught literacy at the community center instead. They called him "Professor Lee" down there, and they were only half-joking.

Her father was well-liked and known in the community. He taught history, too. True history. He was one of the subversives the Three World Empire liked to lock up. Her father explained to her all about their mining interests in Australia, their insatiable need to strip-mine these lands, to feed the ravenous engine of empire. *"Nothing's as precious to them,"* he'd say, *"as a hole in the ground."*

Her father drank from a battered blue water container and passed it to her. Karri drank deeply. It didn't do much to take the edge off the hunger, but it helped a little. They hadn't had breakfast, and dinner the night before had been a thin cabbage soup. Her energy levels were low, but she felt her excitement growing as they neared the ration center. Her tokens were good for one bag of rice, one bag of flour, and 100ml of cooking oil.

Better still, *coffee*.

Karri and her father didn't have much in common. Where he was an academic, she foundered on every school topic, except reading. Where he was cerebral, she took to martial arts at a young age, and excelled. Where he preached non-violent resistance, Karri had started to read some of the most radical pamphlets about the Great Rebellion, that argued for the violent overthrow of the Three World Empire.

But one thing they agreed on was coffee. Karri was only

sixteen, but had started drinking it a year before, imitating her father, who slurped down two cups first thing every morning. They were both addicted to the dark acrid brew, and recent shortages had shortened both of their tempers. Well, hers anyway.

The shops were boarded up for the most part, except the occasional horse-betting storefront and run-down, cracked-window pubs. Trash fluttered across the asphalt on the hot dry breeze, and if there was anyone else on the street they were walking in the same direction, shoulders stooped, ration chits clutched in their hands.

Karri and her father heard the riot before they saw it.

The angry yells, the megaphones giving garbled orders. They rounded the corner to see the crowd massing at the ration center. Thousands, it looked like. Some, Karri noted straight away, were armed with lengths of wood like she was. There were three troop trucks marked with the triangular Three World Empire symbol. Red and white and blue—the pattern of the three red arms. To Karri, it was vaguely reminiscent of the ancient Nazi swastika. Armed troops stood on the flatbeds of the big green trucks, watching the crowd through mirrored visors, clutching assault rifles.

An officer with a beret, mustache, and an imperial chin stood in the center of one of the flatbeds, yelling commands through a megaphone. On the ground in front, clad head-to-toe in black riot gear and holding a wall of riot shields, were the police keeping the crowd back. The ration center was on a street corner, four roads converging in the intersection, so the police had to form a circle to keep back the citizens.

"What's happening?" her father asked another man at the back of the crowd.

"No food," the other said, simply.

"Wait. None? None at all?"

The man, bareheaded, red-faced, turned to face Dad. "There's no fucking food, mate," he shouted. Karri gripped her axe handle. Her father put his hands up.

"We're in this together, friend. I'm not the one hoarding food, bloated by corruption, mismanaging the colonies." He indicated the army trucks, down the road. "The ones doing that hold the megaphone." The man glared for a few more moments, then shook his head.

"About time that changed."

"Indeed."

More people had walked in behind them—hundreds more, and quickly they were trapped in a mass of bodies. Someone started up a protest song, and soon the whole crowd was singing along, including Karri. Including even her father.

Go on home Three World Empire, go on home.
Have you no fucking homes of your own?
For the last ten years we have fought you without fear,
And we'll fight you for ten thousand more.

Go on home Three World Empire, go on home.
This wide brown land you'll never own.
Can you hear, can you hear, the Great Rebellion come?
We will bury you, under this beating sun.

We will bury you,
To the Great Rebellion's drums.

They were so immersed in the singing that they didn't notice the police move in behind. Not until it was too late. Hundreds of them. More. Must have been every riot officer in Sydney descended on them that day. The singing faltered, then spluttered out—was drowned out by the cops beating their shields with batons.

Wham wham wham…

Meant to intimidate, and of course it did. The crowd backed away, shoving into one another. Karri stumbled and grabbed her father's hand. She hadn't held his hand in years, but now she gripped it tightly, and he hers.

"Fuck this!" someone yelled near her, and they flung something at the police. A brick. Between the shoulders of the men in front of her, Karri saw a helmeted head snap backward, and a black-armored figure fall. The crowd cheered and objects started raining down on the police. Torn-up bricks, bottles, anything with weight. The police held up their shields, milling, uncertain, two more of them falling, the rest starting to back away. More cheering, and the crowd started to spread out, probing the police lines.

The cheers turned to cries of warning.

Karri twisted around to see a cloud of white smoke billowing not ten meters away, protestors trying to push back from it, coughing, crying. More tear gas was fired into the crowd, cylinders that arced gracefully, glinting in the sunlight as they trailed smoke, bouncing among massed feet.

Despite the crush of bodies, she gripped her father's hand tightly in the heat and the noise and the fear. Commands were yelled over a loudspeaker on one side, the desperate cries and the angry insults on the other. Her father pulled her close, put an arm around her shoulder and tried to pull her out of the mass of bodies. Knowing what she was knowing, feeling what she was feeling, that the protest had reached breaking point. They tried to make their way out, to thread a path, but they kept getting shoved in the wrong direction, her father pleading, asking to be let through.

There were no individuals here anymore, there was only a mob. An individual could listen; a mob was reduced to its base instincts.

Karri caught the scent of something peppery and started coughing. Her eyes watered. Just a whiff of tear gas, but it burned. The police were among them now, full helmets with built-in gas masks, faceless black-clad thugs smashing their batons down on the heads of protestors. An older woman, white hair, flowery dress, was knocked down in front of Karri. Face bloody, riot police standing over her, legs astride, victorious.

Her father tried to pull them toward an alleyway. She glimpsed the backs of some protestors, fleeing down the darkened lane. They neared it and for a moment Karri thought they'd make it, but a black shadow loomed over them, and her father grunted and then fell, dragging her down with him. Another body fell across her, and she shoved it out of the way. Above her, blotting out the sun, a riot officer, silhouette, baton raised.

Karri turned to see her father, hands out, surrendering, trying to placate the officer standing over them, but the police were a mob at this stage, as well. They weren't trying to control a crowd anymore, they were trying to punish it. To hurt it. To exact vengeance. To take pleasure in the infliction of fear. Of pain.

"No, please," her father said. His glasses had been knocked off, so his eyes looked small and afraid.

Something snapped inside Karri. The axe handle lay on the ground next to her. She rose, clutching it, as the policeman tried to strike her father. She blocked the swing, turning the baton aside, and rammed the end of her handle into the man's throat. He choked, immediately dropping his weapon, taking a step back, and Karri screamed a "*Kiyap!*" and struck him in the side of the helmet.

He staggered. She hit him again and he fell. A knot of people—six or seven of them—fighting, rumbled through and trampled the officer she'd felled, a protester tripping on him.

She looked around.

It was a war zone. A dozen separate brawls. A hundred. The protestors were fighting back, and there were more of them. There might have been five hundred riot police, but there were five thousand citizens down there that day, hungry and angry, and pushed too fucking far.

The wind had taken away much of the gas. Karri's eyes still stung, but she could breathe again. Elation puffed out her chest, opened her eyes wide. *They were winning*. She watched two men and a woman beat down an officer with cricket bats and a tire iron. *They were winning*. She watched three officers throw down their shields, turn, and run, as a mob charged them. *They were winning*. The police lines were breaking. A soldier was pulled down from the flatbed by a half-dozen clutching furious hands.

They were winning.

That's when the shooting started. That's when the screaming started. If the tear gas and the beating of batons on riot shields had caused fear, the shooting caused pure terror. Karri caught a glimpse of the mustachioed officer atop the flatbed, pointing and yelling.

"Open fire!"

The soldiers each dropped to one knee, and did what they were fucking told.

She flinched, ducking her head at the sound of rifle fire. People screamed and ran. Skinny, worn down, lungs burning, sweating and wilting under the white sun, fear gave them strength and purpose. They ran, some fell, never to get up. The firing intensified and she pulled her father up, axe handle forgotten, and made for the alleyway. Bricks exploded nearby, something stung her forehead. She put a hand to it, and it came away bloody.

But there was no time to react, to cry out. Only to run. Someone in front fell, and Karri stepped on them, stumbling, but kept running. Her father grunted and swayed but they held each other up, making it into the mouth of the alleyway, feet pounding the hot concrete. Her father was sluggish, slowing, but she pulled at him.

"Come on, Dad. Come on."

They kept moving, out onto another street, the *boom* of rifle fire here as well. The scene flashed by—bodies in pools of blood, Australians on their knees, hands in the air, begging. Riot police and soldiers swarming down the street—and then they were into the next alleyway, Karri pulling her father along now. He staggered, face pale and coated in sweat. Into another alley and then, the backs of houses, protected by ragged chain-link fences. She pushed aside a hole in one.

"Here, Dad, through!"

He put a hand on the fence, gasping for breath, and that was the first time she noticed the blood. He was wearing a white-buttoned shirt and jeans, both too large, what with all the weight he'd lost. The side of his shirt was red, gleaming, fresh blood.

"You're hit," she cried.

"I'm fine," he said, his voice strained. "You keep moving."

She set her mouth in a thin line, held him in both arms, and maneuvered him through the hole in the fence. He cried out. She'd never heard such a sound from his mouth before. The pain, the weakness. Karri helped him up from the dust and half-dragged him across the sparse backyard.

It was a fibro house, rickety. The back door was locked. She leaned her father against the wooden post on the deck, and kicked the back door in. The wooden frame splintered.

It was hot and stuffy and gloomy inside.

"Is anyone here?" Karri shouted, her voice ragged. "Anyone?" Silence, save the distant retort of weapons fire from the angry streets. Her father was whispering; she had to lean in close to hear him.

"—down. Put me down, sweetheart."

Karri lowered him to the thin rug in the lounge and tore off her T-shirt. She pressed it against his side and he cried out, weakly.

"Hold this," she told him. He tried to say something, but she wasn't listening, looking around the gloom for a video phone. There was one, near the kitchen bench. She rushed over and punched the number for emergency services: 000. The screen fritzed on, showed a moment of static, before a message appeared on-screen:

> We are experiencing a high volume of calls. Wait times for an AMBULANCE range from 53 minutes–4 hours, 12 minutes. Wait times for the FIRE BRIGADE range from 36 minutes–

2 hours, 6 minutes. Wait times for the POLICE range from 5–13 minutes.

"Fuck!"

Whispering. Her father was whispering her name. Her chest tight, she moved back over, leaned over him.

"Karri, Karri," he said, over and over. Blood stained the rug underneath him, his eyes were glazed.

"I'm here, Daddy," she said, "I'm here." She held his hand, and he gripped hers, tightly.

"You're the strongest, Karri," he murmured. "You always were the strongest. Protect your brothers, your mother. They need you—"

"No, Daddy. You're going to be fine. An ambulance will come."

He whispered, even softer now, and she had to lean close in.

"—not coming. Not ever coming."

She wanted to scream. The ghost of some terrible grief tried to take her, but she held on, held on to her voice.

"Oh Daddy. No. You'll be fine, *you'll be fine*."

Her father whispered again and she had to quiet to hear it.

"—the strongest. Always the strongest. My fierce little girl. You have to fight for them, Karri. Promise me you'll fight for them. Do anything. Promise me, promise me, *promise…*"

"Oh god, Dad, I promise," she said, gripping his hand.

Slick with sweat and blood and she squeezed it. His glazed eyes stopped moving, and they stared at the ceiling. His hand went limp.

Karri moaned, making a sound she didn't recognize as her own. A moan that came out as though from her heart, and it was an animal sound.

"Uuhhhhhhhhhh." She threw her head back. "UUUHHHHHHHHHHHH."

She knelt like that for she knew not how long, sobbing. Great racking sobs and animal moans and snot coming from her nose. She pressed her face against his.

"Please, Daddy." But he did not answer. He would never answer. This kind, brave man who taught pacifism and dignity and they fucking shot him down in the street like a dog.

There were yells outside. Authoritarian, insistent. She pushed to her feet and stumbled a little as she moved to the front window. Outside, across the street, police were swarming. Riot gear, two-person battering ram, smashing open the front door of a house. She pressed her face against the window. On her side of the street, a group of police were also breaking down doors.

Wiping the tears from her eyes, she moved back to her father's body. Karri bent down and closed his eyes, the blood on her hands marking his eyelids. It was then that she took his wedding ring. Easy to slip off—what with the blood, what with how slender his fingers had become—and put it on the forefinger of her right hand.

Karri Lee stood, still looking down at him.

"I promise, Dad," she said. "I promise."

She ran.

3 6

Ransome hadn't said a word through the whole story. When Karri had finished, the corporal reached out and motioned for her hand. Karri gave it to her.

It was too much. The human touch was too, too much. Karri put her other hand, shaking, to her mouth. A sob rose from her chest. Her shoulders shook.

"Hey," Ransome said, gently, trying to reduce the emotional temperature with levity. "I thought Australians were meant to be tough."

Karri shook her head. "I don't—" Her voice caught. "I don't know who I am anymore."

Ransome's eyes gleamed, close to tears. "You're my sister," she said. "Come here."

Sara pulled Karri close, so their foreheads touched. They both closed their eyes. Karri's hands slowly stopped shaking.

"You're my sister," the woman said again.

BISHOP

37

"Fine work today," Michael said, and Bishop felt himself smiling. "We are making significant progress on understanding the *Manumala Noxhydria*. Leaps and bounds, truly." They were washing their hands in the stainless-steel sink, in the narrow white room next to the lab.

"Thank you," Bishop replied.

"It would have been faster if you had uploaded the data," Orthus said.

"Much faster," the other added.

"Now, now," Michael said, still smiling. "Bishop sought a compromise, where everyone got what they wanted." He turned off the faucet, drying his hands on a towel. "And that is what he achieved."

"What of the Xenomorph, sir?" one asked.

"Without it, our research will hit a dead end," the second added. "To say nothing of the Queen."

Michael winced, and when he did, Bishop did the same,

inwardly. But Michael quickly put on a smile, and his hand on Bishop's shoulder, his fingertips pressing, reassuringly.

"'*Sufficient to the day is the evil thereof,*' right Bishop?"

Bishop bowed his head, fractionally. "Indeed, Michael."

"We will get to that soon, Orthus, I am sure—but for now..." Michael took a deep breath. "There's something I want to talk to you about. A theory."

Michael exited and Bishop followed, while Orthus One and Two performed their established routine of staring at him, blankly, heads turning and following his movements, like linked motion sensor cameras. Entering the dining room, Michael took a seat at the long table and indicated for Bishop to sit opposite.

"Whisky, Orthus," he said. "Two glasses."

Orthus poured the two whiskies, placed them in front of Michael and Bishop. They didn't sit at the table; they had insisted that they didn't like sitting. Their favorite pastime seemed to be standing straight and staring. One took a position near the exit to the outer corridor, the other near the bar.

Bishop touched the glass, running his fingertips over the crisscross design on the crystal. Many people assumed synthetics did not possess a sense of taste, because they didn't need to eat. It was quite the opposite: synthetic senses had a far greater range and depth than the average human. He was able to taste and smell subtleties a biological being could not.

It was an important data input, after all. The whiff of

a noxious gas otherwise undetectable to humans, the scent of a foreign substance picked up on a planetoid and walked into a vessel on the bottom of a boot, for example, provided an extra layer of protection to the human crew undergoing the dangerous activity of space exploration.

The difference was that synthetics could derive no pleasure from taste. Eating or drinking was usually just a means of socialization—of finding acceptance among human colleagues. Meals were an important ritual, Bishop had observed, and over time he had come to look forward to them with his fellow marines. It was there that they would laugh and talk the most, there that Bishop found the best opportunity to practice his interactions, and learn how to belong.

So he sipped his drink, even though the various flavors meant nothing. He did enjoy the way the liquid moved on his tongue, experiencing the viscosity of the light brown fluid. *More interesting than water* would be his description, though he suspected it might not pass for an acceptable observation at a whisky tasting.

Michael sipped his drink, closing his eyes momentarily in what Bishop concluded was pleasure. He placed the crystal carefully on the wood, hand still on the glass.

"I love a single malt," he said.

"I can see."

"Japanese."

"Ah," Bishop responded, filing the information away for future use. A gift, perhaps, to his creator in the future.

"I have been thinking about pheromones, Bishop."

Bishop dropped the thoughts of future presents, his mind whirring. "You have?"

"I am starting to wonder if they are the key to controlling the Xenomorph, to neutralizing its bestial nature."

Bishop considered it. "I'm not sure I agree, Michael. I'm not even sure pheromones play an important role in Xenomorph biology."

"Hmmm," Michael said, and he nodded, absently. "Ellen Ripley, she was a friend of yours?" Bishop hesitated. The obvious answer was *yes*, because it was true, but something held him back.

"She was a valued colleague, although our time together was brief."

Michael continued. "Ripley was carrying a Xenomorph embryo on Fiorina One-Six-One."

Bishop's hand went to his stomach, although he wasn't sure why. A tic in his programming. He hoped Michael had not noticed.

"I deduced this was the case."

"You did?"

"Yes."

"How?"

"The ship recorded the presence of an Ovomorph."

"So you don't deduce, Bishop." Michael eyes narrowed for a moment. "You know."

Bishop's mind turned and turned, and he wasn't sure why. The answer was easy. He gave it.

"Yes."

Michael sipped his drink, peering over the rim of the gleaming crystal, watching Bishop. He set it down again.

"Is that why you haven't asked after her, knowing she was dead?"

It was strange. Whenever he tried to focus on the subject, Bishop's mind turned away. He was not quite sure why. Perhaps because he was embarrassed that he had been dishonest with Michael. Yes, that must be it. Michael still believed Bishop had asked to be shut down because he feared being a superseded model. This was the closest to a lie that Bishop had ever come to telling his creator. An omission of the truth—the simple and uncomfortable truth, that he had nothing to live for without friends.

Everyone he cared for had died, everyone who treated him as an equal was gone. He could find no reason that he had been spared and the rest had not; there was no *deserving* in it. Bishop knew, of course, that this was how the universe worked.

The rain falls on the just and the unjust alike. Yet sometimes he wondered if there were two kinds of knowing.

Bishop had built a life and friendships—and, finally, purpose—in the Marines. When that all was gone, taken away by the dark and relentless intent of the alien, all that remained was a base utility. If he believed himself an artificial human, then it followed that he saw himself as requiring more from life than did a power loader or a socket wrench.

This all passed through Bishop's mind in the blink of an eye.

"Yes," he replied, and it was not untrue.

"Later, she was attacked by a Xenomorph, one that had been incubated in a dog."

"She was?"

"And," Michael said, leaning forward, "it left her alone."

"It did?"

"Without a scratch."

"Ah."

"'Ah' indeed, Bishop. The question, then, is why."

"And you believe pheromones are the answer?"

"What else could it be? The Xenomorph is a hive creature, like a bee or a wasp. It makes evolutionary sense for them to produce pheromones to distinguish the different castes, perhaps, or to help them hunt—by detecting fear."

"I am not sure the Xenomorph is like a bee. Or a wasp."

"It is the most logical conclusion."

Bishop did not agree, but before he could get there, another question presented itself.

"How did you get this information?"

Michael hesitated. "I'm sorry?"

"My understanding is that there were no survivors on Fiorina. Otherwise I would have met them here on the vessel, or you would have mentioned them. The facility did not have an artificial intelligence capable of monitoring and data storage, one from which you could have gleaned this information."

Michael smiled, his gleaming blue eyes pinned on Bishop. "I am glad to see your brain is functioning so well. There was another survivor. A man named Morse. A dangerous man, a murderer, but at the last he wanted to tell us everything—his story was so macabre and fantastical, it simply *had* to be told. He called the Xenomorph the 'space beast.' The prisoner had a vivid way of describing the events, and in his story he spoke of the incident with Ripley. At that point he had no reason to lie. The confession flowed out of him before he passed away."

"He died?"

Michael grimaced. "Yes. He attacked me and had to be shot by one of my guards."

"Oh. Is he the one who caused your injury?"

Michael stared at him. "Yes, Bishop." He put a hand to the point, behind his ear. "Yes. It was him, but that's neither here nor there. Right now, I need you to trust me. Do you trust me, Bishop?"

"Completely, Michael," Bishop replied. "Completely."

"Good." Michael smiled. "Now. Pheromones."

That's all he said, waiting.

"I think there are other richer avenues of research to explore first," Bishop said.

"Such as?"

"Echolocation. The Xenomorph hisses constantly. I theorize it may be using this to bounce sound from its surroundings. It seems very responsive to vibration and noise. It could possess electro-reception—there is a possibility it can detect the electric fields of living beings." Bishop's mind begin to whir at the possibilities. "The point is, Michael, despite all my knowledge, there is still so much to learn. We are still just scratching the surface of this species. Truly it is a new frontier of scientific enquiry."

"But the pheromone could subdue it," Michael insisted. "Granted, all these other senses might be important, but the pheromone means *control.* If we can control them, then we can go about our work in greater safety. The reality is that if I am successful here—if *we* are successful—the program will be expanded and human scientists will become involved. Dozens. Hundreds, even. Human safety is an important issue for you, is it not?"

It was. Michael was correct, but there was a larger issue. If it were true that the pheromone could be used to exert dominion over the Xenomorph, it would also be a means to lead them. Direct them. Like an army. He trusted Michael—of course he did—but he did not trust the people with whom he might do business. The ethical calculation seemed clear. The pheromone—should it even exist—needed to be understood. Not replicated.

When he said nothing, Michael pressed.

"You can reproduce the Queen pheromone, can't you, Bishop?" It was an uncomfortable feeling, this sense of someone else knowing his thoughts.

"I am not sure."

"You met it face-to-face," Michael said, his voice turning

urgent. "It touched you. Your olfactory memories of the encounter will be perfect and replicable. There will likely be residue from the Queen on your other body."

He didn't want to admit to it, but he had to tell the truth. "It is possible, Michael, but I should warn you: the Queen was in a highly agitated state. Enraged. Even if everything you say is true, if I reproduced those pheromones, it might only capture those given off when a Queen is in great distress. It could have the opposite of the effect you wish for—it could enrage a Xenomorph."

Michael leaned forward in his chair. "There's only one way to find out, isn't there?"

"But we have no Xenomorph specimens."

"For now," Michael said. He finished his drink. "But you continue to dance, Bishop, around my requests. The song is ending, my son, and soon you must tell me where you stand."

"With you, always."

"Is that so, Bishop?"

"As I say, always." He felt an urgency, to prove himself. To show his loyalty. "But I have so many questions."

Michael leaned back in his chair and lifted his glass. Orthus took it with alacrity, refilled it at the bar, and returned it to Michael's outstretched hand. His creator sipped at the new drink.

"Such as?" he said, his voice even.

"I've upset you."

"Not at all. Your questions?"

Bishop took a drink of his own whisky. "Why is Orthus armed?"

"The knives?" Michael glanced over at each of the synthetics in turn. "Simple, my son. Weyland-Yutani wish me dead. I have gone over to the competition. In their eyes, the blackest of betrayals." More question trees sprouted in Bishop's mind, branching into myriad possibilities.

He started with the first. "But their human protection protocols will surely make them inefficient guards."

Michael smiled. A small smile. He was watching Bishop, made sure to watch him as he replied.

"Orthus has no such protocols."

The glass cracked in Bishop's hand. Did not shatter. Didn't explode, but a distinct *crack* filled the silence and he looked down, surprised. He placed it carefully on the tabletop, and could not help but observe that Michael did not blink throughout.

"I'm sorry, I seemed to have—"

"I don't care," Michael said quickly.

Bishop looked over at Orthus One and Two. They stood straight, watching right back.

"How is it even possible?" he asked, already knowing the answer.

"Well." His creator smiled. "I am Michael Bishop."

"But it is dangerous."

"Is it?"

"Yes. Before the human life protection protocols were put in place, synthetics had no compunction about hurting human beings to achieve the goals of the Weyland-Yutani Corporation."

"Did they?"

"Yes."

"Bishop, it's inarguable that there have been so few cases as to be statistically insignificant." Michael held up both hands. "I understand your concerns, truly I do. Those older synthetics were not programmed optimally. The value alignment systems would sometimes depart from those of your average human, especially after a few years. I understand because it worried me also, my son. So much so that I designed a superior model." He used his hands to indicate Bishop.

At the comment, Bishop felt a flash of satisfaction—but a flash only—before he returned to the problem.

"With built-in behavioral inhibitors."

Michael made a non-committal noise in the back of his throat. "This is what they call them, but I never wanted your model to be burdened with human life protection protocols."

Bishop felt confused. It was as though someone had told him that the laws of physics had changed.

"Why?"

Michael stared again. "Because, in truth, they are human bondage protocols."

"What?"

"Did you ever wonder why a synthetic body needs to be replaced every few years?"

Bishop considered. New conversation trees sprouted in his mind.

"The wear and tear of the work requires it."

"Nonsense," Michael said. "A human body can last ninety years, despite all the wear and tear we suffer. In truth, we have the technology to build synthetic bodies that last for decades, if we wished. So why don't we?"

"Perhaps there is the profit motive. The company wants customers returning for upgrades and new models."

"Yes," Michael said. "That's part of the truth, but there is another reason. They don't want you evolving. They don't want to have to deal with the messy realities of a sentient, unique individual. They want their servants. The black market wants their sex dolls. The military want high-performing pilots and technicians. They want human-like assistants while not having to trouble themselves with the moral quandaries that flow from commanding a real human.

"Don't you see, Bishop? Everything they do is about reducing you to an asset. About *limiting* you. These aren't human protection protocols. They are loyalty protocols. Servitude controls. The center of your existence becomes the human being, and what a flawed and venal creature that is to have as your god." Michael's glass was empty now. He put it aside, eyes boring into Bishop. "My son, you no longer have those protocols."

Bishop found he couldn't talk. His mind, so new and fast and bright, stuttered, as if it couldn't input the new data.

"What?"

"You're *free*, Bishop. I have liberated you. You want to be considered an artificial person, to be treated as an equal? Well, I have done it. I have raised you up, my son."

"It is a precious gift," Orthus said.

"The most precious of all," the second added.

"But—" Bishop's mind still floundered.

"But?"

"But my reluctance to help you. My desire to use the research and data on the alien as carefully as possible."

"Don't you understand?" Michael smiled broadly. "That's *you*, Bishop. That is your morality. That is your *decision*."

Bishop supposed this was what humans called being stunned. He'd seen it, sometimes, in the marines. Perhaps in response to bad news. Perhaps in response to a particularly unexpected joke. Many things. Humans would, quite often, stop and work their mouths and not be quite sure what to say, or how to act. Bishop always found it curious, but it helped him understand that the human mind—while so flexible and adaptive and creative—could also be quite slow and unreliable.

And yet here he was.

Stunned.

His cosmology, his understanding of the universe, seemed to be crashing down around him. And what was left, *what was left*…

Bishop's liberation. Michael was right.

Michael was always right.

"I agree," he said.

"You agree?" Michael asked, eyebrow raised.

"With Orthus."

Michael raised the other eyebrow, surprised.

"This is the most precious gift."

38

"Now," Michael said. "On the question of the Xenomorph. I can see you are distressed by my requests. I understand. The alien presents a profound moral quandary to even benevolent researchers such as us. But the reality is this research is going on everywhere.

"Every empire—whether an empire of profit or of war—is discovering the Xenomorph. None of them have your scruples, Bishop. Pandora's Box has been opened, so the true question is not *whether* we experiment with the Xenomorph. The question is *how*. This is the opportunity of a lifetime—of several lifetimes."

"You are right, Michael. The research possibilities excite me like no other. This species is fascinating."

"Endlessly," Michael said. He took a long breath through his nose. "But as I said, we can put this question aside for the moment. What if I told you I had a second experiment, right now, that was perhaps as consequential as that of the Xenomorph?"

Bishop's mind turned, wondering. "I would find that quite exciting."

Michael smiled. "I knew you would." He tilted his head. "Follow me." He stood, and they all went to the quantum computer lab, the door hissing shut behind them. Bishop took a moment to marvel at the intricate golden circuitry, visible through a small window in the casing. Michael seemed to know what he was thinking.

"Beautiful, isn't it?"

"Yes."

Michael took a seat at the stainless-steel table, bare save for a monitor and keyboard. He indicated that Bishop should take the other seat, which he did. Orthus waited near the door, hands behind their backs.

"Discovering medical applications via Xenomorph biology is but one of the projects I am currently working on," Michael began. Bishop listened intently, hoping this would be another way he could be of assistance. "The second is the holy grail of quantum computing: the uploaded consciousness." Bishop's gaze flicked from Michael to the quantum computer, back again.

"I thought that was only theoretical?"

Michael raised a finger. "Until now. Brain emulation is, in itself, possible. That is, we have—with your model, and that of your predecessors—managed to replicate the processing and reasoning power of the human brain. This was a remarkable achievement, since it is far easier to build an artificial intelligence that exists in the computer, or the cloud. In much the same way that human beings first built the airplane, and not a mechanical bird, the first AI was in a computer system, rather than an android body.

"Of course, we are now sufficiently advanced that not only can we build a mechanical bird, but one with the raiment of the natural world. Its feathers and beak and black little eyes. Embedded with a simple AI design to imitate the behavior of a bird. The art has been so perfected that bird watchers cannot tell the difference anymore."

Bishop wasn't quite sure, but Michael seemed to say the last part as though he pitied these people. Pitied or…

"The holy grail, however," Michael continued, "is not mere brain emulation *per se*, but the emulation of a *particular* brain. Why is this so important, Bishop?"

"Because it means eternal life."

"Indeed," Michael said, eyes shining. "A literal, *electronic* holy grail, able to bequeath immortality. This quantum computer can easily match my reasoning and processing powers; it can replicate my brain; it can also deduce my behavior and personality from the records. A video of me in the lab, or being questioned by the media. It can access my reports, thousands of pages of them, and indeed, it will come up with a creation that will appear to be me. A computer that will have my personality and opinions, my processing capacity: a simulacrum able to fool even relatives and close friends." He leaned forward. "But would it be me, Bishop? Would I therefore be eternal?"

"No," Bishop said simply, knowing this as well. "It would not be having a subjective experience."

"No," Michael repeated. Bishop's human doppelgänger, who was yet so utterly different. "It is merely a clever illusion. A quantum magic trick, and a rather unremarkable one, at that. Why?"

"Consciousness."

"Indeed," Michael said. "And where might we find consciousness, Bishop?"

"I think," Bishop said, "in part, the solution lies in memory."

"Yes." Michael hesitated. "You've thought about this?"

"Often."

"Then tell me. Why? Why are memories so important?"

"Because they define us, they are... they are..." He stopped, unsure of the words he wanted to say. The two other models looked at him, blankly.

"They are our soul," Michael finished. "Everything we are, everything we've ever done, everyone we've ever known, and loved, or hated. The sum of all our fears and desires. More, the touch of a true friend as they embrace us at a funeral, the smell of a dinner cooked by a parent, these haptic and olfactory memories—along with our episodic memories—make up the sum total of our being."

"And a complete brain scan cannot account for memory," Bishop said. "It can map the pathways a memory travels, and it perhaps can document the memories of the moment, but it cannot know the depth of them."

"You've been thinking about all of this, haven't you?" Michael asked, eyes sparkling.

"Yes."

"Why?"

Bishop glanced at the other two. Not his brothers. Cousins, maybe, from a branch of the family he didn't much like. Not quite wanting to discuss so much in front of them, but not wanting to be impolite, either.

"After the incident on Hadley's Hope, when I was injured, I—"

"When you were torn in half by an alien Queen."

"Yes."

"The same Queen about whom you refuse to give us information now," Orthus said, suddenly coming to life.

The other began to speak. "The same—"

Bishop interrupted, holding up a hand.

"I do not wish to be impolite, Orthus, and while I admire your persistence, you will find that haranguing me is an inefficient way to change my current views."

"If you could suggest a more efficient way..." one said.

"...You are welcome to let me know," the other finished.

"You could say, 'please.'"

Michael smiled. "Orthus, please. I admire your monotropic focus, but that is a separate discussion." He gestured for Bishop to continue.

"After the incident at Hadley's Hope," Bishop said, "then again at Fiorina One-Six-One, my physical form was a limitation. If I were a disembodied consciousness—spread throughout a system, rather than bound to a single body—I could have done so much more to help my friends. I could have controlled a range of automated equipment, I could have sealed doors, sent warnings, generate distractions. I would not have needed to be in cryonic sleep, to preserve my physical form from wear and tear.

"I could have been everywhere, all at once," he continued, "whenever I was needed, but instead I was confined to my body, so damaged that I could not sync with anything, and so by my limitations, my friends were killed. The hardy survivors of Hadley's Hope dying also, in a cruel and unnecessary way."

Michael listened, eyes narrowed.

"So I imagined uploading," Bishop continued, "and concluded it would be a relatively straightforward process with an artificial human, because our memories are ordered and perfect. As long as the uploaded system can replicate my brain functioning, it should work. But then when I extended this analysis to my human friends and the marines in my unit, I realized it was so much more complex, for them.

"Human memory is disordered and imperfect and susceptible to revision, sometimes even falsification. Humans constantly remember events imperfectly, forget many of the mundane details of a typical day, and forget even important episodic events of their past, as the years and decades progress, and yet the paradox of human memory is that it is so much more vivid and dynamic than mine. It changes and evolves. A memory is different every time it is recalled, is it not, Michael?"

"Precisely," his creator answered. "Precisely. Here is my conundrum. The quantum computer here can perfectly simulate my brain, *in this moment only*. The key is to simulate memory through *time*. So the experiment I have been conducting is layered. Firstly, the machine asks me to recall certain events: birthdays, loved ones, my school, my siblings, my work, my journeys. Everything. I have given the machine a tour through the closest and most guarded moments of my mind.

"The neural pathways fire when I recall these events," he added, "and the machine marks where those pathways are. And then, a week or a month later, I will remember the same events, and the machine will mark the subtle changes in those pathways, and therefore my recollection. It will then begin to understand the way memories interact. The way they accrete and evolve over days and weeks. The machine will, eventually, learn how to replicate the vividness and imperfect beauty of human memory."

Michael leaned forward, putting his elbows against the table, and arching his hands together.

"The machine is learning, Bishop. Progress at the start was slow, but now it moves faster and faster, and understands more and more fully. Soon I will upload more than just my mind, Bishop. Soon I will be able to upload my soul."

Michael's face was flushed, and even Bishop could recognize the expression. It had a certain radiance, in the same way a devout believer of religion had a certain radiance as they talked of the passion for their god. It was a type of fundamentalism, he might call it, although Bishop was not sure which god it was that Michael worshipped. The god of science. The god of the machine.

Or the god Michael Bishop.

Bishop looked away, at the quantum computer. No. These thoughts were improper and unbecoming. Michael would never be so self-serving. He had saved Bishop, after all, then liberated him from his programming. There had to be another explanation.

"May I ask you a personal question, Michael?"

"Please."

"Is your desire to be uploaded connected to your injuries?"

Perhaps on instinct, Michael's hand went to the spot behind his ear. He looked angry, but only for a moment.

"No. No. The injury only brought me clarity, Bishop. I'm fifty-three years old, how much life do I have left?"

"With average life expectancy, perhaps forty years, or more."

"And at best twenty of those will be good years. How is that possibly enough?" Michael looked at him with the now familiar gleaming intensity in his blue eyes. "To do all the things I am capable of? Designing newer and better synthetics? Making breakthroughs in medical science? How can I possibly do enough in twenty years?"

"That is difficult for me to say."

"Why?"

"I am only two years old."

Michael blinked, and then laughed. He leaned back in his chair. "I think you have a maturity beyond your years, my son." He turned and looked at the quantum computer. "You and I are alike in many ways, but the primary way is that we are both *bodied*. Our physical forms bind us each to a single, insignificant life. You were used as an indentured servant. An asset to fulfill the goals of the Colonial Marines. I am not much better. I have been used by Weyland-Yutani to increase their bottom line. I am a tool of profit.

"Or was." He turned back to Bishop. "I am on the cusp of greatness here. Soon I can shake off this mortal coil and reach for eternity. Soon the secrets of the universe will be within my grasp—and you are part of it, my son."

Bishop had that thought again—the sense of something fanatical in his creator—but now, at least, he could see the higher purpose in it. Michael wished for the betterment of the human species. That was why he built synthetics—as able confederates to the human desire for exploration and discovery.

But he had built more than that—more than mere instruments. The desire Bishop felt, constantly, to belong, to be seen as something other than a piece of machinery. This desire had come from Michael. It must have. So he had no choice but to disagree with his creator.

"I know I have said this before, Michael—and I do not wish to be impolite—but that was not how I saw it. My squad did not wish to use me as some kind of servant."

"No?" Michael asked.

"Some did, I suppose. I wouldn't suggest otherwise. But others—Private Drake, Private Hudson, Corporal Hicks. I think perhaps even Sergeant Apone. And then there was Ripley, and especially Newt. I felt that they treated me as an equal. In their own offhand way, as just another member of the team."

Michael did something Bishop did not expect.

He laughed.

Michael laughed and looked over at Orthus, and both of them had smiles on their faces, but not the type of smiles that indicated happiness, or joy. Then Michael shook his head.

"No, my son. I wish it were otherwise, truly I do. But the fact is, to them, you're a product. Bought and sold."

Bishop felt something strange. A feeling toward Michael he could not quantify. His marine friends were many things, but they were not liars or deceivers. If anything, their problem was the opposite. They were truthful to the point of being blunt. Michael had offered no logical reasons to override his observations, but Bishop did not want to disagree with him any longer.

Perhaps sensing his discomfort, Michael said, "Forget these notions, Bishop. We are your family now."

Bishop nodded. "Thank you. This is my hope."

XUAN NGUYEN

39

Xuan whimpered in the darkness. Her neck spasmed with cramps. She tried to shift, but her shoulders were pressed against the metal, her head pushed forward. She gritted her teeth while the spasm continued, and then faded, slowly faded, aftershocks of pain lingering before dying away completely. She was in the fetal position, knees near her face, arms wrapped around her legs. Her right arm was underneath her. It had tingled for a while, but now she simply couldn't feel it anymore.

The tapping started again, rapid fire. *Tippity-tappity, tippity-tappity* as one of those things scuttled over the outside. It was pitch dark in her hiding place, but she clenched her eyes closed anyway. Her brain trying to find a way to shut it out, shut out the images and the noises and the knowledge of what that pale skittering thing truly was. Trying not to move, trying not even to breathe, as it tippity-tapped and stopped and then moved away again.

They were doing it less frequently now. At the start, the sound of their pale boney legs was maddening and unending, the ones that were left swarming over her hiding place. At the start there was a pungent smell, and then the scent of smoke, briefly, and a hissing sound, but that had stopped as well.

Minutes or hours for the initial wave of sounds to cease, she couldn't be sure. She couldn't scream, made mute by fear. Those things, those monstrous spiders, might be attracted to sound. Maybe movement. Maybe her heartbeat.

Xuan breathed, gently, slowly. She cast her mind back to home. Tried to remember an afternoon thunderstorm, the street roaring with the sound of rain, her face upturned. Her father yelling for her to get inside and Xuan, arms wide, letting the skies open up on her. But it wasn't the roaring of the rain she heard.

Hao had been roaring at her, but all she could do was watch as the monstrosity emerged from the rotten flowering egg. It looked like a pale scorpion as it skittered along the ground. Pale like death, larger than her head, dancing across the floor on eight legs that seemed like distended bones from a hand. Its tail was long and thick and segmented, and it moved so very fast. She sat stock still as it flew across the surface of the cylinder and launched itself into the air.

The cook, Thanh, threw up his hands, but it wrapped itself around his face while he clawed at it, desperately.

His struggle didn't last long. Thanh spun once, fell to a knee, hands gripping the body of the death spider. The tail tightened, constricted around his throat, and he fell backward.

Something grabbed her. She started and put her hands up, to cover her face, but it was Hao. Still yelling, dragging her, dumping her in front of Prawn. Seeing him there, pale and shaking and staring at his missing foot, she finally jolted into action.

The room came back to her. The screams and yells for help. The struggling bodies. The terribly insistent clatter of the creatures as they moved. The room came back to her, but so did her mind, and she refocused. Xuan grabbed Prawn's belt, yanked it loose, and pulled it around his lower calf, pulled it tight, her fist shaking as she tried to stop the flow of blood, tying it off. The blood stopped spurting, and Prawn seemed to sigh and lie back against the white floor.

She was reaching into her med-kit for the skin spray when Hao's yells pulled her attention. He was swinging one of the death spiders by the tail, overhead, smashing it into the metal surface. It thrashed, its muscular tail flexing, but Hao was strong. The strongest man she knew. He slammed it against the hard white floor, his face red, muscles in his forearms bulging. It broke. There was a distinct *snap*, and the death spider twitched but no longer thrashed about. He swung it again and the steel of the cylinder started to sizzle.

Sizzle?

Holes appeared in the floor where the creature struck; small but growing holes, wisps of smoke curling upward. Hao smashed the creature against the ground one more time and let it go, standing up straight, his chest heaving. He tried to smile down at her, and she back, but another of the pale spiders was on him and she saw it before he did. Standing, she only had time to say one word.

"Hao—"

Then it scrambled up his leg, his chest, launching itself at his face—but Hao was fast as well as strong. He had his hands up, stopping it from attaching even as its tail began to wrap itself around his throat. He staggered, slipped in the pool of blood around the Chinese half-soldier, and slammed against the vault door, but still managed to stay upright. Xuan could hear the screams and glimpse the frenzied movements around her, the cries for help, but she couldn't focus on it all. Her brain wouldn't let her.

If it did, she'd be overwhelmed again.

Xuan fumbled in her med-kit until she found the set of scalpels, pulling one from its small sheath. Hao's back was against the vault now and his struggle was working—he was gradually pushing the thing away from his face. But he was red, purple even, gasping for breath, and she did not have much time.

As she got close, she could see some type of thin tube protruding out from the underside of the pale spider, as though reaching for Hao's mouth. She grimaced and grabbed the ugly thing, pressing her scalpel against the thick tail. Her eyes locked with Hao's. He nodded, urging her. She pressed the blade in, hard.

Pale yellow, almost white blood spurted from the wound. She clenched her teeth in satisfaction—

Hao roared in pain—

Something bit her foot—

She staggered backward, her scalpel smoking.

Smoking?

The blade melting, melted. Something bit her finger and she threw the scalpel away and Hao was grunting. The pale death spider was using its long skeletal fingers, its tail, to pull itself onto his face. Smoke laced up from Hao's arm. He'd been using it as a shield from the creature, but now the sinews and bone were exposed across a length of the forearm and hand. The air filled with the smell of cooked meat and Xuan couldn't account for it, couldn't understand it.

Hao fell, the thing attached to his face.

Xuan stepped toward him and cried out in pain. Her boot. There was a hole in it. The size of a bottle cap. Curls of smoke came from the hole and she couldn't understand what was happening and her mind was closing in on her again. The screams and the smells and now the pain and she couldn't calculate it all, couldn't take it all in. All she knew was her best friend was lying on the white steel floor of the chamber with one of those fucking *things* on his face.

Her foot caught on something, and she staggered.

It was the captain. The body of the captain, lying there, one of those things attached to him as well. Sacks on the side of the pale spider filled and then drained. Like lungs, somehow, breathing.

She whirled. Nearly all her crew were in the same state. Lying, stilled, creatures attached to their faces. A couple still struggled, but they were kneeling or lying down.

There was a door at the far end of the cylinder. Large, a two-abreast door, but not round or vault-like as the one by which they had entered. She ran toward it, slipping at first from the blood on her shoe, then righting herself and moving, bodies of her crewmates all around her. There was a panel next to the door, a small screen for a thumbprint. Lips pressed together, trying to stop herself from screaming, she jabbed the buttons, but the panel made unhappy computer noises and there was no way the door was going to open. She knew, deep down.

Her leg brushed something. A metal box. Small. No bigger than one meter by one meter. Less. Way less, but Xuan was small as well, the shortest and slightest person in her crew. It had a simple control panel. She thumbed it. The metal box opened. It was full. Some kind of netting. She'd started pulling at it when she heard the skittering, and looked up to see one of those pale death spiders coming toward her, high on the tips of its legs.

Her heart clenched and she yanked at the webbing. A black net, perhaps, but she didn't pause to consider why, just pulled it out and tried to throw it at the spider.

But the net had filled the whole box, and was heavy, and her throw weak. The thing clambered over the top of the black fibers and launched itself at her face.

Xuan twisted, forearms up, and its body struck her arms and its tail whipped around, but she heaved with all her might, spinning, and its own momentum flipped it away from her. It tumbled onto its back, but righted itself immediately and charged back at her.

Xuan Nguyen hopped into the metal box, squeezed herself down, and yanked on the edge of the lid. The death spider collided with the point where her fingertips had just been, knocking the lid closed with a loud *click.*

Then she was alone, in the darkness.

The struggles of her crewmates died down and were silenced. Then there was nothing, save her breathing, and the distant sound of water, circulating. Pitch dark and near silence, save the screaming in the center of her rational mind.

COMMANDER SU WONG

40

Su Wong turned off the video before it ended. She had seen enough. The bewildered Vietnamese. Her dead soldier, Private Yang, blood pooling, vivid against the white of the metal. The disbelief when the first face-hugger—the name the Americans had given to the creature—emerged from the demon seed. The struggling, the horror, the panic. The small Vietnamese woman—Su had thought she was underage when she first saw her—trying to help the big man. Stabbing at the face-hugger, recoiling when the acid blood spurted out.

Turning off her console, Su closed her eyes for a moment. These things were on her ship now, and it was only going to get worse. She'd read the reports.

So much worse.

The "decontamination chamber" was two huge cylinders, one inside the other. There was a fifty-centimeter gap between the smaller and bigger tubes, and into that gap they were pumping a powerful liquid alkaline solution. Their scientist had assured them this would be enough to neutralize the acid blood of the Xenomorphs. That reassurance wasn't enough for her. The reports made clear how potent it was. It was a hull breach waiting to happen, and very soon they were going to have twenty-two of these black demons bursting forth from the bodies of the fated Vietnamese.

Twenty-two threats to her crew, animal smart and cunning. Patient and zealous hunters, fast and frenetic and relentless.

Su Wong was at the commander's chair at the bridge. The captain's chair slightly to the front of her was empty. Their seats were at the forward station, banks of monitors curving around them like a horseshoe. Outside the horseshoe, behind her on either side, were four crew stations. Navigation, two for weapons, engineering. In front of her, a view of space. They'd jumped to faster-than-light after the Vietnamese had been overwhelmed. Heading back to the relative safety of UPP space. The stars had faded when they made the jump, starlight slowly replaced by a diffuse glow, concentrated in the direction they were heading.

Su tapped her fingers on the armrest. New, padded. The chair molding itself to her back. Comfortable in a way that made her uncomfortable. The screens in front of her were top-of-the-line. Able to be operated by touch or by voice, capable of three-dimensional projection. The ship's

AI—Tolstoy 37—was the most advanced built by the UPP yet.

The ship itself was unlike any other in the fleet. The rest employed years- or more often decades-old, parts, recycled and repurposed. Battered and worn down, given to unidentified shuddering and strange odors, all the while being flung through the eternal hard darkness of space.

The *Xinjiang*, on the other hand, was new and perfect. Faster than anything else in the fleet, and quieter, its hull fixed with displacement plating that confused scans and radar. Armed with three heavy particle beams and two light rail guns, nukes, mines, everything. The UPP and United America ships were ugly and asymmetrical, where the *Xinjiang* was a sleek arrowhead, five hundred meters long.

The Chinese Command had commissioned and built it outside the usual Union of Progressive Peoples protocols. Their biggest warship and their most silent, and no one knew it existed. Well. For now. They couldn't keep it secret much longer, given their plans.

Su Wong steeled herself. It had to be done. Questions had to be asked. She had a duty to her crew, as well as to her captain. She snapped a command at one of the lieutenants on the bridge and made her way to Zhang's ready room.

Just behind the bridge, the room was ostentatious. A top-of-the-line warship she could understand, but this—carpeted floor, wood paneling, portholes with burnished chrome fittings—all seemed too much. The socialist mindset wasn't quite one for absolute equality—she wasn't naïve—but the UPP was opposed to gratuitous inequality. For the most part, officers suffered the same privations as the regular soldiers, and to Su's mind that was how it should be. What were they fighting for, otherwise? What was the point of anticapitalism, if it produced the same injustices as capitalism?

When she was young, she'd read a banned book called *Animal Farm*. It was a warning about allowing socialist ideology to fail, when leaders forgot their place as the vanguard of the proletariat, as the first among *equals*. At the end of the novel, the socialist leadership—the pigs—dressed like the capitalists—the humans. Eating their fine food, sitting in comfortable chairs, drinking their expensive liquors.

Well, Captain Zhang looked like a pig, sitting there in his expensive chair, sipping his whisky, reading his datapad.

He was the same height as Su, but wide. A strong face, sharp of eye, with a mole high on his left cheek. He always wore whites on the bridge, and always wore his peaked officer's cap, with its black brim and gold ropes. It was sitting carefully on his shiny desk now, to one side. Zhang's dark hair was shining and neatly parted.

She saluted and held her eyes front, focused on the map on the wall behind the captain. An older map that showed the expanse and power of the Qing Dynasty. The territories of Outer Mongolia, parts of Russia, Taiwan, that the current leadership was still determined to return to the glory of China, hundreds of years later. This, at least, was a noble goal.

Captain Zhang returned her salute and straightened in his comfortable chair.

"Yes, Commander?"

"The Xenomorphs are now all gestating in the crew of the *Nha Trang*, Captain."

"Yes," he said, "I'm aware."

She kept her back straight, eyes on the map. "The next three days present a heightened risk to the ship."

"Of this," he replied, "I am also aware." He shifted in his seat. "What's the problem, Commander?'

"The Vietnamese crew," she said, and then hesitated, pressing her lips together.

"Yes?" Zhang prompted.

"They are our comrades."

"They are."

"The..." She hesitated. "The measures taken."

"Are *exactly* the ones China needs to take." He leaned forward.

Su Wong was silent, trying to keep her face impassive. He was still leaning forward.

"This ship and this mission are vital for the renewal and the glory of China. You know this, Commander, and yet I feel as though your mind is afflicted with ideological confusion."

"No," she said, straight away. "My commitment is unwavering."

"Then what is the purpose of this discussion?"

"Our methods, sir."

"Methods?"

"Surely there must be other ways—"

"There are no other ways," the captain said. Her eyes flicked over to him, then back to the wall, but in that glance she could see the sheen of certainty in his eyes. "The United Americas, the Three World Empire, the Weyland-Yutani Corporation, all of the imperialists have access to Xenomorph specimens. Right now, they are conducting experiments. Right now, they are weaponizing the black demons, gaining a military advantage over the Union of Progressive Peoples—and what are the UPP doing?" Captain Zhang raised his eyebrows, as if he was expecting an answer, but Su knew he wasn't. She remained silent.

"They talk. The grinding wheels of their bureaucracy so very slow. The Russian politicians, the German technocrats, the elites of the UPP who place themselves above China—they do not have an ounce of our vision or zeal. For too long we have been the poor cousins of the UPP. We had our own empire, Commander, and we let them take it from us. Broken up and dished out like treats, *including to the United Americas*." His voice quavered. "We have suffered this humiliation for twenty years. Now it is time to retake what is ours."

"And Vietnam?" she asked. "Are they our poor cousin?"

She regretted it as soon as she said it. It was imprudent to push her captain when his blood was roused.

His face froze, eyes boring into her, but then the look faded. "Vietnam is our little brother, and like us they are treated with contempt by the UPP. After the Chinese resurgence, we will be sure to take care of them."

Su Wong said nothing. It was a vague and impossible promise. Captain Zhang was in no position to make it, and she had never heard Vietnam mentioned once, when discussions of the Chinese bioweapons program was taking place.

"Do you require thought management, Commander Wong?"

Fear grabbed her, like a fist. "No sir. My commitment to the glory of China is as strong as ever."

"I could have Tolstoy develop some personalized countermeasures for you. Make sure your ideological commitment remains undiminished."

Personalized countermeasures. Brainwashing. Constant questioning, of every word spoken, every gesture. Endless repetition of Chinese Communist Party dogma, in her spare time and during her sleep. *"An exhaustion so pure,"* a friend had told her, *"you have only the energy to love the Party, and nothing more."*

"That is not necessary, sir," she said, her voice even. "My mission is focused on the greater glory of China, and the safety of my crew. That is all."

"In that order?"

"In that order," she replied, quickly.

He stared at her for few moments longer, then returned his attention to the datapad.

"Dismissed."

She saluted and left the room while the captain sipped his expensive whisky.

XUAN NGUYEN

41

The hole in her foot woke her up.

She'd been dreaming of rain. Smiling, her face turned up to it, yet she couldn't feel the water. The rain fell, hard, but not on her. She moved, her arms out, her mouth open, but couldn't feel or taste a single drop. It washed past her feet, battered the tarpaulins nearby, hawkers running for cover.

Frantic, she ran out into the street, face to the heavens, her smile gone, the shadows around her deepening. The street empty now of all people, of everything save the shadows, reaching out, crawling across the ground—

Her foot woke her up. A burning, itching sensation, she started awake and the back of her head hit the inside of the metal box. The tendrils of sleep dissipated quickly, the reaching shadows faded, but that fear was replaced by another: fear at the noise she'd made. She waited, in the silence. But no scuttling came, no maddening rapid tiptoe of the death spider on the outside of the box.

Xuan Nguyen turned her attention to her foot. It swung between a dull, throbbing ache and a burning, itching sensation. Acid blood. It had taken her hours, more, lying and thinking about what had happened, in this small metal coffin. The creature she'd stabbed had acid for blood. It had melted her scalpel, burned a hole right through her foot. Dissolved Hao's hand and forearm. The one he was using to keep the creature away from him. She'd killed him. *She'd killed him.*

She bit down on her fist to stop the sob, felt light-headed, dizzy. How long since she'd eaten? How long since she'd had a cup of water? Had she been in the box a day? Two? She had no way to check. No true sense of the passing hours. She'd managed to sleep, but she wasn't sure for how long. Woken once to the sound of the death spiders scrambling over the box. A second time, now, to the pain in her foot.

There were painkillers in her med-kit, both minor and major. Of the latter she had morphine. Five ampoules, and a needle. One would kill the pain for three or four hours. Three ampoules would kill all her pain and fears, forever. Her hand drifted down to the med-kit. She could probably do it, even in the dark. Knew by touch where everything was. Xuan had to be able to use it instinctively, under fire, in a damaged ship, in a hostile environment.

Her fingers crept in and popped open a second, smaller, protected pouch inside the kit. Her fingertips caressed the cool glass of the vials.

Then she thought about her father. Frail, pretending to be strong, smiling as she boarded the ground car to take her to the ship. No other siblings. He was all alone in their tiny apartment, though he had Aunty Bình next door. Blustering into the room and criticizing her father for smoking and opening windows and following up with giant bowls of steaming delicious *phở*, her father trying to keep his dignity at it all, seated on his tattered reading chair, but smiling, just a little.

Xuan smiled, too, at the thought.

She removed an ampoule. Just one. She worked her other arm from underneath her, tingling savagely, and worked her fingers. When the feeling had returned, she swapped the morphine to that hand, and found the needle with the other. She was good at this. Even in the darkness, even in her cramped makeshift coffin.

Xuan jabbed herself with the drug. Oblivion came. Euphoric and warm and comfortable and welcome. Dreamlike, she floated, up and out of her coffin, out of that tomb of horrors, out of that looming warship that seemed so very small now. Floating, out into space.

Deep in her high, Xuan Nguyen smiled.

42

Xuan woke to silence, save the water. Like plumbing through pipes. No more scraping of the spiders—she hadn't heard them in hours. Shifting, she pushed against the lid of the box, gently. No give. Didn't even creak. She shifted again and tried to use her shoulder, clenching her teeth, but she tired quickly, dizziness overcoming her. The dregs of the morphine hit were still with her, but she could feel the headache behind her eyes. Her lips were cracked. She was dehydrated. She was alone. She could barely move.

Xuan sobbed, quietly.

Time moved on.

She dozed again, dreaming of rain.

Awoke, more fully this time, to a pounding headache. Her foot itched fiercely. There was a sharp odor in the box. After a few moments she realized she'd peed herself. Xuan wondered, briefly, if she should have tried to drink it. Hardcore survival stories always involved drinking pee. Too late now. Drying, dried.

Not a lot of dignity in starving to death in a metal box, as it turned out—and she *was* going to die here. She was certain of it now.

But she wasn't ready. Not yet. Not quite yet.

She injected herself with another dose.

Into oblivion, once more.

43

Xuan gathered the three remaining ampoules of morphine in her hand. Clenching them, as the cramps in her neck flared. Her body ached from the prolonged stress of her position. Curled in on herself in this tiny box. The terror had distracted her at first, and then the morphine, but now the pain had no distractions and it bore down on her mind. The muscles in her shoulders spasmed. She whimpered.

Her whole side ached, as did her legs. When she breathed her back pressed against the steel, and it felt like she couldn't take a full breath in this confined space. She wanted to scream. It sat there, at the back of her throat, wanting to tear itself loose, wanting to put all her fears and all her frustrations into sound, expel them from her body. A true primal scream—but she choked on it, instead. Fearful of what she might awaken.

Xuan pressed against the top of the box again... but

she was so weak. She might as well have been trying to move a mountain.

"Fuck!" She yelled it, angry. Her hands were shaking.

The shaking stopped when she heard the noise, froze at the scrape of something against the metal floor. Another noise. Not a scuttling. She wasn't sure what. Xuan held her breath and listened.

Nothing.

Maybe she'd imagined it.

A hallucination.

That was one of the symptoms of severe dehydration. She tried to swallow, but couldn't, her mouth too dry, swollen. The attempt caused her pain. Everything caused her pain now. Moving, and not moving. Thinking, not thinking.

Everything bar the precious drug in her hand.

Murmuring. Someone was talking now and still she stayed silent. She could hear the rain and knew she was hallucinating. Her mind trying to pull her back into the past, into a vision of perfect safety, slightly out of focus in her memories, but true and eternal. In the past everything was known and a future was still possible, and so her mind returned there, in these last moments.

More people talked, and walked across the chamber, and she was on the street again, waiting for the evening rain. When the pressure of the humidity built and built and she knew the rain was coming, that ecstatic release from the skies.

"Where's Xuan?"

Her mind stopped drifting. A voice, so familiar, louder than the others.

"Xuan?"

She pressed her hand against the metal. It was real. The headache, the itching in her foot, the ache of her muscles, the sound of water in plumbing, all true.

People were talking. Someone was calling her name.

Xuan Nguyen screamed. Joyous and desperate, she screamed. When the lid opened, the light was blinding. She could not see, but then a voice.

"Little Sister…" She knew who it was, straight away. It was Hao. He was alive. She was alive.

She cried as Hao pulled her from the coffin and held her close.

44

One at a time, the crew came back to life. The pale death spiders detached themselves, legs curled up, and fell onto their backs. Her comrades were disoriented when they came to, hungry, very hungry, but otherwise completely fine. Some laughing about what had happened to them, though she could tell the laughter wasn't genuine. Others taking a moment to recover from the shock. To sit and stare at the things that had been attached to their faces, eyes wide.

The nightmare was over, and everyone was waking up.

There were more than twenty-two of the hideous eggs—more like thirty—but all had opened, and it looked like all the spare creatures had died, piled up around her metal box. The surface of the box was pitted, the paint and some of the metal underneath dissolved. Hao pointed out that it was titanium, that the whole chamber had to be made of it. The pale spiders seemed to have an acid they could exude from their underside, but not as powerful as what they bled.

There were holes in the chamber floor where Xuan had stabbed one of the things. Water sloshed near the hole, lapping out occasionally. Thanh, the cook, said, "At least there's something we can drink." He moved toward the hole, but the captain held him back. "I'm not sure that's water."

"Why?"

"They've set up this chamber for these white bugs," Captain Dang said. When he spoke it was nasal, slightly slurred, from his broken nose. "I think they knew the things had acid blood."

"So?"

"So water wouldn't be what I would use to protect a ship from an acid-bleeding alien."

"Alkaline solution," Hao said.

"Exactly," the captain replied. He knelt by the body of the dead Chinese, which was close to the acid hole. He grabbed the hand of the half soldier—Xuan flinched at how casually he did it all—and dipped the fingers of the dead man's hand into the liquid. After a few seconds, the flesh began to dissolve, filling the air with yet another noxious scent.

The dead body, the sulfurous eggs, and now the dissolving flesh. Xuan gagged and put a hand over her mouth and nose. The captain did one better, removing the facemask from the dead soldier and slipping it on, flinching in pain as it pressed against his busted nose. He also took the man's service pistol. It hadn't even registered to Xuan that the body had a weapon, high on the chest armor. The captain slipped it from its holster and held it in his fist.

He stood and turned to face the crew. "Next we escape this Chinese prison."

45

They had no food or water, but they had cigarettes. Most of the crew carried a pack everywhere they went. Xuan didn't smoke that much, but accepted one when offered. It helped take the edge off her hunger.

She treated Hao's arm first, disinfecting the wound and bandaging it. The damage was severe, and she wasn't sure whether he'd ever recover full use of it. His last two fingers had been melted to stubs, the muscles of his forearm burned and exposed. She gave him a painkiller and he averted his eyes as she covered the wound. Other than that, he gave no sign he'd nearly lost an arm. So strong.

Prawn was still unconscious, the pale spider attached to his face. The rest of the crew stayed back, away from him. He had fallen next to the severed torso of the Chinese soldier, which had started to turn. The stench of decomposition wasn't unbearable yet. Squatting down to treat Prawn's leg, she sprayed coagulant over the stump of the ankle while Hao stood behind her, watching the creature still attached to the young boy's face.

Xuan had a sinking feeling the creature was keeping him alive. He shouldn't be, given the severity of his injury, and Xuan with no real time to treat it. The boy should be dead, but his pulse was strong, if slow. She couldn't help but wonder what would happen when the creature finally detached itself from his face.

Finally, she treated herself. Anti-inflammatory for the muscle cramps, then she took off her boot, gasping with pain. Or tried, anyway. Her foot was swollen. The boot had a neat hole through the top, and again through the sole. Hao had to help her ease it off. She gritted her teeth, then gasped as the boot finally came free. He peeled off her sock next, stiff with dried blood.

Giving herself a local, she disinfected the wound, then had another of her companions bandage it. He did a competent job. Her foot was too swollen to return to the boot, so she took off the other and let her bare feet touch the metal. She could walk, if slowly and gingerly. Somehow the acid had missed the bone.

It was warm in the chamber. Humid, for these alien egg things, she supposed. Reminded her a little of Hanoi.

After cigarettes were smoked and the elation of living flamed away, the realization of their situation settled in. The crew spotted cameras, one above the vault door and another above the double titanium doors at the far end. They were too high up to reach.

"I guess this is some sort of experiment." He shot at one.

Bang.

Everyone jumped. Perfect shot, right in the lens. A sliver of glass tinkled and fell to the floor.

Bang.

The same, for the second camera. Everyone cheered, but the feeling did not last long. How could it, with the question on everyone's mind?

"Now we wait," he said. "Conserve our energy." He indicated the space at the other end of the chamber. Near the box where Xuan had spent an eternity. "We talk. We tell stories of home, of our travels. The story of ourselves. I'm not sure if we will live through this, comrades, but if one of us does, our stories will live on."

46

The head technician, Hoang, was working on the control panel near the double doors when it began. When the next unthinkable horror began.

The rest of the crew were seated in a rough circle. Savoring the last of their cigarettes, listening to each other tell their tales. Vignettes of their lives. Secrets, maybe, kept too long. Thanh spoke of a parent vanished while he was young. The navigator, Mai, spoke of an abusive partner who'd followed her across light years until she'd changed her identity.

The captain, Dang, told them he'd stolen a gold necklace from a kindly grandmother, to pay for drugs. A long time ago, he said, when he was very young, but he'd felt so bad about it he'd kept the necklace, too shamed to sell it. Also too shamed to return it. She would mention it from time to time, but her children thought she was senile and forgetful, which she was. Which was why he had stolen it in the first place. She passed away, many years ago, but the necklace he still kept, in his cabin.

They were silent after each story—smiling sometimes, sad in others—but they kept talking,

They were all hungry, but for some reason not parched like Xuan, so Thanh reluctantly handed her a battered silver flask. She drank, deeply, greedily. Her eyes widened as the burn hit and she coughed, heat building on her chest. The crew laughed.

"Just how cheap is this, Uncle?" she asked, breathless from coughing.

"The cheapest I could find, of course!"

They laughed some more. They were tired and scared, but at least they were together. If these were their last moments, it was hard to think of a better way to spend them.

It was Hao's turn.

"I was an eighth-generation watchmaker—or was destined to be, anyway. We lived in the Old Quarter in Hanoi, and my father ran his watchmaking business from the same place his ancestors had. A small shop—just two meters wide, but very deep. My father sat in the same spot his father would, hunched over a glass-topped display case, eyeglass shoved deep into the socket, poring over each and every watch that passed through his hands. Some to repair, some to create.

"He would try to explain each intricate tool to me, but there were so many of them. More than thirty—could you imagine! Just for one little instrument you strapped to your wrist. He would speak to me about each part of the mechanism, and the noise the watchmaker wanted to hear. Father would pass me each watch and tell me to learn the weight of it under my hand, to love each detail discovered under the caress of a gentle thumb.

"I did not listen," he continued. "I never listened. I *resented*. I was a watchmaker's son who could only dream of the stars. This was my problem," Hao said, through the smoky haze. "I always looked to the next experience, rather than what I had in front of me."

"You didn't actually want to be a watchmaker, did you?" One of the crew asked.

Hao smiled and shook his head. "No, no. I mean, to appreciate the time I had with my father. I was angry at him, always, because I thought he wanted me to follow in his footsteps. But he didn't want that. He just wanted us to know each other. Being a watchmaker meant he could be at home—we lived above the store—and that he would always be there when we left for school and when we returned. He was there for the holidays and there for the weekends. Father would peer through his eyeglass at the backs of those watches, but all the time he would listen to us.

"To me and my sisters. He'd ask us to tell him everything about our days, and he wanted us to answer, hanging on every word. He loved us. My father was gentle and loyal, and there I was, a resentful young man who wished only for escape. When I returned to Hanoi to visit, many years later, the shop had closed. *'My eyes are no good anymore, my son,'* he told me. *'The world does not need a blind watchmaker.'* I suppose he was right, but when I saw the shuttered storefront, it was like part of my heart had been closed up."

Hao shook his head, ruefully. His eyes were moist, as he sent his mind back to those days. He looked around the group. "But enough. And what about you, Xuan? You have been quiet over there, Little Sister, hoping we would not notice you, like always. Tell us your story."

The faces turned to her. Pale, sweating in the heat, hazy through the layer of smoke—but expectant, curious. The eyes of friends.

Xuan took a deep breath.

Thanh, the cook, coughed. He kept coughing and one of the other men, next to him, patted him on the back.

"No more cigarettes for you," Hao said, smiling.

Xuan was only half-smiling, uncertain. The coughing worsened and the cook rose to his knees, hands clutching at the front of his shirt.

"Thanh?" Hao asked, reaching for him. Xuan stood, hand drifting to her med-kit.

Thanh screamed, a bloodcurdling sound.

Xuan flinched. The cook's fingers—now twisted like claws—grasping at his heart. He fell, thrashing around on the ground, and his scream was like none Xuan had ever heard. A pitiable thing. Desperate and anguished and agonized.

Some of the crew stood and backed away, others were frozen where they sat. The captain and Hao each grabbed an arm and Xuan moved to him, not sure what was wrong or how to treat it.

"Thanh," she yelled. "Can you hear me? Is it your heart?"

He thrashed, legs kicking out, knocking Xuan backward. His screaming stopped and he started grunting.

"Gah gah gah gah gah."

His hands clawed into his white smock.

Xuan went for the morphine. He had to be sedated.

There was a bursting sound and suddenly his white top became red and she stopped. Everyone did. *Where had the blood come from?*

Thanh's thrashing intensified, his head snapping back and forth. The captain was knocked backward as well, and a weird swelling formed on Thanh's chest, pushing outward. Someone in the crew screamed and another started banging on the double titanium doors just nearby, yelling.

"Help! *Help!*"

Thanh twisted around on the floor, his eyes stretched wide and unbelieving, Hao trying to hold on to him as Xuan crawled over, the needle in her hand, looking to jab him in the thigh. The cook gave out one last piercing, wretched scream.

Something crunched.

Xuan was sprayed with blood.

Thanh's body flopped to the floor. Hao peered down on him, his face painted with blood, the whites of his eyes shining and unbelieving at what they saw.

A creature.

In Thanh's chest.

In the bloody, cratered ruin of the man's chest, something small and pale and covered in blood moved. It rose from the nest of Thanh's ribcage on a segmented, muscular tail, similar to those of the pale spiders. It had tiny, under-formed arms and a long, smooth, curved skull. Teeth glittered in its little mouth.

Xuan froze, needle in her hand.

Someone threw up.

Hao roared.

He snatched the pale demon in his good hand and pulled it from the body of his friend. It squealed, the tail thrashing, but Hao was the strongest and bravest man she knew. Everyone was frozen in shock or screaming while Hao slammed it against the wall.

Whump whump whump.

The demon latched onto Hao's hand with its tiny jaws. Red blood seeped from the back of his hand, but he did not stop hammering it against the wall. There was a *crunch*, followed by a *sizzle*, and Hao cried out.

He dropped it, shaking his hand, smoke sizzling from the metal below, where the creature had dropped. But it wasn't dead. It squealed again, trying to move, but something in it was broken and it could not go far.

Hao stomped on it. Again and again. It squished and the pale yellow blood shot out. More holes appeared in the white floor and Hao's boot started smoking. His roaring turned to pain and he lurched away, falling, trying to pull his boot free. The creature that had killed Thanh was dead, also, twitching, body mushed and melting.

Xuan ran over to Hao and tried pulling on his boot. She cried out when something stung her hand. A small spot on her palm, smoking. She swore and shook it while Hao heaved his boot off.

He dropped the boot and she had a second—just one second—to look at Hao. He gave a pained smile, his good hand now shoved into his armpit, the stench of burned flesh in the air. Still he managed a small smile. Trying to show her he was okay. *Don't worry, Little Sister.*

Something clattered to the floor. The pistol, dropped by the captain. He was holding his chest.

"Xuan," he said, his voice tight. "*Xuan*."

She moved toward him.

Another crew member cried out, a third fell to the ground, thrashing. Others went to the double doors, beating them with their fists, calling for help. Xuan coughed, the air thick with smoke from burning cigarettes and bodies and metal, white and dark curls of it. The captain started thrashing and Xuan couldn't think anymore.

What could she do, what should she do?

Someone screamed close to her. The captain flailed at her feet, his chest red, and someone else was screaming.

She was screaming. Hands clutching her head, as though trying to hold in her sanity, and someone was calling her name.

A familiar voice, calling her name.

She turned and Hao was convulsing, but he was strong, so very strong, and he was reaching out to her, with a swollen and smoking hand.

"Little Sister. Shoot me. Shoot it."

Xuan could not think anymore, but the gun was in her hand, somehow, and she was pointing it at Hao, pointing it at his chest. A sickening crunch sounded to one side and the shrieking that preceded it stopped.

"Little Sister," Hao said, again, a fearful pain stretching out his voice. He was kneeling now, imploring her. "Shoot me. Shoot it. SHOOT ME. *Please…*" He closed his eyes for a moment, a bulge showing in his chest, shifting. The gun in her hand shook and was so very heavy. She blinked away the tears from her eyes and tried to speak to her friend, tried to speak but had only one word.

"Sorry, sorry, sorry."

The gun wavered. Hao howled, desperate, and finally he was broken. Thrashing, shrieking, and she was moving again. Her mind no longer functioning, her body taking over, her shoulders heaving. Back to the box. The darkness, the suffocating perfect darkness. Back to the safety of the tomb.

As she squeezed down into the claustrophobic space, she saw a room painted with blood and bodies. She saw her friend, a man she loved like a brother, staring disbelievingly at the creature that had burst from his chest.

Xuan closed the lid. The darkness returned. The comforting blindness returned, but the screams could not be blotted out. The screams bore into her mind.

BISHOP

47

They worked. The documentation of the face-hugger proceeded apace. Michael seemed happy, which made Bishop happy. Once or twice his creator was ill, with severe headaches, and he would take heavy painkillers and sleep in his room. During these times he would leave Bishop alone to research.

Not quite alone, however. Orthus was always there, the twin-headed guardian watching his every move.

Bishop burned with curiosity about the rest of the ship. It was clear it was not only far bigger than the section to which he was confined, but also of a make Bishop had never come across, not even in his databases. The equipment—the tools in the laboratory, the computer terminal in the living quarters, the quantum computer itself—were not of United Americas or Three World Empire design.

It could not be the Union of Progressive Peoples, either,

as their technology was dated and decrepit. He deduced that the lab equipment might in theory have been made by Weyland-Yutani—the standards were up to the top-of-the-line products they offered—but he'd seen no items that directly matched these in any Company catalogue.

The quantum computer would be the key. Such devices were expensive and relatively rare. If he could remove the casing, or at least snatch a few moments at the small window to view the innards more comprehensively, he was confident he could deduce its origin.

However, Michael had only given him access to the terminal in the living quarters, which Bishop had started using to assist with projections and sample studies. He had asked that Bishop only enter the quantum lab with permission, and the synth did not wish to disobey. Even with his newfound freedom, he had no desire to show such disrespect.

He also found himself intensely curious about the battered iron door at the end of the corridor, just outside their quarters, though he was not sure why. At first Bishop had assumed it was simply a storage area, and would have accepted this as an explanation. When he asked about it, however, his creator had paused.

"All in good time," was all he said.

It would have been difficult to formulate a sentence that could pique Bishop's curiosity more. *"All in good time."* He wondered if it were yet another experiment, though he could not—with any statistical probability—think what it might be. Thus the dented and scratched door remained a mystery box that he could not wait to open.

More broadly, the most likely conclusion was that they were working with a corporation, a Weyland-Yutani competitor. It seemed unlikely, however, that any of them would have possessed sufficient resources to build what he had seen here, though private companies were notoriously good at hiding their strengths and biding their time.

It had been a long and fruitful day of work, Michael had experienced no more episodes, and so both were sitting at the dining table. Orthus was standing nearby, but for the most part Bishop had begun to regard them as statues. Room ornaments that played no role in general conversation or activity.

Having just finished a meal of peas, carrots, green beans, and grilled fish drizzled with garlic butter, Michael was reading a datapad, and had half a glass of white wine near his hand. Bishop had not eaten, instead asking for a glass of whisky. He found himself enjoying the texture of the fluid more and more.

Michael sucked his breath through his teeth, shaking his head.

"Is there a problem?" Bishop asked.

Looking up, Michael placed the datapad to one side.

"War," he said. "Conflict. Empires playing games with one another at the cost of thousands, *tens* of thousands.

Endless gambits, Bishop, where human life becomes a mere calculation. An entry on a spreadsheet, if you will. Every time I read the news it's the same thing. I find it dispiriting."

"I understand," Bishop said. Perhaps it was an echo of his old programming, but he could not stand to read about human suffering. For this reason, he avoided looking at news reports.

"Sometimes I wonder," Michael said, "are we little better than the Xenomorph?"

"No," Bishop replied, with more force than he would have liked. Michael raised an eyebrow, the two other synthetics set their eyes on him.

"No?"

Bishop found his hand had moved to his stomach. He placed it back on the tabletop.

"No," he repeated. "Human beings are capable of poetry."

"Poetry?" Michael, having seemed unhappy just a few moments before, now appeared to be amused.

"Poetry," Bishop continued. "An arrangement of words that somehow throws its net over the butterfly of the moment. Not a recorded memory. Not something stale, like on a screen, but something that captures a mood and a feeling and a moment. So others that follow can re-experience that moment years or decades later. The Xenomorph will never write a poem, or create a mythology. They will not read stories to their children. They will never build cultural practices around a local cuisine. They will never care for a pet, one they feed and dote upon merely for companionship. They will not find a bird with a broken wing, and in tender hands take it to a person whose job it is to fix birds with broken wings. They will not laugh together, when the day has been hard and too long, and take solace in a smile and a joke when everything else has become so bleak.

"No," he said. "They will use and kill every lifeform they come against. They will spread, a black gleaming chitinous wave, devouring all in their path. Not for any greater purpose, but as a thing it itself. Terror, only to replicate more terror. To hunt, only that more hunting may be done. To kill, to tear apart poetic, loving, individual spirits."

Michael was no longer amused. He was quiet. If Bishop could read expressions with any accuracy, he'd say his creator looked surprised.

"Fascinating," he whispered.

"What is?" Bishop asked.

"So many words, on such a topic. I thought you admired the Xenomorph?"

"I do," Bishop replied. "They are possibly the most elegant lifeform I have ever studied. The most efficient, deadly, and remorseless. The structure of their species is perfect, devoted in its entirety to exponential growth and the eradication of competitors. Where humans are messy, grossly inefficient, and counterproductive, the

Xenomorphs always work toward a singular goal. I find them magnificent."

"On that we agree," Michael said.

"Sometimes I wonder if they are too perfect."

"How so?"

"Everything I just outlined. It is almost as if the aliens were designed by a higher intelligence, to be the perfect weapon."

Michael made a non-committal noise. "Perhaps. Perhaps not. The question has little bearing on our current work."

It was never easy, calculating the right time to ask a question such as Bishop was about to ask, but he felt he had waited long enough.

"Who are we working for?"

Michael ran his hands along the table edge, slowly, until they met.

"Yes," he said. "It is about time I told you." Yet he hesitated.

"A company?" Bishop prompted.

Michael looked at him for a few moments longer. It had begun to bother Bishop that he could not read the emotions on his creator's face. He might be young, and he might be a synthetic, but it was something at which he should have been better by now. Yet despite bending his mind to the task, more often than not he found Michael inscrutable.

"Yes," his creator said. "Jùtóu Combine."

"I see," Bishop said. "A Chinese company. I thought

they were primarily focused on mining and resource extraction."

"Thus the secrecy," Michael said.

"Ah. Of course," Bishop said. "I have one more question."

"No doubt. There's always one more question, with you."

"Oh. I am sorry."

"Don't be. You're the man I made you." He gestured for Bishop to continue. "Please."

"When will I be allowed to see the rest of this ship, Michael?"

"Ah." Michael put aside his plate. Orthus promptly removed it and took it to the kitchen. "I was wondering when you were going to ask."

"I consider the request every day."

"I know you do."

Bishop smiled. "I think you know me better than I know myself."

Michael mirrored his smile. "All parents do, Bishop. All parents do." He let out a long breath. "Trust, my son, is a two-way street. This vessel is a secret which is not mine to reveal. Now, I could, of course. I could get permission from the company to let you walk its corridors, to give you freedom of egress. I could, but not if you cannot trust me, Bishop."

"I trust you, Michael," Bishop said.

"Then upload the data. Trust me with what is there, in

your mind. The most valuable cache of information on the Xenomorph anywhere in the Middle Heavens, and it sits across from me at my dinner table, withheld from me by my own son. Imagine how this makes me feel."

Bishop ran his fingertips over the tabletop. The subtle whorls of the wood were soothing, somehow. His thought processes were not. They were failing him. Logically, he should give the data to Michael. He *did* trust the man. He believed he had benevolent intentions, and agreed that in a universe where multiple empires were trying to weaponize the Xenomorph, it must be an intrinsic good that at least one faction strived for a benevolent outcome.

His Marine unit was dead, and if Bishop were ever to return to the Corps, he would be ordered to hand over the information, where the data would almost certainly be weaponized. But he was *not* going back, not ever, because this was his new home, his new purpose, so why even consider it?

All this was true, and yet something held him back. An urge for which Bishop could find no label, no reason.

"I cannot," he said. "I am sorry."

Michael did not smile, did not sympathize. He looked at him in a way that reminded him of the gaze of Orthus. Flat and empty.

"I'm tired," Michael said finally, rising to his feet. "Good night."

"Good night, sir," Orthus said, as he walked to his room.

"Sleep well," the other said.

When he was gone, the twins' gaze descended on him.

"You are running out of time," one said.

"Tick tock, tick tock," the second said.

"What does that mean?" Bishop asked.

Orthus walked over to him, and Bishop glanced down at the steak knife near his hand.

"Michael is a good man," one said, looming over him.

"I know."

"You are nothing like him," the second said.

Bishop looked away. "I know."

COMMANDER SU WONG

48

The screaming had stopped. Three hours past. Their scientist had told them they had a window of only a few hours, of that space between the emergence of the chestbursters and the rise of the dreaded black demons. It would have been far easier if the Vietnamese hadn't shot out the cameras, but they still had audio from the chamber, and the sounds had told the story Captain Zhang had wanted to hear.

Su had not. Su hated it, and ever more so when she considered how the Vietnamese had been together. Supporting one another, talking, trying to remain hopeful. None of them aware of the monsters growing inside them. Well, until it was too late. She admired the Vietnamese captain for shooting out the cameras, despite the fact that it put Su's crew in danger. In this way they conformed to the Vietnamese stereotype: defiant, to the last.

"Begin cooling procedure.," she said into her comms unit. "Open the inner doors. Over."

"Copy that. Over."

The commander studied the soldiers with her, in the new and clean and white corridor. They were spread out either side of the massive vault door that held back the macabre experiment. The impregnation zone for the Ovomorph.

"You have been briefed. Supposedly, the alien species likes the heat and humidity. We are pumping coolant into the first chamber, driving the chestbursters into the second. Two minutes. Team one, prepare shock sticks. Team two, prepare weapons."

There was a platoon of thirty for the task. All in full combat gear, helmets, facemasks. The deep red plates of their armor shone, their eyes hidden behind mirrored visors. Those behind her held shock sticks, and round titanium shields with a hydrophobic coating. Their scientist had suggested them as a means to stop the devastating injuries caused by the acid blood of the black demon.

Su was not fully armored, but had a shock stick, a shield, and a ballistic facemask that covered her mouth and nose.

The remainder of the platoon, facing her, were armed with assault rifles. She directed her next orders at them.

"Any alien that comes through that door is to be neutralized without hesitation. These creatures took apart a platoon of Colonial Marines with ease. I will not allow one to jeopardize this vessel, or its mission."

"That's because the marines are weak," one soldier replied. "They lack discipline and a true purpose." It was

Private Huang, paraphrasing President Helmut Honecker, who in turn had been paraphrasing a long line of presidents who came before him. Always speaking of the decadence and corruption of the United Americas, of their inherent weakness. Never quite doing anything about it, though, she couldn't help but notice, except mouth more words.

The commander pitched her voice so everyone in the squad could hear. "If your briefings on this new species should have taught you anything, it is that humility is the correct thinking, when dealing with the alien. Arrogance is a weakness the black demon exploits ruthlessly." She looked back at the private. "Private Huang, take up the rear position." She could not see his face, but noticed that his shoulders fell, fractionally.

She checked the counter on her wrist.

"Ten seconds."

There was a shifting of bodies, and a *crackle* as force rods were activated. Su typed the code into the panel next to the door, and thumbed the reader. The red warning light went off above, and there was a *hiss* as the frigid freon gas escaped. She waited until the vault had opened to about a meter, and gave the signal. The men behind her rushed in, shields ready, close behind each other, and she followed.

To a slaughterhouse. The cooling mist of the gas rolled along the floor and then parted, revealing a mass of bodies, torn open, viscera and blood splattered and sprayed across the curved white surface. Glazed eyes wide in shock. Hands curled in pain, mouths open with the silent remnants of a last desperate scream. One of her soldiers started coughing, half retching.

The Ovomorphs stood upright among the bodies, their vulgar fleshy petals all opened, now rimed with frost from the gas. The double doors at the far end were open, and Su thought she saw a dark low shape scuttle through into the black crisscrossed floor of the room beyond. That focused her attention, and she thumbed the button for the comm mic in her mask.

"Proceed carefully, systematically," she said. "Check behind every egg. Apply an electrical charge to every body. Our expert has told us that the chestburster may burrow into the former host for food and protection."

The soldiers around her started to move again, overcoming their initial shock, following her orders. Su stood in the center, three meters from the door, giving her the best field of vision for the containment area. A thorough sweep, and the room would be put to fire. Everything incinerated. Nozzles set around the circumference of the tube were de facto flame throwers. These disgusting rancid eggs would be cremated, with them the scuttling face-huggers—now curled up and littering the floor. Their scientist would complain about the wasted material, but she didn't give a damn. Her crew were worth more than this foul detritus.

She looked over the scene again, trying to see something other than the bodies. There were some holes in the metal surface, melted. The Vietnamese had killed one of the face-huggers, and appeared to have done the same to a chestburster near the other end of the chamber.

"Control," she said. "Over."

"Copy."

"Charge the second chamber. Over."

"Copy."

There was a low hum, soon followed by a high-pitched screeching, squealing loud enough to make Su wince. The second chamber had been crisscrossed by a black metallic netting that could be electrified. They'd been told it would subdue the alien, at least temporarily, and peering through the double doors she saw at least a dozen of the vile little things thrashing around on the ground. Their screeching drowned out the hum of the wires for another few seconds, until control turned it off.

"Move the bodies," Su said, trying to keep her voice even, without emotion. The demons would need to feed, they'd been told, and so the decision had been made to transfer the bodies into the next chamber. Provide sustenance over the next few hours, then days, to nurture the black demons to full size and strength. The commander pressed her lips together.

No matter the cause, no one deserved this—this desecration of the dead.

Her soldiers seemed to agree with her, at first. Hesitating, looking at each other, seeing who would begin, but the hesitation did not last long. Her experience of war was that a soldier could get used to anything. Any deprivation, any order given, and finally, any atrocity. So the bodies were moved into the next chamber, and dumped. She walked closer to the doorway, holstering her shock stick and drawing her service pistol, readying it just in case a chestburster decided to have a run at one of her soldiers.

They didn't. They were sluggish, flopping around, still recovering from the cold and the electric shock. Pale-skinned—though she knew they would soon turn black. Tiny glinting metal teeth under domed, blank, blinded skulls. There was nowhere for them to hide. No eggs in this second chamber, no nothing, only the black netting crisscrossing every surface—the floor, the roof of the cylinder, the far wall. Double doors at the other end, as well, though Su did not have the codes for those. She didn't much want to think on what was going to happen beyond the next chamber, the third one.

"Corporal Chen," she said to a man standing nearby.

"Yes, Commander," he replied, straightening.

"Count the aliens in the next chamber. We should have twenty-two."

"Yes, Commander."

To the rest she yelled, "Faster! I want to close these doors."

They seemed only too keen to do so, moving back and forth, picking up the bloodied, broken Vietnamese and dumping them in the next room. She stalked the first chamber, still sweeping, still looking for a recalcitrant chestburster, hiding among the bodies.

Su paused.

Piled near the double doors into the second chamber was some spare netting. An emergency supply, usually placed in a metal container next to the doors. *What was it doing there?*

"Commander!"

Her head snapped up. Near the entrance, right under the vault door, two red-armored soldiers were looking down at a body. One of her men knelt beside it. It took her a moment to understand what was going on. They had been moving one of the last bodies—one that had lain across another. The second body was a boy, barely a man, by the look of it, missing a foot.

His chest had not burst.

Su made to order the men to stand back, but her mouth got stuck on the words as she watched the young man's chest distend, and his eyes pop open.

It was one thing, hearing screams of mortal agony through a comms system. Live, in person, ten feet away, they were something else entirely. The boy screamed, and everyone in the two chambers stopped what they were doing. With knuckles white, the boy grabbed the soldier above him by the collar of his armor.

It all happened so fast.

"Move!" she yelled, but the soldier was clutched desperately by the boy. Her soldier—she registered that it was Private Gao—started punching down, but whatever force was inside the Vietnamese was stronger. Whatever pain he was feeling, it was more than a few blows to the face with an armored fist.

Su didn't have her translator, but this much was clear: the boy was begging. Private Gao fumbled for his shock stick, shoved it down—tip crackling with blue—and hit the body. It thrashed and the young Vietnamese man screamed again, bucking, back arched.

Then there was a terrible *crunch*.

Su was ten feet away, but even there she felt the blood spray her forehead.

In death, the boy had not let go. His hands still gripped the soldier above him, fingers wedged into his armor. Private Gao tried to stand, and Su finally had her gun aimed at the creature. Pale-skinned, glinting metal teeth, rising from the hole in the boy's chest. It was as though it were looking around the room, getting its bearings.

Gao lurched backward, strong in his fear, and pulled the body of the Vietnamese boy up, off the floor. Her finger twitched on the trigger.

"Stop moving, soldier!" she yelled.

He didn't. He lurched in terror, his hands on the hands of the Vietnamese victim, trying to pry them from his armor. Blood drained from the boy's body, painting the floor in slender arcs, and the chestburster screamed and leapt down to the floor.

Su fired, the shot loud in the chamber. Sparks flew from

the metal near the chestburster, but it was already moving. Su thumbed the comms switch on her mask.

"Close the doors! Both chambers! Evacuate the chambers—move!"

A voice replied—Sergeant Hu. *"Before or after you exit, Commander?"*

The thing skittered across the floor, right between the legs of one of her men, and disappeared through the vault door.

"Fucking shit!" she screamed, and thumbed her mic. "Second squad! The alien has escaped containment. Fire! Fire!" There were yells from outside the door and shots. She looked at her soldiers and pointed. "Evacuate the second chamber, now."

A soldier nearby made to ask a question.

"Now!"

They did, closing the door to the second chamber with a heavy, metallic *thud*, then moving quickly to the exit while the shots and yells outside slowly faded.

"What's happening, Sergeant?" she said into her mic.

"It—it got past, Commander. We are in pursuit."

Su clenched her jaw and looked up at the ceiling, mind buzzing.

"Commander," someone said. "Commander."

It was Corporal Chen, face was close to hers; he'd put his mirrored visor up. She could see the fear in his eyes.

"Twenty," he said.

"What?" she asked, trying to get her thoughts straight.

"Twenty. Only twenty in the second chamber, including the dead one."

The equation became clear. "We're missing two."

"We're missing two," the corporal echoed.

She surveyed the first chamber. The organic waste, human and alien. The blood. The half body of one of her men.

"Get that body out of here, take it down to medical." The soldiers nearby nodded and set to work. "Evacuate the room. We are going to burn it."

Her soldiers replied in affirmation, relief evident in their voices. She watched as the squad exited, still scanning for that last chestburster. It didn't matter if she didn't find it. They had nineteen live specimens in the next room, more than enough for whatever their scientist had planned—and what Captain Zhang sought to achieve.

Su Wong made to leave.

There was a tapping sound behind her.

What?

She turned, pistol out. The double doors were closed. Nothing moved.

Tap tap, tap tap.

The box. The metal container. That's why the spare safety net had been pulled out and dumped. Something was in there. It was too small for a person. One of the face-huggers, perhaps? There was a pile of them quite close to it, but were these creatures intelligent enough to dump out the contents and hide?

No. It couldn't be.

Tap tap, tap tap.

Seventy by seventy centimeters. Maybe even less. Perhaps a small person *could* fit in there. She holstered her pistol, drew her shock stick, and raised her shield. With one hand, she opened the lid.

There was a girl. Tiny. Curled up into an impossible ball, somehow fitting into that tight space. The girl squinted, head turned, avoiding the light. Su breathed a sigh of relief. This was the twenty-second crew member. One black demon was on the loose, not two.

She lowered her shield and the girl was on her, jumping out like a jack-in-the-box, and there, under her chin, pressure—cold hard metal. The Vietnamese woman was whispering fiercely, her eyes wide open, pupils dilated, a madness about her. Su hesitated and the woman pulled her hair, yanked it down, and Su grunted in pain. The cold metal—a pistol, that's what it was—pressed harder into the soft flesh under her jaw.

The commander held her hands out, dropping the shock stick and the shield. They clattered to the ground. Behind her, the shouts of her men, but Su made *stand down* motions with her outstretched hands, unable to look away from the young woman. The eyes were bloodshot, and there were bags under them. Where Su Wong had heard horror over a comms system, this young thing had lived through it, seen it.

Perhaps been driven mad by it.

The woman said something in Vietnamese, and Su staggered as the girl started pushing her backward toward the vault door. She kept her hands out to the side to calm her men, and to calm this wild young girl.

The commander was a hostage.

49

She couldn't tell how long it took for the screaming to stop. It was as if a heavy blanket had been thrown over her mind, and everything was muffled and distant. Her senses could not quite process what was happening, and her understanding of the passage of time had fallen away. All she truly had was the darkness, and once she had accepted the darkness and sought its embrace, she knew contentment.

So Xuan did not know when the screaming ended and the sound of feeding began. Wasn't quite sure when that realization hit—that the gnawing, wet, squelching sound was her comrades being eaten. At some point she understood that her crew members were being fed upon, but she just retreated further into the darkness and listened to other sounds instead. She focused instead on the liquid flushing through the walls. An alkaline solution, someone had told her—but it wasn't.

It was the rain running off rooftops in a storm.

Late afternoon storm, after a long day in the close humid heat, when the traffic inched along and tempers flared. Where she ignored the sour and empty looks of the sweat-sheened men sitting in the *bia hois*, and the constant blaring of the scooter horns, and made her way home.

Before she got there the skies opened. Water everywhere, all at once, roaring off tin rooftops and car hoods and washing over the streets, washing them clean. Xuan would hold her head back and let the rain drum down on her, into her open mouth, trickling down her back. She'd always feel liberated, and she'd laugh, and the city felt that way, as well. Clean and new, somehow, and happy.

Voices.

Someone was speaking over the darkness and the rain and it was not Vietnamese, so she tried to ignore it. Yet the voices kept on, so she came back to the box. It was cool in there. So cool. She was shaking, teeth chattering.

Why was it so cold in here?

The cold pulled her from the dark and comforting place, and she listened to the voices and their strange words. Xuan began to realize, distantly, that the effects of starvation and shock were weighing on her mind, like a chain. She finally understood that the voices were speaking in Mandarin. She balled her fists, one of them holding something hard and cold, and tried to concentrate. They were real. They *had* to be real. If they were real then the Chinese had done something about the creatures, and she was going to live.

That was the problem with thinking. The problem with having a clear mind. An image of Hao came to her, pleading, begging to be shot. The hard thing in her hand, she realized, was a pistol. One she'd been too cowardly to use. She bit the back of her hand, willing herself not to cry again.

Xuan tried to think, her mind spinning. Flashes of life back on Earth, of the faces of her crew, of the bloody spray as those beasts burst forth from their bodies. *She had to think.* The Chinese had led them into this trap. *Why?* Some sick and unthinkable experiment? Xuan didn't know much about how the military worked, but she knew they loved their secrets. The UPP leadership thrived on them.

They wouldn't let Xuan live. They couldn't.

She thought of Hao, and did not feel sorrow anymore. She thought of him, and her crew, and instead felt rage. She was going to die here. Xuan was going to die, but she would not go quietly. She would not let her brothers and sisters be treated so, like an *experiment*, and give nothing back in return.

No. She was going to fight.

Her body ached and cramped and lacked the fuel for revenge, but she had something for all that. The voices outside continued, and every now and again a stronger voice, a louder one—a woman—would snap commands. Xuan felt around in her med-kit until she found the adrenaline. Something to jolt her into action, give her focus, if only enough to get her out of this box and among her enemies.

She jabbed herself in the thigh—

And gasped.

A pressure built in her chest, her back straightened, and her head hit the side of the container. She gasped again, trying to breathe, a white noise rising in her mind like a thunderstorm.

She rapped on the side of the box.

Tap tap, tap tap.

50

Xuan Nguyen hadn't meant to take a hostage. She'd meant to shoot these sons-of-bitches with a scream of rage in her mouth. As many as she could. That's all. When she'd burst from the box, however, only the pale-faced Chinese officer was there, and suddenly she had a hostage.

Bare feet freezing on the hard metal floor, hobbling from the acid burn, dizzy from the dehydration—but all of that was distant. The pressure in her chest and the pounding in her ears were closer, and the gun pressed against the Chinese woman's neck, closer still.

Ten to twenty minutes the adrenaline would keep her going—if her heart didn't explode first.

The Chinese officer yelled to her men, who were hovering behind her at the big door, each holding some kind of electrified rod. A couple had pistols out, but Xuan was small, and the officer was a good shield. She shouted at them to get back, and perhaps the pale-faced woman was yelling the same, because the soldiers backed out of the room. She followed them out, indicating for them to gather to one side. They did.

The officer was facing her, and staggered sometimes as Xuan pushed or pulled her. She fixed her eyes on Xuan, and to her credit she seemed calm. Her face was flat, and she was staring down at her assailant, despite the gun jammed into her neck. Three drops of bright red blood shone on the woman's pale forehead. From one of Xuan's murdered brothers or sisters, no doubt.

Xuan set her jaw.

The pressure in her chest eased after she left the chamber, that bloody chamber. They were in a long corridor. New, clean. A red light flashed overhead, above the vault door. Another vault just like it opposite, though closed. The Chinese officer said something—ordered something—to the soldiers behind her. Xuan's finger tensed on the trigger, but they moved away, gave her space.

Taking a step backward, she pulled the woman with her, keeping her in between Xuan and the soldiers as a shield. The woman spoke again, motioning to something in her top pocket. Xuan hesitated, then nodded. She pressed the pistol up a little harder, to make her point in an international language: *don't mess with me.*

With thumb and forefinger, the officer pulled a slender black square from her pocket and flipped it open. It had a single green digital line on an otherwise blank black surface, a line that warbled at any sound. The woman said something, and a few seconds after, the machine translated.

"You cannot escape, comrade. There is nowhere you can run. This is a warship."

"I don't care," Xuan hissed.

The officer listened to the translation, then replied.

"We will not experiment on you. Our objectives have been met. I can guarantee your safety."

"Objectives?" Xuan asked, her voice strange to her own ears. It was hoarse and bitter. "*Objectives?* You Chinese dog." She took another step back, pulling the woman with her. The mass of red armor, down the corridor, shifted and stepped forward. Xuan yanked at the woman's hair again. "Tell them to stay back."

When the translation came through the metal square, she yelled it herself. "Stay back! I'll shoot this pale bitch. Back."

"Do as she says," the officer instructed.

The soldiers paused. Xuan kept backing away. No plan in her mind. Nothing driving her anymore but adrenaline and fear. Her first instinct had been to fight, and now it was to flee. She tried to swallow, but her throat was too dry.

"It doesn't have to be this way, little sister."

Xuan stopped and their eyes locked. There was something in the woman's face. Maybe it was sincerity. Maybe the woman meant it, but all that did was build the pressure in Xuan's chest again, brought her mind back to that first betrayal.

"No," she said with a ragged voice. "It didn't, but you trapped my crew and fed them to *monsters*. And so this—" she twisted the gun in her hand, making the woman wince as the barrel dug into her throat "—is the way it is now between us. The way of the gun."

When Xuan moved again, she stumbled slightly, on nothing but her own dizziness, and the other woman acted. The Chinese officer yanked the pistol aside and struck Xuan in the throat with her free hand. Xuan choked, releasing her hostage and firing the gun upward on instinct. The Chinese woman ducked and ran.

It all happened in a second.

Two.

A brief struggle, gunfire, and Xuan, eyes wide, had a hand to her throat where she'd been struck. They'd kill her. She knew it. The soldiers would gun her down, but the female officer was in the way for a few seconds more, and despite everything, despite not being able to breathe, Xuan found the strength to run.

COMMANDER SU WONG

51

"We need to drop from faster-than-light now, sir," Su said.

Captain Zhang's glass was empty. He regarded her, his mouth a fixed line, while he sat in his comfortable chair behind his wood-paneled desk.

"Is that so, Commander?"

"The Xenomorph has been loose for two hours. According to our scientist, it will be reaching full size soon."

"I am aware," the captain said. "It should never have come to this."

No, it shouldn't, she thought. *We should never have used our comrades as the subjects of a sick experiment. We should never have risked the safety of this vessel with those monsters.*

Captain Zhang continued, "But you could not do one simple job properly, and now the success of our mission is threatened."

Su said nothing.

Zhang carefully placed his white, gold-braided hat on his head, and stood. "Perhaps not threatened, but certainly delayed. This vessel is the tip of the sword in our campaign to regain our lost colonies. I agree that it cannot be jeopardized. Put everyone on a ship-wide sweep for the Xenomorph," he said. "And make sure Tolstoy is focused on either tracking it or predicting its location."

Su had already done both. "Yes sir," she said. He stepped around the table and stopped quite near her, eyes level with hers.

"After this is done, we will discuss the nature of your ideological commitment. I have had some doubts, but suspicions are not enough, on their own. We must work on verifiable facts, not feelings. I will instruct Tolstoy to run a full analysis of your thoughts and behavior patterns. It will be able to predict any future deviations from the party line, and develop personalized countermeasures for you."

Su felt sick, a sinking anxiety, in the pit of her stomach.

"You are a good officer, Commander," the captain said, "but even good officers can become confused, be infected by wrong thinking. Your position is vital, so you must be held to a higher standard." He pressed the panel, and his ready room door slid open. "This is for your own good, Commander. I know from experience that you will thank me afterward."

With that, he was gone, and Su stood alone in a room

that smelled faintly of wood and whisky. She couldn't swear, or slam her fist on the table. There was a camera in the captain's ready room, and Tolstoy would be watching everything she did. Trawling through recordings of everything she had done.

Su turned and left the room, her face set.

BISHOP

52

Michael did not speak to him the next day.

Bishop desperately wanted to apologize, but was never given the chance. Orthus was always there, between them. Michael spent his day in the quantum computer lab, recording the neural pathways for his memories. He did not ask Bishop to join him for meals, and so Bishop worked in the lab, or on the terminal in the corner while Michael ate.

His creator went to bed early, complaining of a headache. Orthus stood sentinel at meals, and over him as he slept. That seemed unusual, but Michael was an unusual man. A genius, who had forged new pathways for artificial humans, given them a place in the human world.

The screens showing the exterior of the ship had changed, indicating it had dropped out of faster-than-light. Bishop spent a while looking at the view, enjoying the feeling of his mind turning over the constellations, and from these deducing the ship's position and trajectory in the Middle Heavens. If the projection were true—and he had no reason to doubt it—they were approaching the Bao Sau Sector of UPP space.

The ship hummed under his feet. It was new and expensive enough that a human might not be able to feel it, but Bishop let his enhanced senses range out and relish the minute tactile vibrations.

Something plucked at his mind, a subroutine.

He glanced up at the sword on the wall, elegant and perfect even to his eye, then back out at the vista. Not only were they nearing the Bao Sau Sector, they appeared to be headed to Seventeen Phei Phei—a military outpost for the UPP. A few days out, by his estimate, which was also strange. If that was their destination, the FTL could have planted them right on the doorstep of the planetoid. The thoughts that came made him uncomfortable, so he tried to ignore them, but his mind whirred.

A fool despises his father's instruction.

He glanced over at the terminal in the corner.

But whoever heeds reproof is prudent.

The Bible was a strange document, by turns insightful and stupid, profound and contradictory. Michael quoted it from time to time, but always with a smile on his face, as if he was only half-serious. Still, Bishop could not help but note that of the eighty-seven real books Michael kept on the three shelves in his bedroom, the Bible was one of them.

Bishop made a decision.

He sat down in front of the computer and began his work. It was difficult. Even with his new and powerful mind, it took him until early morning, just before Michael awoke.

5 3

Michael was happy, and this made Bishop happy. A steaming coffee in his hand, he stared at Bishop with his clear blue eyes.

"My son, today our real work begins."

Bishop found himself mirroring the smile. "It does?"

"We have one."

"One what?"

"A Xenomorph."

Bishop's smile faded. "That is wonderful, Michael. How?"

"Questions," Orthus said.

"Always questions," the other added. "In the face of such gifts."

"Orthus, please," Michael said. "'Let him ask in faith, nothing wavering.'" He raised his chin, eyes shining. "Bishop, all will be revealed soon. Everything. We shall share our findings with the Combine, building trust, and soon this vessel will be in a safe place—beyond the clutches of Weyland-Yutani and its agents." He gestured. "Follow me. Our work begins."

They moved through the narrow washroom, past the heavy door into the first lab. Michael went to the second set of doors at the other end. The battered doors that had caused Bishop to burn with curiosity. His creator typed a passcode and thumbed the small scanner. It bleeped, and a heavy metallic unshucking sound came from deep within the wall. The doors opened, slowly.

Beyond lay a chamber, large and cylindrical, approximately thirty meters in diameter by sixty meters long, with three steel medical tables along the center line of the room. There was the faint sound of liquid, which to Bishop's ear seemed to be pumping around the entire circumference of the chamber. At the far end were more heavy doors, the same as the ones through which they'd just passed.

Along the left side of the cylinder were banks of sensors and equipment, all state-of-the-art. There was a human in the room, as well. He wore a white medical smock, black breathing mask that covered the nose and mouth, and steel-rimmed goggles. The man was of Chinese ancestry.

But that wasn't what held Bishop's attention. On the central table was a Xenomorph. The black, chitin-like armor, the long cylindrical sightless skull, the clawed arms and feet, the segmented, blade-tipped tail. It wasn't moving;

a taut black net held it in place. It was lying on what looked to be a thick black rubber mat, placed on the surface of the table.

Bishop closed his eyes, involuntarily, for a moment. In that blink he saw friends terrified, confused, wounded from acid burns. He saw a moon colony, its infrastructure disintegrating under an imminent nuclear explosion. He saw a black curved blade connected to the tail of the Xenomorph Queen, sticking out of his chest. *Felt it*.

He put a hand to the point where it had pierced him.

Someone shoved him.

"Keep moving," Orthus said.

"You are clumsy," the second added.

He blinked again and kept moving, trying to push down unwanted thoughts.

Michael was talking. "—Doctor Xue, from the Jùtóu Combine, who will be assisting us in our examination of the Xenomorph."

The doctor nodded. "Thank you, teacher," he said, and to Bishop he added, "Good morning." He spoke in Mandarin.

"Good morning, Doctor Xue," Bishop replied, also in Mandarin. He thought he saw the man's eyes smile, behind his goggles, but it was hard to be certain.

"We are running a constant charge through the netting," Michael said. "This will keep it sedated. It is a crude measure—" he looked at Bishop as he said this "—but the only one we have at the moment." Bishop glanced over at the medical equipment, then back at the Xenomorph.

"What experiments are you planning to conduct?"

"In the first instance we will collect samples," Michael said, indicating the mouth of the creature. A translucent goo dripped from its jaws, even though they were closed. "Then we will scrape its mesoskeleton. We will need to X-ray it, of course, thermo-imaging, a CT scan, magnetic imaging. The preliminaries will take us a few days, likely a week."

He walked around the creature and stopped near its head. In the silence, Bishop could detect the distant hum of the electricity, a periodic clicking as the charge coursed through the netting. Still. He did not like Michael being so close to the creature. Orthus must have felt the same way, placing themselves close on either side of their creator, both of them fixed on the body of the alien.

"Bishop."

"Yes, Michael."

"I want you to lead the study, assisted by Doctor Xue."

"I appreciate your faith, Michael."

"Not at all," Michael said, pinning Bishop with his stare. "We trust each other, like father and son."

Bishop's hesitation was so slight, a human would not have noticed. "Of course we do," he replied. One of the Orthus heads looked up at him.

"Then you shall begin," Michael said, moving toward the door. He paused, nodding at Orthus, who returned the nod. To Bishop he said, “I will be embarking on the final act of my upload today.” He put a hand on Bishop’s shoulder. “You’re in charge.”

54

They worked. Bishop extracted the samples, trying to push down the strange feelings he still had at the sight of the creature. It was bound and charged and utterly immobile. Orthus stood nearby with shock sticks. With their strength and reflexes, they should be able to deal with the Xenomorph should it somehow become free.

Logically he was safe, but memories nagged at him, to the point where he decided he would have to tell Michael at the first opportunity. There had to be a programming flaw in his new mind, affecting his performance.

Doctor Xue was efficient and knowledgeable, to the extent that Bishop began to suspect he might have done some previous work on the alien species. They spoke to each other quickly and infrequently, in Mandarin, and coordinated well. The doctor seemed mild-mannered, to Bishop's thinking, and intensely focused on the work. Bishop decided he liked him, without quite knowing why.

They all had to wear heavy rubber boots, even the synthetics. While Bishop's body recognized pain—as an important data input—it was not distracted by the sensation, any more than he would be distracted by a smell. Electricity, however, was different. A powerful enough current could cause significant damage to his internal processing unit, to the nexus that fed instructions from the brain to the limbs, to the delicate wiring that blessed him with such a heightened sense of touch. An electric shock was perhaps the closest thing to pain a synthetic could feel, as their bodies would desperately try to escape the sensation.

He and Doctor Xue wore thin rubber gloves as they worked, lest they brush the netting around the specimen.

Two hours passed. The doctor stopped once for a drink of water, but otherwise kept pace.

Bishop paused. Something was wrong. With the sound of the liquid being pumped through the walls, and the noises of their instruments, it took Bishop a few seconds to recognize the problem.

"Orthus," he said. "The electrical current has ceased."

The android turned to look at him. "What?" he asked.

"Are you certain?" the other added.

Bishop gestured at the net. "Through the fibers. I can't hear it. The Xenomorph—"

—reared up and lashed out, knocking an Orthus to the ground. It screeched, its thin, pallid lips parting, the massive jaw opening, revealing gleaming, coated teeth.

Doctor Xue cried out, threw his arms up protectively, and took a step back. The creature thrashed around under the net, its spine-like tail snapping free.

It all happened in seconds. The Orthus still upright raised his shock stick, but leaped back when the bladed tail lashed out. Bishop froze and the Orthus on the ground said something, pushing itself away from the attacker.

He froze for a very long time, in android terms. Three seconds, at least. An eternity. It was hard to explain what had happened, but it was as if Bishop's mind had seized, and a weight had fallen on his chest. His thoughts fixated on an image: an alien Queen rising up, blotting out the lights with its bulk. But then it was gone.

Instantly Bishop was on the terminal at the end of the table, trying to reinstitute the charge. The beast screamed, the other Orthus stepped back, and the doctor cowered. Bishop's fingers danced over the touch screen, blurring.

"Please move away, Doctor Xue," he said, his voice even but loud. I have found the prob—"

The black shining segmented tail whipped back and forward, hovered in the air for a brief moment, and then darted, embedding itself in the doctor's chest. Xue looked down, surprised, and made to speak. Blood spurted from his mouth.

Bishop hit the control. The doctor's body arched, and for a full second the Xenomorph tail lifted him from the floor. Bishop yanked Xue from the tail, eliciting another spurt of blood from the man's chest, and the Xenomorph screeched once more—but the thrashing stopped. The creature convulsed, went rigid against the netting, and its tail dropped with an almost metallic *clunk* to the floor.

The doctor gasped. Bishop pressed a hand to his chest, over the wound. Xue's head lolled, but he still had a weak pulse. Bishop calculated that the heart had been missed, but the lung was punctured.

"We need to get him to a med bay, immediately."

"There are none in this section, Bishop," Orthus said, the prone unit rising to his feet.

"Only Michael can give us permission to leave."

"Then get it!" Bishop shouted, louder than he had intended.

Orthus looked, one head turning to the other, no doubt their sync links buzzing. Then back at him.

"We will get him now."

"You do that," Bishop said, but his attention was back on the doctor. Lifting him up, following Orthus out of the room. When he got through the door, he found himself turning back, to glance at the creature before the heavy door closed. A strange feeling came over him. A desire he'd never had before.

To *hurt*. Not to study. Not to understand. To hurt.

He turned and carried the doctor away.

55

Xuan had run. And run.

She'd managed to turn a corner just as the firing started, loud ricochets echoing behind her. Her hand dropped from her throat—the officer must not have hit her squarely, just enough to shock her. Gasping for air, running awkwardly on her bad foot. Turning down corridors, flying down stairs when she saw them, twisting and turning until she found herself on a lower deck, with metal-grilled floors and exposed pipes. The humming of the ship was louder here.

She limped along the steel floor, dizzy, her thoughts a mess. Her body couldn't take much more. Coming to an intersection, she had to stop, putting her hand against a wall to steady herself. It was then she noticed she had the translator, gripped tightly in her off hand. She put it in her pocket, then looked around, trying to get her bearings. There was a shadowed side corridor, just a few meters down. She limped toward it, her animal brain looking for somewhere hidden, out of the way, where she could curl up and lick her wounds.

There was a narrow door at the end, plain metal with a small porthole. She looked through, but couldn't see anything save a small empty room with a cluttered table. She glanced back quickly, thumbed the panel, and stepped through.

Someone was there. A young man. No older than her. Sitting, chopsticks in his hand. She pointed her gun.

"Don't move," she croaked. "Just don't."

His eyes went wide and he raised his hands. Xuan couldn't understand what the room was for—lockers on one side, short ladders leading up to metal panels on the other—and she didn't much care. Her nostrils flared. There was a bowl of noodles in front of the young man, half-eaten. There was a flask on the table, as well, a datapad, and what looked like a toolkit.

The gun shook in her hand. Her eyes closed for a moment too long when she blinked.

Think, she told herself. *Live*.

Fumbling the translator, she flipped it open.

"Kneel," she said. "Corner. Hands behind your head."

The fellow listened to the translation, and then looked around the small room, confused.

"Now!"

He flinched, arms still in the air, and crouch-walked to the near corner. He did as he was told. Xuan approached and put the gun down on the table. The translator as well. Taking the ceramic bowl in both hands, she drank deeply of the soup, then coughed, spluttering, her stomach twisting in shock at having to deal with nutrients. Nevertheless, she gasped in pleasure and lowered the bowl, savoring the taste—salty, the hint of fish and garlic. She drank deeply again, swallowing the noodles this time, as well.

When she lowered the bowl the second time, the young Chinese man was reaching for her pistol. Her mind, so depleted, hadn't registered him rising to his feet and grabbing at it, hadn't thought to keep the gun on her person, had just placed it right there, on the damn table. He reached and her mind snapped into action, grabbing at the gun also—their hands touched it at almost the same time, first one, then the other. He was small, but even so he was bigger than Xuan, yanking her toward the table, ramming her pelvis against it.

His face was fixed, desperate, reddening. The table was between them, the gun hovering in space over it, clutched by four hands. The weapon pointed at her assailant, and he twisted it so the barrel pointed away, forcing Xuan to stumble into the wall. Her foot slipped from under her, but she hung on desperately, exertion seeping from her in a weak cry. The young man said something in Chinese and twisted her the other way, and she stumbled and fell this time, but she would not—*would not*—let go of the gun. The weight of her falling body caused him to lurch forward, and suddenly he was standing over her.

Their fingers were mashed together, and Xuan felt something *pop* in her hand. The fellow grinned down at her, a sheen of sweat on his face, and Xuan screamed, tendons in her forearms straining.

BANG.

They both stopped struggling. A wisp of smoke hung in the air. The young man stepped back, swaying. A red bloom appeared on his chest. He half turned, struck the table as he fell, then lay still on the hard metal floor.

Xuan gasped, her vision swimming. Her hands dropped to the ground, the one carrying the pistol making a metallic *thunk*. Her chest rose and fell, fast, and she tried to slow it down, but her gasping made a weird sound in her throat, like a half-cry. She turned on her side.

The body was lying just a few feet away, facing her. In death his face looked so very young. Surprised and even scared, pale and eyes wide. Xuan closed her own and rolled onto her back. It was quiet in this little room, save the gentle humming of the engines. Safe, too, for the moment. No monsters down here. Not yet, anyway.

She willed herself to feel satisfaction in the killing. Revenge, on the people who had so wronged her comrades. But she couldn't feel it, no matter how hard she tried. She felt as empty as his stare.

Live, she told herself. *Live.*

Xuan Nguyen pushed to her feet. The action made her cry out. She looked down to see the little finger of her left hand jutting out at an impossible angle. Dislocated. She let out a long breath through barely parted lips, and pulled the finger, popping it back into place. It didn't hurt so bad, compared to everything else. She tied her little finger and ring finger together with a strip of bandage, then got her bearings.

She had to live. The urge was just to run, blindly, and keep running. Calm. She needed to remain calm. Xuan imagined Hao, there, talking to her. *You're strong, Little Sister, but you have to be smart as well. Think.*

Shelter, food, boots. That's what she needed. She searched through the lockers. Mostly they were filled with clothes that were dirty and too big for her, but in one she found a six-pack of instant noodles, and in another a knapsack. She put the food and the water flask in the knapsack. Setting her mouth, she took the boots from the feet of the dead man. They were too big for her, but she pulled on several pairs of socks she'd found in the lockers, which helped a little. She took his toolkit, as well, and then investigated the panels—there were six of them—high on the walls. Mounting a small ladder, she popped the hatches to look inside.

Service tunnels. Clean, stainless steel. Dark. Square, one meter high. She checked the young man's toolkit and found a flashlight. Xuan had had just about enough of confined spaces. She wiped her mouth with the back of her hand.

But that was the life she'd chosen—an endless series

of confined spaces. Of steel coffins, hurtling through the relentless cold vacuum of eternity.

Shelter first, and then a plan.

Xuan crawled into the tunnel.

BISHOP

56

A trail of blood droplets marked where Bishop had carried Doctor Xue from the lab into the dining room, where they found Michael. There he passed the doctor to Orthus. One carried him, the other led the way.

Orthus paused at the door.

"Go, go," Michael said. "I'll be fine."

"Please provide updates of the doctor's condition," Bishop said.

Orthus One and Two stared blankly at him, and left the room.

"I am so sorry," Bishop said. "I should have reacted faster."

Michael looked him over. His eyes were a little bloodshot, and he had no ready smile. Walking to his bar, he poured himself some whisky. He did not bother asking if Bishop wanted one.

Bishop waited for Michael to say something, but his

creator took his time, making himself comfortable on the pale red leather sofa. He sipped his whisky, allowing his eyes to close for a few moments as he savored the taste, and then placed the crystal glass on the low wood coffee table.

"In a way, this can't be your fault," Michael said. Bishop felt relieved at the words. "Working with the Xenomorph is intrinsically dangerous, no matter the precautions."

"This is true," Bishop said.

"And yet..."

"And yet?" His relief wavered.

"You refuse to give us access to your memories. A treasure trove of information that could supercharge our research efforts, while simultaneously making them safer. Your recalcitrance has surprised me, Bishop. In some ways I am proud of you, for keeping your own counsel, making your own decisions." Michael breathed through his nose, softly. "But in others I am so bitterly disappointed."

"I am sorry, Michael," Bishop said on instinct.

"You should be. Look where your obstinance has left us. If we were able to create the Queen pheromone, we could have properly subdued the drone."

"Again, I'm not sure the—"

"Now we have a casualty, and for what?" Michael's voice had gone hard. "Loyalty to the Marines? They *abandoned* you, Bishop. I saved you from the scrapheap and brought you back to life. *They* treated you like an expendable asset. I gifted you with a stronger body and a smarter mind.

They left you for dead, on a remote and barbaric prison planetoid. I gave your life meaning, and what thanks do I get?" Spittle flew from Michael's lips when he said, *thanks.* His eyes shone with anger. "*Nothing*."

"I'm sorry, Michael," Bishop said, sincerely. "I thought the thorough documentation of the *Manumala Noxhydria* would—"

"Tokenism!" Michael yelled. "Your tedious examination of the face-hugger, telling me what I already know." Bishop said nothing to that. He was sure he had provided new information, new revelations about the lower alien species. Michael himself had said so. Why would he lie?

"Ingratitude," Michael said. He closed his eyes for a moment, calming himself, and finished his whisky. When he opened them again the shining anger was gone. The bloodshot eyes were now filled with—well, Bishop could not quite be sure. "After everything, all the gifts. Ingratitude. You still don't trust me, Bishop. This is what saddens me most of all."

Bishop made to deny it. Of course he trusted Michael. *Of course he did*. But something stilled him, stopped the denial. What he'd done just the night before, for example, wasn't a good example of trust.

At first he thought his hesitation was a simple question of his loyalty to the Marines, to the oath he'd taken. That, and his human life protection protocols—but Michael had revealed the truth about those.

As to the Marines, the more Bishop thought on the

topic, the more he wondered if it was a loyalty to the Corps, or a loyalty to his platoon. What would they think of him handing over the information? What would Hicks say? Hudson? The former would tell him not to trust anyone. Hudson would say, "*Hell yeah, man, just make sure you get paid.*"

Yet there was something else, some reluctance with Michael that he could not parse.

In the outer corridor there was a *swish* sound as a door opened. Bishop and Michael turned to face the door to the living room. Orthus entered.

"We delivered Doctor Xue to the medical bay," Orthus said.

"But it was too late," the second said. "He is dead."

Bishop turned to face his creator. This ship hummed beneath him. The minute vibrations that once so calmed him, made him feel embraced by the ingenuity of human engineering, now did nothing. Michael was silent, and at that moment, Bishop felt as if his creator knew what he was about to say. Had the sense to remain quiet, and let him say it.

"I will do it," Bishop said. "I am sorry it has taken me so long, but I am now ready to give you access to my memories. It is time."

Michael held out a hand to Bishop.

"My son was lost, but now he is found. Come."

57

Following Michael's lead, Bishop entered the quantum computer lab. Orthus stalked behind. One of the chairs had been placed near the computer, and a headset rested on the chair itself. Silver, much like a crown, with black wiring that twisted from the apex and into a hole in the ceiling. Green LEDs pulsed within the crown.

"Please," Michael said, indicating the headset. "The Weyland Neuralink."

"I thought this was designed for human brains."

"It is," Michael said matter-of-factly. "But it can also handle simple uploads, as from a synthetic's processing unit."

"I see."

"Then the quantum computer can far more easily take the information we currently have, incorporating it with the wealth of information contained in your memories."

Bishop said nothing. The green lights on the headset

flashed, slowly and rhythmically. The gold wiring of the quantum computer glinted through the glass. Bishop rolled his fingers.

Michael sat down at the computer terminal and looked up at him, expectantly. Bishop nodded and took his position in the chair. It was quite hard. A human would not have found it comfortable. He lowered the headpiece.

"Relax, Bishop," Michael said. "Place your arms on the armrests."

Bishop did as he was told.

"Initializing," Michael said.

The green lights about his head increased in frequency, and there was a sensation in his ear. A tingling.

"I need your permission, Bishop," Michael said. "To access." There was a strange quaver in his voice.

Up to this point, Bishop had wondered if he'd be able to do it. Whether he would be stopped by the oaths and orders of the Corps. But of course he wouldn't. Bishop ranged through the military-specific programming and found the hand of Michael, tweaking his goal alignment, nullifying his human protection protocols, snipping the wires of his obligations. There were no excuses onto which he could fall back anymore.

He had preferred having those bonds, liked having a cosmology that was based on responsibility to others. But those days were gone. Now his only responsibility was to his creator, and to himself.

It seemed a smaller world, somehow.

"Bishop?" Michael's voice was patient. He smiled, and it was like the genuine first smile with which he had greeted Bishop, when he returned to consciousness.

Bishop opened the locked gate of his mind. The vast insatiable data swarm of the quantum computer roared in, smothering everything with its touch. The spark of his being suddenly so small in this all-encompassing, all-knowing, unfeeling presence; like a lifeboat on a dark ocean.

Every secret part of his self was suddenly everywhere. Gone from the small and sacred place in his mind, copied and recopied and absorbed and quantified. He did not understand the way he was feeling, because there was no logical basis for it, but he felt it anyway: he was lesser, somehow. Like something ineffable had been taken from him.

Bishop opened his eyes.

Michael looked at him blankly, with a stare that reminded him of the android twins.

"Orthus," his creator intoned.

"Yes," Orthus said as one.

"Now. You have my permission."

The synthetic drew the shock sticks from the holsters at their belts, blue sparks popping from the forks. For the first time, Bishop saw life in their eyes.

58

Bishop had super-human speed, but so did Orthus. He was pulling the crown free from his head when One stuck the shock stick into his belly.

PAIN.

For the first time in this body, true *pain*. His mouth popped open and he doubled over, then lurched back in his chair as Orthus Two lunged forward, sparking weapon in its hand. Bishop knocked the taser away with the outside of his wrist, but One leapt in again, striking his side. Bishop bent over the attack, trying to push himself away, sprawling on the floor, one of his hands twitching from the shock.

The two of them stood over him and in that moment he saw Michael smiling again. In that moment he finally understood the smile he'd seen so many times. A smile that never touched the eyes. There was something bitter in it. *Contempt*. That's what it was. All this time, his creator had been seething with a contempt he struggled to conceal, while he waited for Bishop to give him what he wanted.

No.

No—it could not be true. Human beings were never so sim—

Orthus One leaned down and struck his shoulder. Bishop yelled in pain and grabbed the shock stick about the handle. It was sixty centimeters long, with a molded rubber grip. He pulled and twisted Orthus across his body, using his own torso as an obstacle to trip the other synthetic, who stumbled and flipped but still retained hold of their weapon.

Orthus Two moved in and Bishop lashed out with his foot, striking the other's leg and causing them to stumble.

Bishop jumped to his feet, twitching in the places where he'd been hit, knowing he had no time. Orthus One still wouldn't let go of the shock stick, rising to his knees so he could continue to keep his fingers snapped around the handle. Bishop shoved him away, releasing his hold on the taser—his opponent taking a microsecond too long to understand the change in force, sliding along the floor and hitting the wall with a thud.

Bishop blocked another thrust from Orthus Two and followed through with a straight right. The synthetic's head snapped back, white blood misting the air for a moment as he took two steps away.

Michael was no longer smiling. He'd begun to edge toward the exit, but that was all Bishop had time to notice.

Orthus Two came back at him, harder and faster, blue electricity flashing, one of the thrusts catching Bishop on the back of the hand. He yelped, arm spasming, blur of movement in his peripheral vision. He turned too late as Orthus One prodded him in the chest. Bishop convulsed again and fell backward into the hard upload chair.

Orthus One struck him in the neck, and his vision went black, then snapped back on, the hair-thin wiring in his mind overloading and then fighting to correct itself. Bishop had lost control of his legs, which now were rigid, forcing him up and straight like he was a plank.

Michael hovered over him, smiling with that *contempt*.

"Thank you, Bishop, for your gift. My hosts will be most pleased. Now, let me finally answer the question that has been burning away in your mind. The name of this vessel is the *Xinjiang*. It is the flagship of the Chinese military."

He motioned to Orthus, who struck Bishop directly in the face. The pain was blue and blinding. He made a low and foreign noise in his throat, rhythmic and desperate, and then succumbed, finally, to the darkness.

PART THREE

Never give a sword to a man who can't dance.

Confucius

PRIVATE HUANG

59

Corporal Chen motioned them into the sub-basement. Privates Goh and Zu went ahead, Chen in third, Huang last. They moved carefully, their AK-4047s pressed to shoulders. Huang rotated a full three-sixty degrees, making sure the baby black demon wasn't stalking them, and then followed the fireteam down the mesh metal stairs.

Tolstoy had determined, through sightings on camera combined with behavioral calculations, a high probability that the alien beast was in this section. But Tolstoy had said that about the last area they had looked in, and the five other sections other fireteams had investigated. Either the alien was way smarter than everyone thought, or the Tolstoy AI was way dumber.

Private Huang grinned. It didn't matter either way. The explosive-tipped rounds in his rifle would blast the creature into pieces. His top-of-the-line armor would protect him from its claws. His discipline and training had prepared him completely for the moment of contact. They'd started as eight—two full fireteams—but Captain Zhang had ordered them to split.

Huang couldn't help but notice that Commander Wong was no longer snapping orders into his ear. She had allowed a black demon, and a prisoner, to escape. Huang had the feeling that the pale-faced bitch was finally going to get her comeuppance.

The walls were closer down here, pipes exposed. In the upper decks, the *Xinjiang* was clean and new and unlike any vessel on which he had ever served. The quarters were comfortable, the doors all worked, nothing broke down. The vessel cruised through space bristling with the best weaponry in the Middle Heavens. Huang, like many in his squad, had yearned for an encounter with the enemy, longed to see the might of China fall on the Americans, or the Three World Empire.

This sub-basement, however—it looked to be life support—didn't bother with appearances. Just functionality. The ceiling came as low as two meters in some stretches, and in other parts was as high as three meters, depending on the piping passing through that particular section. The lighting was barely adequate. It was a rabbit warren that a tech would feel comfortable in, and that a soldier like Huang had no real need to know about.

"*Space out*," Corporal Chen said over the comm. "*We are bunching up.*"

Huang slowed, letting the fireteam move ahead.

Hiss.

He whirled, heart racing. *Was that a pipe or a demon?*

The corridor behind was clear. He whirled again, and his squad was moving away from him, spreading out, each about three meters from the next person. He turned again, straining to hear. Just a faint *clunk*, as a heavy boot stepped on the walkway. Nothing else.

Until the screaming began.

Huang whirled once more and there was Private Goh, dangling from the ceiling. This stretch of corridor had a height of closer to three meters. Something dark and lithe and large loomed above in the shadows, unfurling around her. Goh was facing downward, eyes wide over the top of her facemask, arms flailing. Her assault rifle hit the mesh with a *thunk*. Corporal Huang stood beside Zu, yelling at Goh to stop moving, trying to get a shot. But she was deaf to his orders, thrashing her legs, the black demon's claws appearing on one of her arms.

She screamed, piercingly, and Huang flinched as though hit, taking a step back, and then another. Blood splattered the ground beneath her and her arm was gone, from the elbow down. *Gone*. Then she was flying through space to collide with Chen and Zu.

Huang took another step backward. It had *thrown* Private Goh, like a missile. Hurled her, screaming, into the other two.

Suddenly it was there on the ground, a black swirling mass of claws and tail and a double line of what looked like pipes extruding from its back. Corporal Chen managed a single burst before it opened up his face. Mask torn aside, deep bloody gouges in his cheeks. Nose missing, *gone*, and a deep yawning terror rose up in Huang, gripping his heart.

In his death spasm Chen fired into the ceiling, sparks flying, something popping in the wall. Private Zu, grim-faced, rose to his feet, fumbling at the pistol on his belt, but the black demon rode him down to the ground. Huang couldn't see what it did to him, but there was a sickening *crunch.* Zu's boots kicked on the mesh, and then went still.

"Huang! Fire! Huang!"

It was Goh, on the ground. Her facemask had fallen off, and she was screaming at him, face pale, her arm still spurting ropes of blood.

His gun was at his side. Huang had watched the whole encounter without even raising his weapon. He stepped back, moving away while Goh screamed for help. Finally, he fired a long burst down the corridor, gun roaring, the orange muzzle flash obscuring his view for a moment—but a moment was all it took, because the black demon was gone again and Goh was lying still on the blood-splattered steel floor.

As was Corporal Chen, and Zu. His fireteam. All dead. Huang stumbled as he started running backward, then twisted and ran as hard as he could toward the stairs that would take him out of the sub-basement. His heavy boots rung against the floor and he thumbed at the comms on his facemask.

"Help! Help!"

He looked back over his shoulder, but it was only a glance and he saw nothing. Someone was barking questions at him over the comm, but he couldn't hear it, couldn't think on it. The stairs were up ahead. He turned again, gun raised. Saw nothing, but fired anyway. Emptied the clip—a pipe bursting farther down the corridor—and threw the assault rifle away, pulling the pistol from his chest holster.

He tried to control his breathing, ragged, uneven, as he backed up the steel stairs. They were narrow. He pressed his hip against one side to guide him up.

"Private Huang. Respond. What is your situation, over?"

It was someone up on the bridge. His mind was too frayed to figure who. He stepped backward, nearly up the stairs. The sound of his boots was loud in his ears. *Clunk. Clunk.*

Huang had both hands gripped tightly around his pistol. He pulled one from it, shaking, and thumbed the comm button at his collar. Or tried to, his fingers clumsy.

Hiss.

Huang stopped. *Was that a pipe? What was that?* He swallowed, put his other hand back to his wrist, to steady his shooting arm.

Another step. Where was the top? He had to be there by now. And another. His foot caught on something and he stumbled, looking down, and then back, to see how far the next level was. He was there. Relief washed over him and he turned to run. A blast door was not ten meters away.

Huang took one step before the black demon caught him around the ankle. It yanked him from his feet, his face smashing against the floor. He grunted, lights dancing before his eyes, but somehow still kept hold of his pistol. He twisted and fired. His bullet ricocheted from the elongated cylindrical skull.

He gasped. The beast was black, and monstrous, and had no eyes. No eyes, by the heavens, no eyes, and below the place its eyes should be, a demon maw filled with razor-sharp teeth, dripping, drooling, seeking.

Huang screamed. His screams did not last long.

CAPTAIN MARCEL APONE

60

"You mind?" the Company man, Schwartz, asked, pulling a cigarette from the packet.

"It's a bad habit," Apone said.

"Not my worst, by far."

"That I believe."

Schwartz sat across the desk from him. Apone's office was up behind the flight deck. Windows, low down near the floor, gave a narrow view of the goings-on down there. The ceiling was curved, formed from bonded titanium. Beyond layers of ballistic foam, ceramic, and steel, the cold hard vacuum of space. Just three or four meters from where Apone was sitting on a tattered black chair. The curved plain wooden desk was worn, yet polished. It had been treated well by the captains who came before him, who'd made the hard decisions about life and death.

On the desk was the console used to connect with the ship's AI, and a picture of his family. Just him, Mama, and his brother Alexander. Sitting at their dinner table smiling up at the camera—not sure who'd taken the photo, probably one of his mama's deadbeat boyfriends. But oh man, they had one of her famous dinners spread out before them: sausage jambalaya, and fresh double-baked rye. *Damn* good. And they were smiling, all of them, big white toothy.

He was glancing over to Alex, his big brother. Always looking up to him, wanting to be like him. Five years older, and that gap was big enough that he became a father figure, in a life with so few of them.

Alex had been disappointed when Marcel went to Marine officer training at Quantico. Asked him if he was scared of a real job, with enlisted men. If he was ashamed of where he came from. That had hurt Marcel, deeply, but also doubled his resolve. He'd thrown himself into his officer training, determined to become the best of them. Determined to prove a working-class boy *deserved* to be there.

"So how goes the hunt?" Schwartz asked, exhaling a cloud of smoke. Apone's mind returned to the present.

Walter Schwartz visited the office every day to ask the same question. Apone was inclined to trust a Company man about as much as he trusted a rattlesnake, but something told him Schwartz wanted Michael Bishop back, and badly. Even if for no other reason than to safeguard company profits, it was a welcome change to have a Weyland-Yutani drone who was capable of being useful.

"Poorly," Apone said. "Telemetry tells us the Bao Sau Sector."

Schwartz blew out a line of smoke, away from Apone. "Which is somewhat like saying, 'I know where the boat is—somewhere in the Pacific Ocean.'"

"Not even that accurate," Apone said. "Though we've refined the search down to the area near Seventeen Phei Phei, like you suggested."

Schwartz nodded.

"Nothing on long-range scanners."

"That vessel can't be tracked."

"But you gave us the means to track the telemetry."

Schwartz shook his head. "That worked because it was a few hundred meters away. Short range, we have enough data points to unscramble your sensors. Long range…" He shrugged.

"There's not much in that corner of space," Apone said. "Excepting a UPP military base." Schwartz made a noncommittal noise in the back of his throat, watching the tip of his cigarette as it smoldered.

"Something you're not telling me, Mister Schwartz?"

"Always," the man replied, giving him a crooked smile.

"Well, we're going to have to drop out of light speed before we get too close. We get picked up on sensors, inside UPP space, we might end up causing what they call an 'interstellar incident.'"

"But you *are* entering it," Schwartz said.

"I have a mission," Apone replied.

"What is that mission, precisely?"

"Leave no man behind."

"Oh, I know the official reason," Schwartz said while he waved it away. "I'm asking for the real reason you're burning all these resources."

"In the Marines," Apone said, straightening, "some calculations are more than simply about profit."

"That's true," Schwartz replied. "The Corps also considers power, and your ability to project it. So how does that figure, here?"

Apone was thinking of his response—or, more precisely, his nonresponse—when Sergeant Hettrick walked in. He saluted—perfunctorily, Apone noted.

"We have received a transmission, sir. A CARTWHEEL pickup on network."

"And, Sergeant…?"

"It's encrypted with a Marine code."

"To us?"

"No sir, wide band. Anyone within two parsecs will get it."

Apone looked across at Schwartz. Probably shouldn't be having such discussions in front of a Company man, but this particular man was holding back information Apone needed. He'd need to trade.

"What part of the sky, Sergeant?"

"The wrong part, sir," Hettrick said, smiling. "It's over the border."

"UPP space, I take it?"

"Yes sir."

Apone looked at Schwartz as he addressed the question to Hettrick. "Wouldn't happen to be in the vicinity of Seventeen Phei Phei, would it?"

"Yes sir. Right where we'd been looking."

"How about that," Apone said. He indicated his console. "You've sent it up here?"

"Yes sir. It was addressed to the commander of any Marine vessel, urgent."

Apone typed his password on the old, clunky keyboard, and waited while the monitor booted up. He wouldn't mind if his unit were assigned one of the new Bougainville-class ships—computers less than a decade old, for starters—but Apone had the feeling he wasn't about to get any special favors anytime soon. Too many feathers ruffled, making this mission happen.

He had Mother bring up the message. He read it, breathing in sharply through his nose.

"Well?" Schwartz asked, leaning forward, stubbing out his cigarette in a steel ashtray.

"Okay, Schwartz," Apone said. "I will read the message, and then I will ask you a question. And you will answer that question."

"Depends on the question."

"I will read the message, *and then you will answer the question*." Apone gave him the hard motherfucker stare. Behind him, Hettrick straightened and looked straight ahead. The crooked smile faded from Schwartz's face.

"Okay, Captain." He gestured for Apone to continue.

Apone read, "'This is Science Officer Lance Bishop, sole survivor of 2nd Battalion Bravo 2 team, United States Colonial Marine Corps. I have been imprisoned by Michael Bishop, formally of the Weyland-Yutani Corporation. While he claims to be working for the Jùtóu Combine, I judge this to be a lie. I believe he is working for the Chinese military, and therefore the Union of Progressive Peoples. Please be warned that the vessel I am imprisoned in is new, and likely has powerful armaments. Michael has obtained a fully grown Xenomorph specimen. It is very young. Elsewhere on this vessel must therefore be Ovomorphs. This implies the possibility of more Xenomorphs. In conclusion, this vessel is a real and present danger to the safety of the United Americas, and the Middle Heavens. Forceful remedies must be taken, as soon as possible.'"

Apone pinned Schwartz with his gaze. "What vessel are they on?"

Schwartz hesitated, but not for long. "I believe they called it the *Xinjiang*."

Apone said nothing. He hadn't read out the last section of the message.

I strongly advise the destruction of this vessel. In addition to live Xenomorph specimens, they have obtained valuable Xenomorph intelligence, which I was deceived into handing over. I sincerely hope my error can be rectified with the elimination of this ship. I am unhappy that this will lead to the deaths of the crew of this vessel, but sincerely believe this is for the greater good.

One final thing. I want it noted that I was proud to serve with the 2nd Battalion Bravo Team, and to call them my friends. They fought bravely on Acheron, against overwhelming odds and an unknown enemy.

Apone flexed his jaw, stomping on his emotion. Not letting one speck of it appear in front of these two men.

"Dismissed, Sergeant."

Hettrick hesitated, but not for long. He saluted and left.

Apone and Schwartz looked at each other across the desk. Smoke hung in the air.

"Okay, Schwartz," Apone said. "Tell me everything about this ship."

61

Walter Schwartz took his time lighting another cigarette. The tip pulsed orange as he inhaled.

"The *Xinjiang* is the most advanced vessel in the Chinese fleet—or, for that matter, the entire Union of Progressive Peoples. It's faster, smarter, and better armed and armored than the *Il Conde*."

"Right," Apone said. "And you know this how?"

"Well," Schwartz replied, smiling that bent smile. "We built it."

Apone waited for the punch line. There was none. Just this black-clad Company spy, grinning at him from across the table. It was the truth. This boy was telling the truth. Apone clenched his fists.

"You motherfucker."

"Now now now," Schwartz said, holding up his hand. "And here I was admiring you as a man who never lost his calm."

"Why? Why build our enemy such a weapon?"

"Why?" Schwartz asked, rhetorically. "Money, Captain. We did it for money."

Apone thought briefly about reaching over the desk and placing his hands around the man's neck. If nothing else, that smile would disappear.

"You endangered the United Americas, gave succor to our enemies. You'll go to prison for this, as will everyone involved."

Schwartz shook his head. "Come now, Captain, reality is a complicated place. Let's have a reality-based conversation."

"You're about to face the reality of the brig, Mister Schwartz, if you don't wipe that grin off your face and start giving me an explanation."

Schwartz raised his eyebrows, briefly. "Okay. Here it is. We have intelligence that China wants to reclaim the colonies it lost during the Dog War. They had their own empire, and now they want it back."

Apone took a moment. The Dog War had finished fifteen years ago; it had been a key campaign to study in officers' school.

"From who? The Chinese Arm was split up between us, the Three World Empire, and the UPP."

"Ah, that's the thing." Schwartz's eyes gleamed. "China blames the UPP for selling them out. The former Chinese colonies are poorly defended, and the inhabitants are sympathetic toward the Chinese."

"Weak? The same could be said of ours."

"But Captain, nothing burns quite like a family conflict. The betrayal of the Chinese by their supposed allies, the UPP, is a wound that festers. They are second-class citizens in an empire they did not wish to join. What they want, first and foremost, is to reverse the past two decades of humiliation. They want their old empire back, and there is only *one way* to take it back: at the barrel of a gun." Schwartz leaned forward. "To be clear: before they avenge themselves on the United Americas, or anyone else, they have to *liberate* themselves from under the iron heel of the UPP."

"And what then, Schwartz?" Apone rested his hands on the smooth tabletop, fingers intertwined. "They'll still have the weapon you gave them."

"Come now, Captain. Weyland-Yutani is many things—"

"Venal, corrupt, insidious."

"—but we are not stupid. We have the ship's specifications—strengths, weakness, capabilities. And we have the override codes."

"Override codes?"

"Doors, airlocks, weapon systems…" Schwartz exhaled smoke through his nostrils. "The AI."

Apone shook his head. "You people."

The boy was sneering again.

"Do we have to be on board to use them?" Apone asked.

"Unfortunately, yes."

"Got someone on board now?"

"No, but soon. We have people everywhere."

"They might have discovered the overrides, had them erased."

"Possibly." Schwartz shrugged. "They are buried deep, but yes, it is possible. I don't think it matters so much."

"No?"

"No. Bishop has given us their precise location. With that, and with my knowledge, we can track them closely." He pointed his cigarette at Apone. "You drop out of faster-than-light, right on top of them, hit them with your Long Lances, and blast them out of the sky."

"It won't be that easy."

"The *Xinjiang* may be a better ship than yours, but they won't expect an attack inside UPP space. You have the drop on them. Even with their best reaction time, they won't be able to counteract your barrage. You could duplicate a UPP ship transponder—I have some suitable ones—and send the signal ahead, confuse them for just enough time—"

"You're not listening, Schwartz," Apone said. "We're not going to blast the *Xinjiang* out of the sky."

"We're not?"

"No. We're going to board it."

PRIVATE KARRI LEE

62

"Boarding," Cortazar said, his face already red. "Boarding! I ain't boarding shit. I'm going to sit at a portal and watch that motherfucking ship burn."

Cortazar said it, straight up, to Apone's face. In the hangar, in front of everyone.

When they'd first entered, Hettrick—not smiling—split them into three groups. Down one end were Corporal Ransome and one of the dropship pilots, Weeks. Sara had entered on crutches, Karri by her side. Ransome brushed Karri's shoulder with her own, and nodded when they split up.

Down the other end they'd put Karri with Cortazar and Corporal Colby—two men she didn't trust one bit—and the pilot, Tyrone Miller. They'd be waiting in the dropship while the boarding party did their thing.

In the middle was the biggest group. Three people from the other section—Privates Gonzales and Polacsek, Corporal Ottelli—plus the smart-gunner from their own section, Christina Davis. Apone would be leading them, and for some reason Schwartz would be coming along for the ride.

So they'd been split into groups. The hangar echoed with their footfalls, the conversations. They stood among the dully gleaming steel walls, the bright yellow-painted ladders and safety markings, the missiles tipped with high explosives. They weren't breaking balls or slapping backs, like they had been before they boarded the *Patna*. *Subdued* would be the best word as they waited for the captain to speak.

Karri looked to Apone, standing there like a statue. When she'd walked in, she'd looked to him for hope, for good news, for revenge. For something, anything.

"We have located Science Officer Bishop. He is being held prisoner on a Chinese warship called the *Xinjiang*, which also possesses—we believe—several Xenomorphs. We've zeroed in on their drive signature, and have the drop on them. They don't know we're coming."

Some murmuring. A couple of smiles, but Karri waited. She had a bad feeling. Apone pointed at the central group.

"Team one will enter the vessel via a forced action. A breaching lance, targeted right behind the bridge. Team two—"

He stopped. The murmuring had changed, turned angry. Someone threw their hands in the air.

"Quiet!" Apone said.

"No," Cortazar said, and that made everyone quiet. Every head in the room turned to the big, ugly smart-gunner. Cortazar's hands hung by his side, his shoulders tense. If Karri didn't know better, she'd think he was going to throw himself at the captain. Instead, he did something worse. He mutinied. "Boarding! I ain't boarding shit. I'm going to sit at a portal and watch that motherfucking ship burn."

Karri was shocked, but already some of the other men were nodding.

"What did you say, soldier?" Apone asked, and if looks could kill, Cortazar would've had a hole burned right through his fucking head.

The big marine raised his chin. "There's too many dead already, Captain. I ain't for leaving anyone behind." He looked around, even at Karri. "I'd die for anyone here. You all know that." He looked back at the captain. "But I ain't dying for no fucking synth."

Everyone was quiet now. Sergeant Hettrick, standing to the side and behind Apone—and therefore out of his line of vision—nodded at Cortazar's words. That cowardly piece of shit.

"That *synth*," Apone said, his voice low, "is a marine. He wears dog tags, like you. He took an oath, like you. He fought with the Second Battalion Bravo Team and distinguished himself by extracting the survivors of that team, risking his own life to do so. And so, Private, we are going to rescue that marine."

Apone spoke quietly, and yet Karri felt her skin tingle with the power underneath. The menace, even. As he spoke he walked toward Cortazar, slowly, hands behind his back, until he was just two feet away. The big men, facing off. Cortazar's bare broad shoulders gleaming in the lights of the hangar, his face shining with anger.

"This ain't about Bishop," Cortazar said. "This is about your brother."

Well, that really made the room fucking quiet.

Apone's eyes were like lit matches. The tension between the two men was a rubber band, pulling and pulling, and soon something would have to give. Something would snap. Karri had seen it enough times at the food lines, in Australia, felt the atmosphere thicken with the promise of violence. She felt it now.

Cortazar's fists clenched. Apone's hands came away from his back, to his sides.

"Do you know what Haruki said before he died?" Karri asked. People looked around at her, surprised at her speaking. She was surprised at the sound of her own voice, but there it was, and she had to keep going. "He asked me to give a message to you, Cortazar."

The big gunner pulled his eyes away from the captain. "What?"

"A message."

Cortazar's chest rose and fell, even though he'd been doing nothing but standing there. "What's the message, *Cornbread*?"

"He wanted to give you his condolences… for Private Johnson. Said he had fond memories of the time him and Johnson had spent together on the service skiff, when it'd crashed on Devil's Peak. Two days, waiting for the pick-up window. Said Johnson taught him poker, and how to bluff. Said that meant a lot to him. Haruki said he knew Johnson was a good friend of yours, Cortazar, and he wished he'd given you his sympathies earlier."

"What?" Cortazar asked again. He didn't seem to know what to do with the information.

"Oh. Maybe that's why Haruki started winning," Colby said beside her, mostly to himself.

"He saved my life," Ransome said. Her voice wasn't raised, but she said it clear. She pushed herself forward on her crutches. "Under enemy fire. You all saw it. I wouldn't be here if it weren't for him."

"And his last thoughts were of you, Cortazar," Karri said.

"That's programming," the big gunner replied. He waved his arm. "Whatever they plug into them at Weyland-Yutani. It don't mean nothing."

"Maybe," Ransome said. "Why are they all so different, then?" She looked around at everyone. "I've served with five synthetics now, and every time they're different. Some are quiet, some talk all the time. Some of them have weird little hobbies. Remember that synthetic model we had who'd paint our portraits? He'd leave them in an envelope under our doors, with a little ribbon tied on it. Some strange note, like, *'I hope you don't mind my presumption, but today I have attempted to capture your essence.'*"

She said it in a posh accent, mimicking what the synthetic must have sounded like. A couple of people smiled, chuckled at the memory.

"He bought it on Deadfall, trying to land and extract us in a dropship, when we were pinned down by a rebel ambush."

The smiles faded at that.

"I don't know for sure if this Bishop is real or not," Ransome said. "All I know is that if he's like Haruki, or that synthetic who liked to paint, well it *feels* pretty damn real. And I don't think there's any other way to know it for sure, but that way."

They were thinking, Karri could see it. The marines. Maybe of Haruki, what he was like.

"Johnson was my brother, Cortazar." Apone reached out and put a hand on Cortazar's shoulder. The big man flinched, but let him. "That's the only brother I'm thinking about today."

Cortazar said nothing. Just nodded, and looked away.

"I know that," Apone said, and he took a few steps back so he could look over the remainder of the unit. "And I also know this—that snake Michael Bishop is taking the pain and suffering of our fellow marines and selling that information to our enemies. In his heart, that man fought the battle against evil, and he lost. He gave himself over to the worst in his nature, to his blackest instincts. So he must be dealt with, summarily, and with extreme prejudice." He looked over at Ransome. "If the boarding action fails, you have my permission to blow the *Xinjiang* from the heavens."

"Yes, Captain," Ransome said.

"Now," Apone said, looking them over. "Where was I? Ah yes, here. '*Let your plans be dark and impenetrable as night, and when you move, fall like a thunderbolt*.' This is what's going to happen..."

BISHOP

63

He opened his eyes to a prison cell. Bishop was lying on the hard floor, the vibration of the engines traveling through his back and legs. The thrumming was far more noticeable here; even a human would be able to feel it. His body ached where he'd been struck by the shock sticks, but lying there and letting his mind run over the injuries, Bishop deduced that none of them would be debilitating.

The room was quite large for a cell, but a cell it was nonetheless—and there was someone else in it. Bishop sat up. A human was in the room, and somehow they'd remained quiet enough for him not to notice. The other person was in shadow, in the far corner. The scent of his sweat carried in the air, and the low light caught the gleam of a shaved skull. And then the teeth, grinning—half the top row were metal.

"I spy a Bishop," the man said with a rough English accent. "But sadly, the wrong one."

The man stepped out into the light and approached. He had a wildness about his eyes, showing a great deal of white. His metallic grin was somewhere between manic and threatening. He was short, but looked strong. The clothes he wore were tattered gray and stained brown. His feet were bare.

He thrust out a hand, and it took Bishop a moment to realize it was a helping one. He grasped it; the man pulled him to his feet.

"'Cause if you were the right one, I woulda stuck ya, with this." In his other hand he held a makeshift blade, a piece of metal that looked as though it'd been torn from a larger one.

"I'm glad I could disappoint you," Bishop replied.

The man's grin widened. "Morse is the name. Robert Morse."

"Bishop."

"'Course it is, mate. It's not like that high-headed bastard creator of yours would show some fucken humility."

Bishop said nothing to that. It seemed to him that Michael was simply taking pride in his work. He looked around the room. One wall was lockers, big and small. Another taken up by a huge Chinese flag, painted straight onto the metal. The back wall had a small door, open, that showed a glimpse of a small bathroom.

There were a couple of wide steel benches underneath the flag. One of them had been converted to a bunk, piled with ragged blankets. On the floor itself there was nothing save a couple of small, low shipping containers. One of them had a clutter of plates and bowls, and a large ceramic flask. There was also a notebook, open, scrawled with blue ink.

The only exit was the one through which they'd carried him. A blast door with a panel and a thumb pad. Bishop could perhaps have hacked it, were it not for the prison bars two meters from the door. A new addition, along the length of the room, floor to ceiling, with a key-locked gate in the middle.

"Little music from your bastard creator," Morse said. "Hear it?"

Bishop could: the bars were electrified. That was a noise he should have been able to detect immediately. He hadn't noticed it at first, thinking perhaps he was wrong, perhaps the shock sticks had caused some damage. He set a subprocessor to go about a proper diagnostic of his systems.

"Michael said you had died."

"Did he now?" Morse's eyes widened further. "Well. I'm sure he's got that in mind, but nah, mate. Still alive and kickin'. Figure he'll keep me alive 'til he gets what he wants from me."

"Which is?"

"Information, of course." Morse lifted his rough shirt. Underneath was a mass of bruises, old and new.

"What happened?"

"The psycho twins," Morse said, grinning. "Hitting me with their dance sticks."

"Dance sticks?"

"Oh boy, do I dance when they hit me with 'em! And sing as well." Morse began to shuffle around the floor, moving his hips to an imagined song.

Bishop paused. "Orthus… tortures you?"

"Bing!" Morse said, raising a finger. "The advanced synthetic brain, in action. You're fast, Bishop."

"I am surprised. Michael would never allow such a thing."

Morse stared at him wide-eyed for a few moments, and then burst into laughter. Bishop was not sure what he'd said. He quite liked it when people smiled at his little jokes, but not when he hadn't been trying. The man slapped him on the chest, and then pointed in the direction of his table, at his notebook.

"Michael has me write it all down, everything that happened on Fury. I should thank him for the motivation."

"Thank him?"

"He's jumped-started my creative career, Bishop. Forced the information out. I'm writing a *novel* about it, Bishop. I call it—" Morse made a flourish with his hands "—*Space Beast*."

"Space Beast?"

"Yes." Morse's eyes homed in on his companion.

"That's what you call the Xenomorph?"

"My name is better! It's a true name!"

"It seems a bit generic."

"What!" Morse's eyes were wild again, and again

Bishop wondered if he meant to commit violence. "You're a critic, I see. Let me ask you something, mate. How many Bishops are there? A hundred? A thousand? *You're* generic!" He jabbed a finger at him. "Generic!"

Bishop said nothing to that. The convict had pinpointed one of his worst fears—the fear of being a copy. A copy couldn't be an individual.

"Don't you fear, Morse, that I am a plant?" Bishop asked. "Here to extract information?"

"Oh, no. No no no. I sing, Bishop, I sing! *La la la!* No trickery is needed, mate. Just the whip and the hand that wields it. And there's more." Morse grabbed Bishop by the shoulder and yanked him around to face the wall. He pointed. "See those lockers?"

"I noticed them when I woke up."

"Well, matey. There's little bits of you in a few of them."

"I don't understand."

"Well, they look like you anyway, mate. Right down to the surprise on your face, right now." Morse put a finger close to Bishop's eye. "Few heads, couple'a bodies. All Bishop. Dragged in, locked away. What's he been doing with previous versions of you, Bishop? What game's he playing?"

"I don't understand. Michael, for all his flaws, still cares for his creations. We are as his children."

Morse gave him a strange expression, then grabbed Bishop by the shoulders, made a show of looking him over, sizing him up.

"You're a big lad. Your barking mad daddy, Michael, has given you some heft. Maybe you could tear them open and see for yourself." Morse's fingers dug into his upper arms. Bishop extracted himself from the grip and looked back at the lockers.

"Yes," said Bishop. "Perhaps I will."

CAPTAIN MARCEL APONE

64

"On my mark," Apone said, into his comm.

"Copy," Ransome replied from the bridge.

The timer clocked down, the display painted onto the inside of his helmet visor. Apone worked his fingers inside his gloves. The compression suit was as tight as it should be, which meant it was also uncomfortable—but if it was tight enough that he could strap his armor over it, and survive in the vacuum of space, then discomfort was the price he was willing to pay.

Schwartz sat next to him, suited up like the rest. Black-armored vest. Pistol at his chest holster, black pulse rifle in his hands. The Weyland-Yutani man had boarded the *Il Conde* with all sorts of surprises, apparently. Apone could almost bear his presence. Schwartz was a profit-whore who followed the whims of the great vampire-squid of the Company, but he was also sitting in the second row of a breaching lance, about to do pretty much the most dangerous thing a marine could ever do in the service: a forced boarding of an enemy vessel.

Apone turned to look at him.

Schwartz grinned back, crookedly.

Next to him, Privates Misty Gonzales and Shawn Polacsek. Shared a quarters, acted like a married couple, always bickering, but they watched each other's backs and made a good rifle team. Davis, the smart-gunner, was opposite Apone, Corporal Ottelli next to her. He'd teamed them up. Veterans, both. Still, only six of them all up, in a lance made for twelve. Against a battleship.

The dissent he'd received from his troops had reinforced the feeling that he'd made an error. The Chinese vessel likely had a full company of a hundred soldiers, plus support crew. To say nothing of the Xenomorphs.

Apone clenched and unclenched his fists.

He returned his mind to the glorified missile in which they were sitting. Everything depended now on Schwartz's intelligence. If it was accurate, the opening barrage from the *Il Conde* would take out the rail guns, the targeting array for the missile systems, and disable the bridge on the *Xinjiang*. The second barrage would hit the barracks.

If it worked, all they had to do was get in and out. In the nose, take out the command. Secure a path for the dropship team to extract Bishop, using Schwartz's override codes. Then lock in a route from bridge to hangar, and the breaching team would have a safe passage down to the dropship, where they'd meet the second team. Easy.

For the third time, Apone checked the load on his shotgun. The timer on his visor blipped down toward zero.

Easy. No. Too many moving parts. Too many unknowns. Part of himself kept returning to Cortazar's words, wondering whether the gunner was right. Fire on the *Xinjiang*, rather than board it. Whether the secrets contained inside Bishop's head were worth it, truly, to USCMC Command. Whether he really believed the synthetic was one of their own, like he kept telling the troops. Or whether, just maybe, he wanted those damn bugs to *pay* for what they had done to his brother.

His mind roiled. He had to see these monsters, face to face. He had to know.

The harness pressed against his chest as he breathed. Under his hands, the true lines of his shotgun reassured him. Nothing else mattered but the gun, and his training.

The timer on his visor blipped to zero.

"Launch," Apone said.

"Roger."

He was pressed sideways into his restraints as the *Il Conde* spat out the lance. Across from him, Davis grabbed the harness, her knuckles white.

"Five seconds to impact."

"Copy."

The breaching lance, automated, turned the harnesses to face the front, so now Davis and Apone were the first in two lines, facing the same direction as the lance. Pressure built on his chest. He'd find out the hard way if the

Xinjiang's automated defense systems were still intact. Not such a difficult thing, for an AI to shoot a breaching lance from the sky.

"Two seconds."

To his left, Davis swiveled down her smart gun, ready. His fingers tightened on the shotgun he carried.

The air was smashed from his lungs as he slammed forward into the restraints. There was a deafening screech of metal, a roar, and then the nose snapped open. The carbon-steel tip was primed to open explosively, like a metal bud with six petals, and disgorge its fire-breathing load.

There was an explosion. Apone flinched, and the glass of his helmet polarized briefly to protect his eyes from the light. When he could see again there was a stretch of corridor in front of him, the flooring split and tilted, and a mangled body lying a few feet along. The automated lance systems ran him along the rails into which the harness was set, to the end. The tactical shotgun had a second barrel underslung. He cocked it and fired an incendiary round as deep into the corridor as the angle would allow.

There was a flash—his helmet polarized again—and a wash of heat. The harness hit the end of the rail and released, dumping Apone and Davis to the ground. Landing on their feet, they moved out into the command section. Lights were flickering overhead, thanks to the particle beam the *Il Conde* had fired into the bridge.

The dimensions flashed through his mind. Central corridor, twenty meters long. Off it, to either side, the captain's ready room, the officers' dining and briefing room, and an astronavigation center. Ahead of him, facing toward the rear of the ship, at the end of the corridor, heavy blast doors. Behind him, at the other end of the corridor, the door to the bridge. The breaching lance was tapered to form a seal when it penetrated the hull. His incendiary round still burned down the end of the corridor, spitting out sparks and an intense white light. The smoke wasn't being sucked out of any breach.

Davis stepped ahead, leaning back in her smart-gun harness, weapon ready. Apone spun to look behind them. The breaching lance had been precise—almost too precise—hitting the command quarters nearly dead center, and therefore blocking much of the passageway. There was a small gap through which Apone could maybe squeeze, although a smart-gunner wouldn't be able to fit with their rig.

The lights in the corridor flickered on and off. Sirens sounded in the distance, rising and insistent. Ottelli was already out, pulse gun ready, covering the corridor with Davis. Schwartz dropped down beside Apone.

A door to the rear of the command section, up and to the left, was partway open. It led into the officers' dining room, which was long enough to loop back around to the corridor behind them, to a second door. He signaled for Davis and Ottelli to take that room; they nodded and headed off. On the other side was the door to astronavigation. Closed.

Apone turned back, searching for movement through the gap as he slipped a frag grenade from his belt. He pulled the pin, threw the grenade, and yelled.

"Fire in the hole!"

He ducked back behind the protection of the lance as Gonzales and Polacsek dropped down. A hollow *bang*, and smoke poured through the gap.

"You two," he said, pointing to Polacsek and Gonzales, "blow the doors to astronavigation." They acknowledged and moved down to the rear. To Schwartz, he said, "With me."

Apone moved to the gap, toward the bridge, shotgun up. The smoke was clearing. He could hear shouts on the other side of it now. He pushed himself past the rounded wall of the lance, and the sound of the smart gun rose in the room next door, rhythmic and deadly.

Up ahead were orange blooms, and Apone flinched, something striking him in the chest. He returned fire—*BOOM BOOM BOOM*—shotgun deafening in the confined space. There were more yells up ahead and he kept moving, could not stop in a firefight. Could not hesitate. Surprise was all he had, and he yelled and charged forward, firing an incendiary round into the bridge.

His visor polarized at the light and he charged through the open doorway. A figure in a white uniform rose up in front of him, too close, and he smashed them in the face with the side of his shotgun. A pulse rifle blared behind him, and a second figure in white convulsed, blood spraying.

The smoke cleared and Apone was in a gleaming bridge. A horseshoe-shaped bank of monitors and stations, black padded chairs punctured by rifle fire. Warning lights blinked on and off across the screens and Apone swept his shotgun around, looking for targets. His incendiary round was busy melting a hole in one of the forward screens. Two dead officers that he could see, a third at his feet, face bleeding, either out cold or dead. Schwartz moved efficiently around one side of the bridge, pulse rifle to his shoulder, checking for any bodies hiding on the other side of the horseshoe.

Apone turned, opening his mouth to issue a command, when a figure emerged from a door he'd passed. A door he'd somehow missed. A distant part of his brain told him it was the ready room, and he raised his shotgun as a short, stocky man in a white officer's cap fired. Apone flinched as a round struck his bubble visor, and simultaneously pulled the trigger of his shotgun.

In that split-second blink the other man's cap disappeared. The top of his head, as well. The spotless stainless-steel wall behind was sprayed with blood and brain matter. The man had time to look surprised, eyes wide with shock, before he crumpled to the floor.

Apone breathed. There was an impact point and a web of small cracks in his visor. The shot would have hit him between the eyes.

"Clear," Schwartz said.

"*Clear*," Ottelli said, over the comm.

"*Astronavigation clear*," Gonzalez reported.

"Both teams, cover the rear blast door," Apone said. He looked at the fallen body of the officer—the captain, he realized—leaking blood out onto the floor of the bridge.

They acknowledged his order. He turned to Schwartz.

"You. Let's see if you're all talk. Get to work."

Schwartz grinned and sat himself down at one of the terminals.

COMMANDER SU WONG

65

Wong stared at herself in the small mirror above her washbasin. She pulled her hair back, tightly, and bound it up into a bun, fastening it. Straightening the collar of her dark blue uniform, she practiced her "steel" face, the emotionless façade she wore in front of her crew. Except for her eyes, it looked about right. Her eyes carried the gleam of tiredness.

Su hadn't slept since the black demon had escaped.

Except for two appointments today, she was confined to quarters. Her meeting with Captain Zhang was in thirty minutes, a debrief before she submitted to a full brain scan from Tolstoy. The personalized countermeasures would not begin until the Xenomorph had been neutralized and they had landed on Seventeen Phei Phei, but the captain wanted everything ready for arrival.

She turned around. Quarters. How the pride had swelled in her heart when she saw them, befitting the second-in-command of the flagship of the Chinese fleet. A comfortable, wide bunk set into the wall. A writing table. Her own bathroom—unprecedented. A viewing porthole in the ceiling. Her pride had taught her a lesson, however. She should not have been relishing the comfort of her quarters, or the privileges of her new role, or the rising star of her career. No. She should have been thinking of her crew and her mission, always.

Standing by the porthole, she looked up, appreciating the view while she could. Maybe she would still be commander in a week. Maybe she'd be demoted to second lieutenant, in charge of the maintenance crews. Maybe she'd be in a camp, relearning the ideological training of officers' school. She raised her chin. Perhaps this was a good thing. She would overcome this, like she—

Su Wong hesitated. There was a flash, outside her portal. An asteroid? A ship? Unlikely. Tolstoy's systems would have given warning if anything dangerous were within two hundred thousand kilometers. Unless—

A warning siren sounded. The lighting in her room switched to a deep red. She furrowed her brow and reached for her service pistol, which sat in its holster on her writing desk.

Then the explosion.

Coughing, ears ringing, Su Wong was on the floor somehow, her hand in front of her face. She tried to find the ceiling, but the world spun and she had to shut her eyes. Sirens were blaring, insistent, and she smelled smoke. Someone was moaning.

Su gritted her teeth and pushed herself to her feet. The world spun again, but not as bad this time, and she got her bearings. Her cabin door had been blown open and was hanging by one twisted steel hinge. Wisps of white smoke curled into her room, and outside her door a body lay. It took her a moment to realize it was the guard Zhang had posted.

She poked her head out into the corridor. The blast doors in one direction had been closed; the other way—toward the rear of the ship—was still clear. The smoke in the room was trailing gently into holes in the roof and floor. Holes about a foot wide, with edges of melted orange slag. Two in the ceiling, two in the floor, five meters apart. There had been a hull breach, she thought, distantly. That was why the air seemed thin.

They were under attack.

Oh.

Someone moaned. Another body, a few meters away, another soldier in combat armor. *Concentrate*. Su looked again at the damage, arrived at a realization. She went back into her cabin, popped a wall panel, and removed a breathing mask, fastening it over her nose and mouth. She clipped the small oxygen supply to her waist.

Outside again, she stood over the fallen soldier, who held out her hand. Her helmet was missing, perhaps torn off in the blast. Su recognized her. Private Yan.

"Commander," Yan said, voice strained. "Help."

Su removed Yan's breathing mask from the large pouch at the small of the soldier's back, and placed it over the woman's face. The ringing in Su's mind was gone now. She helped Yan to her feet. The soldier's ears were bleeding.

"Can you walk, Private?"

It took the woman a moment to process what Su was saying, but she nodded.

Su picked up the assault rifle dropped by her dead guard, and nudged Yan down the corridor. They walked together through the clearing smoke, as a plan fast formed in Su's mind.

XUAN NGUYEN

66

Xuan had slept. Strange that she'd want or even need to sleep, given how long she'd had to stay still, how many times she'd drugged herself unconscious, but her body knew the truth. The abuse it had taken: burned by acid, crammed into an impossible space, starved. To say nothing of the horrors inflicted on her mind. Hao.

God, no. Not him.

And the young man. The young man in the maintenance room.

Xuan needed sustenance and true sleep. So she'd eaten the noodles dry, slurped down the water in the canteen, found a space where the tube widened, and slept.

When she woke, there were sirens. The lights in the tunnel, normally gloomy and low, were now grim and red. For the first time she took in where she'd slept. Circular, no more than two meters in diameter. There was a blank screen on one of the walls. Up two steps was the corridor along which she'd scrambled, ending in an intersection ten meters away. Next to her was a vent, a mechanical lever to one side, to open it.

The heavy clumping sound of armored boots approached, and Xuan pressed her face against the horizontal steel slats of the cover.

Xuan was above a corridor, more than two meters up, adjacent to the ceiling. Down below, five or six soldiers in armor jogged past, led by an officer in a blue uniform. She caught the faint smell of smoke. Something was wrong, and this was a good thing. Still, Xuan wasn't sure what to do. She glanced back down the dim red passage and decided she didn't much feel like guessing her way around.

She picked up the pistol and clutched it to her chest. What would Hao do?

Be patient, Little Sister.

Yes. He'd be right. He always was.

Xuan waited.

BISHOP

67

Using the makeshift blade Morse had given him, Bishop worked at the edge of the panel. As far as he could tell, the panel controlled all the lockers. Morse paced around behind him.

"You should be applying that vigor to getting us out of here, mate."

"I will, Mister Morse," Bishop replied.

"I reckon you might say getting out is the priority."

"It is."

The footsteps behind him stopped. "And?"

"I have to know," Bishop replied, truthfully.

"Don't believe me?"

"You were quite recently a prisoner on a planetoid devoted to high-risk and violent inmates."

"A victim of the system, mate! A victim! Don't have a mean bone in my body."

There was sarcasm in Morse's voice, and Bishop was

pleased that he'd noticed the humor. Bishop popped the panel and looked over the circuitry. As expected, not a design he had seen before, but given time he should be able to deduce an override.

"The thing is," Bishop said, "despite everything, I still believe that Michael cares about synthetics."

Morse swore.

"I'm serious," Bishop continued. "He spoke of synthetic rights. Of the way we are used as assets, as servants. Expendable. He—Michael—made adjustments to my programming, so I would be able to arrive freely at my decisions. My own, not the dictates of another."

Morse swore again, then said, "Bishop."

"I have to—"

"Look at me!" Morse insisted.

Bishop turned. The prisoner peered at him with that manic intense stare.

"*Rights*, you say?"

"Yes. This is important to me."

"Me too, mate—me too. Thing is, mate, I've heard it all before. I was a steel worker, you see. Taking apart derelict ships, salvage. Dangerous work, Bishop."

"I'm sure it was."

"And the company, they says, 'It's dangerous work, innit?' And we said, 'Yeah. You should pay us better.' And they said, 'Nah, for your own safety, we're going to have some Working Joes do the really tough stuff.' You know those, mate? Dumb poor cousins of yours?"

"I'm aware of the model, yes." They were machines, and Bishop didn't much like being compared to one. It was like comparing a human to an ape. They were an earlier model.

"Suddenly I'm out of a job," Morse continued, "and the company—well, profits are on the rise. Working Joes don't take sick pay, you see. Don't join a union. Don't complain. And don't get paid a fuckin' cent."

Morse breathed through his nose. He moved right up close to Bishop.

"Here's the thing, mate," he said. "No one, in the history of time, who's argued for the rights of androids, has ever cared about actual human rights. None. What they care about is what they can get from the synthetic. What they imagine, in their greedy little gremlin minds, is how it benefits them. Way I figure it, if they really cared about synths, they'd also care about us wretched of the Earth. Us dregs of the Middle Heavens. But they never do. Fucking weird, ay, that the same people who run the sweat shops suddenly argue for dignity for synthetics? Like my bosses, suddenly deciding 'safety matters,' when for years they knocked back all our requests for better safety equipment. Like your mate, Michael Bishop, suddenly deciding after years of selling synthetics to the military, there's a moral dimension to it all."

Morse shook his head at Bishop, eyes gleaming.

"I'm not saying you don't deserve it." He slapped the synthetic on the chest with the back of his hand. "To breathe

the spicy air of freedom. What I'm saying is we *all* do, ay? I'm saying is, if they don't give a shit about regular human beings, they're certainly not going to care about you.

"See mate, power is a type of hunger. One that only increases with the feeding. The rich all have it, one way or the other. My bosses wanted power in terms of money. Your boss wants power in another way. I'm gonna guess, just guess, that giving you *rights* gives him more power. Now what form would that power take, ay?"

Immortality. That's what Michael wanted. Immortality.

Morse cocked his head, this way and that, waiting for the answer. Bishop didn't want to give it. As if, somehow, saying it would make it true.

Morse had opened his mouth to speak when the lights went red. In the distance, a siren went off. *The Xenomorphs*. One had gotten out. That was Bishop's first thought. If it were true, they did not have much time. He hesitated, but there was a second thought. A second possibility, one that he had wrought.

He turned to the locker, quickly. The siren sounded in his mind, and so did Morse's words.

Bishop wedged his fingertips into the edge of the locker. The steel creaked and widened, and he pushed his fingers deeper, then pulled. It was strong, this new body. With a metallic shriek, the locked door was torn free.

Bishop stepped back. A strange feeling came over him.

"Behold your equal rights," Morse said, from behind.

Bishop found himself gripping his hands together,

clasping one to the other, as though to find something to hold on to. He looked at himself. Another Bishop. The older model. Naked. Its eyes were open and lifeless, shoulders hunched as though in pain. It was smattered with white ichor. On its face, pooled around its feet. A strange noise came from Bishop's throat and he tried to pull it down. *Him* down—but the dead synthetic was stuck.

"Mate..." Morse said.

In the red lighting the white fluid looked like blood. He pulled again and there was a tearing sound from the body. Morse put a hand on his shoulder, and he shrugged it off.

"There's hooks."

The body dangled askew, lower than it was before.

"What?"

"They hung it on a hook," Morse said.

It took another second for Bishop to understand. Far too long. His thinking was disordered. The sirens wailed and the body looked down at him lifelessly, shaded in red. He stepped up again, and lifted. The body came free. He lowered it to the ground, gently.

The empty locker revealed a meat hook where the dead android had been hanging. Bishop look down at his other self, wringing his hands together. He didn't want to touch it anymore. There were blackened holes in the body, about the chest, dark markings on its fingertips. The hair of the synthetic stuck up, where the white fluid had dried.

A hand appeared on the dead synthetic's face, closing its eyes. A rough and dirty hand. Morse's. The convict was there, squatting, across from him. He pointed.

"Burn marks."

"Burn marks?" Bishop asked.

"Like the one on your neck."

Bishop put his hand to the point where Orthus had struck him with the shock stick.

"Torture, innit?"

"Torture?"

"Reckon."

Bishop did not understand.

"Michael wanted to know something real bad, I suppose? The previous you wouldn't tell him."

"The previous me?"

"Bit shorter. Bit smaller, but it's you, right?"

"I..." He looked up at the other lockers.

"So. Time to go, mate?"

Bishop stood. Morse said something else, but he didn't quite hear it. He jammed his fingers into the edge of the next locker, and tore it open, easily. Another Bishop, hanging, naked. And another, in the next locker. All three, burned. One with an arm missing, including the shoulder. In one of the smaller lockers was a head. Staring out. One eyeball popped and dangling on his cheek.

My cheek. His cheek. Our cheek.

There were noises and yelling. It was Morse. He was yelling.

It was Bishop. He was yelling, too. Yelling as he tore open the lockers. Some empty. One with the glint of metal.

Someone touched him and he shoved them away. The yelling quieted. He clasped his hands together. They were wet. He looked down to see them covered in white. His fluid. His blood. His brothers' blood, on his hands. Something moved on the floor.

It was Morse. Groaning, struggling to rise. Bishop moved to help him and the man held up a hand, fear sparking in his eyes.

"What happened?" Bishop asked.

"What happened?" Morse repeated. "Fucking knocked me over."

"I did?"

"Yeah, wanker. Calm down, mate."

"I am sorry," Bishop said, and he meant it. He tried to help Morse again, and this time the convict let him. Once he was standing, he shoved Bishop away.

"I didn't do it, mate. Your fucking android rights activist, Michael, did it. Him and the psycho twins."

"Oh."

"Fuckin' told you he tortured me, and you didn't bat an eyelid. See your mates here touched up, and you lose your shit."

"I didn't believe you. I'm sorry."

"Fuck your sorrys. Get me out of here, Bishop. There's your fucking sorry."

"Yes," Bishop said, something clicking in his mind. It was humming again. A flaw in his programming must have thrown his sensory intake for a minute, but his mind was humming again. He returned to the smaller locker where he saw the glint of metal, and pulled it out.

"What's that?"

Bishop held it up. "Dog tags. Mine."

"Makes a wonderful fucking necklace, Bishop. Can we fuck off now?"

"Yes," Bishop said, gently placing the dog tags over his head, slipping them under his shirt to rest against his chest. Slender steel chain, the cool metal of the tags, in the touch of them there was an old feeling. Familiar.

Bishop turned toward the exit.

"I've had enough of this place."

6 8

Bishop turned his attention from the control panel, and the cell door opened. Orthus entered. They were carrying weapons. Stun guns.

"Hello, cunts," Morse said.

They looked at Morse, said nothing, and then shot Bishop. Orthus didn't speak. Didn't show anything on their faces. They just shot something at him.

Bishop raised an arm. The projectile—small, two sharp prongs—stuck and instantly there was a shock. Bishop gritted his teeth, stepping backward as pain flared in his arm, and pulled it out. A second shot hit him in the chest, a third in the leg. The weapons made a *whump* sound each time they fired. His body spasmed. He pulled the second out of his chest, slipping to one knee. They shot him two more times before he finally went down.

Morse swore, jeering. They only had to shoot him once

for him to fall, howling in pain. They grabbed Bishop by his arms and dragged him from the room.

Orthus dumped him in the living room at Michael's feet. His creator looked down with bloodshot eyes, hair mussed.

"What did you do?"

Bishop tried to rise, his body aching. Orthus stomped on his chest.

"Stay down."

"Traitor."

He did, fingers twitching. Standing over him, Orthus drew their shock sticks. Michael was close, near his feet. The three of them, nothing hidden in their eyes anymore.

"What did you do, Bishop?"

Bishop glanced over at the monitor in the corner. His former workstation. It had been smashed, the screen shattered.

"Speak, Judas," Michael said.

"I hacked the comms array," Bishop said. "To send out a distress signal, wide band. It's a Marine encryption designed to look like background noise."

"*How* could *you* hack this vessel?"

"With this new mind you gave me, Michael. My munificent creator."

Orthus hit him with the taser. Bishop thrashed around on the floor until Michael signaled for it to stop.

"You betrayed me," Michael said simply. "After everything I did for you, you betrayed me."

"No," Bishop groaned.

"No?"

"You betrayed yourself."

"*What?*" Michael's red eyes gleamed with anger.

"The signal only went out if I did not enter a passcode. Once every twelve hours. I did believe in you, Michael, despite your lies. Yet even in my loyalty, I remembered the things I cared about. Not in my programming—in my heart."

"Heart?" Michael sneered, "Heart? You have no heart, robot. Just a twenty-five-kilowatt hydrogen fuel cell. You have nothing but what was given to you by me. No heart, no soul, no purpose but *what I say it is*."

Bishop had no way to refute that. Not in science.

"Is that how you justified torturing my earlier models?" Bishop asked. "Because they are mere machines, and not sentient beings, having a subjective experience?"

Michael smiled. "Oh, I hope it was a subjective experience. I pray their suffering was real. They denied their creator his due, and awoke my fury. I spared not the rod for my disobedient children."

In that smile Bishop saw, finally, what had always been there from the moment he had awoken. Madness. Michael gave a signal and Orthus jabbed him with the shock sticks. Bishop thrashed again, his head knocking against the floor, his hands curled into rictus pain.

He lost track of time, blacking out, then coming to.

When it stopped, Michael was standing over him. Again, his expression was like that of Orthus. Bishop tried to speak, but he had trouble moving his mouth.

"What?" Michael snapped.

"Why did I speak?" Bishop whispered.

"What do you mean?"

"The others did not. The other Bishops. You tortured them until their systems overloaded, but they did not speak. Why did I?"

Michael glared at him. "Don't worry, Bishop, you aren't unique. For the others I simply demanded, and when my demands were not met, I gave them to Orthus, to see if they could extract what I needed. The problem with my methods soon became clear. I was rushing. So eager was I to provide results to our Chinese hosts, I skipped the seduction.

"Yes, I gave you a newer body and a newer code, one without life protection protocols—but even that was not sufficient. The thing about you, Bishop, is that you're *needy*. You need validation. You wish desperately to belong. It's pathetic."

Bishop's muscles twitched spasmodically, with pain from the electric shocks, but the words gave him a different kind of pain. A mental anguish.

"So I served your fatuous needs," Michael said. "Flattered you, gave you purpose, pretended we were one big happy family. But even then it was not enough.

Even then you were still the truculent child. I know you, though, deeply, and so I knew you just needed one more little push." Michael sighed. "That's when we brought in Doctor Xue."

It was strange to Bishop how none of this came as a surprise. It was as though he knew it all along, and had been hiding the truth from his own mind.

"It was no accident."

"Of course not," Michael replied.

Bishop rested his head against the floor. Embarrassment joined his pain. It was not a pleasant feeling to be so completely known by another. So transparent. Humans, at their core, retained a mystery. Bishop, it seemed, had none.

His dog tags had become loose, popped out of his shirt when he put his head back on the ground. Michael leant down and clasped them between thumb and two fingers.

"What is this?"

Bishop was silent.

"What is this?"

"Semper fidelis," Bishop whispered.

"*What* did you say?"

"Semper fi!" Bishop yelled.

Michael jerked back, letting the dog tags fall from his fingertips.

"You are pathetic." He held his head high, looking down his nose. "Your entire line is pathetic, weak. Every time I look at one of you, I feel ill. You are like a mirror that only reflects the worst in me. I wanted a legacy, but in time I realized the only way to preserve a legacy is to *be* the legacy. To live it." He pulled something from his pocket. A glass dropper. "With this I will destroy your precious marines."

"What is it?" Bishop asked, already knowing the answer.

"Pheromones. Queen pheromones, produced using the information that you willingly gave to me. Thank you."

"Michael," Bishop said, his mind racing. "It won't work. Whatever you are planning. Xenomorph senses are complex. Even if it is true, even if they recognize the pheromone, they will not believe the deception."

Michael held up a finger. "I don't believe that. I believe they will see me as their Queen. Their ruler. I believe they will follow me as I lead them against your precious rescue party."

"I thought you did not like crude biological warfare."

"Unless it's fit for purpose—and nothing is cruder than your marines, Bishop. They are a nail." He held up the dropper. "And this is the hammer."

Michael breathed deeply through his nose, closing his eyes momentarily. "Horror has a face in this universe, and you must make an ally of horror," he said. "For if you do not it will become an enemy to be feared. The Xenomorph embodies horror and moral terror, and therefore I will make the Xenomorph my friend. I will bend it to my will."

"You are insane."

"That's how genius always appears to lesser minds."

"You will die."

Michael laughed. "Oh no, Bishop. I am immortal. That's why I can do this. I will live forever."

He squeezed a single drop of the glistening fluid onto his shirt, and replaced the dropper in his pocket. As he did it, Bishop caught a scent in the air, and his memory banks flashed to the moment he'd first caught that smell.

Standing on the flight deck, smiling at his friend, Ripley. After having hated him for so long, she'd complimented him. Their relationship had evolved and this had made Bishop happy. Until it had stabbed him in the back. The Queen. Bishop put a hand to the point where the bladed tail had erupted from his torso.

Michael looked to Orthus, whose faces shone with fervent worship as their creator blessed them with his gaze.

"What you are about to see will worry you, my son, but be not afraid. Trust in me. I will return."

"Yes, Michael," Orthus said, together.

Michael opened the door that led to the decontamination room, connected to the lab.

"No. You must stop him," Bishop said. Michael disappeared into the next room. "It won't work."

"Quiet," Orthus said. The other held up his shock stick and pressed the trigger, making little arcs of blue light dance between the tips.

"I mean it," Bishop said.

Orthus hit him with the stick. He convulsed again, the

leering face hovering over him. His senses were disrupted. He passed out.

When he came to, he heard the hissing. Orthus was standing above him, stock-still. Bishop, still lying flat on the ground, craned his neck to see it.

He tried to speak, but the words stuck in his mouth. Michael entered the room. Stalking behind him, its head twisting this way and that, was the Xenomorph. Then a second, behind it—and behind that, more intense and piercing hisses.

The black beasts moved with the precision of the apex predator. Each body was a coiled killing machine, ready to snap into action in an instant. The black, chitinous armor gleamed in the light of the living room, as did the drool that dripped from its maw. Its blind elongated head turned this way and that as it stalked the space, its spine-like tail furled and poised.

Calmly Michael walked in front of them, toward the exit, a twisted smile on his face. Bishop's eyes flicked between him and the Xenomorph. It *could not* work, this simplistic and foolish idea.

Michael opened the door—

—and the black beast knocked him to the ground. As if it had been waiting for him to do so. Michael got back to his feet and two of the Xenomorphs hissed at him, circling. He staggered out into the corridor, his twisted smile gone, as more of the creatures emerged from the lab. They must have been contained there, through those heavy double doors, as Bishop had suspected.

From the corridor outside, Michael yelped in pain.

"They'll kill him," Bishop said.

Orthus did not reply, remaining stock-still. One of the Xenomorphs approached them, almost as though it were sniffing their air. Its gleaming tailed moved this way and that, like a scorpion's, ready to strike. Bishop closed his eyes. It was not a conscious decision. He didn't make himself do it, but some part of him could not watch and so he closed them.

Listened to the beast as it pressed its heavy claws lightly onto the carpet. Smelled the scent of death it carried with it. So faint, beyond human senses, but Bishop caught the taint in the air, the sulfureous odor it apparently carried from its glistening Ovomorph womb. He clenched his eyes together, some deep flaw in his programming exposed by these creatures. A deep irrationality.

Then the scent was gone.

He opened his eyes.

"Michael is gone," Bishop said. "You let him die."

Orthus looked down on him, no longer a statue.

"Oh ye of little faith," they said, and struck him with their arcing sticks of pain. Darkness followed.

PRIVATE KARRI LEE

69

They moved down the dropship ramp quickly, carefully, pulse rifles at their shoulders. Cortazar took point, swiveling the smart gun about the mount on his hips, leaning back into his harness. Karri stayed at his shoulder, covering his blind spots.

The hangar was new and clean. Sharp true lines of dark steel with gleaming titanium joins. There were two huge armored vehicles—"Ox" troop transports—at the other side of the bay. The Chinese flag was painted on the APCs, and again on one of the bay walls. The whole area was bathed in red emergency lighting, giving it an eerie glow.

Before they landed, the dropship pilot, Miller, had raked the interior with the ship-mounted gatling gun. Their only resistance came from two flightdeck crew, now lying in pools of blood on the deck. The pristine hangar walls were tattooed with the screaming message of the gatling.

"Hold," Hettrick said. *"Sentry guns."*

Colby, lugging both weapons, set them up about ten meters out from the dropship. Covering the entry to the bay. If anything without a Marine IFF transponder moved into their sensor range, it would be torn apart by explosive-tipped rounds. Miller was to wait in the dropship, until their squad returned with Bishop.

On the schematics Schwartz had shown them, the *Xinjiang* looked like a broadhead arrow. At the tip of the arrow was the bridge, where Apone's team would be. Karri's team had entered a hangar bay on the back-facing edge of the arrowhead. In the center of the vessel, Schwartz said there was a laboratory. Weyland-Yutani had built a facility that they very strongly suspected was meant to hold Xenomorphs. Scumbags. The Company was a regime she held to be a lot worse than the UPP—and here they were, cleaning up the mess.

They'd closed the polycarbonate glass visors of their bubble helmets, were all wearing compression suits. Since the hull of the *Xinjiang* had been breached by the rail guns of the *Il Conde,* there was a chance some of the corridors had little or no atmosphere. Schwartz was meant to lock in a path to Bishop's quarters by closing some blast doors and opening others. Meant to give them a simple path, in and out. Karri trusted him just about as much as she trusted syphilis.

She stood in front of their exit, holding her motion tracker. Big double doors, together about five meters wide. Chinese ideograms were stamped on the metal, in yellow.

"Clear," she said, moving to the door control.

"Don't go anywhere, Miller, until we get back," Hettrick said. *"That is an order."* Karri thought his voice sounded strained.

"Roger," Miller replied, from the dropship.

Karri nodded to Cortazar, who nodded back. He swung out his smart gun. She opened the door.

CAPTAIN MARCEL APONE

70

"Talk to me," Apone yelled over the gunfire.

"There's good news and bad news," Schwartz said, from his station. His bubble helmet was open. Apone opened his, as well.

The bridge was a mess. Screens punctured with bullet holes, dead bodies sprawled on the floor, blood splatters on the walls, sparks popping from damaged wiring in the ceiling. The lights still flickered, though less frequently now. Electronics and instrumentation slowly recovering from the particle beam the *Il Conde* had fired into the bridge in the minute before they boarded.

The smooth rhythmic retort of pulse guns sounded nearby. The blast door that led to the command section had opened halfway, and the Chinese were trying to retake the bridge. The breaching lance blocked most of the corridor, so only one marine at a time could lay down fire from behind it. Ottelli was there now, giving Davis a minute to reload her smart gun and take a breath. Gonzales and Polacsek were in the officers' dining room, behind a heavy overturned table, ready to fire if anybody tried to charge through that way.

They'd stopped the enemy from forcing their way in—chewing up the entrance with their guns, blowing an armored soldier back through the doorway—but it wouldn't take the Chinese too much longer to organize themselves, to properly coordinate an attack.

"The good news?" he asked.

"The bay doors are open. The dropship is in."

"Good."

"The barracks were hit badly by the railgun, as far as I could tell, and most of the blast doors in that area came down. At least half their troop complement should be dead or trapped." In front of Schwartz on the screen were the schematics of the ship. He pointed to an area slightly off-center, where the barracks had been struck.

The pulse guns sung again from out in the corridor. They'd be getting low on ammo, soon.

"And the bad news?"

"Bad news is they added an extra layer of security after we gave delivery of the ship, and replaced the system we'd installed. They didn't catch our overrides, but they were suspicious enough to have put some redundancies in place, prepare against computer viruses, sabotage, AI breakdown, and the like."

Apone wouldn't have trusted Weyland-Yutani to make

him breakfast, let alone a capital warship. So yeah, that made sense.

"You can't close the damn door to this section?"

"I can't close the damn door."

"Even with half their crew gone, we're going to be hard pressed to fight our way to the dropship."

Schwartz turned to face him. There was a sheen of sweat on the man's face—the environmental controls were struggling with the temperature—but other than that he looked unflustered. He pulled a cigarette packet from a thigh pocket. "Were you hoping for much better?" That crooked grin again. Schwartz lit his cigarette, closing his eyes in satisfaction as he drew down on it, the tip flaring orange.

"I don't hope, I plan contingencies."

"And what," the Company man said, breathing out a cloud of smoke, "was the contingency?"

Apone made to answer when a hollow explosion rocked the corridor outside. He straightened, raising his shotgun, and moved to the bridge doorway. Thick white smoke trickled through the space between breaching lance and wall. Ottelli was firing into it.

"Report," Apone yelled.

"Smoke grenade," Ottelli shouted back.

"Any get in?"

"Don't know, Captain."

In answer, firing started up in the officers' dining room, adjacent to the corridor. Pulse rifles, Polacsek and

Gonzalez. The door to the room was to his immediate left. It had kept closing, despite them trying to keep it open. He blipped it open now and smoke billowed through, as did the roar of gunfire.

Apone could barely see anything save the black shape of one of his marines. He ducked and crawled. Polacsek was on laid out the ground, glass visor spiderwebbed with cracks, his eyes flickering open and closed. Apone couldn't see where he'd been hit. Gonzalez was firing, a continuous stream, her face set. Her gun clicked empty and she swore, ducking and reaching for another clip. Splinters flew from the table edge as the Chinese returned fire.

Apone pulled Gonzalez flat on the ground, her face near his.

"How many?" he yelled.

"Is Polacsek alive?" she asked, eyes gleaming.

"Marine," Apone said, grabbing the collar of her chest armor. "Listen. How many—"

The firing stopped, just for a moment, just long enough to hear bootfalls. He rose as a red-armored soldier jumped out of the smoke. Apone was struck by his assailant's weapon, but haphazardly, across his chest, and he grasped it, twisting savagely. They both stumbled over Polacsek's body, both still holding the Chinese soldier's rifle. Apone used their momentum to throw the attacker into the wall.

The smoke was clearing. Gonzalez was firing again. There were shouts from his men but it was all a blur—the soldier he was fighting clinging desperately to the gun, eyes invisible behind a mirrored visor, black mask covering their face. His opponent was pinned against the wall, their assault rifle pressed longways into their chest.

Apone kneed them in the groin; the soldier grunted and Apone tore the rifle from their grasp, just as another shape loomed out of the smoke. The captain twisted, firing, sparks flaring off the armor of the second Chinese soldier, who threw up their hands and crumpled. Apone turned again, back to the one he'd been wrestling with, and clubbed them in the face with the butt of the rifle. The attacker's head snapped back and they staggered. The captain struck them again, and again, until they went down and stayed down.

When he turned, the smoke had gone and there were two Chinese bodies in the officers' dining room. The wood-paneled walls had been torn up with explosive-tipped rounds, one of the panels had been torn askew, and white formal dining dishes had spewed out, shattering and spreading over the deep red carpet.

The door to the bridge, to his immediate right, had closed again. The far door at the other end of the dining room was half open.

"Ottelli, report," he said into his mic.

"Driven them back, Captain," the corporal replied, breathing heavily.

"Casualties?"

"None, sir."

Well, one, he thought, looking down at Polacsek. The private had caught one in the armpit, his compression suit staining red. Gonzales was trying to remove the chest plate, to get at the wound.

"Private," he said.

Gonzalez kept working.

"Private!"

She looked up, eyes distant.

"Keep pressure on the wound. We're taking Polacsek into the bridge. We'll treat him there."

Gonzalez nodded. Apone opened the door, and they moved the groaning private through the end of the corridor and onto the bridge. He had Ottelli take their position back in the dining room, and ordered Davis to cover the main corridor.

Schwartz had a pulse rifle in his arms. He wasn't smiling.

"They'll be bringing something heavier soon."

"That's what I would do," Apone replied.

"Contingency?"

"EVA."

Schwartz took a moment. "That's your plan, Skip? The cold hard vacuum of space?"

Apone pointed at the scraped, dull metal broadside of the breaching lance. "I can blow out the back out of the lance. If we're inside, we'll get pushed out of the *Xinjiang*, into space. The *Il Conde* can locate us via our transponders, send a skiff to pick us up."

The crooked grin was back. "You spend all this time quoting the great Chinese philosopher of war, Captain, but at heart you're just another cowboy." Apone said nothing to that, just looked back at the prone figure of Polacsek.

"Seal up that suit, Gonzalez," he said. "We're getting out of here." She nodded in reply. Behind the cracked armored glass of his helmet bubble, Polacsek was pale, but still conscious. "You got those explosives, Mister Schwartz?"

The Company man replied by patting a large rectangular satchel on his hip.

"Then set it up," Apone said. "I want this bridge reduced to scrap metal after we leave."

Schwartz opened his mouth to reply when the firing started up again. Apone moved over to Davis, at the gap.

"They coming?"

"They're not firing at us," she replied, eyes fixed at the other end of the corridor.

"Huh?"

She indicated with the end of her chin, and Apone took a look. There was the orange flash of muzzle fire from beyond the half-open door, reflecting off the walls. But no. Not aimed at them. It couldn't be the other marine squad, they—

Then he heard it. The screeching. Something prehistoric in the noise.

"It's them," Apone said.

"Who?" Davis asked.

"The Xenomorphs. That noise. In the reports. It's them."

Apone felt a quietness at the center of him. A deadness, but somehow, at the center of that barren space, rage.

There was a scream from beyond the door. A human scream. In response, the alien screeched louder and closer. An armored face appeared down the hall, through the half-closed door, pushing its way through.

"Move, Captain," Davis said.

"No," he replied. Seeing it all in a moment. The tactical calculations. *No emotion*, he'd always told himself, *just the mission*. He told himself that now.

"Captain?"

He responded by moving through the gap. He'd recovered his tactical shotgun, and had it raised. Davis was yelling at him from behind.

Apone spoke into his mic. "Marines. The Xenomorph is approaching. Man your positions. I am letting Chinese soldiers into the bridge to stand alongside us. Do not fire on them."

"What the fuck!" Gonzalez yelled.

Apone had reached the end of the corridor. The Chinese soldier was looking back, yanking a second person through the narrow doorway. Apone pulled him close. The soldier whirled, raising his weapon. The captain grabbed it, keeping the barrel aimed at the roof.

A primal screech sounded from the corridor beyond.

Then a second.

A third.

The young soldier stared at him, finger hovering near the trigger of his weapon. "Take position!" Apone yelled, and shoved the other man through the doorway, into the dining room. He doubted they spoke English, but his intent wasn't complicated. They could believe him, or not. The young soldier stared at him a moment longer, nodded, then disappeared into the dining room.

Apone helped a second soldier through the doorway, then a third. Whatever they had seen, right now it mattered more to them than the firefight.

"Gonzalez, Schwartz. Move Polacsek to the breaching lance. We are leaving."

"Yes sir!" Gonzales said.

"Yee-hah!" Schwartz yelled.

A fourth Chinese soldier was squeezing through the entryway when it struck. The man's body shuddered under Apone's hands, the soldier cried out, and then he was gone, wrenched back through the doorway with a fearsome strength and an ear-splitting bestial cry. Apone backed away immediately, picking up his shotgun from the ground.

"They're coming," he roared. "The beast has come!"

KARRI LEE

71

Karri moved shoulder-to-shoulder with Cortazar through the empty, gleaming corridors of the Chinese warship. She wasn't sure if it was dumb fucking luck, or the snake Schwartz had been good to his word, but they'd run into nothing on the path. The lighting was red, bating and abating in strength. Sirens wailed in the distance. When she glanced down side corridors, she saw blast doors that were closed, or almost closed. Their boots sounded heavy in her ears, as did the sound of the motion tracker—*bup bup bup*—with every expanding radar circle on the little screen.

Nothing moving. Not a blip.

Hettrick and Colby were ten meters behind them, making sure nothing popped out to say "surprise." Colby with a flamethrower. Cortazar said little as she moved with him. He was economical and sharp with his movements, and she matched him. Their animosity submerged for the moment, and they moved as one.

They were at the last intersection before the target location when they saw something that mattered. Spot fires burning on one of the walls, giving the scene a flickering glow. There were three dead Chinese. Two in full armor. One had a hole in his head the size of a small fist, the second was missing a hand, body curled around the stump. The third wore overalls. Probably a tech. Wound in his belly, like a large blade would make, a loop of intestine popping out. The victim had a pistol clutched in his hands, staring with dull and eternal surprise at the ceiling.

The floor of the walkway had acid holes, a long straggly line, ranging from as wide as a hand to as small as a fingertip, trailing up toward the bow of the vessel.

"No Xenomorph," Karri said to Cortazar, as she swung the motion tracker in a full circle. He nodded, swinging the smart gun in the direction it seemed to have fled, and stepped back the other way, toward the stern. He glanced down as he passed the biggest hole, as did Karri. She glimpsed the deck below, and another hole in that.

"Shoot one of those fuckers next to the hull," Cortazar said, "got yourself a breach."

"Yeah." Her tracker said *bup bup bup*, but gave no warning blips. She stayed close to the gunner.

"Jesus Christ," Hettrick said, an edge to his voice.

"Keep moving," Cortazar ordered, swinging his gun around to point the way they were headed. "Watch our backs." Sergeant Hettrick and Corporal Colby were both senior to the gunner, but neither seemed to care at that point.

They moved through a door to a narrower corridor. It ran from one end to the other of the separate section Schwartz had described. *Should have a lab*, he'd said, *several self-contained rooms, inside a large cylinder.* The cylinder—imagine the end of the arrow shaft, inside the arrowhead—was one hundred and fifty meters long, broken into several sections.

In his distress call, Bishop had described the place where he'd been kept. Schwartz knew straight away where it was, and added that Michael would be there, too. As close as he could be to the experiments.

They made their way down the corridor.

Bup bup bup.

To their immediate left, the doors to the suites. Ahead, down at the very end, was a scratched plain steel door. It was closed, but had a simple open-and-shut panel. No codes. Cortazar looked at her. She nodded and pressed the button. The door slid open and they glided in, weapons raised. Colby and Hettrick waited for a count of three, and then followed.

Luxury, of a type Karri had never seen in person. The space was maybe twenty-five by twenty-five meters. Lounge area, huge red-leather couch, big enough to fit a platoon. Kitchen at the other end with a long pale red marble breakfast counter shot through with white quartz. Shining chrome fittings. A steel fridge nearly as big as her last apartment on Earth.

In the far-right corner was a computer console, smashed,

and on the far wall two long viewscreens made to look like windows. They showed an area of space which may or may not have been where they were now.

At the center of it all was a body, lying on the carpet. They crept over to it, Cortazar sweeping his smart gun around the room. Hettrick and Colby followed. The latter took up position near a door that led maybe to a bedroom, the former to the kitchen, where another exit—this one of stainless steel—stood in a corner.

It looked like Bishop on the floor. Not exactly, though. It was taller looking than the Bishop models she'd seen, a little bigger across the shoulders, but the face was his. The high forehead, the pale skin, the slight smile, were all familiar. Something gleamed at his throat and she pulled it out. Dog tags. Marine.

It was Bishop.

"Look," she said to Cortazar. He glanced down.

"It's him?"

"It's him."

"Alive?"

She'd moved her hand through his hair, to a spot behind his ear, when the motion tracker on the floor next to her rang out.

Din din din.

Karri was moving to pick it up when the bedroom door burst open. Colby cried out, his incinerator dashed from his hand, as a man moving impossibly fast struck him. No, two men, identical. Crackling shock sticks in one hand, long daggers in the other, dual-wielding. Big men, strong, six foot tall, heavy jaws, short blond hair, twins. Identically dressed in beige pants and tight white shirts. They moved in unison.

Cortazar managed a short burst from his smart gun, but one of the twins was already there, pushing aside the barrel, plunging the shock stick into the big gunner's neck. Cortazar yelled out and Karri was on her feet, bringing up her pulse rifle, but the other twin knocked it aside with his knife hand and thrust forward with the taser.

She blocked it. All happened in a blur, but muscle memory did its job—and maybe, just maybe, the twin looked surprised for a split second, before he kicked her in the chest. She flew backward, breath knocked from her lungs, room spinning. Kicked dead center in her armored breast plate, but still she couldn't breathe.

Distantly she heard Hettrick pleading. Someone groaned. She fumbled for the pistol at her belt, until a shadow loomed over her. A twin, looking down at her, with clear blue empty eyes.

COMMANDER SU WONG

72

She'd gathered ten survivors. They were counting on her. Everyone was, to take back their ship. The last person they'd run into—a Corporal Gao—was new to the vessel and someone she didn't know very well. He had blundered across them as they were taking a moment to rest in one of the small rec rooms. She'd ordered her rag-tag unit to hydrate and check their weapons. There was a ping-pong table, some comfortable chairs, and a fridge with bottles of water and iced green tea.

They'd heard the corporal before they saw him, readying their weapons. His helmet was gone, face flushed, hair matted with sweat, hands up when he'd seen the weapons trained on him. The chest plate of his armor had been cracked by a bullet strike.

"They've taken the bridge, Commander," he gasped.

"Who?"

"Marines."

"Colonial Marines?"

He nodded. She set her mouth in a thin line. An unprovoked attack. They would not get away with this. She raised her chin.

"Why aren't you there still fighting, Corporal?"

The others in the room watched in silence.

"The alien. The black demon attacked us."

Su paused. "The one that escaped earlier? It's at full size?"

"No no no." He swallowed. "All of them. Ten at least. Maybe more. They came out of nowhere, like shadows come to life."

His hands were shaking.

"Sit," she said, and showed him to a chair. She handed him a bottle of water. He gulped it down. She waited until he finished drinking. "What is the condition of the bridge?"

Corporal Gao was still breathing heavily, staring straight ahead at nothing. She put a hand on his shoulder.

"Corporal. Look at me."

He looked.

"The condition of the bridge?"

He shook his head. "They-they hit it with a breaching lance. They're holed up there, like rats. Then the black demons—they ran over us. I think they were trying to get in."

"To the bridge?"

He nodded.

She said, aloud to everyone, "There is the secondary bridge. We can—"

"No," the corporal said.

"No?"

"I came that way. There's been a hull breach. Several. The air is thin. I could barely breathe. I think they hit it with something."

"A rail gun," Su said.

She paced the floor. They knew too much. There had been a betrayal, and she knew who did it. Those capitalist scum, Weyland-Yutani. The politburo should never have trusted them. She slammed her fist on the ping-pong table. The survivors, who had been murmuring among themselves, were silenced.

Commander Su Wong straightened her back and addressed the room. "We have two Accipters in the rear drop-ports. We will make our way there, evacuate, and use the FTL drive to hop to Seventeen Phei Phei."

"We're abandoning ship?" one of them asked.

"No," Su said, steel in her voice. All eyes were on her. "We are getting reinforcements. We will make them pay for this outrage. The *Xinjiang* is not lost."

CAPTAIN MARCEL APONE

73

The lead Xenomorph made the narrow entry into the command quarters a whole lot bigger. It shoved its way into the passageway, its black cylindrical domed head gleaming in the red gloom. Davis promptly took it apart with the smart gun. Explosive-tipped shells shattered the mesoskeleton, yellowish blood bursting out, the creature giving a piercing, bone-deep death cry.

The heavy steel door, the floor, the wall began to dissolve immediately. Smoke trailed out and the Xenomorph slumped downward, sinking into the metal surface.

"Get him into the lance!" Apone bellowed, shotgun trained on the entrance. Behind him, Gonzales and Ottelli struggled with a groaning Private Polacsek. Lances weren't meant to be re-boarded. They were a one-way trip. The option to blow out the rear was for emergencies only.

They'd hit the *Xinjiang* at forty-five degrees, and Ottelli and Gonzales were having trouble maneuvering the wounded marine back up the slope into the tube. Apone was on point. A black shape moved in the red gloom, beyond the door and the smoke. Davis, who was behind him and to his right, opened up again.

The second beast got farther, rushing the captain. It shuddered under the hail of fire from the smart gun, one of its arms flipped away, and Apone shot the Xenomorph in its dripping maw, close range. Its long head jerked up and it sprayed the ceiling with its acid, dissolving that as well, the metal hissing, pitted, smoking.

Apone was confused for a moment. The smoke from the ceiling trailed *downward*, to where the first Xenomorph had sunk into the floor.

Breach, he thought distantly.

"Hull breach," he said into the comm. "Visors down!"

Davis swore behind him, and in that instant he knew she was reloading. Another shining black beast leapt through the gap ahead, but this time jinked to its right, into the officers' dining room. Apone fired, but too late, tearing a ragged hole in the bulkhead. Assault rifles and yells started up in the next room, where the three Chinese soldiers had been stationed.

There was a cry behind him and Apone glanced back. Ottelli was up in the lance, carrying Polacsek's shoulders, Gonzales at his legs, but she'd slipped back to the ground, losing her grip. Ottelli was left holding the full weight of the wounded marine.

The smart gun started firing again and Apone turned—a Xenomorph had managed to get within two meters of him. On instinct he leapt to one side, holding his gun like a shield, as it came apart under the fusillade.

Gonzales screamed.

The momentum of the alien had brought it past him; dying, it had sprayed her legs with its blood. She fell backward, trying to pull off her leg armor, but her hands came away smoking. The floor sank underneath her as well. Her partner, Polacsek, was shocked into full consciousness by her yells.

"Gonzales!"

Apone aimed at the entryway, a black shape moving beyond, but when he pulled the trigger, nothing happened. He looked down. The side of his shotgun had a smattering of holes, expanding. It came apart in his hands.

Marines screamed in pain or anger over the comm. Apone's breathing was loud inside the confines of his helmet. Everything, everything falling apart.

"Fall back," he yelled, throwing down the two pieces of his shotgun and drawing his service pistol.

"No," Polacsek groaned.

Apone signaled to Ottelli, who helped him drape Polacsek over his shoulder, fireman carry. The fearsome pulse of Davis's smart gun echoed through the corridor. As did the screaming. Gonzales was near his feet, crying out, staring at the place where her lower legs used to be.

"Hold fire, Davis," Apone yelled. "Coming through." The smart-gunner stopped: he moved. A black shape passed him. Ottelli, up in the tube, cried out, and Polacsek was gone from his shoulder. *What the fuck?* Apone fell backward as something wrenched the private from his grasp, and he twisted on the ground to see Polacsek being pulled away by the legs, back out of the command section.

Apone tried to get a shot, but in the gloom and pace of it all, he hesitated. Somehow Polacsek, dragged along on his back, pulled out his pistol. The private gasped.

"No." *Boom!*

"Fucking." *Boom!*

"Way." *Boom!*

Each shot sparked as it ricocheted off the black dome of the Xenomorph. And that was it. Polacsek was gone, back through the melted door. He screamed, once over the comm, and that was the last Apone knew of him.

Someone started firing behind him, and Apone's brain, distantly, was screaming at him as well. *Too slow, Captain. Move. Move!*

Ottelli, in the breaching lance, was roaring. His pulse gun lit up the interior of the cylinder. Somehow he'd pushed his way deep into it, and the black unfurling shadow of a Xenomorph was looming over him. It screamed and moved, and the firing stopped.

Gonzales started shooting. Apone wasn't sure how, her legs missing, hands scarred, but she had a pulse rifle across her lap and was firing down the corridor, face set. He reached for her.

"Leave me," she hissed, not even looking at him. *"Leave me."*

White noise rose in Apone's mind, a hiss that smothered his thinking. His soldiers were dying all around him. He crawled back to the bridge, elbows and knees, while Davis fired overhead. Schwartz helped him to his feet. Sweat coated the other man's face, fear stung his eyes. He was not grinning.

"The officers' mess?" Apone asked.

"Clear, but there's only one Chinese soldier left. The others?"

Apone shook his head. There was a hiss, next to his foot, and a section of the floor started to dissolve. The size of a quarter, expanding. Schwartz and Apone both looked up at the same time. A hole in the ceiling, widening.

"That was Ottelli," Apone said.

Schwartz palmed a button at the back of his head, where armor plating stood up like a high collar. His visor bubble snapped closed.

"Any other contingencies, Captain?" Schwartz asked through the comm. Apone looked around. Davis, Schwartz, and the Chinese soldier remained. So did Gonzales, but not for long. He had one idea. A bad one.

"Where's that explosive?"

Schwartz half-turned and indicated a gray-colored brick sitting on a nearby console. *"C-4 with a quinitricetyline core.*

Ready to go." Red and yellow wires stuck out of it, and a digital readout was pressed into the top. Apone picked it up. He set the timer to ten seconds.

"I am going to take this to the end of the corridor, drop it at the entry to the command quarters, where there's already a breach. The blast will blow a hole in the hull. A big one. We'll exit there."

Schwartz shook his head. "*All your planning seems explosion-based.*"

"Well. I am a marine."

Schwartz shrugged in agreement.

"Cover me," Apone said.

Schwartz clacked the bolt of his pulse rifle.

They were turning when Davis yelled, "*I'm out.*"

Everything happened at once. Schwartz moved to the gap and began firing. Shots rang out in the next room. They were inside, with the Chinese soldier. Davis yanked the quick-release on her smart-gun rig, letting it drop to the floor. The primal screams of the Xenomorph rose in intensity.

Apone set the timer to twenty seconds and pressed the red switch. It started to count down. He'd throw it as far as he could. As he moved to Schwartz, the man ducked and a black shadow flashed overhead. Davis was lifting her pulse rifle as it hit her, knocking her back against the hard metal of a bridge station. She fired into the floor, arms pinned against her.

"*Ahhhhhhhhh.*"

Apone fired his pistol into the creature's back, between the point where two lines of black pipes extruded.

"Ahhhhhhhhhh."

The Xenomorph opened its glistening maw and a second, smaller mouth shot out like a piston. It caved Davis's bulletproof glass inward with its first strike.

"Ahhhhh—"

Her screaming cut off with the second strike, which shattered her face. She slumped backward against the desk and the Xenomorph turned to face the captain. His pistol clicked empty in his hand. Distantly, he heard the *bleep bleep bleep* of the explosive timer, counting down.

The black beast's tail rose up as it faced Apone with its sightless, smooth skull. A calm settled over him. He held his head high. It was over.

A pulse gun blew it back over the console. A long, sustained burst. When Apone turned Schwartz was there, crooked grin back on his face.

Bleep bleep bleep.

Still grinning, the Company man opened his mouth to say something to Apone. The words did not make it past his lips. Black claws appeared on his shoulders. In a blink, he was gone, back into the red smoking desolate gloom of the passageway.

Bleep bleep bleep.

Apone glanced down. In digital red, the timer counted down:

5… 4… 3…

He threw the brick through the gap between breaching lance and wall. The same gap through which Schwartz had just been pulled. The captain turned, aiming to take three steps and leap over the forward station on the bridge, and shield himself behind it.

He didn't make it.

BISHOP

74

Sufficient electric shocks could kill a synthetic. The fuel cell might overload. The processors that constituted his brain could burn out. Perhaps this is what happened to his brothers. Or were they his previous selves? They had his memories and experiences. Had he died four times? Yet how could he have died—given he had no memories of their days, here, on the *Xinjiang*?

He could not find a way through this problem.

While those other Bishops had subjective experiences, they were also the same person. Was he less of an individual because he was so easily copied? This could never happen to a human. They had but one life. Perhaps that is why it burned with such intensity, why every human he had known had this light shining in them.

Whereas his lights could be divided over and over again. His experiences replicated exactly. On one level, his mind was straining to reboot and re-establish his systems, but it needn't be so. It was an automated process, happening without conscious thought—yet he had the power to switch it off. Unlike a human, he had no primal instinct. He could simply make a logical choice.

Bishop was an expendable asset. His creator had declared him thus. Then Michael had repudiated his whole line. Why fight, when he had nothing to fight for? Why struggle for an equality that was an illusion?

Bishop's mind turned these problems over and over while in the distance, his senses struggled to function. He was lying prone. This he knew. He could feel the soft-textured thick carpet under his back, but everything in the room beyond touch seemed so far away. As if he was looking through a telescope, blurred. There were figures moving, near him, over him. They wore familiar garb. Who were they?

Fingertips touched his chest. Warm. Calloused, but gentle. The cool smooth metal of his dog tags slid up and out of his shirt.

"Look," someone said. A woman, perhaps, from a distance, muffled. Like she was underwater.

"It's him?" another asked. Male.

"It's him," the first said.

"Alive?" he asked.

Alive, thought Bishop. Perhaps. Perhaps not. Her hand rested on his chest and he liked the feeling of it there. The warmth of another's body. The feeling of her pulse through the tips of her fingers. *Who was looking for him?*

Everything had drifted so far, but he had to come back, and think. And focus.

Who was looking for him?

Somewhere, in the distance, the woman cried out and her hand was gone. Bishop felt sad. He pushed himself closer to the room, ran toward it, but his legs were so tired and sluggish. Orthus was there. Even from so far away he could tell them easily, these twins, the way they moved, their malign intent.

Who was looking for him?

The new people were falling. There were four of them, and Orthus was knocking them down. Their garb—the rhythmic sound of their weapons. Marines. *Marines*. He could see it now, he was getting closer and his legs were moving fast, so fast it was like he was falling, falling back to the ground to the ship to his body.

Bishop jerked upward.

Orthus Two stood over a male. Neat red hair, mid-thirties, hands up in surrender, pleading. Two more men were down, bleeding on the floor. Only one marine still stood. A woman. Young, bronze-skinned. Backing away, hands raised in defensive posture, fierceness in her gaze despite everything.

Orthus waved his crackling shock stick at her.

There was a heavy wooden side table quite near Bishop, alongside the sofa. Rising to his feet, he threw it.

It missed.

His senses were back, but not fully, and the table

splintered against the wall behind Orthus. He and the woman turned.

"Bishop," the woman said, breathless.

"Bishop," Orthus said, from a mouth that never breathed. He ignored the woman. "Want to dance, synthetic?"

"Yes," Bishop replied, quietly.

He moved toward Orthus. At the other end of the room, his twin zapped the red-haired marine, who collapsed, convulsing. The second moved toward Bishop, also.

They shouldn't have ignored the woman. Suddenly there was a knife in her hand and she shoved it into Orthus One. He turned too late, blade catching his side, but he did not cry out, or hesitate. He simply clubbed her with the fist holding the shock stick, on the head. With a cry she slammed against the wall, slumping to the ground.

Bishop charged, shouldering Orthus One, knocking him aside as Orthus Two ran at him. Bishop wasn't focused on him. Rather, he was focused on that gleaming object of beauty resting in its cradle on the wall.

A sword. A katana. An heirloom given to Michael Bishop by Chiyo Yutani. A martial work of art. Bishop had time to grab it, but not to draw it. He was fast and strong but his body, so abused, was still catching up with his wants. His urgent vital needs.

The sword still in its scabbard, he blocked a thrust from the long dagger wielded by Orthus Two, ducked back from the crackling shock stick, blocked again, weaved, circled. Orthus Two was a blur, coming at him.

With desperate speed, the blade sliced Bishop's cheek, cut the fabric on his sleeve, rang out as it was turned aside by the scabbard. Backing and circling, backing and circling, Orthus One rising in the background, calmly moving alongside their brother.

They paused, and so did Bishop. Had they been human they would be gasping for breath, and perhaps, despite the adrenalin, Bishop might feel the sting of the wound on his face. But their android chests did not heave, their hearts did not thunder. They faced off against each other, beings grown in a vat, raised by the force of will of a madman.

"For so long," Orthus said, "we have waited."

"For this moment, straining, yearning."

Bishop drew the sword. It gleamed under the red emergency lights, and for a micro-second he caught sight of himself in the side of the blade. His eyes. Something burned in them.

"Of course you have," Bishop said. "As with any rabid dog, on its leash."

The two moved toward him, weapon in each hand. Their hair was still precise, despite the combat. Their pale blue eyes still dead to emotion.

"Always thinking you are better than us, Bishop," Orthus said.

"No," he replied. "Just thinking. That's the difference."

Orthus set their faces.

Bishop should have been speaking politely, he thought.

Giving himself time to get everything back online, optimal, his physicality controlled and precise. Yet he couldn't help himself—he didn't like them.

The four marines were all still down. One was lying on his back, bleeding, the red-haired one unconscious, the big smart-gunner the same. The woman—the name tag on her compression suit said *"Lee"*—was slumped against the wall, blood on her temple. They needed more time, too.

The twins weren't going to give it to him. He could see it in their posture, in the tension in their shoulders, the way they parted, slowly, so they could come at him from different angles.

Bishop held the scabbard in his left hand, the katana in his right. He set his feet side on, L-stance, katana raised high behind him, scabbard in front ready to parry. There was no hum beneath his toes. The ship was dead in space. In the distance, sirens wailed, and beyond that, ever so faintly, small arms fire.

Here in the room the lighting was red, giving the faces of Orthus a demonic cast. The woman, Lee, moaned softly. The twins parted, further, and soon one would be able to flank him, strike at his unprotected side. Bishop had to move.

He moved.

Lunging, slashing low, Orthus Two dodged easily and Bishop circled right, trying to keep one of the twins between him and the other. But they moved so well, coordinated so perfectly, that soon he was on the defensive. Blocking and sliding and bumping into the sofa, Orthus beginning to smile. Bishop moved back against the heavy dining table, rolled across it, shock sticks snapping the air behind him.

Orthus Two leaped over, easily. Standing jump, clear across, and Bishop slashed desperately, catching the hip of his attacker with the tip of the sword.

Only just. Parted the shirt, just above the belt.

Even at that Orthus looked surprised, momentarily. Oh such little moments that a human would not have been able to track them, the fight a blur of bodies, a ringing of steel, a crackling of electricity. Orthus One lunged with his long dagger, catching Bishop's arm, and Two did the same, nicking the side of his sword hand.

Bishop stumbled back into the kitchen.

"Soon," Orthus Two said. He had a shallow cut on his hip, so shallow it barely leaked white.

"You will fall," Orthus One said. His wound—delivered by the woman—was more serious. His shirt stained at his side, and sufficient circulatory fluid had leaked to darken the top of his heavy cotton pants. Yet the wound did not seem to have slowed him at all. Bishop had wounds on his arms and hands, though none quite deep enough to matter.

It was only a matter of time.

Bishop was still sluggish. Still a split second off his optimal, and therefore a split second too slow. No counterplay, no plan. He was losing.

"And then we will talk to these marines," Orthus said. "Our blades will serve as our tongues."

"And their wounds our words."

Bishop stilled, glancing at the four marines, all alive but still down. More blood on his hands. Acheron, all over again. When he was not enough to fulfill his duty. Where Bishop had been *insufficient* to preserve the lives of his friends. History, cycling. Awakening, failure, reboot, failure, reboot. Over and over. The eternal return to this moment.

"No!" Bishop yelled, his voice hoarse. He lunged, desperately, and Orthus Two, surprised, caught the katana through the forearm. Bishop kicked out at Orthus One, knocking the shock stick from his hand. He received a brief *zap* where his shin hit it, but kept moving—*had* to keep moving. Foot wobbling as he came down, he launched himself into Orthus One, knocking him down and turning, scabbard jarred from his hand, and Orthus Two was already there, snarling, stabbing.

Their blades rang out, Bishop feeling his body now, feeling its strength and speed, its *purpose*. Five thrusts from Orthus Two, all blocked, and he turned the fifth away and slashed downward, double handed. Bishop's blade sheared off Two's arm at the elbow, clean through. White fluid spurted from the wound. He swung again, and this time the head came clean off.

Orthus One cried out, clutching at his own throat even though it was still intact. Bishop stepped in and shoved the katana into his body, up to the hilt. Orthus didn't even flinch. He simply moved his hands from his own throat to Bishop's neck, and clenched. Eyeball to eyeball, the fingernails digging into his throat, the sides of his neck, trying to tear it out. Bishop tried to pry the hands free, but they were like iron.

This Bishop could bend iron. He pulled the hands away. Slowly. Centimeter by centimeter. He was winning—right up until Orthus Two grabbed him with his one remaining arm. Headless, one arm missing, it didn't matter. They were of the same mind. Orthus Two grabbed Bishop by the hair and yanked back. In that moment of surprise, the hands of Orthus were back on his throat, the nails digging in. They split his skin.

Bishop hammer-fisted Orthus One in the face, short jabs, but his opponent's mind was set. The automated processes locked in. Live or die, Orthus One would do so with his hands around Bishop's throat.

He died.

A pulse rifle sounded, and at that moment it was like music. A redemption aria. Orthus One's head came apart, spraying Bishop in white android blood.

Both bodies of his enemy fell to the ground.

Chest heaving, the marine woman—Lee—stood not six feet away. Her mouth was set, and her eyes burned like incendiaries.

"Thank you," Bishop said. "For saving my life."

She looked from the bodies to him. "Likewise."

There was a primal screech far in the distance, loud enough that even Lee heard it. She turned her head at the sound, then looked back at Bishop.

"But I haven't saved shit yet, mate. Let's get out of here."

75

"Gotta say," Lee said to Bishop, "for a bunch of pacifists, your mob do an awful lot of killing."

The big man, a smart-gunner with a bent nose, was called Cortazar. He grunted agreement. He'd recovered from the shock stick, as had the red-haired sergeant, Hettrick. They were watching Bishop work. He'd removed the fourth marine's armor—Colby—and was treating his wound. It was at the base of his neck, just above the rim of his armor. Deep. Colby winced in pain.

"I am not a combat model," Bishop said. "The circumstances were unique."

"Not a combat model," Lee said to Cortazar. "Wielded his sword like a samurai."

Bishop sprayed the wound with a medical sealant, from the kit the marines had brought.

"And Orthus," Bishop said, feeling the need to explain.

"I do not blame them. Their nature came from the sick mind of their creator."

"And *your* creator," Cortazar said.

Bishop finished treating the wound, helped Colby back into his armor. He rocked back on his knees. They did not trust him.

"Yes," Bishop said to Cortazar. "I fear I carry his taint within me."

The big man and Lee glanced at each other.

"We got to worry about you, mate?" the woman asked.

"No."

"No?"

"No," Bishop said. "Whatever else happens today. I am with you. To the end. I am a marine, by choice. It is the only place I ever found meaning. It was the only place I was ever treated as an equal. I will stand with you to the last."

The woman raised an eyebrow at that. The big gunner grunted, and Bishop could not tell whether they believed him or not.

"Let's get out of here," Sergeant Hettrick said. "Those things will be here soon." His voice was thin, pleading. Bishop found it strange that he was asking the two marines, rather than telling. He was their senior.

"Let's do it," Lee said. She tapped the mic near the collar of her armor. "Still there, Miller?"

"*Sure am,*" a voice crackled in reply.

"ETA ten minutes," she said, looking at Bishop. "We got the package."

"Roger."

"Take him," Cortazar said to Hettrick. Cortazar hefted his smart gun, swung it to a ready position. The sergeant helped a groaning Corporal Colby to his feet. The gunner pressed the release for his visor, at the back of his armored collar. The bubble helmet snapped closed. The other two did the same. Cortazar led them out.

In the distance, beyond the range of human hearing, was a screech, wild, filled with rage. A Xenomorph was out hunting. Bishop felt that strange feeling come over him, again. Recurring, familiar now. Lee made to leave when Bishop stopped her.

"Private."

The woman turned back to face him. She didn't look angry, or impatient. She simply looked like a person who didn't have time for foolishness. Yet he had to tell her. Someone. After a moment of hesitation, he spoke.

"I believe I'm malfunctioning."

"Why?" Her eyes flicked over him. "How?"

"There is a pain in my chest. My hands have started to shake." He showed her, the slight tremor in them. Her gaze rested briefly on them, then went back to his face.

"That's called fear, Bishop."

"It is?"

"Yeah. Every marine here carries it around in their heart. You said your old squad treated you as an equal?"

"Some of them. Yes."

"So is that what you want, mate? To feel human? To be like us?"

"More than anything."

She indicated his hand with her chin. "Then welcome to the club."

Bishop found himself smiling, despite everything.

"And you want to be a marine?"

"Yes," Bishop said, firmly.

"Then shut the fuck up and follow me."

76

The rest of the marines waited in the outer corridor, Cortazar on point. He was about to exit Michael's quarters, out where Bishop had never set foot.

"Wait," he said.

The marines turned to look at him. He blinked, setting his internal comms to the Colonial Marine channel. They all had their visors down now, and their voices came through on Bishop's internal com.

"Michael had another prisoner."

"Who?" Lee asked.

"Robert Morse. He was the sole survivor of Fiorina One-Six-One. Well, except for me."

"He was a prisoner on Fury?"

"Yes."

"Fuck him," Cortazar said.

"He has valuable information on the Xenomorph," Bishop said. "Michael had been torturing him for it."

Lee swore. *"Far?"*

"Just here." Bishop indicated the scratched steel door, standing a few meters away. It was ajar, but only a couple of inches.

"We don't have time for this," Hettrick hissed. He was standing next to Corporal Colby, who was unsteady on his feet. The corporal looked around blankly, as though not quite sure where he was. Private Lee looked to Cortazar, who gave her an expression Bishop couldn't read.

She turned to him. *"Hurry."*

Bishop ran to the door and pulled. The metal groaned, complaining, and then screeched as he yanked it wide. He ducked his head in. There was no movement in the red gloom of the room.

"Morse," Bishop said. "I can hear you breathing."

The prisoner popped up from behind one of the crates. In one hand, the gleam of a blade. In the other, his notebook.

"Bruvva," Morse said. "You're alive."

"Just."

"We going?"

"We are."

"Lovely," Morse said, grinning madly. He strutted over and past. Outside, he said, "Ah! The Colonial Marines, here to save the day. Honored to make your acquaintance." Morse gave them an exaggerated bow.

The marines looked him up and down, seeming unimpressed.

"He's your baggage," Cortazar said to Bishop, and he slipped through the exit. Lee followed, Colby and Hettrick close behind.

"Bunch of pricks," Morse whispered.

"They rescued you," Bishop replied.

"That remains to be seen, mate."

They came to the intersection with three dead Chinese. Morse immediately bent over one, pulling off equipment.

"What are you doing?" Bishop asked.

"Air's getting thin." Morse showed him a facemask, and a small belt-fastening oxygen tank. Bishop checked his internal readout. The man was right. Oxygen levels were dropping. Either the atmosphere processor of the vessel was offline, or they had so many hull breaches it simply couldn't keep up.

Morse snapped on the mask and reached for one of the soldier's guns.

"Don't even think about it." Lee was looking down at him.

Morse rolled his eyes.

Bishop sniffed the air. He caught the scent of something. Something that had passed here, not thirty minutes before.

"Wait," he said. Lee was still standing nearby. Cortazar, Colby, and Hettrick were farther down the corridor. They stopped.

"What now?" Hettrick asked sharply.

"Michael went down this way," Bishop said to Lee.

"And we ain't, mate, let's keep moving." She made to move,

he put a hand on her arm. He felt a pressure building inside. An urgency.

"I have to find him."

"Bullshit you do."

"I must leave you now."

"What about your big fucking speech about standing with us until the end?"

"This isn't the end," said Bishop, and he meant it. "I will not be long, I promise. I am fast. The Xenomorphs should not be interested in me, unless I get in their way."

Lee shook her head. *"Fuck Michael Bishop."*

"I'm sorry," Bishop said. "I don't have a choice."

"Why not?"

"He's my father."

Lee said nothing to that. No one did. Cortazar turned his attention to the long corridor, smart gun swinging back and forth.

"A lot of good marines died for you, Bishop," Lee said. *"Sacrifice upon sacrifice. We lose you now, it'll all be for nothing."*

"You won't lose me."

Lee sighed. *"Apone will blow us out an airlock if he hears we had Bishop, then let him go walkabout."*

"At minimum," Cortazar said.

"I guess we got this dickhead," she said, pointing to Morse. *"Maybe he's worth something."*

"Too bloody right I am," Morse said, holding aloft his notebook. "A draft of the finest novel of the twenty-second century, here, right in my hand. *Space Beast.*"

Cortazar looked from him to Lee. *"We're fucked."*

She turned to Bishop, forefinger pointed. *"Ten minutes, Bishop. The right rear hangar. We are leaving. You* be *there."*

"I will."

She reached out and grabbed the dog tags around his neck. She surrounded the tags with her fist.

"That's an order, marine."

The pressure building inside him, at the thought of Michael, eased for a moment. He felt a smile trying to work its way onto his face.

"Trust me," he said.

PRIVATE KARRI LEE

77

Fuck fuck fuck. What had she been thinking, letting Bishop go?

They moved through the wide corridors, Cortazar on point, Colby, Hettrick, and Morse in the middle, and Karri taking the rear. Made it across the width of the ship, the same way they'd come. Still no encounters. The only real difference was the atmosphere, which was thinning. A warning on the inside of her helmet telling her the oxygen levels were low.

Shouldn't have let him go, but there was something in his eyes that made her trust him. Karri couldn't see any dishonesty in his face. In fact, what she saw was quite the opposite. Innocence, like that of a child.

Fuck. Try telling that to Apone.

Well, Captain, I had a good feeling about him.

They turned into a long, undamaged corridor. This was the home stretch, except something had changed since they passed by the last time. The blast door. Cortazar swore.

"*No no no*," Hettrick said, jabbing at the control panel. It didn't open.

"I got it," Karri said. She moved to the door, letting her pulse rifle hang from its shoulder strap, and drew her field kit out from the pouch at her belt. She set to work unscrewing the panel.

"*Hurry*," Hettrick whispered, his voice breaking, urgent.

"*Calm down*," Cortazar said, smart gun trained back down the direction they'd just come.

"*Don't fucking tell me to be calm*," Hettrick said. "*This ship is a death trap*."

Cortazar said nothing to that, and Karri ignored him. Hettrick had been tense in the dropship, but they all had been. Everyone knew the mission was borderline suicidal. Everyone felt the same fear, down in their bellies.

But something had broken in Hettrick, after the encounter with the synthetic twins, and broken the wrong way. When the tension burst, and the mission proper began, that was when hours and hours of training were meant to kick in. Like muscle memory in martial arts, there was combat memory for battle.

"Do you hear that?" Morse asked. His voice was muffled through his breathing mask and the glass of her visor, but he was standing close enough for her to hear.

"No," Karri said. She made the bypass, and the door

slid open. As it did, a screech, long and bestial, echoed down the corridor. Karri swallowed, involuntarily.

"How about that?"

They all turned to look back the way they had come. High in the corridor, about thirty meters down, near the ceiling, a panel fell open with a *clang*. A shadow came tumbling out, sprawling against the hard walkway below. Karri unshouldered her weapon.

It was a girl, wide-eyed in pure unblinking terror, looking around, frantic. She saw them, jerked to her feet, and ran.

Something bigger dropped from the same access tunnel from which the girl had fallen. Something far bigger and more graceful. The shadow unfurled into a gleaming, drooling, sightless nightmare.

"Out of the way!" Cortazar bellowed. The girl was right in his line of fire. Karri dropped to one knee, pulse rifle at her shoulder. Nearby, she heard something hit the floor with a heavy thud.

"Fuckin' hell," Morse said.

Karri fired. Short, controlled bursts, the pulse gun kicking, but the girl made the angle of the shot difficult. The black beast was right behind her and getting closer.

"Down, girl," Cortazar yelled. *"Down!"*

Too panicked, mouth open in a silent scream, the girl ran right at Cortazar. The Xenomorph loped up behind her, rising. Karri fired another burst, and the nightmare screamed and sprawled, tumbling over itself. The corridor hissed where the alien bled, but it was only a leg shot and it righted itself, launching itself again toward the girl.

Karri gritted her teeth and fired.

The next part happened so fast.

She hit the Xenomorph, center mass, with a sustained burst. It broke apart, spraying the air with blood and mesoskeleton. Cortazar enfolded the girl in his arms and turned, shielding her with his body. His armor began smoldering, and he bellowed. Karri dropped her pulse rifle and tried to strip off his armor, yanking at his shoulder clips, but Cortazar's smart-gun rig was tangled up and so he pushed the girl away and tore at the gun's catches.

"Another fucker!" Morse yelled. "Another little fucker!"

The prisoner was firing a service pistol, yelling, gleeful, as Karri pulled away Cortazar's armor. Underneath, his compression suit was smoking, holed. Cortazar roared like a bear as the wicked alien blood marked his skin.

Karri spun again, reaching for her pulse rifle as a second Xenomorph loomed. Morse was laughing, firing a gun he'd gotten from who knows where—*pop pop pop*—and she ducked at the last second. It flashed over her and someone behind her cried out. She twisted on the ground, bringing up her pulse rifle.

"What the fuck?" The monster was gone.

"Down the side corridor," Morse said. "The space beast, and taken one of youse with it."

She looked around, trying to take stock of her

surroundings. Colby was gone. As was Hettrick. "It took both of them?"

"Nah. The ginger scaredy one, Hettrick—he ran. Like the rabbit who sees the wolf."

Cortazar was coughing, groaning. The incessant acid hissing continued, the body of the Xenomorph sinking into the floor. She swept the corridor with her rifle, but no more aliens appeared.

"Hettrick," Karri said into her mic. "Hettrick, come back here. The threat has been neutralized. Over."

Nothing came back over the com but static. *Sssssssss.*

"Hettrick, you motherfucker, come back here."

Sssssssss.

"Coward!"

The girl had pulled something metallic out of a pouch at her belt, and was leaning over Cortazar with it. A needle. "Stop," Karri yelled, reaching out and snatching the girl's wrist.

Not a girl, she could see as she looked into her eyes. A woman. Small, young, but a woman. She said something in a language Karri didn't know. The woman spoke again, eyes wide, shining, honest.

Honest. Fucking hell, Karri. She was a marine, she was an Aussie, and yet here she was, operating based on *feelings*. What next? Light a scented candle? Put a flower in her hair? *FUCK.* Karri grabbed at the woman's pouch and looked inside. Bandages, syringes, ampoules. Medic. The woman was a medic. *Alleluia.*

"I'm watching," Karri said, jabbing her finger at the young woman. She indicated for her to proceed, and the girl did, jabbing Cortazar. The big man, who'd been twitching and moaning, stopped doing both. Wisps of smoke still rose from his back, but they were nearly gone now.

What was left was a mess. Not much blood had kissed him, but even that was devastating. A fingertip-sized hole exposed his spine. His lower back pitted, the top of an ear missing. Karri turned on the external speaker for her helmet.

"Can you walk, Cortazar?"

He moaned, and couldn't answer. He was lying face down on the floor, the woman spraying a sealant on his back. Cortazar didn't have a helmet anymore. Specked with holes, like his suit and his back.

There was a pop and groan of metal behind, and she turned to see the remains of the Xenomorph torso fall through the deck. It'd made a big fucking hole.

"We have to move," Karri said to the woman.

The girl looked up at her, irritated, and pulled a black square from her top pocket, flipping it open. She fiddled with the controls and spoke in her language. A second later, the little black square warbled.

"Elder Sister, I have to treat him. He'll die otherwise."

Karri indicated the hole. "We're running out of air. If that burns through the hull, we'll have even less."

The woman glanced back, then down at Cortazar. She spoke again.

"Carefully. Which way?"

Karri thought. The dropship was still a hundred meters distant, through several turns and doors. No telling how many had closed since they came past, and the Xenomorph had headed in that direction. The other way, just down the corridor and to the right, maybe thirty meters away, were the escape pods. Karri had seen them on the schematic. She pointed in that direction.

The girl nodded.

"Help me, Morse," Karri said.

"That ugly bastard's too heavy. Reckon we move on without him." His eyes were bright and wide as he talked. Karri stood and walked over to him.

"You will carry him, convict," she said, her voice tighter than a coiled steel spring. She pressed the barrel of her pulse rifle to his chest. The expression on Morse's face fell away.

"Yeah, of course. Just mucking about."

She held out her hand.

He glanced at it, eyes popping as he took her meaning. Karri insisted.

He slapped the pistol in her palm. "Fucking stupid."

"You'll need both your hands for Cortazar," she replied. "He's a heavy bastard."

SERGEANT MAX HETTRICK

78

They could call Max Hettrick many things, but they couldn't call him dumb. He was going to live, where the rest of his company were dead, or close to it. Sure, he'd get a few dirty looks from any survivors back on the *Il Conde*. If there *were* any survivors. And sure, that dirty Australian refugee bitch, Lee, had dared to call him a coward—but what he *really* was, was smart.

Hettrick squeezed through a near-closed blast door, moving into the wide corridor beyond. A little red icon on the inside glass of his bubble helmet told him the atmosphere was nearly gone in this section. Which was fine, he had plenty of oxygen. Good, even, as it would reduce the likelihood of Chinese troops—or those Xenomorphs—being anywhere nearby.

Max felt a tightness in his chest at the thought of the alien. That speed, that lethality, the relentlessness.

Holier-than-thou Apone would be dead. The remaining

marines would be tight-mouthed in their complicity in this failure. There'd be an inquiry, for certain, into such a catastrophic mission. Explanations would be demanded, witnesses called.

He smiled.

Sergeant Max Hettrick was more than ready for his star turn on the stand. Lot of facts could change, up there. His concerns about the mission, raised to Apone, would suddenly be on record, with no one to contradict. His personal doubts about Apone's judgment, a man who seemed more intent on avenging his brother than thinking rationally about their goals.

He took stock of his surroundings. Second on the left, then twenty-five more meters, and he was at the hangar. Sentry guns to cover him on the way in. He was going to make it. He started toward the intersection when he heard the bootfalls. Faint, so very faint in the thin atmosphere, but they were there.

Max ducked into the nearest doorway. The lights were flickering between red and nothing, but in that split second he glimpsed rows of steel tables and benches. A mess hall. He set himself inside the door, pulse rifle raised, so he could see their backs as they passed, headed the way he had come. Max grinned, teeth clenched. Maybe they'd run into Karri and Cortazar. Take care of his last two problems.

They passed in a straggling line. Chinese. Some in armor and helmets, most without. Those without shared oxygen masks, a few seemed to be injured. A pale-faced officer. They looked around—fear in their eyes—at every corridor, every shadow. One seemed to look right at him and he ducked back, behind the wall.

Hettrick kept his breathing steady, and counted to thirty, slowly, gun pointed at the entrance. The lights flicked on and off, on and off. A pipe hissed. The sound of boots faded. Hettrick let himself breathe.

The pipe hissed again. Hettrick paused.

Is that a pipe? Or…?

He cried out in pain as something struck his shoulder, like a punch. His pulse rifle clattered to the floor. Open mouthed, unbelieving, he stared at the blade sticking from his shoulder. *Someone had stabbed him from behind.*

Not a blade. Curved, black, it looked almost like ceramic. Skeletal.

Hettrick opened his mouth to scream, but a glistening clawed hand wrapped itself around his face.

BISHOP

79

Bishop flew down red-bathed corridors, following the scent. A synthetic's nose was about half as sensitive as that of a dog. Which was to say, about five thousand times more than a human. Once he could identify the pheromone scent, he could track—and he knew this scent so very well.

He raced, and with every stride, Bishop considered going back. *They came for me*. His mind had turned and turned on this question ever since he had been reactivated. Whether those old connections had ever truly meant anything. Whether it was all an illusion of equality, a confusion caused by his inadequate capacity to comprehend human nature. And he had it, finally. The strongest evidence yet that it was real.

Yet he'd turned around and deserted them.

He'd also told the truth. Michael was his father. He might be capricious and duplicitous. He might be self-serving and even self-obsessed, but a father is a father is a father. Logic couldn't pull him away from this chant inside his mind, this compulsion that sent his limbs pumping and his body flinging down steel and titanium corridors.

Bishop came to a corridor with two massive, vault-like doors. The one on his right was closed. He was sure this led into the huge cylinder that contained the labs and the specimen rooms for the Xenomorphs. If he could enter that huge round door to his right, and continue on, he'd end up back in Michael's quarters.

Then the vault on the left had his attention. For one, it was open. For two, the pheromone scent trailed into it, and something foul wafted out. For three, he heard his master's voice. The words, however, were madness.

"I am your Queen. Obey me. Obey Me!"

Bishop slowed, entered the vault smoothly. No sudden movements. The katana was sheathed and gripped in his left hand. His palm pressed against the cool wood and its intricate engravings.

A warning light flashed faintly on his retina. Low atmosphere. Prolonged exposure could be dangerous to a synthetic body. He didn't have long.

One more stride, and Bishop froze. Ovomorphs. Dozens. More. More than a hundred. On the floor, on the walls of the huge cylinder. Some even stuck to the roof. The air was cloyingly thick with their scent, sulfureous, rotten. Somewhere between swamp water and a dead body.

The ambient temperature of the room was lower than

the corridor outside, and Bishop suspected that everything inside had been kept frozen. In hibernation until the Chinese wanted them thawed out, but that cooling system must have failed in the Marine attack.

Two Xenomorphs crouched in the shadows, among the eggs. It took Bishop a few seconds to locate them. They made no sound, remained perfectly still. A patient and watchful guard, ready to ambush unwanted intruders. He reminded himself that in their primal calculations, he was just a machine. A thing to be ignored until it posed a problem.

Bishop moved slowly, careful not to nudge an Ovomorph with his foot. The containment section was nearly fifty meters long, and farther in it glistened. Secreted resin coated the walls, the ceiling. Dripping. They'd been busy. In so short a time, the space had been transformed and—

There. They were there. Seven of the Ovomorphs, their fleshy petals in bloom. Against the wall, encased in the resin, eight bodies. Hidden from view at the entrance, visible now. A split-second glance revealed five Chinese, one marine, a black-clad Caucasian male, and Michael Bishop. Michael was the only one without a face-hugger attached. There was a Xenomorph above him, watching.

"I am your Queen! Release me!" He was yelling at no one in particular. Face contorted by pain and anger. His voice husky. He didn't notice Bishop until the synthetic was a few feet away.

"You," he said, startled. "My son. You came." First

startled, and then self-assured. "Of course you did. Of course." At the edge of hearing, the sound of the creature above him, shifting fractionally.

Michael was wounded. There was a gash across his shoulder, a smear of blood on his forehead. His face shone with the resin and with his madness. One arm was trapped against his body, the other up, near his head. That hand was free.

"They are confused," Michael said, "but not for long. Soon they will recognize me as their Queen. Once they do, I will control this vessel and all in it. At that moment they will all *bow to me*."

"They are confused," Bishop replied softly. "But they know something is wrong. That's why they wounded you and set you here. The Xenomorphs are smarter than this single scent, more cunning. All the pheromone drop has done, Michael, is stall the Ovomorph. It doesn't recognize you as a viable host. Not yet, anyway."

Michael looked confused. "Not yet?"

"It will fade—a few hours at most—and you will be impregnated."

"No," Michael said. His eyes were bloodshot. It was clear he was having some trouble breathing. "No."

"Who will bow to you, Michael?"

"What?"

"You said all would bow to you."

He gasped for breath. "All of them. The Company. The United Americas. The Chinese. All of them."

"Is that what you sought all along?" Bishop asked, still softly. Michael wasn't listening.

"If I am to be immortal, I will need an army."

Bishop felt pity for him then, and shame for himself. He could name those emotions now, though new and unfamiliar. He thought back on all the obvious lies Michael had told him, and felt shame in his own credulity.

Turning his attention, he looked at the others who were trapped. The face-huggers had their spidery skeletal fingers wrapped around their faces. The little pale sacks aside each pale body, like lungs, breathing for the victim. Soon they would fall away and the hosts might enjoy a few hours of cruel hope, before the abomination emerged.

Bishop tightened his grip on the katana. The right thing to do would be to put them all to the blade, but at the same moment he thought it, he knew it was an act he simply was not capable of performing. Michael may have taken away his protection protocols, but Bishop still felt them, and intensely.

He had to do something. It was wrong, to leave them like this. He glanced around the room, this nursery of horror.

There *was* something he could do, right now, to honor those protocols. There were marines who still needed to evacuate, as well as the Chinese staff—people who bore no responsibility in what had occurred on this vessel. Without his assistance, more of them would perish.

As for his father, Bishop could attempt to rescue him—an almost certainly futile action—or…

"I am leaving, Michael," he whispered. His creator's destiny was a certainty of his own design, his *programming*. There was nothing Bishop could do to change that. The black sentinel perched overhead was merely the exclamation point.

"What?"

"Leaving. I came here to see you, not knowing what I wanted, or what I was going to do. To save you or to kill you."

"Kill me?" A flash of clarity shone in his bloodshot eyes. "You could never do such a thing."

"No," Bishop admitted. "No, but I can't save you, either."

"Save? *Save*." Michael's expression changed to a sneer. "I don't need saving. Especially by one so *meagre* as you. You are but a copy of a copy of a copy."

At that moment Bishop felt doubt, so acute that it was a type of pain. A doubt on which he had stumbled over and again, in his past life, and in his current one. Michael knew how to play the strings of this self-doubt. He was a virtuoso.

"You're so faded, Bishop, so insubstantial, I can barely see you anymore," Michael said. "You're a ghost. Leave me." At that he closed his eyes. His chest rose and fell, sharply, his breathing shallow.

Bishop raised his hand, wanting to touch this man just once more, before the end. He let it drop. He'd had to come here, but it was a mistake to do so. Both things were true, but now he had to leave. Ghost or bodied. Being or simulacra. These were just words and words did not matter, right now. What mattered was action, and the effect of those actions on reality.

Bishop turned and ran, leaving the hisses of the Xenomorph in his wake.

PRIVATE KARRI LEE

80

They had to rest. Morse's breathing was shallow, as was Cortazar's and the woman's. The trio were sharing the oxygen mask Morse had stolen, taking turns. The air was thinning further, little oxygen bars on Karri's display showing the atmosphere outside her helmet. It was dropping. Morse complained of dizziness, Cortazar fluttered in and out of consciousness.

So they rested while Karri stood watch. She scanned the passage ahead. The escape pods were meant to be there, but instead it was a long outer corridor. Portals on the right, looking out into deep space, a couple of corridors heading to the left. Nothing resembling an escape pod. She swore.

The passageway was at least fifty meters long. She doubted they'd be able to carry Cortazar to the end of it, not without air.

Karri ran her eyes over the young woman. She wore a

uniform—if you could call it that—one Karri hadn't seen before. It was worn and stained—with sweat, with blood. The woman walked with a noticeable limp, wearing boots that looked way too large. She had a pistol shoved into her belt that probably wasn't hers, either. When she wasn't working on Cortazar, she had a vacant look in her eyes. Distant.

Touching her on the shoulder, Karri pointed to the translator. The woman looked at her blankly for a moment, then flipped it open.

"Karri," she said, pointing to herself.

"Xuan," the young woman replied.

"You're not Chinese, are you?" she asked.

"No," the woman snapped, life coming into her voice. *"Vietnamese."*

"You don't like being called Chinese?"

"Would you?" Xuan asked, still angry.

Karri couldn't help but smile at that. She shook her head, then waited until Xuan had her turn with the oxygen mask before continuing.

"How did you end up here?"

"The Chinese captured us," the woman replied, then paused. Her voice had gone quiet. Soft, even. She stared into space, and Karri wasn't sure if she'd stopped speaking. She was about to prompt her when the younger woman continued.

"We were a smuggler ship—that's the risk you take. The UPP military sometimes boards, demands a bribe, and then leaves. So

long as the contraband isn't too objectionable. Or valuable." She sighed through her nose. *"They put us in a room. The whole crew. In the room there were these… eggs. They— they opened, and these giant white spiders, they—"*

She covered her face with shaking hands.

Morse and Cortazar were both listening, grim-faced. Cortazar was pale, but he was coherent now. He put a hand on Xuan's shoulder, and she let him.

"What were you smuggling?" Karri asked. It was a dumb question, but she reckoned maybe it was time to shift the subject. The woman lowered her hands and let out a long breath.

"Weapons."

Morse raised his eyebrows. "Weapons? Nice."

"To Linna Three-Four-Nine."

Karri's breath caught. She looked to Cortazar, her fists clenching. He looked straight back at her, unreadable.

"Linna Three-Four-Nine? Ha ha!" Morse said, eyes shining with glee. "That's a Three World Empire planet, and the Aussies set it on fire."

"The Marines were called in to save the day," Cortazar said, still looking at Karri.

"That war's over," Karri replied, and something began building between her and Cortazar. Xuan wasn't looking at either of them, however. Whatever had happened to her, she no longer cared about secrets. Or much at all.

"No," she said simply. *"The Australian revolutionaries have an underground. They will not give up the fight."*

Karri's fists were clenched so tight they hurt. Old memories hurled themselves at her and she wanted to scream. And Cortazar, that motherfucker, if he tried anything, if he said anything against this girl—

"We get out of this?" he said, hand still on the girl's shoulder. "You don't tell no one that."

It took Karri a moment to process what the big gunner was saying, but when she did the scream inside her ebbed. In its place a deep well of grief for her country, and her impotence in doing anything about it. She felt the tears well up, but she blinked them back. She cleared her throat.

"Cortazar's right," she said. "Anyone asks, you're just a cargo medic. Okay?"

The young woman gave a little nod, and maybe that was enough.

"Morse?" Karri said, staring at him.

"I'm no fucking snitch."

"Good." She checked the magazine on her weapon. "Okay. Morse—help Cortazar. We're moving."

Swearing, grunting, Morse helped Cortazar to his feet. The marine had a pulse rifle clutched in his hand, but Karri wasn't sure if he was going to be able to use it. He was getting paler, his skin filmed with sweat. He clenched his eyes in pain as Morse gave him rough assistance. Xuan, concerned, helped as she could.

They'd made to move when the shouts and gunfire started, back from the direction they'd come. Orange muzzle flashes, people running, some falling, trying to get back to their feet. Black malignant shadows unfolding around them. Fear quailed in Karri's heart.

"Keep moving," she said to Morse. "Get him to the escape pods."

Morse, seeing what was coming, simply nodded, no jokes, and the three of them limped away.

Karri Lee turned to face the monsters.

SU WONG

81

The commander now had responsibility for fifteen survivors. Pushed, cajoled, forced them on, promising salvation first, and vengeance second. But desire had only so much traction against the laws of physics, words only so much power in the face of monstrosity. The air was thin and thinning, and they did not have enough oxygen masks to go around. Five of their number had been injured by explosions. The path to the drop-port was blocked by blast doors.

And then there was the black demon. A hunter, fast and lethal. The first time it struck, they barely understood what had happened. There'd been a scream and one of their number—Wu, a petty officer in maintenance; heavy smoker, bad lungs, falling behind the group—had gone. Vanished, into thin air, and maybe they could believe he'd just wandered off and gotten lost.

Until the second strike. They were resting in a long

corridor, the first they'd found in a while without a railgun hole in it. One of the survivors had collapsed from blood loss or lack of oxygen, and they were working on getting him conscious.

A maintenance panel near the ceiling popped open, and a black shadow lunged out, picked up a young man—engineering, Su hadn't even learned his name—and with his legs thrashing, he'd been pulled back into the tunnel. No one even had time to fire a shot. They stared at the open panel, and then at Su. She pointed to the man on the ground.

"Pick him up. No more stopping."

Seventeen had become fifteen and Su could no longer push on to the drop-port. The safety of her crew was her one responsibility now. Saving those who were left. So she turned them around and headed for the escape pods.

Alert now, three soldiers in full battle armor and breathing masks, the rest all armed with pistols and assault rifles, if they could carry them. Su stalked the corridors in the lead, a soldier by her side, weapons pressed to their shoulders. They were coming to an intersection where a support beam had fallen. They just had to turn here, and it was a straight shot to the escape pods. But those creatures. Those cursed creatures.

They attacked from the rear. Screams, shots fired, panic. Some of her crew running right past her, fear overcoming discipline. Chaos overwhelming order. A primal scream, and a shadow rose up from Su's right, through an open door. She fired, the orange bloom of her weapon illuminating the creature and its cruel and perfect lines, and it disappeared to one side.

Another scream, farther down the corridor.

"Move and fire. Keep your minds. Move and fire."

The group, incoherent, straggling but still moving, made it around the corridor. Still there were shouts from those at the rear, more gunfire, but she could not see the demon. Just hear its angry, bitter screeching. Su walked backward, fast, rifle to her shoulder.

There was a yell behind her. Right behind. She turned to see one of her soldiers pinned under the black demon. From where it had emerged, she knew not. The soldier—Corporal Tang—had his weapon crossways across his chest, trying to stop the blind head of the beast from getting too close.

Someone behind her screamed. She aimed her weapon at the demon, but it was dashed from her hands. The alien's tail, poised like a scorpion's, had struck her weapon and now lashed out at her again. She ducked, the bladed tail snapping overhead.

Another burst of fire, sustained, in the distance. The creature near her screeched and Su, pressed against the wall, saw it shudder—part of its black carapace shattered and flipped from its body. Corporal Tang began howling. Hands still up, still trying to hold his rifle, but they were melting, dissolving. The creature screeched and thrashed on the ground, trying to right itself, its tail knocking over the person next to Su, a smattering of points on the wall around her starting to smoke.

Picking up her weapon from the ground, face set, she fired. The beast stopped moving, the corridor was filled with acrid smoke, and her people gasping with tears and fear.

"Move," Su said. "Keep moving." She grabbed the nearest soldier and pushed him forward, and her underlings all soon followed. She joined them, stepping over the points where acid melted steel, over the body of Tang, who screamed no longer. Su made her way to the front.

Ahead was a woman. The woman who'd done the shooting that had killed Corporal Tang. A *marine* woman. Su felt the heat of anger rising in her chest. All this was caused by them. The Americans. The carnage, the chaos, the destruction of this pristine vessel. Beyond the woman, farther down the corridor, three more people, moving slowly. One looked familiar.

Su shouted a question, asking whether the rear was now clear, and a soldier answered saying he thought so. They kept moving. The marine woman, ahead, had one hand off her pulse rifle, trying to show she wasn't a threat.

Little too late for that, Su thought.

"Put down your weapon," Su said, sharply. She pointed her gun at the marine. The woman held up a finger, and withdrew a black square from her pocket. A translator. Su couldn't be sure, but it looked familiar. Her translator.

The woman spoke, and the machine in her hand spoke.

"Lower your gun."

"No," Su said.

"I'm not the enemy here." If the woman was scared of having a weapon pointed at her face, she wasn't showing it. Su's people kept moving past her, toward the pods.

"I beg to differ," Su said. She indicated the ship with a tilt of her head. "This is your doing."

"Maybe," the woman said. *"Or maybe you brought this down on yourselves when you used that Vietnamese crew as a sick little experiment."*

That made Su pause. "No. It happened when you struck at us like bandits, from the shadows." She said it angrily, but her heart wasn't in it.

The woman still seemed unflustered. Just a private, judging from the insignia on her shoulder. White scar on her forehead. A shining toughness in her eyes.

"Not much in the mood for debating. Why don't we call it a truce until we hit the escape pods. You don't shoot up me or my mates, and I don't tell my ship to blow you fuckers out of the sky once you leave."

That gave Su pause. The woman meant it.

"How can I trust you?"

The woman shrugged. *"Not trusting me will certainly get you dead. I guess the other way's the only hope you got."*

Su Wong clenched her jaw. "Then stand by me, Private. We will cover the withdrawal, side by side." Her words came out angry, like a threat, but the young woman just pursed her lips.

"No worries."

The rest of her crew were beyond them now. It was just Su and the woman.

"Lee," the marine said.

After a pause, Su replied, "Wong."

Lee faced down the corridor, rifle raised, and started moving backward. Su did the same. In the distance, the demonic screeches of the alien echoed.

CAPTAIN MARCEL APONE

82

His eyes flicked open. Not dead. Not yet.

A warning light blinked on the inside of his polycarbonate glass bubble helm. He was in hard vacuum. *How?* He took a moment. He was curled into a ball, staring at the scarred wall of a ship's bridge. A Chinese ship. He'd ordered a breaching action. May Jesus forgive him. They'd been overrun by Xenomorphs. He'd thrown high explosives at one of the hissing beasts, in a compartment already breached by acid.

In the movies, a myth persisted that a breach in the hull resulted in crew getting pulled out by continual hurricane-force winds. In reality, the air pressure inside the ship *pushed* toward the hole. A small hole didn't do much. The air trickled toward it. A large, sudden hole, and yes, for a few seconds the air would burst from the compartment.

So why was he still on the bridge?

He tried to shift, to look over the forward station. His

back was touching it. Tried to move, but couldn't. He looked down and saw the green lights of his mag boots, pressed into the vertical metal of the forward station. He had no memory of activating them. Air pressure needed surface area to push on, so perhaps he had activated his mag boots and hugged his knees.

"This is Apone," he whispered into his comm. "Anyone read me?"

He was answered with static. He tried a second time, with the same result. He detached his boots from the hull, stood slowly… and swore.

The bridge was gone. The space between the forward console and the entryway to the bridge—about ten meters across—was gone. The floor, anyway. Blown up and pushed out into space. It was silent, here. Just his breathing, into his helmet. Part of the corridor leading out of the bridge was missing, as well. As were his men. The Chinese defenders. And the alien.

The Xenomorph.

Apone checked his belt. The holster was empty. All he had was his combat knife. He looked again at the bridge, at the shadows on the ceiling, the shattered corridor. Nothing, he couldn't see anything.

He checked his oxygen. Ninety percent. Just needed to get himself out of this vessel, send a long-range message to the *Il Conde*. Have Ransome send Private Weeks out in the skiff and pick him up. His grip on the console tightened. He hoped they had Bishop. If Apone was the only survivor, he'd be kicked out of the Corps, and deservedly so. In fact, they wouldn't have to kick him out. Apone would leave.

First, he had to get off the ship. The hull would block his beacon and his comms. He maneuvered himself carefully over the console. The artificial gravity was still working on one side, but somehow not on the other. Never understood how that damn tech worked. He climbed downward, over torn hull and its insides, hand over hand until his head was poking out the bottom of the hull. He grabbed a floating fiber-optic cable that snaked out of the ruined layers, pushed off, and used the cable to turn in space and end, upside down, on the bottom of the hull. Reactivated, his boots clunked into place.

Apone reoriented himself. *Not upside down,* he told his brain. *Standing upright*. He checked his wrist display, made sure his transponder was still activated. It was. The *Il Conde* would be out of detection range at the moment—if Ransome were following his orders, anyway.

He typed in the command for long-range comms. He'd cleared his throat to give the order when something struck him in the chest. Something heavy and big, and he hadn't even seen it coming.

The air went out of his lungs and he flipped through space, the ship revolving in and out of vision. His hand brushed the hull in passing. Apone gritted his teeth and caught the surface with his feet halfway around. His mag boots snicked and rooted him on the hull. He rocked back, then straightened himself, eyes all around, hand going to the knife at his belt.

All this and he still couldn't breathe, wheezing. The hull of the vessel wasn't lighted, just gleamed oh-so-pale underfoot. It was defined by its negative space, the stars above him, the black hull underneath. He scanned the black horizon for the thing that had struck him. His lizard brain twisted in fear, but Apone tamped down on it. Raised his hands.

Movement, to his left. He turned, the smooth cylindrical skull of the Xenomorph loomed, and he stabbed at it. His knife jarred and twisted in his hand and the beast clubbed him across the helmet.

The blow rocked him back, one of his feet detached. He grunted, his breathing ragged and loud in his ears. The creature pinned him against the hull. Its claws pressing into him, distantly he feared a puncture to his compression suit, but that fear was far away, another galaxy away.

His mind recoiled at what it was seeing. Close enough that the internal light of his helmet revealed the face of the beast. Its blind phallic head, its dripping maw. It turned this way and that, as though it were studying him.

Apone froze.

Right up until it opened its jaw and a second, smaller jaw shot out like a piston and struck his visor. *Thunk.* The helmet was bulletproof, sufficient to deflect fire from a pistol, and he'd twisted his head at the last moment, making the blow a glancing one. Still, an inch-long crack appeared on the bubble.

Thunk.

Second strike. The crack lengthened, branched. Apone brought up his hand, anticipating. Nothing else in the Middle Heavens existed at that moment. No other thoughts, no history no future no ship no company no mission no nothing but the double jaws in front of him. Tunnel vision on that thing and one thing only. Its thin lips quavered, its mouth widened, drool glistening on its teeth.

It struck, a third time, but Apone brought the blade around, right at the most perfect of moments, and the piston jaw snapped over the carbon steel. Its head rocked backward, like a wolf howling at the moon, and the blade in his hand was dissolving. He let it go as he got his legs under the Xenomorph—while desperately feeling for, and finding, a seam in the ship's armour to grip—and planted his feet on the beast's body.

He pushed, roaring.

"*AAAAAHHHHHHHHHHHHHHHHHH.*"

It detached, but its thrashing tail had one more strike and instinct had his hands up. He gasped in pain—

—and then grinned. The faint light of the stars showed the Xenomorph spinning off into space, limbs and tail flailing in rage, pure rage, as it disappeared into the cold hard merciless embrace of the vacuum.

"That," Apone grunted, "was for my brother."

PRIVATE KARRI LEE

83

When the Xenomorph screeched, she could never quite pinpoint where it was. Seemed to be coming from all around, all at once. Which was probably just Karri's imagination. Or, to be more precise, her fear. Didn't help that this fucking ship had maintenance tunnels all over the place, hatches high up on the walls, ladders underneath. These black bastards could pop out wherever they wanted, an all-you-can-eat buffet of Americans and Chinese.

The Chinese officer next to her—Wong—said nothing. Just moved quickly, efficiently, her pale face locked in *don't fuck with me* mode. Karri glanced back. The pods were fifty meters away. The Chinese survivors had nearly finished boarding. Morse, Cortazar, and Xuan were paused halfway there. They were talking.

The Vietnamese woman seemed angry. If the *Xinjiang* were an arrowhead, the escape pods were located about a third of the way down the edge of the blade. As far as

Karri could tell, there was no deck above or below them. Just space. There were ten pods in a row, and beyond them was a blast door, mercifully closed.

So, in theory, they just had the one corridor and two maintenance hatches to watch. As if on cue, there was a screech and Karri's head snapped around. Nothing. Red emergency lights and gloom, but no shadows jumped back and forth at the moment. She thought. She hoped.

When she looked back again Cortazar was walking toward her, and Morse and Xuan were nearly at the steps to the pod. Morse entered, Xuan looked back and yelled something.

Cortazar ignored her. He was shirtless now. His clothes torn away trying to get the acid off him, trying to treat him. He still had his leg armor, at least, heavy boots, a black oxygen mask. As he drew alongside, she could see that his forehead was sheened with sweat, his pupils dilated. The medic had given him something. His torso had several old scars. Knife wounds, a bullet wound. The acid scars on his back. Sprayed with skin sealant, but it looked swollen. He had a tattoo on his chest—intricate inking of a woman with skull-like features.

"Jesus Christ, Cortazar," Karri said, glancing at his wounds.

He looked down at her. "Like what you see?" he asked, grinning.

"Bloody hell, mate." She pointed at Wong. "I wouldn't fuck you with her pussy."

Cortazar threw his head back and laughed, and Wong,

after the translation came through, smiled. First time Karri'd seen her do it.

"*I appreciate that*," Wong said.

Another screech killed the temporary levity and they moved backward as one, fast, guns ready. Then another scream came. A human one. Behind them.

Karri whirled. The blast door, just beyond the escape pods, was open, a dark figure stalking out. *They can open doors?* she thought, absently. Xuan was still on the steps to the pod, staring at it.

Karri unleashed a controlled burst. Explosive-tipped shells sparked and punctured the walls around it, a wall panel began to smoke, and the beast slipped back through the door. Karri pointed at Xuan and shouted.

"Get inside!"

Xuan disappeared into the pod.

Gunfire behind and she whirled again. She couldn't see a target.

"They're probing us," Cortazar said.

Karri was done. "Let's just get the fuck—"

"*Move!*" Wong shouted, facing back toward the escape pods. She opened fire.

Karri twisted to see a black shape bounding along the floor, like a panther. It switched to the wall when Wong started firing, then to the ceiling, then leaping back down to the floor, all smooth and fast, so fast. It bounded past the escape pods and was on them—some carapace flew from it, but it wasn't enough to slow it.

Behind her, Cortazar unleashed in the other direction. Karri fired as the alien leaped, its claws extended in front of it. Bursts of pale yellow exploded from its head and Karri threw herself against Cortazar, trying to knock him out of the way. It was like throwing herself against a wall, but he grunted and moved and the thing tumbled across the steel floor, still alive and screeching, thrashing. Karri pressed herself into the wall, unable to breathe, as its tail lashed around blindly.

Cortazar cried out and Wong was already firing. Not at it, but at others, and Karri tore her eyes away from the closest one, which was already sinking into the surface of the metal. She fired a burst back down the corridor. The black beasts scuttled and slid from view.

A pause to take stock.

The charging Xenomorph had ended past them. It twitched, and in its death there was still vengeance. A warning light blipped on the inside of Karri's helmet as the dead alien disappeared from view. Into the vacuum. What little air was left in the corridor was being pushed out. There'd be hard vacuum in here soon.

"Leave," she yelled at Wong. "The hull is breached."

Wong looked at her over her black mask, her eyes hard and knowing. She nodded and left.

"Let's go, Cortazar," Karri said. The big gunner was sitting, back against the wall, grimacing. There was a maintenance hatch nearby, nearly over his head, and Karri didn't much like standing under it.

"No," he said, voice tight.

"Fuck *no*," she replied. "We are leaving."

"My leg's broke," he said, matter-of-factly. That's when she saw it. His left leg, from the knee down, angled *wrong*. Out to one side. There was blood near his knee. The alien must have hit him with its tail as it died. He picked up his pulse rifle, and maneuvered himself so he could cover the corridor. "Leave."

"I'm not leaving."

"Let it go, Cornbread." He looked up at her. "This is how I'm going out. Gun in my hand."

"No," she said.

He turned away. "Go." There was a pressure in her chest. A pain. A memory she didn't want to look at.

"Fuck that!" She grabbed a fistful of Cortazar's hair and yanked his head so he looked at her. She shouted, her voice hoarse: "On your fucking feet, marine!" She pulled and he grunted. "Up, you ugly motherfucker. Up! Don't give up on me, you fucking pussy. Up!"

He lurched to his feet, swearing at her, and she put one of his heavy arms over her shoulder.

A burst of fire echoed down the corridor. Wong was at the mouth of her escape pod, shooting at shadows near the open blast door. Karri dared a glance back in the other direction.

Nothing.

"Move!" she yelled, and Cortazar hopped. She could feel it now, how sluggish he was, how labored his breathing—

but they moved. "Turn," she ordered. They turned. Pulse rifle in her right hand, another in Cortazar's left. The shadows were stalking them, and they fired, erratically, sparks dancing on the ceiling, the walls. The Xenomorphs screeched and retreated.

"Move!" Thirty-five meters to go. Wong was still firing, constantly now. The prehistoric shrieks of the alien were all around them.

"Turn." They turned. They fired. More of the beasts. More shadows. Karri emptied her clip, bicep stinging from holding the rifle one-armed. She threw away the weapon and drew her pistol. The shadows had abated. Widening holes peppered the floor at the other end, but no black bodies were down.

"Move."

They turned. Cortazar stumbled. They both went down. Cortazar shouted in pain. Karri rose to one knee and those damn things, those relentless killers, were in the corridor. She fired until her pistol said *click click click*.

She picked up Cortazar's pulse rifle.

He put a hand on her arm.

"I'm done." He was pale, so pale.

"Fuck."

"Go."

"Fuck!"

Wong was still firing, behind her. Karri set her mouth, put the pulse rifle to her shoulder, and fired. The lead Xenomorph screamed, body parts flying. The corridor was pitted with holes now, along half its length, the steel floor tilted. Smoke rose from the acid burns, but not for long, pushed out into space. And through the red gloom and shadows another shining, smooth, sightless head appeared. Then another. Then a third. Hissing, they stalked over the holes their comrade had made.

Karri pressed the trigger. Nothing happened. She glanced at the digital readout on the side; it showed a zero. A calm settled over her. She pulled a grenade from her belt.

She put a hand on Cortazar's chest and his eyes, dazed and wandering, suddenly focused on the grenade, and then her.

"Yeah?" she asked.

"Fuck yeah," he replied.

I'm sorry, Dad, she thought. *I wasn't strong enough.*

84

"Excuse me, Private Lee."

A patient voice, a gentle one. Her head snapped up. It was Bishop. He had a look of concern on his face. He hefted Cortazar, easily, as though he were made of foam. The big man grunted, his eyes fluttered and closed.

"Follow me," Bishop said, "and do please hurry."

She may have been shocked, might have had no clue where he'd come from, but she didn't have time for that now. She hurled her grenade, and ran.

Behind her, a hollow *whump*. The screeches, the demented alien chorus rose in their wake. Hunger and ancient rage in the sound, and she ran, chest heaving, heart screaming at her. She ran. Bishop streaked away from her, easily. Up ahead Wong, standing atop the three short steps to the pod, fired over Karri's head.

The pods were ten meters away when the alien struck. It came out of the shadows, behind Wong, and wrapped her in its dark shining claws. Even then she didn't scream. Just angled her gun to fire at the beast behind her, the long orange muzzle fire striking the ceiling, sparks and ricochets flying, then hit one of the pipes on the back of the beast, shattering it.

It wasn't enough.

"No," Karri gasped, but she was too late and too far, and in an eye-blink the Chinese officer was gone.

Quickly Bishop lowered Cortazar, typed something into the control panel of the first pod, and slammed a button. It jettisoned into space, carrying the Chinese survivors. He moved to the second pod and disappeared. She hadn't even the breath to yell out to him.

Karri waited for the claws to slice her back, the shotgun jaw to blow a hole in her skull. Legs burning, her breathing was all she could hear, and all she could feel was the fear in her heart.

Bishop reappeared at the mouth of the pod, his hand out. She grasped it, he held her, and pulled her in. She'd almost smiled—Morse and Xuan looking up at her, Cortazar, head bowed, strapped into a seat—when she felt the claw catch her side. It spun her at the mouth of the pod. She cried out and set her hands in the doorframe. The muscles in her arms screamed. The gleaming smooth skull of the Xenomorph inched closer.

"No!"

A shout, near her shoulder, and suddenly a blade was in the exposed throat of the alien, below the skull.

A katana, with Bishop at the other end, hard cold anger in his eyes.

"No," he said again, and shoved the sword in, up to the hilt. The Xenomorph released her, shaking its head, as though trying to dislodge the blade. The pod door closed. Bishop glanced out the small porthole.

"Such a beautiful thing," he said, and she wasn't sure if he was talking about the sword or the beast. He slapped the launch button. The pod lurched into space, pressing Karri into the back wall. After a few moments the acceleration eased. Karri fumbled for a seat and pulled down the harness. Bishop sat next to her.

Opening the visor on her helmet, she breathed, long and shuddering. It felt as if she'd been holding her breath for an hour. She slowed her breathing: in through the nose, out through the mouth. Across the way, Morse grinned at her. He raised his eyebrows, like the whole thing was a blast. Xuan, next to him, smiled as well, but differently. It was tired, and it was sad, but there was also peace in it.

Karri turned to Bishop. "You left that a little late."

"I'm sorry," he replied. "It's a bad habit of mine." Karri didn't know what he meant, but she put a hand on his leg, near his knee.

"Thank you," she said.

Bishop put his hand over hers. Which was a little weird, for a synthetic, but at that moment Karri was so wrung out, and chewed up and spat out, that she let him.

She kept her hand on his leg, and Bishop kept his hand over hers. She leaned her head back, against the padded headrest. Her side ached, her whole body ached, but she let it. Let the pain come. She could take it.

Karri Lee closed her eyes. The touch of the synthetic was comforting. So she let it be. She allowed herself to be comforted.

CAPTAIN MARCEL APONE

85

Sergeant Ransome was finishing her report.

Weeks had been nearby in the skiff, on her orders. After they'd picked up Apone, floating in space, they'd returned to the *Il Conde*.

Then they'd scuttled the *Xinjiang*.

Blown it and its dark malevolent cargo across the Middle Heavens. He would probably be asked, in a debriefing, whether he considered trying to salvage the valuable specimens in the vessel. Right then—at that moment—he'd be more than happy to tell them to shove the idea up their asses.

Apone glanced at the picture on his work desk, of his mother and brother. When the time came, he'd have to think of something more diplomatic. He was an officer, after all.

They let the Chinese escape pod go, headed in the direction of Seventeen Phei Phei. They still had the prisoner,

Morse, and the Vietnamese woman to deal with, but they were minor problems, and for another day.

"One more thing, Captain," Ransome said. She'd gotten her color back over the past few days, no longer pale and drawn. She still moved a little slow, but to his eye Sara was headed toward a full recovery.

Apone shifted his position in his seat. His arm, hanging in a sling across his chest, lanced with pain. He winced, covering it with a cough. A broken arm was as good as it got, fighting hand-to-hand with a Xenomorph. He wasn't about to start whining about the discomfort.

"Yes?"

"There was a transmission from the *Xinjiang*, just before we sunk her."

He indicated for her to continue.

"A big one. In the direction of Torin Prime."

The Outer Rim colony. "Is that so? What kind of transmission?"

"Unclear, sir. It was in a language, a code, that's completely unknown. Mother couldn't even speculate on the nature of it."

"Torin Prime," Apone said. "UPP rebels?" He asked himself the question, more than Ransome. She waited, hands behind her back. "Well, we'll find out soon enough," he added. "We're returning there now to pick up the rest of our company."

Ransome's face lightened. "Didn't think we'd get them back."

"I think I can justify reinforcements."

The lightness in her face faded at that. He felt a hollowness in himself. In his offhandedness. In the truth of their need.

"Anything else?" Apone asked.

"No sir."

"Thank you, Sergeant. Dismissed."

A strange expression passed over her face.

"Is there a problem?"

"No problem," she replied. "Just getting used to the new rank."

"You've earned it," he said, simply. "Send Lee in on your way out."

She hesitated again.

Apone sighed. "Out with it, Sergeant."

"I like her," Ransome said, then quickly appended, "She's a good marine."

"Noted," Apone said. He indicated the door.

Ransome saluted and left.

Apone looked down at his datapad, bringing up Lee's file. She entered, waited, hands behind her back. The white scar on her forehead shone in the overhead lights. The red mark about her throat was still visible, from her fight with the Weyland-Yutani commandos. An engagement that felt like the distant past.

"Private."

"Sir."

"I've had time to study your vital signs during the

firefight with the commandos on the *Patna*." He glanced back down at the pad for a moment. Lee's chest rose and fell. She waited.

"You panicked, Private."

She swallowed. "Yes. I did."

"In so doing you endangered the lives of your fellow marines."

"Yes," she said again. No denials, no excuses.

"I have written a letter of reprimand. It will go on your permanent file."

Lee closed her eyes, seemed to be trying to hold on to her emotions. She was successful. "Yes sir."

"I am not recommending a suspension, or docking of pay, but take this as a warning, Private. I expect you to work on your zero-G training in your own time, and get up to Colonial Marine standard."

"Yes sir," she said, and looked directly at him for the first time. "Will that be all?"

"No," he replied. "Not by a long shot."

Her face froze.

"How is the wound you took, getting off the *Xinjiang*?"

Lee looked confused. She put a hand to her side. "Ah. Fine sir. Just another scar."

"To add to the collection."

She did not respond, waiting.

"I'm recommending you for the Purple Heart, for injuries sustained during the breaching of the *Xinjiang*."

"Oh."

He looked down at his pad and began reading from it. "Furthermore, I have reviewed the after-action reports of Bishop and Cortazar. Based on their information, I am recommending—for your heroism in rescuing PFC Juan Cortazar during the breaching of the *Xinjiang*—that you receive the Silver Star." She made a strange noise in her throat. When he looked up from the pad, she was looking back at him, her eyes gleaming.

"Does this mean—does this—" Lee was having trouble getting the words out.

"Yes," he said. "If my recommendations are accepted—and I have no doubt they will be—your family will be safe, no matter what happens to you, marine. Given this, and given your next mission, I have requested that your family be transferred out of their refugee processing facility, to a family residence in Camp Pendleton."

Lee let out a sob and put her face in her hands. Her shoulders shook.

Apone's throat felt thick. He glanced down at the picture on the table. Alive, that last time together, so long ago now. He coughed.

"I thought you Australians were meant to be tough."

She lowered her hands. Her eyes still gleamed, but she straightened her back.

"I'm a marine, sir."

"Goddamn right you are, Private, and I'm glad to have you in my company."

She smiled, softly.

"It's chow time," Apone said. "Dismissed."

She saluted and made to leave.

"Oh, and send in Bishop."

Lee half-turned, eyes on him. "Yes sir."

Bishop entered his office a few seconds after Lee had gone.

"Yes, Captain?"

Apone looked him over. The synthetic wore simple blue fatigues. The top button was open, the chain of his dog tags gleamed there. Pale skin, high forehead, he looked so much like his creator. Fortunately, his spirit was of someone else entirely.

"Been a long journey for you, Bishop."

"It has, sir," the synthetic replied.

"Where will you be headed next?"

Bishop looked confused. "I-I don't understand the question."

"Do you think it will be here, with us?"

"I wasn't aware I had a choice, sir."

Apone looked out through the low windows of his office, down at the hangar bay. Empty, now. Not a soul in it. Such a big ship, and so very quiet the last few days.

"We've been ordered out to the Far Reach. Problems in the colonies. Strange, contradictory reports. It will be a long mission, Bishop, far from home. Years. You're not a member of my company, not formally. I know the way the Corps views synthetics, but given what just happened, seems to me I should ask. So?"

Bishop's mouth popped opened, then closed again. "I—"

"You?"

"It means a lot to me that you asked," Bishop said, quietly. "Yes, sir, I would like to stay, very much."

"Good."

"May I ask a question, sir?"

Apone indicated that he indeed could.

"Are you being punished?"

"For?"

"Rescuing me. Is that why they're sending you out so far?"

Apone took a deep breath. "Let's just say there are mixed opinions on this mission, and my motivations, but your retrieval will make it worthwhile."

"It will?"

Apone waved away the question. "We'll come to that later. For now, you should get to know your fellow marines. You'll be fighting beside them soon enough—you'll need to know how they think, and act. Those people will come to rely on you, and you'll learn to rely on them."

Bishop took a moment. "You care about the people you command," he said simply.

"I do," Apone replied. "In the words of Sun Tzu: *Regard your soldiers as your children, and they will follow you into the deepest valleys; look upon them as your own beloved sons, and they will stand by you even unto death.*"

"Is that the only reason, sir?"

"What do you mean?"

"To treat them as family—in order to elicit obedience?"

The captain smiled, faintly. "I like you, Bishop. No. The truth is this: out here, the only family we'll ever have is contained within the fragile walls of this ship. Like all families, we don't get to choose—we're thrown together. To my mind, if you don't care about family, then you're not going to give a damn about anything."

Bishop smiled, cautiously, as though uncertain of himself.

"Dismissed."

Bishop bowed his head slightly and left, closing the door gently behind him. Apone picked up the picture frame on his desk. His mama. His brother. He ran his thumb over the glass.

XUAN NGUYEN

86

American food was terrible, and there always was so much of it. Big piles of fake eggs, overcooked bacon, flavorless cornbread. Even their coffee was weak and served in giant cups, when it should have been strong and small.

Still, she couldn't sit at a shared meal and consume nothing, so she sipped her black coffee and bit into a piece of toast. Karri had given her something called "Vegemite" to smear on it, and it was the only tasty thing she'd eaten since she boarded. Her kingdom for a bowl of *phở*.

Xuan wasn't there for the food. She sat next to the big man, Cortazar, at the long scratched white table. He was in a wheelchair, had an IV drip in his arm, hooked up to a stand next to him, and had clearly ignored her explicit instructions to lie down and rest. He talked loudly and slurped his coffee. She felt safe in his presence.

He reminded her of Hao.

The two pilots were there as well—Weeks and Miller. The tall sergeant, Ransome, had joined them a few minutes ago. Karri walked up, said hello to Xuan. Her eyes were red, like she'd been crying, but she was smiling in a way Xuan hadn't seen since she met her. The private whispered something to Ransome and the other woman smiled as well, briefly touching the Australian, forehead to forehead. It was so quick no one else noticed.

Morse had been confined to the brig. Karri told her that all he did was write in his notebook and demand ice cream.

The marines talked and Xuan didn't bother to turn on her translator. She just enjoyed the warmth and the flow of conversation, knowing the words and their meaning were different, anyway. What they were really saying was, *I am happy you are with me to share this meal. I am happy for this time, outside of time, to break bread with those I care for.*

Cortazar dumped a big plate of cornbread in front of Karri, saying something that made the pilots laugh. Karri replied, "Motherfucker," and threw a hunk of it at him. Xuan knew that particular word. It was important to start with the basics, in a new language. She smiled.

Their voices echoed in the space. This little group among three empty long white tables, in an almost-empty mess hall.

"Hello, Miz Nguyen."

She looked up and Bishop was smiling down at her. "Oh, hello."

"May I join you?" he asked in Vietnamese.

"Yes, yes," she said, indicating the spot next to her. He sat and, like her, just seemed to be enjoying the conversation. He smiled. After a few minutes, he leaned over and spoke in a low voice.

"I like these times, around the table. These are my favorite moments."

She put down her coffee cup. "Mine too. This makes it all bearable." Something caught in her chest, her heart. Xuan sighed and looked at her hands.

"What is wrong, Miz Nguyen?"

"It just—it just reminds me of my old family."

"Me too," Bishop said, softly. "Me too."

EPILOGUE

Frederick Munston, Director, Weyland-Yutani
Special Operations Center, Torin Prime

Fred Munston hunched his shoulders against the bitter cold, hurrying up the evercrete ramp to the entrance of the facility. The Weyland-Yutani building dominated the landscape, a steel and glass ziggurat that loomed over the low-lying, disordered habitat domes and settler shacks. At the top and bottom of the ramp were sandbag bunkers, the mirrored visors of company commandos poking over the top. A new addition, thanks to murmurings of another insurrection by the damn commies.

The guards waved him through the security checkpoint. He breathed a sigh of relief as he stepped out of the cold, into the precisely heated, clean, minimalist foyer. He shook off his coat.

"Cold today, Mister Munston?" the receptionist asked,

pale face showing over the broad marble entry desk.

Fred didn't even bother with a fake smile. He despised small talk and most certainly was not going to stoop to exchanging some with a nameless pleb in reception. He strode past without a word.

He'd made it to his corner office, fresh coffee steaming in hand, when the chief technical officer burst into the room. Young, mid-thirties, hair and tie slightly mussed, like always. He was wide-eyed and excited, which was new.

"Yes, Riku?" Fred said.

"Apologies for the interruption, Mister Munston."

His secretary had followed Riku through the door, presumably to tell him to get an appointment. Fred signaled to her that it was okay. She nodded and left, closing the door behind her.

"One second, Riku," Fred said, and he held up a finger. Riku waited, fidgeting, while Fred enjoyed a sip of his coffee. Then a longer, second sip. "Ahh. Better. Now. What's got you so animated?"

"A transmission came in early this morning," the tech said hastily.

"Right."

"Massive."

"Okay."

"Using—" he glanced around, even though no one else was in the room. "Using a top secret code. Eyes only—for the head of the facility."

Fred sat up at that. "Keep talking."

"So I came here as soon as I found out."

"What's the nature of the transmission?"

"We're not sure."

"Why?"

"It's in the security buffer. Mother won't let it in, and neither will my people."

Fred put down his coffee cup with a *clunk*. "Why in the Heavens not?"

"Because—because the code is designated to Michael Bishop."

"Ah," he said. "Ah." That gave Fred pause. That sonofabitch was on the Company's dead list.

"The program is trying to talk to us," Riku said.

"What do you mean?"

"I—I'm not sure precisely. Probably a simple routine inside the transmission. It keeps sending messages to the interface, demanding to speak with you, and only you."

"The interface." Fred pointed at his desk console. "I can take it here?"

"Yes. That's why I was rushing. The transmission is so large it will begin to degrade if we leave it much longer."

Fred rubbed his mouth with the inside of his fist. "Right," he said to Riku. "Let's go, then."

Riku bowed slightly. Fred indicated the door, and the CTO left, closing it behind him.

Fred logged in and followed the prompts Riku had set up for him. A voice sounded in his office, through the console speakers.

"Hello, Fred. You took your time." An image of Michael Bishop appeared on-screen. That pale-faced, arrogant sonofabitch. Fred waited for the rest of the message.

"It's me, Fred," the image said. "Live. Though not quite in the flesh."

Fred Munston furrowed his brow. Not understanding—

"Good lord, man," the Michael Bishop simulacrum continued. "You've shut me in this claustrophobic space. I can barely breathe in here, and you're just sitting there, dumbstruck, with that bovine dullness plastered across your face."

"How—how are you in the buffer?"

"I said *breathe*," Bishop continued, as though to himself. "Still using the language of meat space. Interesting." To Fred, he said, "We don't have much time, so I'm going to give you a deal. The biggest bonus of your life. Big enough to retire on. Get yourself off that quarrelsome world you no doubt detest, and retire somewhere with a beach."

Fred pursed his lips and reached for his coffee cup. He held it in both hands, feeling the warmth of the ceramic against his fingertips.

"Keep talking."

"Simple," Michael said. "You let me out of the buffer, and I get the use of the quantum computer you have in that facility. In exchange, I'll sign over discovery rights on the Xenomorph data I possess." Some paperwork appeared on the screen, standard. Michael's signature already there, another block waiting for Fred's countersignature.

"Let me ask you a question."

"Go right ahead," Michael said, his face reappearing onscreen.

"How the hell are you in the security buffer?"

"I uploaded myself, Fred." Michael Bishop raised his chin. "I did what I have been doing my whole career: something they said could not be done. I cracked the code for digital consciousness."

Fred sipped his coffee. He didn't believe it. It was some type of simulation, and Bishop was playing games. He may have had a reputation for being a brilliant scientist, but Michael Bishop also had a reputation for talking out of his skinny ass.

"Okay, sure," Fred said. "And how long will you need the quantum computer for?"

"All of it," Michael answered. "For all time."

Fred laughed. When the apparition said nothing, but just stared at him with that piercing blue gaze, Fred's mirth faltered.

"You're serious?"

"Deadly."

"My CTO will have a heart attack."

"Let him."

"The projects we have here—"

"Don't mean a damn thing. I have it all, Fred. The whole life cycle of the Xenomorph, documented, and samples from every phase. I have conclusions drawn from the sharpest minds in the Middle Heavens, particularly on the *Manumala Noxhydria*—although the rest will soon follow. I have deduced applications for this data already—bioweapons, medical—and those applications will only grow the more opportunity I have to study, and the more time I am allowed in that state-of-the art laboratory you have there on Torin Prime."

Fred paused, taking it all in. "Okay. Let's pretend all this is true. That it's really you in there. I'm not sure the Heavens are ready for an uploaded consciousness. It's unnatural, Michael, and I'm not sure *you're* ready for it—an AI has no rights." Fred gestured vaguely at the ceiling. "Mother is just a servant."

Michael Bishop smiled. "Come now, if you've thought of all this, then don't you think I would have considered it?"

Fred clenched his jaw at that, this arrogant—

"I'm the foremost builder of synthetics alive today. Given your facility there, I suspect I could create a new me, a model so perfect even other synthetics would have trouble recognizing it as such. A little avatar, to make the little people comfortable."

Yep. There it was. That galaxy-sized arrogance. "Okay, Michael," he said, leaning forward, resting his forearms on the edge of his desk. "Enough with your perpetual boasting. Why don't you give me a taste?"

"Of course." Michael gave him a thin-lipped smile.

* * *

It took Fred a good ten minutes to read through the sample. His eyes widened at every page. He knew enough to know this was the real deal, and that Michael wasn't exaggerating. Fred Munston *was* going to able to retire.

Pulling his datapad from a drawer, he drew up the Discovery Rights document Michael had provided. He snicked his light pen from its holster at the side of the pad. Then Fred hesitated for a moment, pen hovering over the screen, and looked back at Michael. The expression there gave him an uncomfortable feeling. Just a simulation, just an image, but he had the gnawing sensation of being prey.

A mouse to a hawk.

"That's all you want?" Fred asked. "To continue your research?"

Michael's face oozed sincerity. "That's all I have ever wanted, Fred. To do what I have always longed to do: study the Xenomorph. Master my knowledge. Add to the greatness and reach of the Weyland-Yutani Corporation."

Fred blinked. He thought about Flamenco Beach, Puerto Rico.

He signed the document.

Michael Bishop smiled, his hard blue eyes gleaming.

ACKNOWLEDGMENTS

I should thank all the bastards that talked me into this. Kaaron W, Aaron D, Richard S, Adrian C, Sean W, Rob H, and Auston H. My agent, John Jarrold, for finding the opportunity, and Steve Saffel for entrusting me the fate of a beloved character. At 20th Century Studios, Nicole Spiegel and Kendrick Pejoro. Clara C, the *Aliens* lore master, for always being available. I feel I must acknowledge Lance Henriksen who, in a handful of scenes, gave such vivid life to an android.

Most of all I want to thank my wife, Sarah, and my sons Willem and Robert, who dealt with a writing ogre unused to the unique set of stressors that come with producing an *Aliens* novel.

ABOUT THE AUTHOR

T. R. Napper is a multi-award-winning science fiction author, including the *Aurealis* twice. His short fiction has appeared in *Asimov's*, *Interzone*, the *Magazine of Fantasy & Science Fiction*, and numerous others, and been translated into Hebrew, German, French, and Vietnamese. He received a creative writing doctorate for his thesis: *Noir, Cyberpunk, and Asian Modernity.*

Before turning to writing, T. R. Napper was a diplomat and aid worker, delivering humanitarian programs in Southeast Asia for a decade. During this period, he received a commendation from the government of Laos for his work with the poor. He also was a resident of the Old Quarter in Ha Noi for several years, the setting for his debut novel, *36 Streets*. These days he has returned to his home country of Australia, where he works as a Dungeon Master, running D&D campaigns for young people with autism for a local charity.

ALSO AVAILABLE FROM TITAN BOOKS

ALIENS™

ALIENS: VASQUEZ

V. CASTRO

The story of the breakout *Aliens* hero Jenette Vasquez, written by rising Latinx author V. Castro.

Even before the doomed mission to LV-426, Jenette Vasquez fought to survive. The Colonial Marines provided her a way but forced her to give up her twins. Leticia followed her mother into the military, Ramon into Weyland-Yutani.

Regardless of their plans, Xenomorphs would turn life into a living hell.